A BRIDGE OF STRAW

CHRIS BUDD

W0010140

SilverWood

Published in 2013 by the author
using SilverWood Books Empowered Publishing®

SilverWood Books
30 Queen Charlotte Street, Bristol, BS1 4HJ
www.silverwoodbooks.co.uk

ISBN 978-1-78132-120-1 (paperback)
ISBN 978-1-78132-121-8 (ebook)

British Library Cataloguing in Publication Data
A CIP catalogue record for this book is available from the British Library

Set in Bembo by SilverWood Books
Printed on responsibly sourced paper

If you have four characters playing cards around a table and a bomb goes off in a briefcase hidden under the table, that's a surprise. If you tell the audience about the bomb and the characters continue to play cards, that's suspense.

Alfred Hitchcock

Prologue – 2010

When it Comes Back

The fox watched the bungalow. It wasn't just any old fox, it wasn't *a* fox. It was *the* fox. The fox that, as far as Mack was concerned, had chosen his bins to pillage, over and above all the other bins in the village. Not content with simply going through the rubbish, the fox had then decided to distribute the detritus over the entire back yard, almost as if it had wanted to create the maximum irritation possible.

Mack picked his way across the yard towards the shed he had converted into a recording studio, briefly looking up to glance ruefully across the fields. A large cup of coffee was gripped tightly in one hand, with a short slim cigar, as yet unlit, tucked behind his ear. He made a note of shopping requirements as he went, treading carefully through soggy egg boxes, empty soup cartons, and revealing plastic containers that had until last night held a Chinese meal for one. A little piece of him died inside as he forced himself to accept that at some point he would have to actually leave the house and make a trip to the supermarket.

Crossing the threshold into the studio, he could feel the tension from the night's sleep starting to leave his shoulders and back muscles. It was the same every morning. Life seemed a little brighter when confined to this small room.

Picking up an acoustic guitar that had been handmade to his own specifications, he hummed vaguely to a song he was working on, allowing a melody to suggest itself, if it felt so inclined.

Today was Wednesday. Jay would be coming over that evening, and Mack needed to have something to play him. Knowing that Jay would join him to add keyboards and ambient noises gave him the incentivising deadline that had once been provided by the record company's A&R man almost three decades ago.

The track came to an end and Mack hung the guitar by its neck from a bracket halfway up the studio wall, next to two electric guitars and a banjo. A mandolin and a variety of items to shake or stroke were lying on the floor with the larger items leaning against a keyboard. He turned to stare out of the window, absent-mindedly scrunched his long brown hair in a fist behind his head, then let it drop back onto his shoulders.

The fields looked spectacular in late October, with the early morning mist persistently laying on the ground like a woollen fleece rug, waiting to be burned away by a sun which was threatening to make its presence felt through the clouds.

He couldn't see the fox, but he had a feeling that it was not far away, almost as if it was watching him, waiting, biding its time.

The song 'Rocks Off' by the Rolling Stones began playing from Mack's mobile phone. That meant it was Johnny calling him. He smiled to himself, feeling grateful that his son was still so close to him, still such a large part of his life at a time when most of his friends' kids were just discovering that being back at home was not as much fun as living with mates at university.

"Morning," he said, sitting down again and leaning back in his chair.

"Dad. Johnny."

"Yeah, I know, mate," he said, with mock irritability. "I am able to read a name on a mobile phone. Hey, did you see that programme last night? About the history of folk music, it was brilliant, some great footage of Davy Graham – man, could that guy play guitar! Made me realise that I've been playing Anji totally wrong all these years."

"Didn't see it."

"Well you should have! Come over this weekend, I'm happy to watch it again."

"Sorry, can't. Have a life."

"Okay, I'll come to you then and we'll do your life instead."

"You don't know what I'm going to be doing," replied Johnny.

"Well, no, that is true. With mates returning from uni, I imagine your social life will now develop from its current moribund status to one that involves reprobates of variable gender, recreational drugs, and Jack Daniels. Am I right?"

"You're cheerful."

"Hung-over. Red wine and an Ealing comedy last night. Always feel better with a hangover." Mack reached behind his ear for the cigar. It was flavoured with vanilla. He lit a match and held the flame underneath the end of the cigar, twisting it to ensure an even burn.

"So, I haven't spoken to you for a week or so," he said, breaking the silence. "What's the news? How's Mum?"

"Cool. Bolton this week, new shop."

"Another one? Sheesh. Hasn't the world got enough overpriced jewellery?"

"Not going there, Dad," said Johnny, a warning tone to his voice.

"What, to Bolton, or allowing me to rant about your mother?"

Johnny maintained a practised silence.

Defeated, Mack changed the subject. "And how's Mary?"

"Good."

"That it? Just good. Surely your sister talks to you more than that."

"Okay, pretty good."

"Hey, look, come on, I need your help here. She hasn't talked to me for sixteen years – the only way I get the news is through you. Your mum barely gives me the time of day. If you keep on protecting me from what they're saying, I'll have to keep on being a miserable old git living off past glories. And it's not as if they're particularly good glories. In fact, I'm not even sure they were glories. Thing is, until you get yourself a wife and some kids, which I frankly hope won't be for a number of years yet, but until you do, Mary's kids are the only grandchildren I've got, and I'd bloody well like to see them every once in a while. That's all a man has kids for, you know, to wait until they have kids of their own. That and the nursing home fees."

Mack took a puff on his cigar. One day, when he has kids of his own, that boy will look back in awe and wonderment at the skill with which his father had managed his own son. He blew the smoke vertically into the stale studio air.

"Her kids are fine," Johnny finally replied. "Don't know about anything else, only ever talks about the kids."

"Why can't she just let the kids come and see me? She doesn't have to come too."

"Don't start, Dad."

"I'm not starting! I just want to see my grandkids."

11

"You know why she won't talk to you."

"That was sixteen years ago, Johnny. Can't she move on?"

"Dad," said Johnny, "I've got some news. You sitting down?"

That was a swift change of subject. Did Mack detect a tremble in his son's voice?

"I'm always sitting down, you know that," he replied.

"Cool." Johnny took a deep breath. "You know those 'failed pop star' and 'past glories' comments?"

"Yeah," Mack said slowly.

"Well, not any more."

Mack sat up in his chair, interested now. He adopted a mock fatherly tone.

"Would you care to explain yourself, young man? What have you been up to?"

"Lots. And some more as well." He paused. Mack could definitely detect some nervousness, even more than was standard for Johnny. "Got you a gig."

"Okaaayyy," said Mack slowly. "Didn't know I was actually looking to play a gig, but I'll go along with it for the moment. Where is it?"

"LA."

"Long Ashton?"

"No, Dad. LA. Los Angeles. City of Angels."

There was a pause. Mack puffed slowly on his cigar, and Johnny could hear him exhaling. A considerable amount of ash was now hanging on to the end of the cigar, so Mack rolled it round the rim of the ashtray, keeping the lit cigar end neat and tidy. Eventually, he spoke.

"You want to elaborate on that a little, pal? I know you're not one for the words, but I think you might need to break with tradition here. Start talking."

"I've been putting your music online."

"Online? Where?"

"Facebook, Myspace, your own website."

"I've got a website?"

"Yeah. Only simple though. Just to show off your music."

"How do you show off my music on a website, Johnny? You know

12

I'm not into all this sort of thing. I can send an email and check the weather online, but that's about it."

"I put your tracks on for people to download."

"What?! You've been giving away my music? Are you barking frigging mad?" Mack stood up and took three paces to one end of the room, turned, and took five paces to the other side of the room.

"Easy, Dad. Listen."

"Listen? Listen!? I've been working on this music for the last sixteen years, you know, and you tell me you've been giving it away?"

"It needed to be set free. You wouldn't do it, so I did. You don't need the money. I thought people should hear it."

For only the third time in his life, Mack didn't know what to say. 'Set free'. Nice turn of phrase. Johnny had clearly been preparing for this conversation. His music *was* eclectic. That was its point. Since that awful week leading up to the divorce he had changed his approach to music, from pleasing other people to being a channel through which his consciousness could find expression. But since he couldn't use words – what had happened could never be told, that was a simple fact – he had learned to empty his pain and anger into his music. He no longer had an audience, which meant he no longer had to care what people would think. The music he made was for him, not anyone else. He alone knew what it meant. How it expressed one's emotional responses, creating value and influencing future behaviour, leading to new events, new responses, amended values, and so on, round and round forever, whittling ever decreasing shards of personality.

He had managed to step off that endless loop, temporarily and intermittently, and move from being protagonist to observer, chronicling and translating, creating sounds and noises which allowed a purge of responses. Unable to speak about the one thing he would have wanted to speak to someone else about, the music became a waste pipe; a conduit into which he could empty his frustration and anger. Not even Jay really knew what memories possessed the spirit of the music. How could an audience possibly understand?

So Johnny had set the genie from the bottle. Reaching inside for a reaction upon which he could hang his response, Mack was surprised to discover a part of him that was glad. It seemed to sit alongside a vanity that he hadn't known still burned, and a fear he

13

had been forced to grow accustomed to.

"Dad?" Johnny was not used to silence at the other end of a telephone call with his father. "Dad, you angry with me?"

"No. No, not angry, just a little taken aback, mate. You've set the music free. Nicely put. Where has it gone? Who is listening to it?"

"Lots of places. American college radio is a big one."

"Really? Young people like my stuff?" Mack was so taken aback that he was starting to talk like Johnny.

"There's something else. About 'My Grass is Greener'."

"What about it?"

"It's gonna be used for a TV show. Main theme."

"Really?"

"It's a big show. ABC's next push. Teen angst, The OC, 90210, that kind of thing."

"Okay, we'll gloss over the fact that I've no idea what you've just said, and I'll just take it that it's a good thing."

"More than good. National. Massive. International. You can tour the States on the back of it."

"Oh my God, I can't take this in. Who's been helping you do this?"

"No one," said Johnny, testily.

"Come on, Johnny, someone must have been."

"Well, a bit of help from someone, but it's been down to me, okay? I can do this, you know."

"Sorry, mate. Of course, you've just shocked me a bit. Who the hell am I to be having stuff on telly? I'm not even sure I want this. I've had fame once, Johnny. I'm quite happy sitting here all day doing my own thing. I'm not sure that I really want to go through all that again." He tried to measure his words, conscious of the wonderful thing his son thought he had been doing. He couldn't be angry at the boy, not after what he'd been through.

"Different this time, Dad." Johnny paused for a moment, his breathing audible.

Mack reminded himself of the amount of effort this must be for Johnny. His own exile had been self imposed, whereas Johnny's nervous nature was something that just seemed to be within him. "Look, it'll be on your terms," Johnny continued. "You only do what you want to do. Tour the small venues. College towns, where your audience is. Take your time over it. What you've always wanted. You deserve it. All those grey hairs in your beard from looking after me – about time you had some return on that investment."

"My beard is not grey, it is salt and pepper." Mack stood up, the cigar now forgotten in the glass ashtray housing a picture of Joey Ramone, surrounded by the words 'Hey Ho, Let's Go'. Those words would have inspired him to action as a younger man. These days he didn't even notice the design. "Christ, Johnny, how the hell did you pull this off?"

"Internet. The word just spread. People love your music."

"I can't take this all in, Johnny. Get your arse over here, we've got a lot to discuss."

"Why don't I see you in The Feathers at 8 tonight."

"Fine," said Mack. "I'll call Jay."

Mack pressed 'End' and put the phone slowly back onto the desk in front of him. Contradictory emotions swirled around inside him, wary of each other yet preparing for attack and defence; like a matador and a bull, each aware of themselves and also their precise position in relation to the other, any movement creating a reaction, a change, until they danced around as if held together by an invisible thread.

The parent within him was proud of the son who had stepped from behind his father and proven himself; the latest of a thousand steps on the journey to becoming a man of substance, of heart, of meaning. He was only too aware of the pivotal role his own approval held in his son's dignity and pride.

Opposite these instincts stood the memories of that week sixteen years ago, when Johnny was only six years old. The memories may not have been buried but they had at least been kept hidden. There were people out there who had ruined his career and his life once already. People that he had tried very hard to avoid.

What would tomorrow bring? Let alone the days that stretched infinitely ahead. Was that hope he could see near the horizon, or was a familiar face laughing , taunting him again? And where would Johnny be in this future that seemed so determined to hide its secrets from him?

For the second time in his life, Mack felt as if he was about to be dragged along by a tide of events over which he had little control.

Part 1 – 1994

When it Happened

Chapter 1

The mothers. Like a plague on the playground, Mack thought to himself, as he stood isolated, arms folded, waiting for the school doors to open. Johnny had run off to play with his friends on the giant wooden train as soon as they came through the gates of the infant school. It was out of habit that Mack waited for the children to be called in, Johnny safely inside the security blanket of the school.

He thought back to the days when they played small local gigs: just him, Al, Harpo on bass guitar, and a drum machine. Before the record contract, the tours, and the all too brief mayhem. It might be for a school fundraiser, or fiftieth birthday party. If the organiser was a man, they knew what to expect. Doors open at 8, band on at 9. Eat before you get there. Drink beer, dance. Band break at 10, on again at 10.15, wrap up at 11.30 – everyone goes home happy.

But if the organiser was a woman…totally different evening. Doors open at 7. Food at 8. Band supposed to go on at 9 but pudding is only just being served. Too many tables and chairs; not enough room to dance. Clear away some tables. Band on at 9.45. Almost forgot the raffle. Band on at 10. No time for a break, play straight until 11.15. No encore – someone wants to say a few thank yous.

He returned a coy smile from a lady whose name he couldn't quite remember. Mum of Johnny's friend, Xavier. She walked on to talk to the same mums that she joined every morning. Were they talking about him? Gossip operates in a vacuum. Just because me and Jude don't join in your coffee mornings or whatever you do while your husbands go to work, it does not give you an open invitation to invent and assume, he thought.

How did they judge him? Intelligent? Brash? Did they think he'd look better with shorter hair? He felt he made an effort – chatty enough with people he knew well, only quiet and reserved with everyone else.

Happy in his own company, he thought of himself. Miserable bastard, Jude called him.

Five minutes to go before they opened the doors and let the children into their school. The teachers were wielding their power inside, looking out on a cold day. How Mack hated this period of standing in the playground on his own: smiling at people he hardly knew; talking to mothers about children whose names he couldn't remember; being asked questions about Johnny that he didn't want to answer because it was his son, not theirs. He knew they weren't really interested; they were just ferreting for more gossip.

One day Johnny would be old enough to want to enter the school grounds on his own, and Mack would be only too happy to accede to that demand.

Mack, Jay and Harpo were playing a gig that evening at a small club in Bristol. They were going to be playing some of the old Mamal songs, and Mack was eager to get back and practise the new arrangements. The pop star years… It all seemed rather silly now. He had an idea for a different way of playing one of their songs, 'Shubunkin'. It was a throwaway dance number that the band had recorded for the second album (which flopped), but Mack was eager to slow it down, make it more bluesy. It was one of the few songs that Al had written, and was part of an even smaller subset of those Al had written which Mack actually liked.

The school doors opened, Johnny went flying up to Mack to say goodbye, hugging his hips. Then he grabbed his bag from where he had dumped it at his father's feet and ran into school. With a last wave to his son's back, Mack turned to start the twenty-minute walk home to the other side of the village.

What had become of Al? After Mamal split up he went to Hollywood and found minor success in the movies, at least for a while. What an idiot. An ego on legs. Disappeared from Mack's life when he went to America and disappeared from public life a few years later. It occurred to him that Al may have been in his thoughts more often than he realised, like a fox in a city: always somewhere nearby.

If Mack had known that Al Smart was, at that very moment, watching him from the passenger seat of a white Peugeot 306 parked seventy-four metres away, he would have reacted by being friendly and realising that he didn't actually bear a grudge after all this time. If he knew *why* Al was parked there, or, perhaps more importantly, why the young woman was sat in the driver's seat next to him, he would have reacted altogether more aggressively.

That evening, soundcheck over, Mack sat in a small room behind the stage. The Tesla was a boat that had been converted into a music venue and bar, and now hosted live music most nights of the week. On Tuesdays such as this, the artists would either be young groups trying to sip from the well of fame, or older groups still scraping at the parched ground, their water having run dry a long time ago.

Mack hated the feeling that he was reliving past glories. The poster for the gig hadn't helped. It showed his name and his picture, and then, to hedge bets, 'From 80s band, Mamal'. If he never had to play 'A Bridge of Straw' again he would be happy, no matter how much money it continued to generate. Well, maybe that was rubbish. With the amount of income it brought in, he could reluctantly play it again.

Harpo came into the room, holding two pints of Guinness. He put one on the table in front of Mack and took a long drink from his own, the journey across the room taking marginally less than a second. The walls were covered with old posters for bands that had played at The Tesla over the years, and smelt vaguely of beer and disinfectant. Around the edge of the room was an assortment of chairs, many of which were being used as receptacles for bags, feet and guitars.

"All set?" asked Mack.

"Yep. Guitars tuned and fresh batteries in the drum machine." Mack took his pint and looked at the man who wasn't so much a friend, more a person who was always there. Harpo was like a roadie – he had great attention to detail. His real name was Harper Smith, so named because his parents had been big fans of the book, *To Kill a Mockingbird*. Mack had originally invited him to join Mamal as a harmonica player after seeing him in a blues band, a gig which came to an abrupt end after Harpo assaulted the singer for continually singing over Harpo's solos. As Mack had been having his own battle of egos with Al, he had to admire anyone with such an uncompromising attitude towards lead singers. Bored of the harmonica, Harpo changed to bass guitar and his simple but solid style suited the music.

When Harpo went to college to train as a hair stylist, he continued playing with the band, although they wouldn't allow him to appear in any of the photographs. He had always considered music and the cutting of hair as equally artistic endeavours. His was a perfect marriage of hair and music, particularly in the 80s when that peculiar combination of talents was in great demand.

The door opened abruptly, interrupting Mack's thoughts, and Jay came into the room. He placed two bottles of beer down in front of the men, bending to the low table with all the grace of a baby giraffe.

"I couldn't decide which beer to get, so I got one of each," he said. "Those okay? You can swap with mine if you like. I'm not fussy which one I have."

"That's cool," said Mack, smiling at Harpo. They drank from the pints in their hands, but Jay still didn't notice. He seemed to be a little edgy, which Mack put down to pre-gig nerves.

"Did you see the poster?" Mack asked them, with a wince.

"Yeah," said Jay. "You know what you need, mate? You need a name."

"Thanks, but I've already got one," Mack replied.

"No, a band name. Something that will move you on from Mamal."

"But aren't people coming to see us because I was in Mamal?" Mack asked.

Fame is a cruel mistress, and she had decided to withdraw her charms many years ago. Al may have gone running after her, but Mack felt quite content to be without her seductive yet fickle features. But he was here, wasn't he? Wasn't he still getting up on stage? What was it within him that needed this adulation, or was it just habit that kept him coming back for more? He felt like a good character in a bad novel, drawn by fate into endlessly repeating the same mistake.

"I'm not actually sure too many people are coming to see us at all," said Harpo, matter-of-factly, raising his bottle to his lips.

"Thank you. Thank you, Harpo – I can always rely on your pre-gig pep talks to get me in the right frame of mind."

Harpo tilted his head back to take a long swig from his bottle and pointed his finger at Mack, winking at the same time: a bravura display of multitasking.

"Well at least you're not called Mamal anymore," said Jay, drinking from his bottle of beer and suddenly looking at Mack sheepishly. "Sorry, mate. Still. It wasn't the best of names, to be fair."

"It was a terrible name. The record company came up with it. But a lot better than the other ones we went through. God, Al and I were in various bands over the years until the record company persuaded us that we could make it as a duo. What were we called? There was Butterfly Teardrop, which became Flaming Teardrop for a while, before deciding to abandon the reference to crying altogether. We were also Hot Chilli Sauce, Manga Massala, The Fire Throwers, and, in a moment of rebellion, The Freezers. Eventually we settled on The Flaming Hearts."

"That's actually quite a good name," said Jay.

"Yeah, I liked that one. We designed a logo – a heart engulfed in orange flames instead of the letter 'a' in each word. Then when the record company got involved we discovered there was a doo-wop band in America with the same name, who'd had a minor hit in 1958, so we had to change it."

There was a knock on the door. Harpo got up and opened it. He said a few words to the person outside. He left the room to continue the conversation, shutting the door behind him.

"What's he up to?" asked Mack.

Jay smiled. "You know Harpo, fixing something up, no doubt." He took a swig from his beer and sat back in the chair. "Nice," he said, pointing at a small badge on Mack's lapel. It was black, with the word NIRVANA in white.

Mack looked down as if he had forgotten it was there. "Oh, yeah. Nicked it from Mary. She's got loads. Think she's got a teenage crush on Kurt Cobain. Not that she'd admit that to her dad. I'm the last person she talks to these days. In fact, I'm not entirely sure she talks to any adults in anything other than a grunt."

They lapsed into silence for a moment. Jay picked up the copy of *Estates Gazette* that he had brought with him and thumbed its pages, disinterestedly.

"Why do you read that?" asked Mack. "I know you're not really interested."

"Professional habit, I suppose," replied Jay. "It's what people in the village expect of me." He put the magazine down.

Mack got up and walked around the room. It was about half an hour before they were due to go on stage. He didn't get nervous like Jay, hadn't done for many years now, but he did get sullen. Not a good counterpoint to Jay's heightened need for small talk at these moments.

There was a full-length mirror in the room which was clearly stolen from a circus, as it made the viewer look slimmer. It was an old trick for a Green Room, intended to give the artist an ego boost just before going on stage. Looking at himself, Mack felt that age had been kind with his body, at least when viewed from the outside. The last fifteen years had changed him, but not as much as he knew the next fifteen would.

Tall, a little over six feet, and only a few pounds heavier than Mary continually told him he should be, he was pleased with his physique, especially for someone so lazy and unwilling to undertake any form of physical exercise. He knew his luck would run out at some point, but until then, there was as much chance of him seeing the inside of a gym as there was of him letting Harpo sing.

The door opened narrowly and Harpo came back, sliding through the gap and shutting the door quickly behind him. He went over to the table, looked down at the bottles and turned to Jay. "Which one is mine?" he asked.

"I've had a swig from all of them," teased Jay.

"Not funny," said Harpo.

"Oh, come on mate, it doesn't matter. Take a chance – there's probably only a small bit of my saliva left on the bottle."

"Don't wind him up, Jay," said Mack. He looked up at Harpo and smiled. "No one's touched them, mate. They're all safe for you to drink from."

"Thank you," said Harpo pointedly, taking a bottle from the table and putting it to his lips.

"Oh, apart from that one," said Mack. Harpo lowered the bottle and looked at him through narrow eyes. Mack winked extravagantly.

Harpo put the bottle back on the table and proceeded to pick at his fingernails with a studied nonchalance. "So," he said, casually. "Fancy an interview, Mack?"

Mack looked at him blankly, momentarily confused by the request. "You what?" he said. "An interview? Who..."

"It's a student," said Harpo. "Trust me on this one. It's for the university magazine. She's doing a review and wants an interview." He paused. "I, uh, recommend you do it."

"You *recommend* I ..." Something about the way Harpo was looking at him stopped Mack short. "Okay, Harpo. If you *recommend* it." Mack looked at Jay, who was smiling broadly. Mack furrowed one eyebrow at him, still not quite sure he understood.

Harpo opened the door wide. "All sorted," he said to the person standing outside. "Come on in. This is Kimberly. Mack, Jay." Harpo pointed at the two men in turn.

"Thank you," said a female voice with a strong American accent.

Probably from New York, thought Mack. A young woman joined the voice in the small room. Mack felt the room was suddenly a great deal smaller thanks to her presence.

She was tall in a rather imposing way, with dark black hair and dark eyebrows. Her hair was tied back, but poorly, allowing a few wispy strands to fall around her face. The hair at the sides of her head petered out into delicate sideburns, merging into soft downy hair which clung onto her cheeks, delicious and ethereal. Mack instantly had the thought of stroking that downy hair, gently and slowly; first with his fingers, and then with his own cheek. Coincidentally, Jay was having those very same thoughts at the very same time, whereas Harpo had already been through the thought process some five minutes earlier when he had first met the girl.

Her cheekbones seemed to have been baked using the same mould that would have produced a heart-shaped Valentine's cake, the two sides of her face sliding down in perfect symmetry to meet below her expressive mouth. It was the pointiest and most perfect shape of a face that Mack had ever seen, set off by a small nose and deep, expressive eyes that held him in their thrall from the moment that she took off her sunglasses.

"Hi," she said, confidently moving forwards to shake Mack, and then Jay, by the hand. She took her seat behind the door, which Harpo shut, moving to stand against the wall, his hands flat against the cold plaster behind his back. She was just a few seats away from Mack,

25

and turned herself towards him. Jay continued to sit on the other side of the room, now with an excellent view to study the girl and the conversation without being noticed.

"How can I help you?" said Mack, with just a little more chocolate velvet in his voice than he had intended.

"I'd love to ask you a few questions, if you don't mind," Kimberly replied, smiling at Mack.

It was immediately clear that she wasn't interested in Harpo or Jay, which made Mack more uptight and Jay relax. Harpo retained his air of detached amusement.

"Will you be playing 'A Bridge of Straw' tonight?" she asked, conversationally, as she reached forward into her black leather bag to retrieve her notebook. The top of her blouse yawned open as she leaned, and Jay and Mack instinctively moved their heads slightly away from her direction. Their eyes swivelled in their sockets, the gaze of both men remaining firmly fixed on the dark promise that seemed like it might reveal something rather special. Only Harpo did not join in the deception, as he simply stared down her top.

"Yes," replied Mack, still pretending to stare at the wall. "I think people expect it. I don't suppose you remember that song when it first came out?" He laughed ever so briefly, and both Harpo and Jay squirmed ever so slightly.

Kimberly sat up holding her notebook and smiled at him, a patient smile of a person used to having to overcome the burden of their beauty. "No," she said, "I don't. To be fair, I would have been about six years old at the time. And living in Michigan."

Mack brought his hand to his chin. He tried to decide if the girl in front of him was mocking him or not, but couldn't tell from her smile. Still, something within him felt chastened.

"But you have heard it now?" he asked her, the chocolate and velvet tone turned down a few notches.

"Oh, of course. Who hasn't," she said, settling into her chair. Her smile was a little warmer now, as she met him halfway. "That song is ubiquitous. They play it on college radio back in the States all the time. But it's not really my kind of music."

"Oh?" said Mack, moving forward on his seat. He sensed her desire to prove herself, and fed off it. "And what is your kind of music?"

"Ah, well, something with a bit of style, I guess," she said, still smiling, not taking her eyes off his.

In the background she heard Harpo say, "Ouch!" and Jay suck in his breath.

"And you don't think my music has style?" asked Mack. He was focussing his stare onto her left eye, having moved upwards and slightly right from the bridge of her nose.

"Sure," she replied, holding his gaze. "When you allowed it to. There are moments of beauty in your music. 'A Bridge of Straw', for example. That's a very true and honest song, a lovely lyric. A possible accusation of your music could be that such emotion isn't allowed out of you too often, however. I think it was Kent Nicholls who said of you, in the famous NME article, that 'you have a tendency towards inanity that doesn't do you or your music justice'."

The four of them were silent for a few moments, then Mack leaned forwards in his chair and looked at the woman.

"Do me a favour," he said, in a voice that made it clear that he wasn't looking for any favours whatsoever. "Do not ever mention that man's name to me again." He paused for a moment, as if a thought had just struck him. "And let's not mention his article either, okay? He's done enough damage already." He got up from his chair, walked around the room once, then sat down again and looked at her. He forced a smile. It wasn't her fault. She didn't know. And yet... he was confused as to how she even knew about the article if she was that young. But for the time being, he had to play the game. She was going to write an article about him, after all. "So...what do you want to know?"

Kimberly looked down at her notes to the first question. Mack noticed that it was typed.

"Why do you make music?" she asked.

"Hmm, good first question," said Mack. "I'm tempted to say something like, 'I don't make the music, it makes itself', but although that is true, it sounds a bit facile." He paused for a moment, looking at the wall.

"It can be a deeply unromantic and technical experience, making music. When I hear a song, perhaps on the radio, I'm listening to how it has been put together. In fact, in some ways, being a musician has rather ruined music for me. I criticise it, analyse it, picking out the arrangement, or a clever bassline, rather than letting it get inside me. I don't know if you guys get that too?" He turned to Jay and Harpo.

Jay mumbled an agreement; Harpo shrugged.

"It begs the question," Mack went on, warming to his theme, "what do people get out of listening to music, or perhaps reading? If you read a great book, do you not think 'I wish I'd written that'? If you heard a great guitar solo, do you not think 'I wish I could play that'? I make music and play music because I want to, because I love it, and because I can." He sat back, pleased with his answer.

"There's a new Mamal 'Best of' album out. Are you proud of your back catalogue?"

"Some of it, yes. There are some songs that stand up. You mentioned 'A Bridge of Straw', that's one I think has aged well. There are others, we're playing some tonight."

Kimberly nodded as if in broad agreement, and Mack noticed that she wasn't making any notes, nor had she brought a tape recorder. He wondered how she was going to manage to remember all this.

"Of course, there are some tracks that haven't stood up to the test of time so well," he said. "And there are others that never had a fair hearing. Like 'Shubunkin', for example, which we're playing tonight. Actually quite a good song, beneath the horrible 80s overproduction. Well, a fun song, anyway. One of the few that Al wrote."

"I think we do that song quite well these days, actually," said Jay, craning his neck a little to make sure Kimberly had seen him.

She turned to smile at him, then returned to her notes. "You won't have heard it yet, of course," Jay continued, "but I've added a lot of percussion parts that make it much more contemporary."

There were a few seconds of silence in the room, punctuated only by a brief awkward laugh coming from Jay, as if to suggest that his interjection had been light-hearted. Kimberly smiled at him again, this time only fleetingly, before turning back to Mack.

"When was the last time you saw Al Smart?" she asked him.

Mack paused for a moment. "A long time ago," he answered. "A lifetime ago, you might say."

She had noticed him looking at her notepad, and now she was writing, rather self-consciously, he thought. It gave him a chance to look at her a little more closely for a moment. She looked a little old to be a student. He had an odd feeling for a moment, as though a future self were trying to send him a message, but he couldn't make out what it was.

She looked up suddenly, still writing, as if trying to catch him doing something he shouldn't have been. Instinctively he smiled awkwardly, and she returned the look with interest. You don't have me, he thought to himself. Far better women than you have tried to seduce me. And very few have succeeded.

She paused briefly as if to underline the point she thought she had scored, before asking her next question. "What was your relationship like when you were in the band together?"

"Depends when you're talking about. When we were at school together, Al and I were never that close, but we just found each other because I was good at playing music and he could sing. Or maybe the point is that he *would* sing. He did, after all, have a great voice for singing pop music, and that's rare. And he was happy for me to be writing all the music and doing the hard work while he flirted with the girls."

Mack took a drink from his nearly empty bottle. He held it up to the light to check how much he had left, then put it down and picked up the pint glass. A fleeting expression of confusion flitted across Jay's face. Mack continued talking. "Over the years Al contracted LSS. As we had some success, everyone wanted his autograph, and he ended up getting all the..." He looked at Kimberly again, choosing his words carefully, "...attention."

"Sorry," said Kimberly, "what's LSS?"

"Lead Singer Syndrome," said Jay, eagerly.

"Ah," said Kimberly, smiling at Jay. "I think I can understand what that means." She looked delete at Mack, expectantly.

Mack looked back at her, not speaking. He wasn't going to make it *that* easy for her. "So what happened?" she asked eventually. "Why did you two split up?"

Mack paused. It might only be for the university rag, but this woman was still going to write what he said and put it in a paper. And things that get said in student papers, if salacious enough, can easily end up in bigger papers. "I think it would just be fair to say that a few people got into his head. Like the aforementioned Mr Nicholls. In the end I wasn't sharing the limelight with him – I was standing in his shadow. It was a shame. We had some good times. I'm sure we'd still be on speaking terms if we saw each other now. He wanted to try acting and an opportunity arose in Hollywood. I wished him luck."

"Indeed," said Kimberly, "after you'd been through so much together it must have been difficult. After the loss of your co-writer, the songs presumably dried up?" She let the point hang for a moment, looking at Mack, almost waiting for a reaction.

"Uh, excuse me, thank you," he said, unable to prevent himself from reacting. "I think you'll find that I wrote the songs. At least the good ones. He was the singer. And a very good one. But he was no songwriter. The only songs he wrote were at the very end, when he suddenly realised how royalties get split." He was working up a bit of steam now, aware that she had poked a finger into a sore spot but unable to prevent himself from reacting. "Royalties follow talent. That's it, that's how it works. The difficult bit, the bit that has longevity, is in the song writing, not in the performance. I wrote those songs, no matter what Kent Nicholls or anyone else has to say about it."

"And presumably those royalties have made you a pretty wealthy man?" asked Kimberly.

Mack held himself back from delivering the first answer that came into his head. After a self-imposed pause, he said, "I think I'd say that's one topic I have no desire to elaborate on." He stared at her for a moment, and she met his gaze.

"Beers?" said Harpo loudly, standing up at the same time.

Jay was still looking dopily at Kimberly.

"Yeah," said Mack, suddenly glad to have been interrupted. "Yeah, thanks."

"Time to go on, chaps," said Harpo, looking at Kimberly, who in turn was looking at Mack. He kicked Jay in the leg.

"Hmm?" said Jay. "Oh, yeah, right, come on then."

Mack stood up and offered his hand to the young woman, who shook it limply while standing up herself.

"Pleasure to meet you, Kimberly," he said. "I hope you got enough for your article."

"Yeah," she replied. "Yeah, I think I got a pretty good idea of how things are."

Harpo held the door open for Kimberly. Although she walked with her head bowed, he couldn't help but notice the self-satisfied smirk that she seemed to be trying to suppress.

Chapter 2

Shutting the door quietly so as not to wake the children, Mack carried his guitar cases through the kitchen and into the garage. Taking a glass from a shelf on the wall of the garage, he poured a measure of Jack Daniels from the table of drinks. It would be considered a generous measure in even the most dubious of establishments. The house had a double garage but only one car, which was never parked in the garage anyway. The second garage was therefore used as a glorified drinks cabinet, with an array of bottles of various types on a large table and a wine rack extending from the floor to near the ceiling.

Diet Coke was poured on top of the ice and Jack Daniels. Mack took a sip. He felt restless. The gig had gone well, albeit to a relatively small crowd. Still, any chance to play his new music these days was gratefully accepted. He didn't want to be in a covers band of his own songs.

Taking both guitars with one hand and the drink in the other, Mack walked up the stairs and into a recording studio built above the garage. It was a large room, with a mixing console, a sofa at the back, several black leather chairs on wheels, and a table in front of the sofa. It even had a vocal booth: a microphone behind thick plastic glass.

Sitting on the chair in front of the mixing desk, he rooted around in a box of disks under the desk, found the one he was looking for, and put it into the Atari computer in front of him. He turned on the power and, while waiting for the machine to start and boot up the programme from the disk, he turned on the eight-track tape player, the midi control unit, the drum machine, the amplifier, and the keyboard. When would someone invent a computer programme to do all these things at the touch of a button?

He wasn't planning on recording anything at this time of night, but he fancied playing along to something, perhaps getting an idea for a guitar line or vocal that he could work on in the morning. After all these years it was as much habit as anything.

The interview had left him feeling uneasy, talking about the old days, about Al. The fickle hand of celebrity had come and gone at a relatively early age, leaving behind a brittle truce between ego and pride. For them it hadn't even been the entire hand but just the index finger of fame, and had not so much put a hand on their shoulders as flicked their ears. Life now not only contained the 'what ifs' and 'what could have beens', but was underlined by the limp truth of 'what had actually happened', always present to torment him.

He sipped the Jack Daniels and Coke, a sip that drained half the glass. Not the best way to quench a thirst, he thought to himself. He was even drinking aggressively. What was it she had said that annoyed him so much? Was it about Al co-writing the songs? That had been the irony, in the end. Al had wanted to be respected as a writer and Mack had wanted to be more famous. They had swapped roles. How stupid it seemed, now it was viewed through the prism of time.

They were only twenty-two when it all finished. And all because of that bloody article, written by that bloody journalist, Kent bloody Nicholls. He knew what he was doing, that man. He knew that if he wrote an article about Mamal that was almost entirely about Al, with only a fleetingly abusive mention of Mack, this would be the mix that would light the fire under Al's ego. What was it he had written? 'The latest album is the fading glory of an already mediocre career. The songwriting on the new album splutters and limps along, like a mortally wounded ferret. While Al Smart has the image and the energy, Mack will look back on his apology of a career – one that has so few peaks it looks like the profile of a small village in Shropshire – and wonder why he didn't set his singer free many years before.'

Kent Bastard Bloody Nicholls. Angrily, he stabbed the Enter button on the keypad and the computer began playing the music, a slow groove. He began to sing, trying to put the journalist out of his mind. The words came out as he was singing, not thinking about them, the lines forming themselves because they scanned with the rhythm of the syllables. Then two more lines came, just because they seemed the obvious next words. The verse finished and he quickly scribbled them onto a pad of paper he always kept ready.

So I am arrogant? Maybe so
You think I'm stupid – how would you know?
If just misguided, then let me be
Because your thoughts have no effect on me

Leaving the track playing to the end, Mack went down the stairs and into the garage to top up his drink, then padded into the lounge. He sat down on the large black leather sofa, placed the drink on the wooden table in front of him and leaned forwards, elbows on knees, rubbing his stubble.

The beers and the gig had brought on the melancholy mood, he was aware of that much. Could it be channelled, used to inspire not inhibit? Melancholia is my muse, he mused. Playing with words, that was how ideas formed. He took another sip and tried to get his mind to think about words, new words, a new song. Lyrics are not poetry, he reminded himself. They are intended to convey rhythm and suggestion; the message or reason can be hinted at, but not stated too boldly. How to conjure up an image in three or four words – that was the art of the songwriter. Was that skill still within him? Given that it was so reactive, he had no idea, no way of finding out until he tested it. Being reliant on something so ephemeral made for a precarious trust in one's own talent. How to shape such ideas, to boil them down – perhaps this should be the subject of the song itself. Irony, yes, that's it, the irony being that in the song he is lamenting the loss of his talent, but written in such a way that his talent is shining through as strong as ever. That first line – that would get him going. The first line so often led to the next, and the next; each pushing forward into the next like dominoes.

He thought of a possible title, I Miss You, which would be the first line of the chorus, or perhaps the last. So, how to build up to that moment when you are unsure whether it is a person or his own talent he is referring to in the third person? He grabbed one of the many notepads with a pen taped to the front that he kept lying around the house; this one on the side table next to the sofa. He could feel the first line bubbling up from the surface of his psyche, exploding out of an almost chemical reaction of his ruminations.

"Are you coming to bed soon?" Jude said, poking her head around the door.

Mack thought he actually heard the popping sound as the idea disappeared back into the fog.

"Soon. Why, does it matter?" He turned back to the pad and closed his eyes, trying to grab the idea. He wanted something to cling on to that he could use to bring it back later, but it just wasn't formed enough to get a decent grip. Jude raised an unnoticed eyebrow in disapproval and disappeared back out of the room.

He made a mental note of a line: If you feel it, then be it. That would be pretty good as his epitaph. Better than the one Jude had suggested: He was never too far from an opinion.

Jude returned, a glass of water in one hand and a book entitled *Bead On A Wire: Making Handcrafted Wire And Beaded Jewellery* in the other. "Goodnight," she said tersely, and disappeared.

"Jude," Mack called. She came back in. "Sorry for being grumpy. I was in the middle of an idea when you came in." He smiled, hopefully. It was too late for an argument.

Jude smiled back. She had a nice smile, thought Mack; it was something about her he still appreciated, even after being so familiar with her face.

"There's a lyric," he said.

"Where?" Jude replied.

"No, I mean *'there's* a lyric', not 'there's a *lyric*' – 'I've grown accustomed to her face'."

"I'm not sure I want to know the reason why you've just thought of that." Jude leaned against the doorframe patiently.

"It's from *My Fair Lady.*"

"Yes, I know. I am the female round here, so I am more likely to be the one out of the two of us to know that fact. Unless you are going to have a gay midlife crisis. The fact that we went to see the newly restored version at the cinema last week also gave me a hint."

"I've been thinking about that lyric. It's actually not very nice."

"Really." Jude said it more as a statement than a question. She perched herself on the arm of the sofa, crossed her legs, placed the booked precariously on her knee and crossed her arms, still holding the glass of water.

"I've grown accustomed to her face," Mack went on. "It's not exactly adulation, is it? I mean, it's hardly 'She's gorgeous and I'd give her one.'"

"I'm not sure that's a line that would work, coming from Rex Harrison."

"Accepted. But if he's falling in love with her, then wouldn't something a little stronger be better? And the next line – 'She almost makes the day begin'. Almost? Why almost? It suggests she's lacking in something." He put on a posh Rex Harrison voice, half speaking, half singing. "You do a pretty good job, luv. I mean, you're not bad. In fact, you almost make the day begin. Do try a bit harder, though, won't you, there's a good girl."

"But that's the point, surely," said Jude. "He's gotten used to her being around. He's only just realising he might be falling in love with her, but he doesn't recognise it as love. He's an old fart."

Mack was warming to his theme and not really listening to Jude's contribution to the discussion. "'Her ups and downs are second nature to me now'. Second nature? He's gone straight from not being in love to having been married to her for twenty years. He completely missed out the courtship phase, the exciting romance, and gone straight into married humdrum. He's missed out the good bit."

"Welcome to the club," said Jude, perhaps just a bit quieter than she had intended.

Mack went on talking. "Isn't there something about 'Like breathing out and breathing in'? I mean, can you think of an analogy more inclined to state that you are taking someone for granted?" Mack put his glass down on the table so that he could gesticulate better. "I know the idea is that he's trying to decide whether to take her back or not, but she's not a dog, you know? It's always bugged me, the second half of that film, especially the very last moment when he asks for his slippers and she takes a step or two towards him, smiling. So patronising. He hardly lets her get a word in edgeways all film, and then condescends to take her back at the end. What an idiot."

"I'm going to bed," Jude said, taking the book from her knee and standing up.

"Hmm? Oh, don't do that. I've had a few drinks, I feel like chatting."

"I know, that's why I'm going to bed." Jude smiled, relenting from her grumpy stance. "Anyway, I'm tired."

She reached over and he gave her a kiss on the cheek. "But I was enjoying talking to you, though," he said.

"Okay. Don't be long, now. I don't want you arriving with Johnny in the playground looking hung-over again."

"He's proud of his dad. Anyway, I've got an image to uphold, you know. This is what ex-minor pop stars do. We stay up late, brooding, thinking increasingly negative thoughts and drinking rock-and-roll-type drinks."

"Stan Cullimore of The Housemartins writes children's books."

"Okay, so one or two ex-minor pop stars spoil it for the rest of us."

Jude smiled at him. After few moments, she said, "What did we used to talk about when we were in love?"

"Hmm, tough one," said Mack, rubbing his chin dramatically. "Dunno. Ask me one about sport."

Jude laughed, lightly. "Goodnight," she said, as she went out.

Picking up his pen and paper, Mack stood up and walked to the window. There was a beautiful, bright moonlit night out there, and he could see into the garden, his own reflection creating a strange morphing effect in the double glazed glass.

Did he really think his talent had deserted him? He could still turn a mean phrase, he felt sure of that. But who was listening? The problem with having had a hit was that no one took you seriously anymore. If he did manage to come up with something as good as 'A Bridge of Straw' (as good as? Hah! He'd written a dozen songs better than that one since), who would listen to it?

He didn't need the income – royalties from 'A Bridge of Straw' would always see to that. But how badly did he need the audience? There was enjoyment to be had from making music at home, massive enjoyment in fact, but if no one heard it, what was the point? If he played his music in the woods with no one there to hear it, would it actually make a sound? Could the music within him matter for its own sake? What it would be like to make music solely for himself? What would come out of him then? What if he finally became a true conduit for his own music, and not the apologetic singer he felt himself to be?

37

Chapter 3

"Come on, Mary, love, it's time to get up. Seriously now, you're going to be late." Jude went out of the bedroom and left the door open.

Mary hated it when she did that. It meant she had to get out of bed to shut the door. That meant she may as well get up properly. So annoying.

Looking up at her from the corner of her bedroom, crumpled in an untidy heap, was her school uniform. A pair of yesterday's knickers lay guiltily on top: the last item of clothing rejected before being replaced by pyjamas. Now the reverse operation took place, with the only concession to hygiene being a fresh pair of knickers garnered from the top drawer of her pine chest, with the old uniform put back on over the top. Mary stood at the top of the stairs running her tongue around the claggy recesses of her mouth, still not fully awake. Monday morning, she thought to herself as she went down for breakfast. Blergh.

Mack took a bite of his toast. "What's on at school today, Mary?"

She didn't bother to answer. All she could hear was the sound of her father masticating. It was such a disgusting sound, and once she had heard it, she felt unable to listen to anything else. Why did he have to always ask her questions with his mouth full? It wasn't like he actually wanted to know the answer. Go back to your stupid conversations with Johnny.

Silently, Jude put a plate of toast covered in lemon curd on the table. Without looking up, Mary took a bite and tried to harmonise her internal noises with those of her father in order to block out his grossness. She stared at the table to better focus on not listening to him, to remove all distractions. Breakfast with my family is a time to be endured, not enjoyed, she thought. Is it supposed to be like this? Is this what is happening right now in every house in the country, or is it just me? Why do I have to be so different?

Breakfast negotiated, teeth brought briefly into contact with toothbrush, she grabbed her school bag and shouted a goodbye as she slammed the door shut behind her. She looked up into the rain that seemed to be coming to an end, and felt cheered. There was something about the randomness of April weather that she enjoyed: one moment it was lashing with rain, the next bright sunshine, blinding with the brightness of the wet pavements.

She loped down the driveway, lost in thought. The school uniform code left little room for individuality, but she wore trousers rather than a skirt. Her hair was closer to black than brown, shoulder length and in the style that suggested she didn't much care for going to the hairdresser. Although the curse of acne visited the sides of her face, she was a pretty girl, something she seemed determined to mask. She wore no make-up – ever – and wore clothes influenced by bands such as Nirvana and Pearl Jam, a fact she would only realise in hindsight.

She saw Stevie Humbert, known as Stretch, waiting at the end of her road, leaning against a high stone wall. He was balancing his school bag on his head and was reading a book, probably the same book he had been reading for a long time now, *Catcher in the Rye*. Good old Stretch. She smiled. Stretch thought that he was walking *her* to school – Mary knew it was really the other way round.

"Right?" she said, as she approached him, jerking her head upwards slightly.

"Right?" he responded, the school bag falling off his head. He closed the book but kept hold of it and picked up the bag. They walked off.

Stretch was stick-thin, tall, and stooped. Mary thought him to be fairly cool, mainly due to his languid demeanour and his hobbies of drumming and knitting. He had lanky, dark hair that sat on his shoulders as if a plate of spaghetti had been poured over his head. He had a face that was the same shape as his body: thin, but with a nose that, had he ever attempted to kiss a girl, would more likely have poked her in the eye first. Mary teased him about this sometimes, just to underline that they were only friends.

His nickname had been coined by their art teacher, Mr Flynn, who had seen him waiting for Mary one day after school, lying on the grass with his hands behind his head. Mr Flynn had begun singing a Smiths song at him as he walked past. "Stretch out and wait/Stretch out and wait/Let your puny body lie down/Lie down."

Some older students had heard this and thought it was hilarious – partly because Mr Flynn was considered pretty cool – so they began calling him Stretch from then onwards. Like only the best nicknames, it had stuck.

Mary was young for her year, and Stretch was already fourteen. To look at them, however, you'd have thought that he was her younger brother, despite his height. They both loped, but Stretch took the word to its logical conclusion, his long, easy stride and hunched shoulders making him look like an extra from a 1970s Robert Crumb comic strip that Mary had seen in one of her father's books. When she watched him walk, head bent with curtains of straight unwashed hair hanging vertically, she half expected him to raise one arm and do the peace sign while continuing to walk and stare at the ground. Mary also took her time, but she loped with a confidence that suggested she would be the one in charge of whatever it was that you asked the two of them to do.

They walked through a housing estate, taking shortcuts through narrow lanes, the houses smaller now, more uniform, row after row of boxes. High garden fences loomed over them, the experience akin to a rolling down a marble run.

Mary looked sideways at Stretch and grinned, only using the side of her mouth that he could see. "You ready?" she said.

"Is it my turn?" he replied.

"Yes. As you well know."

"Oh God," he sighed. "Okay. Give me a second."

"Don't tell me that you were standing there waiting for me and hadn't been thinking of it."

"Not really. Well, not much. Okay, yes. But I've not got very far."

"Well, time's up. Give me what you've got."

"Okay. How about this." He paused. "'I'd like to ignore my life and concentrate on my dreams.'"

"Hey, that's not bad. For you." Mary smiled to show she was joking, even though she wasn't really. "Okay, my turn." She went quiet for a moment, thinking. "Okay," she said. "'I'd like to ignore my life, and focus on my dreams.' How about if the next line was 'If only I had the time.'"

"Yeah, okay," said Stretch. "Followed by 'or the money.'"

Mary laughed. "'Or the bloody inclination.' The end!"

They stopped for a second, unable to walk and laugh at the same time. He put his hand on her shoulder, bending over with a giggling fit, while she cackled loudly. After a minute or so they began walking again, still chuckling.

Stretch spoke first. "Is that what they call irony?"

"I think so," said Mary. "My dad did explain irony to me once, but I wasn't really paying attention." She gave another sideways glance, to see if he'd got the joke. He was smiling, but that could just as easily be trapped wind.

Mary was only too aware that Stretch got a hard time from some of his classmates for being friends with Mary. Mary the Moan, they called her behind her back. Only because it was alliterative, not because it was true – that's just how kids were. That's just the way it is to be a teenager. She knew that.

"Okay, your turn," he said.

"Right, the first thing that comes into my head. Oh, yeah, alright, how about 'You're the first thing that comes into my head.' Your turn."

"Um." Stretch thought for a moment. "How about 'Every morning when I'm lying in bed.'"

"Scans nicely. Okay." Mary paused for a moment, thinking, then said, "'To the darkness of my life you bring light.'"

"'And take me to where only angels can tread.'"

"Ouch! That's actually really cool! I like that lots. Not sure about the bed bit, but I reckon we can improve that. You remember it – we'll work on it at school."

"Okay."

Mary looked around her. They had been walking down a lane between two houses, where trees in the gardens on either side were hanging over the tall, slatted fencing, creating, a dark, tunnel effect. As they neared the end, a man turned into the lane in front of them. He had the collar on his large overcoat turned up and his hands in his pockets, hunched over in the cold and damp, as if unused to such conditions.

Stretch and Mary had to walk single file to allow the man to pass them. As he did so, he looked at them both and smiled. Standing upright he would have been about the same height as Stretch when he stooped, which was always. He had a deep tan, insanely white teeth, and a receding hairline.

"How about 'A strength that breathes within you'," said Mary, as they walked side by side again.

"Hmm, not sure," said Stretch. "Does strength actually breathe? It's vaguely deep without actually making any sense. Classic rock lyrics, I suppose. Okay, let me think."

"Excuse me. Are you Mary?" The man who passed them had stopped and turned halfway towards them, still hunched over but now looking at them with his head cocked sideways. Mary and Stretch turned.

"Um, can I help you?" she said, tentatively.

"That *is* Mary, isn't it? Jeez, you can see your mother in there." He was peering at her face now, moving slightly forwards. She could detect a slight American accent, but it was a confused accent, one she found hard to place.

"Okay, that's officially creepy," Mary said to Stretch under her breath. She then spoke to Al, still around fifteen metres away but slowly walking closer, trying to act as unthreatening as possible. "Do I know you?" she asked him. Unknowingly, she took a step closer to Stretch. Also unknowingly, Stretch stood slightly straighter.

"Mary, do you remember me? I'm Al. Your dad's old partner. In Mamal?"

"Um, I am aware of you, yes, I know about Mamal and stuff. You went to America, right? You're a movie actor. I've heard Mum and Dad talk about you from time to time."

"Do they? That's good. That's kind of them. Are they, um, are they home?"

"Yeah, well around, anyway. Dad will be taking my brother to school."

"Well, yeah, that's great, cool. I was, uh, thinking of going to see them. Do you think that would be okay?" He smiled, and both Stretch and Mary recoiled at the full view of a mouthful of pristine white teeth.

"Sure. Don't see why not," Mary replied, shrugging, trying to convey that she really wasn't sure why this man was asking her.

She looked at him a bit more closely. He wasn't exactly what she had imagined a movie star to look like. He seemed nervous, somehow. His hair was cut very short, almost shaved, as if in reaction to the fact that it was receding. He had a few days' worth of growth on his chin and was tanned, although she was not altogether sure whether the tan was real or fake. Either way, it looked out of place in England in early April. He was dressed all in black, with a long black trench coat over black boots. She couldn't take her eyes off his teeth. They were perfect in every way and quite an unnatural shade of white.

"Thank you," he said to her. He smiled, his lips drawn back, teeth closed perfectly together. "I hope we can speak again soon."

She smiled back and Al turned to walk away from them, hunching over like a man not used to invasive drizzle and the absence of warmth in the air. Mary stood for a few moments, watching him. She smiled a weak, uncertain smile at Stretch, and then they continued on their way to school.

"What was that all about? What's Mamal?" asked Stretch.

"Oh, my dad was in a band."

"Yeah? Were they big?"

"They had a few hits, I think."

"No way!" Stretch stopped walking, his mouth open. He dropped the book he had been carrying, then bent down to pick it up. "How come you never told me that?" he asked Mary.

"Didn't you know?" she replied. "I thought everyone knew about that. Anyway, it was a pretty lame band. It's really not something you shout about, believe me."

"Well, I disagree. I think he's very cool, and to have had a hit and stuff…wow, that's amazing."

"I'm not sure that disagreeing was actually an option." Mary was getting irritated. "Can we just drop it please?"

"But what was the hit called? Was he on *Top of the Pops*? Did he tour and stuff? Did they do albums? I always wondered why he didn't really work but just taught guitar a bit. So cool. Did he write the stuff? Was he…"

"Enough!" Mary almost shouted. "Please, can we change the subject? Thank you."

They walked the rest of the way to school in silence, the lyric game forgotten.

43

Chapter 4

Jude spread the paperwork out across the large dining room table that she and Mack had bought so many years ago, just as Mamal had signed their recording contract. She stood up straight for a moment and read some of the scribbles in various coloured inks. When Mary was a toddler, they had allowed her to draw all over the table, thinking that they would soon replace the cheap pine version with something more expensive. Over the years, however, it had become a memento of her childhood and an integral part of all their lives. Johnny added his own drawings and scribbles, mainly misshapen drawings of Mack with pink spiky hair and a big smile. Always with a big smile.

An array of receipts and orders confronted her. The jewellery had been selling pretty well recently, and the nagging, tempting thought that there might be a living in it danced tenaciously in front of her in the form of sales confirmations from the various shops that stocked her jewellery. There was more time in the day now that Johnny was settling in well at school; time she had waited for patiently for what seemed an eternity. Time to bring her ideas to fruition.

Others made necklaces and rings that were very beautiful, whereas Jude noticed what sold, what people actually bought, and then made more of it. That was the difference between making jewellery and having a jewellery business. These orders were the proof.

A few loose strands of greying hair were reinstated behind the ear with the sweep of an index finger, an automated manoeuvre from someone with a long history of indeterminate length hair. If Jude had been concerned with the opinion of others then she may have been aware that they found it difficult to make a firm assessment. What some called visually unobtrusive, others felt was demonstrating an inner confidence. Jude knew that she exuded such ambiguity, but chose not to concern herself with which side of that particular fence other people chose to lean against while they gossiped.

Mack would be back from the school run soon. Was he teaching today? She thought not, in which case he would go and noodle around in his studio, the two of them keeping out of each other's way in a well practised manner until it was time for Mack to go and pick up Johnny.

Jude got her typewriter out of a cupboard and put it on the table. I must get one of those word processors, she thought to herself. It would make all this annoying paperwork so much easier. Placing a blank invoice into the top of the typewriter, she began to mechanically go through the pile of sales slips. The quicker she could do these, the quicker she could escape to her studio in the shed at the end of the garden.

Mary had seemed a little distant this morning, even by her standards. She would have been meeting Stretch for the walk to school; he seemed to be a good influence. Her mind wandered back to the friends she had spent time with at school. Most of her senior school years included Mack, but not all; he didn't have a completely exclusive right to her youthful memories. Al, of course, he'd been pretty ever present too, although they had never been especially close. Had he been close to anyone? Not an easy person to warm to.

She tore out the first sheet, now completed, placed a fresh sheet in the roll, and wound it into position. Invoicing was a job she didn't exactly relish, but it wasn't taxing, just monotonous, allowing her mind to drift.

Al Smart. Not quite as smart as he thought he was. She recalled when Al first came in with a song. He'd never come up with anything new before. The week previously, she noticed how he had gone quiet when someone was discussing how royalties were shared out within Spandau Ballet, and how Gary Kemp, the main songwriter, received most of the money. She almost heard the clunk as the penny dropped with him. Surprise, surprise, the following week he came along with a song that he'd wanted the group to do. 'Shubunkin' it was called, with a bizarre lyric about fish. He tried to show them how it would fit in with a new dance, and he looked absolutely hilarious in his ankle boots and floppy hair, jumping up and down in their front room. And, as if to prove a point, Mack had come up with 'A Bridge of Straw', a song with poignant lyrics about the fragility of love and a beautiful melody.

45

'I'm the main songwriter in this band,' it said, 'and don't you forget it.'

Another invoice was removed from the typewriter. It had been a good week. She opened a blue notebook and wrote down the quantities of each type of jewellery that had been sold.

What would Mary be doing at school now? Break time, probably sitting with Stretch somewhere, scowling at the world. That's what she did when she was that age, sitting with Mack. They hadn't needed much else. She almost wished they had. There were a few other friends, like Spencer. Why had he popped into her mind? He was a boy in the year above. Sometimes when Mack was otherwise engaged – hanging around in the music block, practising or talking about Led Zeppelin with some mates – then she would spend time with Spencer. He was good to talk to, a thinker, like her. They would just sit on a wall and talk, having those difficult teenage conversations about life. Looking back, she did wonder if Spencer had been just a bit in love with her. She smiled to herself. Of course he had – who was she kidding? That was part of the attraction.

She remembered walking through school towards registration one morning with some friends. Spencer had arrived next to them, and said hello. He had obviously run to catch them up, but was pretending he was just walking the same way. He'd made a comment about Jude looking like she was in a good mood that day because she seemed to have a bounce in her stride. It was the sort of detail that gave away a little more than he meant it to – that he noticed her, always – and he immediately went red. Jude, aware of the slight faux pas, just said thanks, and how kind it was of him to notice. She'd already been attached to Mack for so long by then that compliments were a nice surprise.

Finishing the last invoice, Jude put the typewriter away, went to the kitchen, boiled the kettle, and made a cup of tea. Taking three chocolate biscuits out of a packet left by the bread bin, she took the mug and went back out to the garden and into the shed. This was her real home from home, where all her jewellery-making equipment was kept; the place where she could get real peace and quiet. No one disturbed her here. She didn't even take the telephone out there, the new cordless one that you could take up to a hundred feet away from the base.

Picking up a pair of pliers, hunched over a silver earring, Jude tried again to remember what it had been like to be a teenage girl. Spencer once again came into her thoughts. What had they talked about for such long periods? The meaning of life, for sure, but what had been so important back then? What would Mary be troubled about now? Were they the same things that troubled her then?

Meanwhile, Al knocked at the front door, but got no response. He decided not to leave a note, and instead walked back to the guest house he was staying in.

Chapter 5

Hooking his toe around the edge of the door with his foot meant that Mack didn't need to put down the tray he was carrying. Shutting the door with his bottom, he walked up the stairs to his studio. On the wall, next to the wine rack, were four guitar hooks, two of which were empty. Jay was sitting on the black leather sofa playing the theme from *M*A*S*H* on the Ovation Legend guitar and an acoustic guitar handmade by a local friend of Mack's was leaning against the mixing desk.

A Gibson Les Paul Gold Top, the main electric guitar Mack played ever since the day he could finally afford to buy it, was hanging from one peg. The final hanger held a banjo, but the screws were just starting to come out of the wall. It was as if the hook was embarrassed to be seen clutching such an instrument. Mack could play the banjo, he just chose not to. It seemed fairer all round that way.

Mack brought over a bowl of chilli peanuts and two empty glasses, putting them down next to a bottle of Grand Cru Burgundy from the Montrachet vineyard that he had already opened. Effects units – black metal cases of identical size and shape but with varying arrays of LED lights on the front – blinked at them from underneath the table which held the mixing desk.

Pouring out two glasses of wine, Mack then placed one of them in front of Jay. The other he took a sip from, holding the dark red wine in the floor of his mouth while he sucked in air across the top of it. He placed the glass in front of his stool, picked up the guitar, and sat down, resting his arms across the top of the instrument as he watched his friend concentrating on what he was playing.

Jay Golding was not a great guitarist, but he was an all-rounder: a musician who could get by on most instruments. He had never been able to stick at one particular instrument long enough to be able to master it, and instead flitted from one to another as he needed them. Mack said he had the 'best right hand in Nether Littleton', a sobriquet that Jay saw for the backhanded insult that Mack intended it to be.

He always seemed to Mack to be happy. Happily married, a happy father of two, and happy working as co-owner of Golding & Head, the main firm of estate agents in Nether Littleton. The village had grown considerably since Mack had been a child, and was threatening to transmogrify into a town. Mack often referred to it as a village surrounded by housing estates with a shopping precinct stuck in the middle. It was as if the town plans had been designed by the pupils of the local junior school, still sleepy after their mid-morning milk.

Jay was tall, with hair that always looked as if it had just been washed (usually because it had). A modestly vain man, he made the most of his looks, and was something of a throwback to a previous generation in that he carried a comb in his back pocket. The long, thick hair started in the middle of his head and flowed downwards. The middle parting started at the crown, on the apex of his head, and came forwards in a perfectly straight line. When it reached his forehead, the two sides of his hair simply flowed away from his face and down either side in two perfect wave formations. With bright blue eyes, when he leaned forwards his face looked like it was doing an impression of the parting of the Red Sea.

"Do you know," said Jay, placing the heel of his right hand on the strings of the guitar to stop them from vibrating, "we've got new cleaners in the office." He always referred to the shop as the office, even though it was in the shopping precinct. Jay's personal office was a room at the back, the only room other than the toilet and the kitchen not to face onto the shoppers. Sarah Head sat out front, as she was best at dealing with new customers. "I was still there at six tonight. Everyone else had gone and this girl arrived from the new cleaning company. Dyed blonde hair, big tits, a t-shirt that must have belonged to her considerably younger – and smaller – sister, and a little too much black eyeliner. Not bad-looking, to be fair. And do you know what? I bloody well could have."

"Oh, come on," replied Mack. "Seriously?" He pointed to the plate of peanuts.

"Thank you, no," said Jay, holding up his left hand, the right hand sweeping back his hair, which then fell back into exactly the same position it had started in. "Seriously, she was just kind of looking at me in a funny way – frankly, in a way that no woman has looked at me for a very long time. Especially one who is probably only twenty years old. Weird."

"You're not a bad-looking bloke."

"That's usually a very sexy thing to hear someone say, unless that someone happens to be you." Jay reached forward, took a handful of nuts, and poured them into his mouth.

"So what did you do?" Mack shaped various chord positions silently with his left hand, getting the fingers loose.

"Thought about it a lot, what did you think I would do?" Jay paused to swallow some of the nuts, making it easier to talk. "She was bending over to empty the rubbish bins into sacks, and these whopping great breasts were just dangling around in the most delightful fashion, straining to get out of her bra. You could just imagine standing behind her and cupping them both in your hands."

"I'm sure she would have appreciated the help." Mack leaned forward and took another pull on his wine.

"I've not been able to get it out of my head since. The possibility that I actually could have had sex, in my office, with a girl that much younger than me."

"Except, of course, that it wasn't a possibility at all. It all happened inside your fevered little brain," said Mack, tapping his finger against the side of his head.

Jay looked thoughtful for a moment. "What you don't understand, Mack, is that women are like an island. Specifically, like the island of Saint Nicholas, just off the Northern Coast of Spain."

"Oh, really." Mack folded his arms, tilted his head and raised his eyebrows, all in one fluid show of mordacity.

"I read about this place in a book. You see, there is a rather distinguishing feature about the island. It can be reached by boat or by a good swimmer from the harbour on the mainland. However, the rocks surrounding it make it impossible to land – apart from twice a day, at low tide, when a path through the rocks opens up. It's only there for an hour each time, as if the island will only allow you to enjoy what it has to offer for a limited period of time. And that is how a woman should be viewed. She is invariably willing – she just has to be approached at the right time, and in the right way."

"Good grief," said Mack. "That has to be the most tortured analogy I have heard in a long time."

"Thank you. You honour me. So, you know that phrase 'I'm old enough to be her father'," asked Jay, now warming to his theme. "Well, it doesn't really mean anything until it actually applies to you. Then you suddenly get it. Now I really know just how horrible that phrase is, because it is paralysing. It's one thing to say that you are old enough to be her father when it's only technically true. But when it is not only possible, it's actually bleedin' realistic, you feel very old indeed. Which is so totally not fair, because she did have a really great pair of tits." Jay drained his glass.

Mack laughed. "That's the difference between you and me, mate."

"What's that," asked Jay.

"Culture."

Jay raised his eyebrows and rubbed the side of his nose with his middle finger, aiming the obscene gesture obviously towards Mack.

"Like that girl who did the interview," Jay continued. "If she's a student, there are some very lucky young men in this world. And yet…. And yet…." Jay raised his eyes to the heavens, "My goodness, I could have. And she wouldn't even have had to ask me nicely."

"Why do you say 'if' she's a student?" asked Mack.

Jay tilted his head to one side, a clear indication that he was thinking. "I dunno," he said. "There was just something… not right about her. She looked older than twenty-one for a start."

"It's been troubling me a bit too. She certainly looked older, but then she could always be a mature student."

"She got under your skin a bit, didn't she," Jay said, carefully.

"Yeah, well, I was caught a bit off guard, that was all. How could she have known about Kent Nicholls? That article of his killed the band stone dead. No one's written anything about us since, so how could she have known about him? We're barely a footnote in pop history. Why did she bring it up? Left me with an odd feeling, if I'm honest, like she was poking a stick at me to try and get a reaction."

"Well, it worked."

Mack looked at him, slightly irritated.

Jay smiled foolishly, his eyes wide. "Don't suppose it helped that she was possibly the most beautiful woman any one of us has ever seen that wasn't in a Bond movie."

Mack smiled. "Yeah, she was a bit special, wasn't she."

"Ah, so you did notice! I knew there was a dirty old man in there trying to get out."

"Jay, forget it. If there were to be any chance that I might have sex again in my life, it is most certain that it would be with my wife."

"Oh dear," said Jay. "Like that is it?" Mack didn't reply so Jay changed the subject for him. "So, I was in Bath the other day," he went on. "Went to the jazz shop to see my mate, Tony. That's a shop that sells jazz records, just to be clear. I was walking up the road and this woman was walking towards me. Seriously good-looking in that 'posh filly' kind of way. Nice figure, just jeans and a jacket, nothing too fancy, but a classy looking girl." He paused to take a sip from his wine glass. "So," he continued, "I was looking at her as we approached each other, when suddenly she looked straight back at me. I held her gaze for a second, and she gave me the most gorgeous smile. It was like a spark of recognition, a shared moment of tenderness. It was over in a moment as she went by, but it was such a horny moment."

"Beautiful," said Mack, slightly ironically, slightly wistfully.

"Problem was," said Jay, "as I walked past her I started laughing to myself, because I realised something. There was I, walking along, imagining to myself what she would look like naked. And yet there was her, thinking to herself, 'Aah, he looks just like my dad.'"

Mack laughed hard, Jay joining him. After a few moments, they both took a sip of wine and put their glasses down, still smiling. Mack launched into the opening guitar lick of 'Make Me Smile (Come Up and See Me)' and they sang the opening line together: "You've done it all," both guitars beginning strumming on the final word.

Chapter 6

The following morning, Mack lay in bed, staring out of the window at the top of the oak tree in the field behind the house, a bare chest exposed above the duvet. He had already been joined by Johnny and read him some more of *Treasure Island*. Jude had gone down to make the kids' breakfast, and Johnny had now gone down to join her. Mary was still getting dressed. Mack knew he would need to get up soon himself. Jude wouldn't be making anything for him; he'd have to fix his own toast before walking Johnny to school.

He felt uneasy, unsettled. Why had he let that student get under his skin? Swinging his long legs out of the bed, he sat for a moment, stretching his neck to one side and holding the position, enjoying the feeling of blood flowing into a stiff muscle. He stood, scratched his groin unsatisfyingly through soft pyjama trousers, then walked over to his chest of drawers and pulled open the top drawer. Rummaging through underwear of assorted hues and tie-dyed t-shirts, he saw the magazine. He didn't need to take it out to picture the article that Kent Nicholls had written to get back at him, including the picture of Al. Just Al. A subtle yet powerful denunciation.

The real reason for his uneasiness had been roaming in the back of his mind, prowling, waiting for the moment to strike, for the right time to reveal itself. Now, it came hurtling back at him, past the defences he had constructed over the years. It was a memory of a night on tour, a night influenced by strong drink, and stronger drugs. A memory that had been aroused by the mention of Kent Nicholls.

Agitated, he got dressed quickly, blocking the memory once again. He went downstairs, knocking on Mary's door as he went past and calling her to hurry up.

Five minutes later, as if she had waited in order to demonstrate that it was not as a result of her father knocking on her door, Mary came down the stairs for breakfast in her school uniform. Jude placed some tea and toast on the table for her. Mack and Johnny were already at the table, discussing *Star Wars*, Johnny eating from a bowl of Rice Krispies.

"But Dad, Luke was born to be a Jedi. That's why he could be trained so fast."

"Sorry, I'm not buying that one. Yoda trains Luke for the same amount of time as it takes the Millennium Falcon to be chased back to Lando's Cloud City. They start training, we see the Millennium Falcon get chased, then we see Luke finishing his training. Is it really that easy to be trained to be a Jedi?"

"But this is Luke we're talking about, Dad. He was born to be a Jedi. It's just easier for him." Johnny seemed to have picked up the art of rolling his eyes in irritation, although in his case it was for comedic affect.

"Look," said Mack, "at one point, Yoda states that Jedi training must start as a young child. So how can Luke learn it in a day?"

"Because he's Luke, of course. And because Obi was keeping an eye on him when he was growing up. He probably taught him some cool Jedi stuff without Luke even knowing it."

"Mum," said Mary, "are they really having a conversation about *Star Wars* again?"

"Leave them to it," replied Jude. "They are males. That means they are just a little bit backwards in certain ways. It's not their fault. It's in their genes."

"You leave my jeans out of it," said Mack.

"Oh, Daaad," said Johnny.

Mary just shook her head and shifted her gaze down towards the table.

"I have nothing to declare except my jeans," said Mack, loftily, one hand over a rough approximation of where he thought his heart might be, the other raised into the air. "Oscar Wilde almost said that."

Johnny looked up at him, smiling, his entire face a picture of adoration for his father. "Who was Oscar Wilde?" He took a spoonful of cereal.

Mack stood up. "Ah, 'tis a long story, my child. He was a brilliant man, not dissimilar to myself in many ways."

Johnny's eyes rolled again, involuntarily but happily.

"He was a very funny man, wrote lots of plays, and became famous for being rude to lots of people."

"And he was gay and got arrested for it," said Mary.

"Thank you Mary. Glad to see the genius of Mr Wilde is still taught to open minded teenagers."

"And he died penniless in Paris at the age of forty-six," Mary continued.

Mack looked at his daughter, clearly impressed.

"Didn't you know that, Dad?" Mary said, genuinely surprised at her father's ignorance. "I thought everyone knew that." She returned to her breakfast.

"What's gay, Dad?" asked Johnny.

Mary started to answer but Mack put a hand up to quieten her. "Thank you, Mary, I shall take this one, if you don't mind." He turned to Johnny. "It means a man who falls in love with another man."

"Or a woman who falls in love with a woman," said Mary.

"Indeed," said Mack.

"What, like Luke and Han?" said Johnny.

"Oh yeah, definitely, they are *so* gay," said Mary, her left eyebrow achieving seemingly impossibly arched heights.

"I'm not exactly sure that your input on this subject is helping enormously, to be honest, Mary. That's not quite right, Johnny, because Han fell in love with Princess Leia." He started to sing – "Could it be I'm falling in love, with you bab-y."

Mary took a mouthful of toast. "Did that Al guy manage to find you?" she said through the crunching.

Mack stopped singing and looked at Jude, who raised her eyebrows at him.

"What Al guy, sweetheart?" she asked Mary.

"Dad," said Johnny, "what about Luke and Obi-Wan…"

"Not now, mate," snapped Mack, more abruptly than he meant to. He was looking at Mary, but, seeing the disapproving look on Jude's face, turned to Johnny. "Sorry, Johnny, I just wanted to hear what Mary was saying." He smiled at Johnny, who smiled back without opening his mouth, then went back to playing with a Thunderbird 2 toy that he had been eyeing the entire time.

Mary was looking at her mum. "Al. You know, the one that was in that band with Dad. I saw him yesterday, on the way to school."

"Did you, now," said Jude, a forced smile making itself obvious.

"Yeah. He said he was looking for you. Said he was going to come here."

"And did he come here?" asked Mack, looking at Jude.

"Well of course he didn't. Not that I heard, anyway, you know I can't hear the door from the shed." Jude's eyebrow raised itself accusingly at him.

"Okay, okay, just asking," said Mack, holding one hand up to placate her. "I wonder what he's doing here. Last I heard he was continuing to fail at his movie career."

"That's not nice, Mack," said Jude. "If he has come to visit, you should be nice to him."

"Really?" Mack sank into a sulk, folding his arms.

Mary tutted, not at anyone or anything specifically, just a general tut in the general direction of her family. She got up and put her plate and glass into the sink. Jude automatically took it out of the sink and put it in the dishwasher.

"See you later," said Mary, leaving the kitchen.

"Brush your teeth before you go, please," called Jude. Then, to Johnny, "Come on, you, upstairs and brush your teeth."

Johnny picked up his bowl and noisily slurped down the rest of the milk, before scraping back his chair and going upstairs, leaving the bowl on the table. Mack was gazing out of the window. Jude came over to pick up the bowl, but instead stopped and sat down at the table. She put her hand on his arm.

"It would be nice to see Al again," she said.

"Mm."

"Oh, come on, it's water under the bridge, isn't it? Don't be negative."

"Do you know," said Mack, turning to face Jude, "my immediate reaction is that I can't be bothered. It's done, I've moved on in so many ways. I've no interest in seeing him or going back over that stuff."

"Well, he probably doesn't want to go over things either."

"Doesn't matter. I will, whether I want to or not. At night, cogitating. You know how my bastard brain works. Never gives in."

"Ah, yes, your cogitating. Or, as you could call it, worrying. Come on, be positive for once in your life."

"I am not being negative," said Mack. "And it's not worrying if there's a point to it." He paused for a moment, realising that he was heading down a blind alley at the end of which lay a lost argument that served no purpose. He stared out of the window for a few moments before speaking again. "Dull, dull, dull. I don't need this in my life."

"Come on Dad, we're going to be late." Johnny was stood in the doorway with his coat on, school bag on his back. Mack turned towards him, his arm draped over the back of the chair. Behind the boy, Mack saw Mary walking out the door, allowing it to slam heavily behind her. Jude took the bowl to the dishwasher.

"Excellent work, Captain Amazing," Mack said to Johnny. "However, just one small problem."

Johnny looked back at him, head tilted to the side, eyes narrowed. "What?" he said slowly.

"Well, I'm not wanting to cast aspersions on your character..." said Mack.

"Cast a whoody on my whaty?" said Johnny.

"To suggest that you might be anything other than my perfect son."

Johnny smiled.

Mack went on. "However, the fact that it is a chilly autumn day, with the prospect of rain at some point today, does make me think that shoes might well be a good option."

Johnny looked down at his feet and squealed. He laughed and went to put his shoes on.

"That boy," said Mack, to Jude and yet to no one in particular, "is what I need in my life. No ego. In direct contrast to Al sodding Smart." He stood up, issued a brief "See you later" to Jude, and went out of the kitchen. He stopped for a moment in the hallway and rubbed both his eyes with his fingers. As he did so he took a breath so deep that an innocent bystander could easily have mistaken it for a stressed sigh.

Chapter 7

Stretch leaned back as he sat on the bench outside McConnel's, the newsagents, and clasped his hands behind his head. He gave an almighty push backwards with his head and sighed with satisfaction as he heard a popping sound from several places in his spine.

Mary came out of the shop and sat down next to him, carrying two packets of crisps and a bottle of mineral water.

"Jeez, Stretch, that was loud. You okay? Sounded like you snapped your spine in two." She threw a packet of crisps onto his tummy and he grabbed them before they fell off.

Sitting down next to him, the two of them munched in silence, each in their own thoughts. They still had twenty minutes until the start of school, which was a ten-minute walk away, so they felt little urgency. Mary had not noticed the strange reaction of her parents when she mentioned Al's name.

"I can't see the point of taste," Stretch said, holding a crisp up to the light.

Mary turned her head to face him dramatically. "I'm not sure it actually needs to justify its existence, does it?"

Stretch persisted. "It doesn't have any memory, does it. I mean, I can't remember the taste of bacon, I can't actually think what it tastes like. I can remember a tune by, say, Soundgarden, I could hum it to you, but I can't remember taste."

"I can," said Mary. She closed her eyes. "Victoria sponge, with fresh cream. I can imagine what that tastes like." She licked her lips in comic fashion. "Mmm, gorgeous."

Putting the crisp in his mouth, Stretch stood up and put his bag on. "No you can't," he said. "You're just being bloody difficult." He walked on slowly, waiting for her, but he seemed to be annoyed.

Mary got up, confused. She hadn't meant to annoy Stretch; she was just trying to be funny. Sometimes words would come out of her mouth and their impact would be very different to what she had intended. She knew the other girls thought her too clever and difficult, but she didn't mean to be. It was just the way they seemed to interpret what she said. Sometimes it seemed that everyone was deliberately trying to make her look silly. Everyone except Stretch, of course. And now she'd annoyed him somehow.

She put her arms through the straps of her bag (which had originally been a *Power Rangers* bag, but she'd sewed on patches for Nirvana and Amnesty International) and swung it onto her back, hurrying to catch up with Stretch and make things cool again. Walking over to the side of the road, she looked right to see if any traffic was coming. There was a white car coming down the road, with its left indicator blinking, as if it was going to turn left – except there was no left turning. She assumed that it was someone going to stop in order to pop into McConnel's, and as there were cars behind it starting to move round it, she stood back a pace from the road. Instead, however, the car slowed to a stop right in front of her. In the passenger seat, closest to her, she saw a very pretty lady with short dark hair. She was wearing too much make-up, but it had been put on with great skill. Mary thought she looked like a fashion model, should a fashion model have reason to be in the passenger seat of a white Peugeot 306.

The window went down jerkily, as if the lady was not used to lowering windows using a handle. She saw her say something in an annoyed way to the driver. Mary stood still – the lady was clearly going to talk to her.

"Hi, sweetie," said the lady in a strong American accent. "Are you Merry?"

"My name is Mary, yes." She felt an immediately and irrational irritation towards the woman.

"Mary, hi. It's me, Al."

The American lady leaned back a little, so that as Mary bent down she could see Al sitting in the driver's seat, now leaning across the awful woman so that he could see Mary.

Crouching right down so that she was level with the woman, Mary said, "Oh, hi. Did you not manage to find the house yesterday?"

"Yeah, I did, thanks, but there was no one home."

"Ah, Mum was probably working in her shed. It's in the back garden and she can't hear the front door. I keep telling her to get the bell fitted so it goes off in the shed, but she never does it."

"That explains it." He smiled at her and she smiled back, despite herself. Her gaze was once again drawn to his smile, the broad acreage of whiteness between his lips. The teeth seemed too big for his mouth, somehow, as if he had borrowed them from a larger man.

"We okay to go round now, you reckon?" said the lady.

"Guess so," replied Mary. She felt less inclined to waste words on this lady.

"Will your dad be there, Mary?" said Al. "I really would like to catch up with him. It's been a few years, and we go back a long way."

"Give it half an hour maybe. He's walking Johnny to school."

"Great, thanks." Al smiled. He seemed to do that a lot. "Oh, this is Kimberly, by the way – a friend of mine."

Mary gave an insipid, lips only, no teeth smile to Kimberly, tilting her head as she did so. It was a withering smile, loaded with deliberate lack of conviction.

"Hey, great to meet you, Mary," said Kimberly. "Listen, I hope we can catch your father at home. He's got quite a reputation – I've heard sooo much about him."

The way she said it made Mary feel uncomfortable. Was this woman simply incapable of successfully faking sincerity?

"We've got to go somewhere first, though," Kimberly went on, "so if we don't catch him, we might try and meet him at the school later. What time does Johnny finish school? So we can catch your father there, you see."

"3.15."

"Thanks, sweetie, greatly appreciated."

"Thanks, Mary," echoed Al. "Catch up with you soon, I hope."

"Okay, bye." Mary watched the window go back up, and received a highly annoying fingers-only wave from Kimberly. She gave a polite smile back and stood up, putting her hands back into in her pockets.

The road was now clear. As she crossed, Mary realised that Stretch was stood on the other side waiting for her.

"What was that about?" he asked.

"That guy again, and some awful woman."

"You shouldn't talk to strange people, Mary."

"I talk to you, don't I?" She smiled as sweetly as she knew how, but only succeeded in copying what she had just seen from Kimberly.

Stretch didn't answer. They walked the rest of the way to school in silence, each occupied by their own thoughts.

Emotions seemed to fuel Mary's whole existence. Every moment seemed so intense, so angry, so involved. Her father elicited an almost chemical reaction in her. She knew it wasn't fair, but she couldn't stop herself. Recently, he had tried to rustle her hair and she had jerked her head away irritably. He had looked upset, but she knew that she would have reacted the same way if he did it again, even though she knew it was wrong.

In art class the previous day, the students had been asked to draw a picture of something that represented laughter. She had struggled with the concept, and while everyone else seemed to immediately start drawing yellow haystacks and bright green frogs, she had stared out of the window, unable to conjure up an image, intrigued by the idea of abstract imagery but unable to apply it to her logical mind.

Walking under the shadow of Stretch, she wondered what she would draw to represent her father. It would probably be some sort of large amorphous object made of a hard but unidentifiable substance, and very, very heavy. So heavy and so large that it would fill the entire picture, with hardly any room for background. It would have been dark blue all over, but with some parts in shadow. The strength of her feelings overwhelmed her, prevented her from lucidity, from being able to distinguish between the love she knew must be there, and the anger that seemed to be in the very air that she breathed.

Turning into school, the drive opened out into a large concrete area at the front of the main building which was used as a visitor car park during the day, but in the mornings contained buses dropping off the kids who lived further away. Like most mornings, there were lots of children milling around. A number of older girls seemed to be clumped together in groups, many of them hugging each other.

"What's going on?" said Stretch, breaking their silence.

"I don't know," replied Mary. "Weird."

They walked on through the school towards their own tutor room. There was an atmosphere about the place, there was no doubting it.

Among the pupils and teachers going about their business in the same way as every other day were groups of children clearly very upset. They were either crying together (mostly girls), consoling each other (boys with girls), or standing around in groups staring at each other (boys).

Eventually, they saw some girls from their own class, Clare and Donna, and went over to them. They were sitting on a grass bank, wiping away tears with a shared packet of tissues.

"Hey guys," said Mary. "What's going on?"

"Haven't you heard?" said Donna, as Clare blew her nose.

"No, what?"

"Kurt Cobain has shot himself. He's dead."

Chapter 8

As they walked hand in hand up the final stretch of road to the school, the game that Mack and Johnny had been playing – the band name game – also neared its conclusion.

"Okay," said Mack, "what about New Riders of the Purple Sage?"

"Yes," replied Johnny, "that's a real band."

"Correct. A point to you. What about Dumping from Great Heights?"

"Ummm…no, not a real band."

"Argh! Correct again! Silliness?"

"No. Not a band name."

"Craziness?"

"No."

"Madness?"

"Yes!" With his free hand Mack slapped his forehead in comedy exasperation. "Good grief, how do you know so much? You're only six, for goodness' sake! You shouldn't be beating me at anything."

Johnny looked up at his father, a beaming smile lighting up his face.

"Okay," said Mack, "what's the score?"

"Twenty-five to me, three to you," replied Johnny.

"And how come," said Mack, "you can't remember to put your shoes on in the morning, or concentrate long enough to eat more than two mouthfuls of your tea before drifting off to Johnnyland, but you're perfectly capable of beating me hands down every time we play the band name game? And keeping score for the entire time as well!" Mack's voice raised at the end in mock indignation.

Johnny laughed a gurgling, happy-deep-inside laugh.

Meanwhile, across the road, sat in a white Peugeot 306 which was parked between a long line of cars, Al and Kimberly watched in silence. If anyone had been studying them, it would appear that Al, from his body language, looked uneasy and uncomfortable, whereas Kimberly held herself with a steely determination. She had a notepad on her lap and was making copious notes, while Al occasionally rubbed his forehead.

As Mack and Johnny disappeared through the school gates, Al looked at the dark-haired woman sat next to him. She nodded, he started the car, and they drove away.

Jude stood at the sink and put the last bowl from the breakfast detritus in the dishwasher. She gazed out of the window, arms folded, mug of tea held firmly in one hand. The large tree in their neighbour's garden was so full of different colours, it reminded her of a painting by Seurat. The huge variety of colours in the leaves gave the impression of being painted in the pointillist style, whereby the paint is applied by dots rather than strokes. An object that looked to be brown from a distance was in fact made up of dozens of different colours, including blues, yellows, reds, in a variety of shades. Looking at this tree, it was entirely possible that the colour she thought she saw was not represented at all, the overall hue being made up of thousands of different colours.

There was a lot of philosophy in the pointillist idea, she thought. It echoed her own feelings about the joyous mix of life. The solitude of the shed beckoned, but for the moment, she allowed her mind to drift.

Biting her bottom lip, Jude tried to bring into focus a concept that had felt just out of her grasp for some time now. Inside her lived an idea, something that would bring together her vision for jewellery as popular art. It needed to be something that could be repeated over and over again, but in different ways. Something that would allow her to express herself, and allow the wearer of her jewellery to express themselves too. Maybe the tree was trying to suggest something, a way of epitomising the multitudinous facets of a personality in its seemingly endless hues and shades, the overall impression of colour, and therefore character, being made up of almost infinite variations.

It needed to be something that could be easily – and cheaply – replicated. What could she use to help people to reveal a little of themselves through jewellery?

The noise of knuckles rapping quickly on the front door made

Jude jump as she was hauled out of her train of thought. She hadn't realised quite how far she had drifted off in her thinking, and the jolt made her spill some tea down the slightly tatty, light-blue cardigan.

Putting down the cup, she went to the front door and opened it. She instantly recognised Al, even though he had less hair. He was tanned, his teeth shining from the darkness of his face, and he was dressed in a long black coat. About the same height as Jude, he only looked short when he stood next to people the height of Mack. The good looks were still there but the glint in the eye was not. He had a rather hangdog look – the look of someone who'd had their strongest beliefs tested and had found them to be lacking. He was alone.

"Hello, Jude," he said, with a nervous smile.

"Well, so it's true. You have come to say hello. Come on in, please." Jude stepped back to allow him in, smiling warmly. They stood opposite each other inside the door for a moment, then Jude reached forwards and put her arms around him.

"Come here, you bloody idiot," she said, and she gave him a big hug.

He brought his arms up and hugged her back, and she squeezed him hard for just a moment. It was a squeeze born from happy memories.

"Tea?" she said, letting him go and walking into the kitchen.

"Have you got any coffee?" he called after her.

"So, you've picked up a few other things in America then, as well as the teeth. You're a coffee drinker now."

"Hey, leave the teeth out of it. This is the colour they are supposed to be – white, not yellow."

"Only when you're four." Jude filled the kettle, flicked the switch, and turned to face Al, folding her arms. "How are you, Al? It's been a long time."

"Okay," he said, in a way that told Jude that he wasn't. "It's been an…interesting road since we last spoke."

"Well, we followed some of it in the newspapers. To begin with, anyway. The movie role. The actress. You made a bit of a name for yourself for a while there."

"Hmph. Yeah, well, not all of those headlines could be trusted, you know."

"None of my business, Al. I'm not one to judge."

"Well, I had a lot of fun, I'll say that. In those early days when you're new and people are interested in you. You're a novelty. Then when they feel there's nothing more you can do to interest them you are pretty quickly passed by. The clever ones realise that and get out, go and do something else."

"And were you one of the clever ones, Al?"

"No. No, I wasn't." He scratched the back of his head and drew his coat around him more tightly. "I was one of the ones who stick it out, thinking 'they'" – he held his hands up to imitate inverted commas, something that Jude found instantly irritating – "that 'they' haven't seen the best of you yet. So you try and convince those select few that the same talents and skills that they either used or passed over before are going to be useful to them again. But they are already gone, busy looking for fresh meat. Everything becomes a comparison to before. Until it becomes impossible to be heard or seen at all. You end up like an invisible man, wondering why no one will see you."

"Oh, Al, you make it sound pretty terrible. We thought you were living the high life out there."

"You still do that then?" Al smiled.

"Do what then?" replied Jude.

"Refer to yourself in the plural when you are speaking."

Now it was Jude's turn to smile. The kettle clicked off behind her. She took out two mugs from a choice of twenty or so that covered a whole shelf in the cupboard, put a teabag in one, a spoonful of instant coffee in the other, and poured in the boiling water.

"I forgot you did that," he went on, putting up his hand to indicate that he didn't want milk or sugar. "You always talked about yourself in the plural. 'We thought this,' or 'We both like that.' Hasn't he let you go, even a bit? Haven't you kicked his ass and found your own space yet? Don't tell me he's still bullying you."

"If you've come here to make trouble, Mr Smart, you can turn around right now." Jude was smiling. "He's never bullied me, and don't you patronise me by thinking I'd let him. I'm quite happy with how things are, thank you very much. And if I wasn't I would have done something about it."

Now it was Al's turn to smile. "Okay, sorry. I should have known better about you. You know I always thought that…"

"I don't care to know what you always thought, thank you," Jude interrupted, handing him a mug. "Just come into the lounge and talk sensibly." She saw Al's eyes, and thought she detected a flicker. Why was he so nervous? "Mack is taking our son to school, but he'll be home soon. Come on." Jude walked out of the kitchen, across the hall and past the front door, into the lounge.

Al followed her into the large front room. The walls were crowded with shelves full of books and records. Two matching black leather sofas stood at right angles to each other, a pine table in the middle. Jude had allowed Mack to go and get the sofas one Saturday afternoon, giving him far greater credit for taste than he actually had. When they had been delivered, she had immediately driven out and bought a series of cushions, giving the lounge a feel of extremes between black leather, wooden tables, and brightly coloured furnishings. It was a strangely pleasant mix, as long as one didn't suffer from epilepsy.

The television had been backed into a corner, to try and remove it from what it seemed to feel was its rightful position as the most important item in the living room. Al took off his coat and folded it over the back of the armchair, then sat down as Jude got placemats for the mugs from another corner that Al now noticed held a record deck and stereo system.

"I should ask you about your kids, I guess," said Al. "That's the etiquette with old friends who are now parents, isn't it? Are they doing well at school, all that kind of stuff."

"Well it's good of you to ask, I suppose. A good effort, let's say."

They both smiled, acknowledging Al's disinterest.

"They're good kids. Not without their own complications, but they're good kids." Jude continued to stand, as if her presence in the room was only temporary, a prologue to the return of Mack for the main discussion.

"Oh, I've got something for you," said Al, reaching into the inside pocket of his coat. He pulled out what looked like a crumpled bit of paper, but he straightened it out and Jude could see that it was a small unicorn, made out of gold paper. "A mate of mine is into origami," he said. "He makes these from the inside of cigarette packets and leaves them lying around. I thought Johnny might like it. A peace offering, you might say." He smiled at her.

"Thank you," said Jude, "that actually is thoughtful. I'm sure Johnny will like it." She put it on the coffee table. "It's very sweet."

"Yeah, he learnt it from a film, I think. I've tried to make them, but I'm rubbish. I can barely fold a napkin."

Jude looked thoughtful for a moment, then asked him a question. "How did you know his name is Johnny?"

Al looked awkward for a moment, then said, "Oh, Mary told me. It was quite a coincidence – I stopped to ask someone if they knew of you, and it happened to be your daughter." He forced a laugh but Jude thought he sounded rather like an asthmatic goat.

They sat in silence for a moment, Jude continuing to stare at her old friend. And they had been friends, once, but towards the last days of the band they hardly saw each other. Jude had not approved of his behaviour, and the fact that he wouldn't return her gaze told her that he was well aware of the fact.

As if he had been waiting outside for his cue, the front door opened, and Mack returned back over the threshold to his perceived dominion. He didn't look up, expecting that the house would be empty upon his return from the school run, and that Jude would be in her shed by now, as usual. He unwound his scarf and took off his jumper, leaving him in a black polo neck and jeans. He put his hands though his hair, and kicked off his boots. Jude came out of the lounge to meet him and Al stood behind her, hovering nervously.

"Look who's come to visit," said Jude.

Mack arched an eyebrow at his wife and she stepped aside. Al grinned with one side of his mouth, the other seemingly afraid to join in, just in case it formed a full smile.

"Hello, mate," he said, his voice containing more than a trace of an accent from the years spent in America.

Mack didn't move for a moment. Instead he sighed, even closing his eyes for a moment, unafraid of the awkward silence that befell the small hallway. Jude looked at him, concerned. Opening his eyes, Mack looked at Al for a moment, as if weighing something up. Then he smiled, walked slowly over to Al, and wrapped his long arms around him. Al looked over his shoulder at Jude, as if seeking her agreement; then, receiving nothing but a warm smile from her, lifted his arms and put them gently, nervously, around Mack.

Bringing his arms back down at last, Mack walked past Al into the lounge, not looking at him. He walked over to the sofa, having noticed Al's coat on the back of the armchair. Al sat back in the chair, while Mack remained perched on the arm of the sofa, leaning back but ensuring he maintained the height advantage over his former friend.

"Brew?" Jude asked Mack from the doorway behind him.

"That would be brill, thanks," replied Mack, not turning round to look at Jude as he said it. He therefore didn't notice the flash of irritation that accompanied her out of the room.

Mack drew his hands through his hair again, which instantly fell back to its previous position; the act was more a reveal of his mood than to serve any practical purpose. He looked at Al and smiled deliberately, keeping his lips together and not showing his teeth.

"Mary told us you were around," he said to Al. "It got me thinking about what I would say to you when I saw you next. I came up with quite a few opening lines, actually. But then, when I saw you just then, I didn't have the heart to say any of them. It's good to see you, mate."

Al looked down, abashed. Then he looked up and smiled, lips apart, teeth together, a broad American smile. "You too, dude. You're looking well."

"Thanks. So are you. Nice teeth, by the way."

Al's smile waned a little, then gave up completely. "So what were some of the lines you discarded? Come on, lay it on, I can take it. Chances are I may have deserved some of them." There was no aggression in his voice, but Mack was fully aware of the defensive nature of the question. He decided, defiantly, to answer the query as if it was a genuine one.

"Oh, blimey, I had a few crackers lined up. All unpleasant, of course. There was, 'So, the prodigal son returns.' In a really unkind moment I thought of, 'Had enough of shagging your way round the world, have you?' There was the levity of, 'Are you so desperate for money that you want to get the band back together?' And I'd finally settled on, 'Hello, so what do you want?' Not very charitable all round, really."

"If you like," said Al, "when they come and ask me for a comment for your obituary, I can pretend that you really did say that. It would make you seem more like John Lennon."

"What makes you think I'm going to die before you?"

Al smiled just as unconvincingly as before, the teeth breaking through the space between his lips like an iceberg appearing out of fog. "I suppose you're in control of that as well now, are you?"

"Not in control, so much as not out of control," replied Mack.

Al didn't answer. Round one to me, thought Mack, simultaneously trying to stop himself from having such thoughts.

The door opened and Jude entered. She placed a mug on the coffee table in front of Mack, next to the origami unicorn, which drew Mack's attention for a quizzical moment. She went back out, leaving the two of them to talk, but leaving the door slightly ajar.

"Present for Johnny," said Al, noticing Mack's gaze. "A mate of mine makes them."

"Look, Al, I don't want to start us straight back on that kind of unpleasant banter, okay?" said Mack. "We left on that note, let's not start back on the same one. I don't actually believe any of those things that I was going to say to you, they're just old thoughts that were the easiest ones for me to find. In fact, as soon as I saw you just now, it was the good stuff we did together that came back to me, not the bad stuff. Which, in any case, was only at the end – a pretty short period of time. Why should that be the stuff we remember? It's not fair on the good stuff."

Al smiled reservedly. "We did a lot of stuff all round, didn't we?"

"Well, it depends what we mean by stuff, of course. You did a lot more of it than me, as I recall. But yeah, not many people get the chance to do the things we did."

"And to have a legacy. Something that we created, something that we left behind."

"That *I* created," corrected Mack. "And then *we* made into something truly memorable," he added, charitably.

Al looked down for a moment. Mack noticed that he was breathing hard. He didn't speak for a few seconds, as if catching his breath. When he did speak, it seemed to be a deliberate attempt to change both the subject and the tone of the conversation.

"I saw Mary. She seems a fine young lady."

"Thanks," said Mack. "She's doing okay. She's got attitude and thinks she knows everything, of course, but then she's a teenage girl, so what else could I possibly expect. You must meet Johnny, our son, at some point. He's cool, got a bright mind there. Doing pretty well at school. Doesn't seem to have too much interest in music at the moment, but it's early days for that, I guess." Mack paused, waiting for a follow-up question that might encourage him to carry on talking about his family but Al just stared into his mug. "How about you," Mack asked his old partner, once he realised no such stimuli was about to be offered. "I've not read anything about you in the papers for a while."

"I'm okay," Al replied, curtly. "I look after myself alright. Moving to the States was the best thing I ever did."

Something about the way Al could not tear his eyes away from his coffee and look his old friend in the eye suggested to Mack that this statement might not have been entirely true.

"So are you back for good?" Mack asked.

"Just visiting," responded Al, arching his back slightly and rubbing his legs with his hands. If there was a purpose to his visit, he clearly didn't seem keen to let on.

"They were good days though, mate, weren't they?" said Al, brightly.

The clunky change in the direction of conversation put Mack even further on his guard.

"I can still remember where I was and how I felt when we first wrote or recorded many of our songs," Al continued. "Listening back to some of those demo tapes, singing those songs for the first time, I can picture myself there, see myself as I was at that age…so many details which are so clear. To do something that gave me so much joy and lasting pleasure – I'll never be able to have those feelings again. I can remember it all so clearly."

"So come on, why have you come back?" said Mack.

There was a point to this visit circling around their heads. Sure there was goodwill for his old friend, but there was no point in pretending that he could completely ignore the lies and sneaking around behind his back towards the end. Talking with record companies about solo records; the interview with that bastard journalist, Kent Nicholls. Sure, Al had denied it at the time, but Mack always thought that the two of them had cooked that article up between them: Kent Nicholls for revenge and Al to pursue his solo career. Kent Nicholls' articles appeared in *Rolling Stone* magazine, and Mack was sure that it was him, with his American contacts, who had lured Al away from Mamal with the promise of an acting career.

"So Johnny's the man, eh?" said Al. "Bit of a chip off the old block, is he?"

Mack reached forward for his mug of tea. Standing, he walked over to the window which looked out onto the back garden, now with his back to Al. He watched a solitary robin peck at a ball of suet that Jude had hung up yesterday. He sighed, deeply and slowly.

"Yeah, Johnny's great. Just kind of cool, you know? Spends his entire day going from one thing that gives him pleasure to another. I don't remember being six myself, but going by him, it seems to be the most hedonistic period of one's life. All he seems to do is walk around trying to decide how to have fun next."

"Heh, I've been to a few parties like that."

Mack turned to look at him. There was something about Al's expression that transported Mack back to times he would rather have forgotten.

"Well," said Mack, "given the sort of parties you used to be at the centre of when we toured, I dread to think what vices Hollywood must have exposed within you."

Al smiled, his white teeth seeming to not quite fit his mouth. Then he looked up and realised that Mack had not mean this as a compliment, and his face slowly returned to its default position.

They both sipped their drinks, each lost with a few thoughts for a moment. Al put his down first, then got up, and went over to the bookcase. The books and records covered one entire wall of the lounge, either side of the fireplace, even going up and over the top of the mantle like a wave.

"You still buying and listening to new stuff?" he asked.

"Yeah," replied Mack. "Jeff Buckley seems to have his dad's abilities. He's one I listen to a lot. And I think Pop Will Eat Itself could just be the biggest band of the decade if they carry on the way they are."

"Well, you were always the one with the ear," said Al, with a dismissive wave of his hand. "I've never heard of either of them."

"I'm sure you will," said Mack.

Al smiled, his head now cocked as he read the spines of some of the records.

Sitting on the sofa, Mack folded his arms. The legs followed, and he now looked like he was trying to screw himself round into the arm of the sofa. "Al," he said. "Why are you back? I can't imagine it is just a social visit, and I can't imagine you're house hunting."

Al didn't answer for a moment, but stopped looking at the records and turned around, now staring at the floor. He looked to Mack like an actor trying to remember his lines.

"It's not been an easy few years, mate," he began, his voice suddenly solemn.

"Yeah, so you mentioned," replied Mack, warily.

Al took a deep sigh and rubbed his eyes. "When I first left England, things were okay. Obviously I didn't have the same income that you had from the records, but I didn't worry at the time, everything was working out for me. I was in some pretty cool roles, actually. Had a good agent. Got a few minor roles in films like *Amadeus* and *Body Double*. Bit-part stuff, that's how it goes to begin with, but I got a few lines. Got paid pretty well for a while there, even after the agent took his cut.

"Man, you should see the life some people lead out there, especially in those days. Cocaine was like dandruff – it was everywhere, so cheap. Parties where I saw things that I really didn't think existed outside of Jackie Collins books. Bottom line is that if you had it, you could get more of it. The world will hold a party for those who can afford to hold their own. You'll be invited once, but you have to pay back in some way. Return the invite, reflect some glory – you scratch my back and I'll pay for a hooker to walk over yours."

"Nice line," said Mack.

Al looked at him and smiled, coyly. "Yeah. Kent Nicholls wrote it."

He sat in the armchair and leaned forward. He rubbed his face, then stared at the table, as if he would look anywhere in the room except Mack's eyes.

"You have to join in if you want to be invited again. That's the rub. You have to be seen to be spending. Bottom line. Always spending. Always proving how good you are by spending.

73

"It's a tough world, Mack. You wouldn't know, with the income you've always had from our records. Especially 'A Bridge of Straw', that's always on the radio in the States, you must earn so much from that. But I had to keep working. I went into TV, did some stuff there. Took me a while to realise, but in Hollywood you are seen as either on your way up, or on your way down. There is no in-between. The trick is to stay at the top as long as you can. If you don't get to the top, you start to go down. And once you are seen as on your way down, they generally expect you to go right to the bottom."

Al's finger jabbed downwards onto the table. "I've done some fantastic work they wouldn't use, just because I wasn't the 'star'." Al didn't notice Mack's left eyebrow rise. "They cut some of my best stuff simply because it was so good, because I was making the star look bad. Couldn't have me stealing the limelight. It really pissed me off, and I told them so."

Al looked at the table again, calmer now. "That only made matters worse. If I did make a mistake, that phone call was it. Thought I was doing what they would have expected of me, standing up to them. Didn't get much work for a while after that.

"So I got into debt. Someone…" he paused, fumbling for the right phrase, "an, uh, old friend, he had some other friends in some business I didn't know much about. Fixed up for some bills to be sorted out for me. I thought they were doing me a favour. Now that *was* stupid. There's no such thing as a favour out there. They were hooking me in. Paying my debts off actually meant transferring my debts to them." A long pause. "And now they want repaying."

Al stopped. He was staring at the cold fire. He had reached the end of the story. And yet it seemed to Mack that it was only the introduction.

The room was quiet for a few moments. Mack was the first to speak. "That's really bad, mate. I'm sorry you have problems. But I don't see what this has to do with me. At least, I don't want to think what it might mean. We don't have any money, you know? We don't have any spare cash. Any money we do have is tied up in the house."

Unexpectedly for both of them, Al stood up. "Do you remember recording 'A Bridge of Straw'?" he began. "That was a great weekend. It all came out so easily, didn't it."

Mack didn't reply, but looked at him. He didn't like the way the conversation was turning, but didn't want to join in, to offer encouragement.

"I remember it so well – we were firing in those days," Al continued. "You'd have some ideas, some words, and we'd go into the studio, knock them about and make a brilliant record. I think we should have had more hits, if only the record company would have supported us more."

"I have a feeling I'm about sixty seconds away from asking you to leave," said Mack.

"Did you know that 'A Bridge of Straw' is actually the second most played record on radio stations in the USA, after 'Lay Down Sally'?"

Mack didn't respond, but continued to look Al in the eye.

"Now come on, don't be like that, mate. I'm simply after what is due. We were a group. Those records were made by us. Even if you did write the words to some of the songs, they only came out because of the creative atmosphere that you were in, that I helped to create."

"I was wrong," said Mack, standing quickly. "I was only thirty seconds away. Get out."

"This is not just me, Mack," said Al. He had suddenly turned defensive, standing up and moving sideways, away from Mack, with his hands out in front of him. "These people have access to some powerful lawyers. I'm here with someone who will want to talk to you – Kimberly is her name. She's kind of their representative. She scares me, Mack. They want a share of those publishing royalties. I don't know how much you get exactly, but it's paid for a pretty good lifestyle for you. They've sent me here to tell you that they will take you to court, and it would be easier for you to just hand over the cash."

"Get out."

"Mack, these are serious people." Al was walking backwards slowly, towards the lounge door. "They know stuff. They're blackmailing me. They know about some of the stuff that happened on tour. They know..." Al looked behind him to make sure that Jude had not come back into the room, then lowered his voice to a whisper: "They know about that night. I don't know how, but they do."

Al placed a piece of paper on the table, next to the origami unicorn. "Don't give me an answer now," he said, walking towards the door.

"Think about it. I'm staying at the Manor. My room number is on there. Call me, or I'll call you in the next couple of days."

"I have thought about it," said Mack, in a low voice, also conscious of not being heard by Jude. "I wrote those songs. While you were swanning around getting blow jobs off underage girls, I was writing and creating the music. That night is a memory I do not wish to recall, and I will not be threatened with it. You were a lazy bastard then, Al, and it seems you haven't changed. Get out of my house before I seriously lose it."

Al went out of the lounge, into the hallway, and to the front door. He realised that Jude had been standing in the kitchen doorway and was now listening to their conversation. He changed to a conciliatory tone.

"Mack, listen. I'm only asking for what's mine by right. A share in the royalties. If you give me that, I can keep them happy. Think about it. We don't want this to escalate."

Something in his voice made Mack think that this was not so much a threat, but a plea.

Al looked at him, eyes wide, eyebrows raised. He offered his hand for Mack to shake, but the offer was ignored. Al lowered his hand, then turned and went out of the front door. He stopped for a moment, as if feeling the need to say something else, then his shoulders drooped and he walked down the driveway.

Jude turned to face Mack. The left eyebrow was raised. Mack walked over and put his arms round her.

"Do you think you did the right thing?" she said, into his armpit.

"He's not getting a penny off me. He has no rights."

"He seemed rather scared. I don't like the sound of these people he's got himself mixed up with, Mack."

"Then they can take me to court. But I'm not just handing over our money to them."

Jude looked at the wall around Mack's shoulder. She didn't like the feeling in her stomach that Al's visit had left her with.

Chapter 9

The school playground and fields were covered with knots of teenagers, standing or sitting in groups. Several had a few girls at their centre, arms around each other, with a boy or two standing awkwardly next to them, not really understanding or knowing how to help. There were also the usual games of football and other activities, those children seemingly impervious to the suicide of Nirvana's lead singer. Kurt Cobain's death was either totally changing someone's life, or not affecting them at all. There were no half measures, which seemed to Mary to be an entirely appropriate response to such an extreme action.

She was sitting with Stretch on a wall outside the sports hall. They had been into lunch early, with the first bell, and were now killing time, waiting for the third bell which would call them back into class.

The *Nevermind* album by Nirvana had affected them both deeply. In truth, Stretch preferred Led Zeppelin, and Mary listened to Soundgarden more often. However, they both knew all the words to the *Nevermind* album, had followed the saga of Kurt's relationship with Courtney Love, and had been swept along with the media's obsession with his increasingly tortured existence. For Mary, however, the upset was more about the loss of a person to the world, and to his family, than of Kurt Cobain himself. She couldn't quite put her finger on what it was that was upsetting her so much; new feelings were awoken in her that she didn't yet know how to turn into opinions. It was as if her mind was trying to sort her emotions into a new order.

Clare and Donna came over and stood in front of them with their arms folded. Their eyes were smudged black: the result of a lunchtime of crying. To Mary's knowledge, neither of them had even so much as mentioned Nirvana before, so quite what they had been crying about, she couldn't imagine. Still, Clare and Donna were very popular, so she resisted the urge to comment.

"Right?" Clare grunted.

Mary just smiled weakly at her.

Stretch mumbled a barely coherent, "Right?"

"Crap, isn't it," said Donna. Mary assumed they were talking about Kurt Cobain.

"Yeah," said Mary, uncertainly. Clare and Donna were just about considered friends, but any other person was a potential for conflict, for some argument or misinterpretation of something she might say.

"You were really into them, weren't you?" said Clare, as if goading Mary to show them how upset she was.

"Kind of," Mary shrugged, in a voice that seemed to ache and throb with her attempt to be reasonable and uncontroversial. "It wasn't the band though, was it? It was Kurt. It was the way he lived his life. Everything mattered so much." She stopped, uncertain as to whether sharing herself with the others would be the right thing to do. From their reaction, she decided that on a day filled with so much emotion, it would be accepted.

Donna and Clare sat down on the wall next to Mary, close to her, their movements jerky, their arms remaining folded. It was as if their every movement was designed to contain the maximum amount of drama possible.

"That is so right," said Clare. "He just, just cared so much. It was like he couldn't help himself."

Mary continued, now feeling more confident, unwittingly being lulled into a contest of 'who cares the most'. "The lyrics," she said. "He knew millions of people were listening, yet he couldn't help but pour his heart into everything he did."

"I know," said Donna, "he just loved Courtney so much, and poor little Frances Bean. He must have cared so much about them, it's so sad."

"It's not sad," said Mary, quietly. She stared at the ground in front of her and felt blood rushing to her head. It was the mention of the child that seemed to make her jumbled emotional responses fall into place. "It's stupid. Really, really stupid. And selfish. He had a daughter, for Christ's sake. How could he leave a daughter? How could he kill himself, knowing that his daughter would grow up with the knowledge that her father didn't love her enough to stay alive for her?" Mary was staring at the floor intently now, her face flush and reddening with the realisation of what had been boiling in her mind all day.

Her voice rose gently but firmly, now unaware of the others with her, just needing to voice the thought that had been gnawing away at her ever since she had heard the news. "What sort of a selfish bastard could do that to a little girl? She will have no father ever again. He has taken that gift away from her, stopped her from being able to have a family that cares for her. How can she ever understand what he did without thinking about herself, about what it says about his love for her, his little girl, his baby? Courtney is going to have to explain this to Frances Bean one day. What chance does she have of a normal life now, with the media attention she will have forever? And all in the knowledge that her father didn't care enough about her to stay alive. As well as killing himself, he's as good as killed her, inside, by denying her a father in the most selfish and dramatic of ways." Tears were welling up in her eyes as she spoke.

Mary stopped talking, her mind racing. She looked left, to Stretch, who hadn't moved position, his head stooped forwards at a ninety-degree angle to his neck. Then she looked right, at Clare and Donna. The two girls were sat bolt upright, their arms still folded. Donna's mouth was hanging open; Clare's was quite the opposite, her lips almost white with the pressure of her lips being so tightly pursed. They were both staring at her. Mary's heart was beating fast as she came out of her fervour at last, realising what she had said might not have been a universally accepted interpretation of the situation.

Clare was the first to speak, her words clipped with disapproval. "I cannot believe you just said that. That poor man was so driven to do something so, so awful – how can you say a word against him?" They both stood up at the same time, as if somehow joined.

"You're sick in the head," said Donna, as the two of them walked away, arms still determinedly clamped around their midriffs.

Mary was once again red in the face, but this time with embarrassment. She sat for a few moments, unsure of what to do, suddenly aware of everything and everyone around her.

"Shit," she eventually said, almost to herself. She looked to her left, and Stretch, whose face was masked from view by his hair, seemed to be crying. Oh man, she thought to herself, I really messed this one up.

"Stretch," she said, gently, putting her hand on his shoulder. "Stretch, I'm sorry. I didn't mean to upset everyone. I'm sorry, mate."

He looked up at her, hooked a finger into his lank hair and dragged it away from his face, behind his ear. He looked up at her, his eyes twinkling, his mouth shut as if he was trying to prevent something from escaping through his lips. Then he let out an involuntary snort, and began giggling again, uncontrollably.

Mary smiled uncertainly, making her face look somewhat distorted, as if it wasn't sure what emotion was going to attack it next.

"What?" she said, slowly. She laughed – just once – as she watched Stretch, his eyes shut, giggling silently to himself. It felt like not quite hearing the punchline that everyone else heard, but feeling the need to laugh along with them anyway.

Slowly, Stretch regained his composure. Eventually, after a few lapses back into giggles, he took a deep breath.

"Oh, Mary," he said, leaning his head towards her. "You are classic."

"Why?" she replied. "What have I done?"

"Just keep on being you, okay?" he said.

Mary smiled. "Okay," she said, "though that's not as easy as you make it sound." She paused and looked at the ground in a brief and rare period of self assessment, before quickly coming to a conclusion. "Anyway," she said, "I'm right."

"I know," replied Stretch. "You always are." He ducked to avoid her swinging arm aimed at the back of his head, then continued with the impetus and stood up. "Come on," he said, "bell's about to go."

Mary stood up too, feeling better but not sure why.

After a few yards, Stretch, still looking in the direction he was walking, said, "Your Dad does care about you, you know. I know you think he prefers Johnny, but I'm sure he does care about you as well."

Wide-eyed, Mary said, "Where did that come from? I didn't say anything about my dad!" She enunciated every word, slowly, and deliberately.

They returned to class in a delicate silence, Mary mortified by the thought that she might have said something to give him an entirely accurate impression of what she was really thinking.

Chapter 10

Mack put down his guitar. He had been playing for an hour or so and was getting nowhere fast. Thoughts whirred around his mind and then passed straight out again, like a ring road at rush hour. He decided to take a break, padded down to the kitchen, and flicked the switch on the kettle.

Al's threat, on one level, had been pretty plain. They would sue him for a share of the royalties of his songs. They would claim that Al had been involved in the writing of the songs, and that he had a right to a share of the proceeds. That didn't worry him. It couldn't be proved that Al had anything to do with the songs, and he could call on many people, such as Jude, to prove that he wrote on his own. No, that wouldn't come to court. It was a threat, and it was a hollow one.

It was the memory that haunted him. It was wrong, and it was there. Forever. That's what Al had really threatened him with. "They know about that night," he had said.

It had been after a gig in Leicester. For some reason, they hadn't stayed in a hotel. There was a house that had been rented for them, just for one night. Their tour manager had known someone who was away; he had been trying to save money, or so they found out afterwards. That idiot journalist, Kent Nicholls, had been there, and had brought a girl with him. A few people had come back for a party; they'd all had a lot to drink and there had been dope, speed and cocaine around too. It was quite a night.

It was the first time Mack had taken cocaine. He wasn't one for the after-show party, usually hanging around for a bit then sidling out as Al started to get fired up and take centre stage. But tonight was different, not just because he had snorted cocaine for the first time and felt like he could take on the world. It was also because of Kent Nicholls. Everyone knew of the legendary journalist, and having him join their tour was a real compliment. It was like having an official rock and roll stamp of approval. If Kent Nicholls was going to interview you, then you must be worth interviewing.

Okay, so his heyday had been during the punk era, when he had got lucky and been at some of the seminal shows that set the scene for many years to come. But he also had a swagger, an attitude straight out of punk which seemed to say that being a rock critic isn't for the elite, isn't only for those who went to college; it's for everyone, we can all do it – you've just got to have the balls.

He wrote what he thought, and he said what he thought. He also thought what he wrote was the work of a genius. It was once said that Kent Nicholls had the shortest distance between his brain and his mouth than any other man alive. He was not someone to cross, and after a decade in the business, on both sides of the Atlantic, he had the power to make or break a band if he so chose.

It is fair to say that Mack and Al were a little in awe of him, but it wasn't just because of his journalistic reputation. They had also heard other stories. He could be a bit of a loose cannon. The tales were the stuff of legend, the type that a friend of a friend had seen happen; stories that no one ever quite knew if they were true or not. He claimed to have been at the Marquee gig in London, when the Sex Pistols supported Eddie and the Hot Rods, and the punk movement was born. He made many other claims that were equally as hard to substantiate.

Then there were the stories people would tell each other in clubs and in recording studios while waiting for the drum kit to be set up. The earliest involved how Kent Nicholls had got his first job as a journalist. It was at a Buzzcocks gig, and the chap from the most popular paper of the time, the *NME*, happened to start chatting to him at the bar. When Kent Nicholls realised who the man was and why he was there, he supposedly spiked his drink with LSD. When the journalist started to freak out, Nicholls helped him out the front door, left him in the street, and went backstage after the gig to interview the band, pretending to be the journalist.

He submitted the interview the next day, with a covering letter saying that he'd been writing for a local paper in Ireland for the last few years – also a lie. The editor had been expecting to print a Buzzcocks interview, and he didn't have one. He didn't care why. As it happened, the article was very well written and the editor used it. He even offered Kent Nicholls a job. The original journalist got the sack for taking drugs and for failing to meet his deadline. And so, when the record label said that Kent Nicholls was going to join Mamal on tour for a few nights to do research for an article on them, it was like the ultimate accolade. It said that the band had arrived, that they really were stars.

After the gig, they had gone to a club and partied. The tour was kind of a holding tour: just ten dates around the country, slipping a couple of new songs into the set. The new album was recorded and the first single would be issued in a few months' time, once artwork had been agreed. They really thought that the second album was going to make the success of the first seem mild in comparison.

With no gig the next day, they left the club at midnight and went back to the house. After a few hours there was just four of them left, Harpo doing his usual disappearing act. Mack, Al, Kent Nicholls, and a friend of his, a rather beautiful young woman.

Then things got a bit out of hand. It became one of those nights that make you wake up with a jolt the next morning. Mack could only assume that it was the combination of Jack Daniels, spliffs and cocaine, but when Kent Nicholls and the girl started kissing and then she took her clothes off, he didn't move, and nor did Al. It was like he was too heavy to move. After a night of abuse, his entire body seemed to have shut down. And then when she crawled over to him and Al and started working on them, both at the same time, the part of his brain that knew it was wrong seemed to have been subsumed by the part that was being driven by cocaine. He had finally crawled into bed at 4am.

The following day, he had been sitting at the kitchen table on his own, drinking orange juice, a desperate feeling in the pit of his stomach. He had fooled around a bit with girls on the road before, nothing too serious, but last night was something different, something totally unexpected. Kent Nicholls walked into the kitchen, wearing only underwear and his trademark full-length leather jacket. The lecherous sneer on his face made Mack immediately realise that he deeply disliked this man.

"Morning," he had said.

Mack had not replied. Kent Nicholls poured himself a glass of milk and sat down opposite Mack, so that the two men almost had no choice but to look at each other. The journalist leaned back in his chair and took a drink from his glass, leaving a white moustache in the stubble that seemed to surround his mouth like a forest planted in rows. His smug smile stayed in place for the duration of Mack's recollection of the event. That self-satisfied, disgusting smile was like a permanent scar on his memory.

"Summat else, wasn't she," he said, placing the glass on the table and stretching his hands behind his neck. Then he placed his hands ostentatiously on the table, leaned forward, and whispered to Mack, "How old do you think she was?"

Mack looked at him, eyes narrowing, his forehead furrowing. "I don't know," he replied. "Twenty? Twenty-two?"

Kent Nicholls grinned. "Fifteen," he said.

To any normal person, the look that spread across Mack's face would have been pretty clear. The previous evening, he, a married man, had taken part in a group sex session with an underage girl. There were so many parts of that sentence that were wrong, he struggled to realise which he should be disgusted by first. The fact that he had been unaware would make no difference. He was in shock, his brain trying to process the combination of revulsion at himself, anger at Kent Nicholls for duping him, and disgust at Kent Nicholls for looking so pleased with himself. But then Kent Nicholls had said something which would affect the course of Mack's life for evermore. Presumably mistaking the look on Mack's face for pleasant surprise, he leaned in even further, as if what he was about to say was enrolling Mack into some kind of club, and said, "And I can get them even younger."

Harpo told Mack later that when he had arrived at the house and walked through the front door, he heard the commotion in the kitchen, ran in, and had to physically pull Mack away from Kent Nicholls, who was lying on the floor. The journalist's face was covered in blood. Grabbing Kent Nicholls by the lapels of his leather jacket, Harpo reckoned that Mack had dragged him out of his seat, across the kitchen table, and headbutted him. Harpo had to tell Mack this, as Mack had no memory of his actions. They could only surmise that it was a swift movement, remarkable for its precision at the very moment when Mack had completely lost control of himself. Kent Nicholls was not a small man, but Mack seemed to have lifted him off the table and thrown him to the ground, his brain no longer trying to process the information he had been given, instead being powered by instinct, by his utter disgust and anger.

By the time Harpo had entered the room, Mack had managed to hit the prone journalist in the face several times. In response, the journalist had put his hands over his head and curled into a ball, putting his knees up to his chest. Mack was trying to prise his arms away so that he could hit him some more. He was shouting abuse at him, mainly involving words like 'sick' and 'scumbag'.

After Harpo had managed to push Mack against the wall and hold him there, Kent Nicholls took himself off to casualty and eventually had to have three teeth replaced (one of them was inevitably gold), and his jaw wired.

Mack and Al had never spoken about that evening again. At the time, Mack had left the house immediately in order to calm himself down, walking around the garden several times and only returning when he'd seen the taxi arrive and Kent Nicholls leaving with the girl. He had not talked to Al about it at the time, although he had always assumed that he had known how old the girl was. Whether he knew about Kent Nicholls' general perversions, he didn't know, and couldn't bring himself to ask.

When the album came out, *NME* ran the article that Kent Nicholls had written. In one part, he wrote, "the arrangements on these songs are like their composer: uncomplicated and lacking in any form of emotional resonance." In another section, he was even less subtle. "I would rather chew my own foot off than have to watch Mamal live again. If it wasn't for Al Smart's charisma and talent, there would *be* no charisma or talent on that stage."

It was easy for Mack to see that he had made an enemy for life in Kent Nicholls. And now it seemed that Al had been put under pressure by whoever it was that he owed money to, and had grasped at the closest possible source of money he could think of. He could imagine they would have tried to get Al to think of anything that he might have over his former partner, and that night would have come up pretty quickly. Except...

Mack took his tea, back up the stairs and sat at his desk, still in thought. Al had been there as well that night. So if they tried to land him in trouble with the law, then Al would be in trouble as well. He really must be desperate. What did they know?

He had made a decision. They could do their worst. It was time to face this memory.

Chapter 11

Wednesday at school had been strange for Mary. Rumours kept being passed around about Kurt's death: whether it might have been murder, whether Courtney was somehow involved. It was all so confusing, she just couldn't sort out her own feelings, except for this ongoing notion that Kurt had somehow let everybody down by being so selfish. It had proven such an unpopular theory, however, that she decided to keep it to herself.

The family had just begun eating supper together on the Wednesday evening when the telephone rang in the hallway. Mary was sat nearest the door and got up to answer. As she picked up the phone, she noticed a piece of paper beside it. It read: 'The Manor Hotel, Room 32'. Next to it was some gold foil folded into…what was that, a horse?

"Hello," she said eventually, not really taking in the information on the piece of paper.

"Hey, sweetie, is that Merry?" The American accent immediately told Mary who it was.

"It's Mary, yes. Do you want my dad?"

"That would be cool, thanks."

Mary took the cordless phone into the dining room and handed it to her father without saying anything. She sat.

"Well, who is it?"

"That American woman who was with your friend, Al. She wants you."

Mack looked at Jude quizzically, then took the phone from Mary. He took the phone out of the kitchen, shutting the door behind him. Jude looked at Mary, her eyebrows raised.

"What American woman?" she said.

"The one that was with Al. She was in the car with him when they stopped me this morning."

"I don't think I've come across this person before." Jude tried to sound unconcerned, but her efforts merely served to rouse Mary's suspicions. "What's she like?"

"Oh, you know," said Mary. "Typical American, all tits and teeth." Johnny giggled.

"Mary, please don't swear, especially not in front of your brother." They ate the rest of their meal in silence, each for different reasons.

Meanwhile, Mack took the telephone upstairs to the privacy of the bedroom. He knew that someone was behind what Al was doing; he knew that he could not have been doing this on his own, and besides, Al had almost told him as much. So as soon as Mary had told him that an American woman was on the telephone, he had put the pieces together.

"What is it?" he barked into the receiver.

"Hey, now, honey, no need to be so abrupt. We're on the same side here."

"I don't see how we could possibly be on the same side," Mack replied, walking to the window of the bedroom and looking out as he spoke. He kept his voice low. "Let me see if I can sum the situation up for us both. I have an old friend with his arm behind his back, an arm that you are twisting. And because of that, he comes back to England in search of money. How am I doing so far?"

"Not bad."

Mack heard her take a drag from a cigarette and blow out the air. She even managed to make smoking a cigarette sound sexually alluring.

"You then come and see me pretending to be a student," continued Mack. "I'm not sure why you did that. Perhaps to assess how likely I was to roll over and agree to change the publishing credits and cough up some money for you. Perhaps because you thought flashing your eyes and letting me see down your top would make it more likely. I obviously gave you the impression that it worked, because you sent Al in to see me and ask the question. I'm guessing you wrote the whole script for him. Including changing tack from friendly to threat when I responded in the negative. How am I doing?"

"Pretty good summary," said Kimberly. "Only thing you've missed is that it's not only his arm I have control of."

"What does that mean?"

"Are you going to cooperate?"

"I gave Al an answer to that that yesterday."

"Yeah. You did, didn't you. However, I was rather hoping that you might have changed your mind. You know, after you'd slept on it. Do you like to sleep on it, Mack?" Her voice was soft and warm. It was like talking to a kitten. He reminded himself that she had very sharp claws.

"Look," he said, keeping his voice low. "I don't know what you think you've got on me, but things that happened when Al and I were together were a long time ago. I don't actually care what you tell my wife. And she won't care either. Any such events are long in the past, and you will not be able to blackmail me with them, if that's your plan. Those songs are mine, the publishing rights are mine, and I am not giving them up for you, Al, or anyone else. Whatever he owes you, whatever he has done, it's his problem, not mine."

"Al is a very sensitive man," cooed Kimberly. "He is also a man of limited resources. But, as my boss always tells me, it's not what you know, and it's not who you know. It's what you know *about* who you know."

"And who is your boss, Kimberly? Who is this person trying to blackmail me for money?"

"I'm not sure that matters right now, do you? All that matters is that you know he has a plan to get what he feels he should have, and that it involves you. Personally, I don't know what that plan is, but from previous experiences, I'd suggest you provide the money that Al owes us so that you don't have to find out."

Mack sighed for a moment and looked out of the bedroom window, not focussing on what he saw. "This is pretty straightforward, as far as I'm concerned. I'm really sorry you made Al do something that I'm sure he'd rather not be doing. But hear this. It is not going to work."

"Then we'll just have to find something that does," said Kimberly, her voice an insistent whisper.

There was a pause as Mack thought for a moment. The events in that house were only known to four people, and he could not be certain how much Al had told them.

"Enough doublespeak," he said. "If you are trying to blackmail me, then tell me what with, otherwise it is not going to work." His voice was shaking, although still low in volume.

"You should write your autobiography, Mack. Put in enough of the juicy details and it would sell a whole heap of copies."

Mack realised that he needed to tread extremely carefully. He spoke more calmly now. "You want to give me something more to go on?"

"Not at this stage. But we will if we have to. But I'd rather have you in person. I'm sure we can come to a suitable negotiation position. Or maybe even a variety of positions."

"Drop the act," said Mack. "That's not going to work. Do you think I'd give Al money to have sex with you?"

"I hear you've done that sort of thing before" said Kimberly. "You've a bit of a reputation where the ladies are concerned, Mack."

Mack jabbed angrily at the 'off' button on his telephone. He placed the telephone on the windowsill and let his hands hang by his side, taking short, shallow breaths. Had the bluff worked? Could she tell that he desperately hoped they would not go to Jude?

Sitting down on the bed, Mack put his head in his hands and rubbed his eyes with his knuckles. He felt tired all of a sudden. Had he just done the right thing? What price might have to be paid for something that happened such a long time ago? No, it wouldn't come to that... would it?

The sound of an elephant jumping up and down told him that Mary was going down the stairs. She was a good kid, for a teenager. There was always a suspicion that Mary had been conceived as Jude's way of keeping him faithful. Jude had been on the pill at the time and yet she had still got pregnant. Technically possible, sure, and yet there were doubts. There was no resentment of Mary, he loved his daughter, but he certainly couldn't pretend that he had planned to have a child at such an early stage of his life. The whole experience rather caught him by surprise, one that lasted the eight years until Johnny joined them. By that time he had felt properly ready to be a father.

Ah, life would be so much simpler if such secrets were left buried deep down. No good could come of revelation. All it would cause is a lot of discussion and heartache, wading through unnecessary pain in order to get back to where they currently stood. Any marriage with ambitions for longevity must permit a few secrets.

Downstairs, Mary slammed the door behind her as she left the house, confused and angry at the snippets of her father's conversation that she had overheard.

Chapter 12

Thursday night, and Mack carried two renewed pints of beer high and to the side, avoiding the gesticulating teenagers who had ventured into the main bar of the Fox and Glove to get drinks. He and Jay had taken a table as far away from the bar as possible. The Fox was big enough to contain several parties at once, had there been sufficient people wanting to go out for a pint on a Thursday evening in Nether Littleton.

On the wall of the pub were a number of antique paintings of fat men and women in red jackets on horseback, surrounded by packs of beagles. There hadn't been a hunt in Nether Littleton for, well, forever, as far as Mack was aware. He had often wondered why some long-forgotten landlord had chosen those pictures. Each new landlord simply took the pub on as it was, including the faded pictures of a past few cared to see return.

Mack returned to the bar to collect crisps and his change, which the current proprietor had left on a bar mat for him. Brin was a tall, broad and bored Welshman, who was generally miserable and didn't seem overly fond of his customers, especially the younger variety. He was prone to laughing loudly at inopportune moments, as if laughing at something he had heard ten minutes previously. On Saturday afternoons in winter, when Brin would turn on the television above the bar to show Wales playing rugby, local knowledge held that it was best to drink in Nether Littleton's other pub, the Queen's Head.

Mack threw the packet of crisps into Jay's lap then sat down next to him on the long padded bench, so that they were both facing into the pub. He opened his packet of crisps and offered it to Jay.

"Thank you, no," said Jay, putting his hand up, palm facing Mack. His hand then went to cover his mouth and he sneezed. Waiting for a moment, he sneezed a second time. Mack continued to delve into his packet of crisps.

"Bless me," said Jay, sarcastically.

"Hmm?" said Mack, looking up.

"Bless. Me. Honestly, you can be so rude at times."

Mack smiled at his friend. He did take these small niceties so very seriously.

"So, what's up, mate?" said Jay, happy now that he had made his point. "Not like you to convene at short notice. Is all well?" Jay reached over the table and took a couple of Mack's crisps.

"No, nothing doing. Just a lot on my mind and fancied chewing the fat for a bit."

"Cool," said Jay, "I'm always up for that. Hey, how about that for a song title, actually? 'Chewing the Fat'."

"How about that it's shit?" Mack continued to delve into his packet, speaking with crisp mulch parked in the side of his cheek.

"No, it's not. It could be allegorical. You know, a double meaning. On the one hand it means talking around an issue because you have the time to do so, on the other it means…. Well, I suppose it means having to chew on something for a long time because it's fatty and not easy to break down. You could put both sides of the meaning into different parts of the song."

"No," said Mack, firmly. "What you have done is identified how the phrase 'chewing the fat' came about. Both meanings are the same. Because it's a phrase that is used to describe that meaning. So, without wishing to sound too repetitive here, it's shit. What you have managed to hit upon is the reason why I am the songwriter and you are the slightly nerdy techno geek who creates texture and sounds to give my songs even more character and flavour than I have already imbued in them."

They sat in silence for a moment. Mack munched at his crisps, busy arranging his own thoughts, the first beer only just starting to penetrate and ameliorate his mood.

"I've got a client who lives by the docks in Bristol," said Jay, eventually breaking the spell. "We manage a few properties for him."

"Oh yeah?" replied Mack.

"Yeah, he was telling me he's got a major seagull problem. Out the back, they nest on top of buildings, and make a right bloody racket."

"Perhaps he should shoot them. Is that legal?"

"Ah," said Jay, "that's the point. That's what he and I were discussing. We thought that shooting would be no good. You can't leave dead seagull carcasses lying around the roads."

"Could you poison them? Same problem I suppose."

"Exactly. So we thought of a crossbow. With a long line attached, so that after having killed the seagull you could drag its body back."

"Maybe sell it."

"Exactly. Pigeon is something of a delicacy, isn't it? Perhaps seagull could become a new Bristol dish. It would be great for tourism."

"Hmm," said Mack, "I'd have thought the pigeons you'd be served in a fancy restaurant would be specially reared, with little similarity to the annoying seagulls that pester your toes for food. Still, there must be an easier way to control the little bastards." This is why he had wanted to see Jay. The unbridled optimism was a life-affirming counterpoint to Mack's own current melancholy and negativity. He felt a little better already.

"Okay," replied Jay. "Let's think. What's the natural predator of the seagull?" They both sat in silence for a few moments. "There isn't one, is there?"

"Yes there is," said Mack. "A shark. I've seen it in nature programmes. The seagulls sit on top of the water, feeding, and then the shark comes from below and eats them."

"So we need to get a shark shipped into the docks. Okay, I think we can organise that. But how do we get the seagulls to sit on top of the water? What is the staple diet of a seagull? Fish?"

"Not in Bristol. It would have to be chips. You'd get a skip full of chips and spread them across the water. The seagulls land on the water to eat the chips, the shark eats the seagulls. Bingo, job done."

"Ah," said Jay. "One problem. The docks aren't saltwater. The shark couldn't live there."

"That's okay," replied Mack, "the chips will provide the salt."

They both laughed, Mack especially hard, feeling tension being released. An old man, sat on his own at the bar with a pint of beer and a whisky chaser, turned to look at them. Mack smiled at him. The old man took a packet of cigarettes from his pocket and lit one.

"Please," said Jay, catching his breath, "tell me you haven't got me out on a Thursday night for that."

"No," replied Mack. He picked up his pint and poured beer down his gullet. Wiping the excess from his top lip, he looked up at the ceiling of the pub at the leather straps screwed into the ceiling for patrons to hang from as their evening wore on. It was time to get to the point. "Far more annoying than that. I saw Al on Tuesday."

"Al," said Jay, narrowing his brown eyes. "Al. Narrow it down for me. I can think of three Als off the top of my head, at least two of whom are female." Jay ran his fingers through his hair, which flopped back into position.

"It's the guy I used to be in the band with."

"Oh wow. That's cool. At least, I thought it might be cool until I just looked at your face, and now I don't think it is so cool after all."

"No, it's not. Not at all." Mack took another long pull from his pint. When he put it back down on the table, he didn't say any more.

"You two parted amicably, didn't you?"

"Well, sort of," said Mack. "It's kind of hard to explain, and sounds really, I don't know, wet, I suppose. When you're in a band, you do give a lot of yourself up, especially if you are writing songs and lyrics. It's like a marriage in some ways – you have to let a bit of yourself out, otherwise it doesn't work. And so, when you break up, lots of things get taken personally, as each person tries to hide themselves again."

"Mm. A bit like your badminton doubles partner, then."

"Yeah," said Mack, "identical. Thanks, that's helpful."

Jay picked up his pint again. "So, you left with baggage. When was the last time you saw him?"

"Oh, I don't know, ten, eleven years ago. He went to LA to become a movie star."

"Oh wow. And did he?"

"Not really. The fact that you just asked the question is probably revealing in that regard. Anyway, now he's back."

"Is it not good to see him again?"

"I'll be honest, there were a few things said and done which I will find it difficult to move on from."

"Now we're cooking. Come on, tell Uncle Jay all about them, and don't skip on juicy bits."

"Nah, it's nothing like that. Well, there were a few things like that, but they didn't cause a problem." Mack paused. "Okay, so there was one particular thing that did cause a problem, but I'm not going to tell you about it."

"Why did the band split up?"

"Ah, we made some pretty silly mistakes. I remember one time we had a slot on Radio 1, which was a big deal. It was for John Peel, a late night session where you rerecord some of your songs in a BBC studio in Maida Vale."

"Cool." Jay was leaning forward now, eagerness and encouragement clear in his smile.

"Yeah, it was actually, and quite a coup for us. Having had a huge hit, we weren't a particularly cool band. So we – well, I – thought we should do something different. So we did three David Bowie songs instead of our own."

"Sounds like a good idea."

"Yeah, I thought so. Except it wasn't. We should have plugged the new single. It actually turned out to be our only chance that we'd have of getting on Radio 1 – the daytime shows wouldn't play it. So nobody got to hear the new songs and the album bombed."

"Ah."

"Yeah. The record company was furious at us. Rightly so, to be honest."

The two men lapsed into silence. That wasn't why the band, why he and Al, had split up. Mack knew it, and Mack knew that Jay knew it. The pressure of having something to lose, that is what created the tiny crack through which ego and envy came tumbling. What do you do when you have the thing you've always wanted? He had been the person who achieved their goal, terrified to discover that there is nothing beyond to aim for. Standing at the summit, being hit by the realisation that you'd forgotten to enjoy the scenery and the only steps left to take are down. A single man with no money and no family can take risks. But a successful man with a family, now he has something to lose.

The last few years had been all about recalibration, learning, applying that knowledge. But had he really learned anything? Was he not still the vain arrogant man who allowed his ego to be so affected by one article from a piece of shit journalist? Yes. Yes, he was. A feeling came over him that nothing had changed, despite his attempts to make music for himself, to reduce the reliance of ego on applause and adulation, but still he felt exposed. Now he had a family, a reputation, and financial security under his jurisdiction.

"You know what, mate," he said. "Sometimes I write late at night, after a few drinks. I write what I feel. What I really feel. It surprises me sometimes – what comes out is so angry. It's not often very good. I can't use it, it's not stuff that I can put into songs…it's too me, too much of me. It's just bile. Vitriol. And yet it must be what I actually feel. I want to fill the world with love, with happiness and optimism, but my innermost feelings seem to be dark thoughts."

"It's not always like that though, is it?" said Jay, concerned.

Mack didn't answer. He seemed to be sinking. "I have two beautiful children," he said, finally. "Surely the world I imagine is one of joy and love for them to inhabit. But it's not. It's a terrible place. Full of pretty terrible people, if truth be known. People who will smile at you while shitting on you from a great height, given only a very minor opportunity."

"Bloody hell," said Jay, "and I thought I was feeling stressed about having to pay for a new bathroom for the wife."

"Come off it, Jay, you run a business. I can't even begin to imagine the pressure you must be under every single day."

"Not me, mate. My fellow directors worry about the business – I just do the client stuff. I know my place. I'm Happy Jack."

"What does that make me? Self-obsessed Steve?"

The old man at the bar had fallen asleep, perched precariously on a high stool with the cigarette smoking between his fingers. Mack had been watching him while talking. It seemed inevitable that the cigarette would burn the man's fingers. Still the old man dozed, head lolling forwards. Just at the moment Mack stood to go and take the cigarette from his fingers, the man lifted his head, stubbed the cigarette out in the ashtray, and ordered another round of drinks.

Jay waited for Mack to sit back down before speaking again. "Just a wild stab in the dark, mate, but I assume this has something to do with Al."

"He wants money," said Mack, curtly.

Jay paused. He couldn't remember the last time Mack only used three words in a sentence. One of the reasons he and Mack got on was their enjoyment of verbosity. If Mack was matter of fact and to the point, it usually meant something had got to him.

"Why? What for?"

"Oh, his shitty life in LA has collapsed and I'm supposed to pay for it."

"How much?"

"Half the royalties from the band."

"Ah. I see. The old 'I thought of the title so I deserve half the publishing rights' chestnut, eh?"

"Yup. Except he didn't even think of a title. He reckons that he was there, creating the 'vibe', the creative atmosphere that led to the songs being written."

"And what do you think?"

"That he's full of shit."

"Hmm." Jay paused a moment, taking the opportunity to drink.

Mack stared at his pint morosely.

Eventually, Jay asked, "Does he have something on you, Mack?"

Mack didn't look up. "There are a few things that I'd rather not have come out, that's certainly true. I don't think it would be terminal between me and Jude, but I'd rather not take the chance."

"Don't tell me, let me guess. I can picture the scene. You're on tour, it's Huddersfield, you've been away for a few months, you've tried calling home but Jude's not there, you're in a club, you are approached by a couple of girls who were at the gig that night…"

"Yeah, alright, Jay, thank you. I don't need a blow-by-blow account. And yes, that was a poor choice of phrase, before you say it."

"Am I close, then?"

"Ish."

"So Al does hold something over you?"

"Yes. The fact that he doesn't have a family."

The old man sat up a bit straighter as a woman arrived at the bar, allowing her space. She ordered, then turned to look around the bar. Mack immediately recognised her as the student who had interviewed him. Except this time she didn't look much like a student. She looked much more of a woman.

The woman had short dark hair, tied back but with strands that were allowed to fall over her face. She was tall, wearing jeans and a white blouse with just enough buttons undone to be revealing – actually, really quite revealing now that Mack looked properly. Over the blouse was a black leather jacket, worn in a way that only certain ladies could get away with. Certain ladies who don't normally appear in English pubs.

She accepted the change from Brin and picked up her drink; bitter lemon, it looked like. Her dark eyes surveyed the pub, stopping when she saw the two men. She smiled at Mack; he did not smile back. He saw her look at Jay and nod, as if to say hi. Jay smiled back, and then averted his gaze in the manner of one who was eating a chocolate cake when he knew the chocolate cake was not his for the eating.

"Interesting," said Jay. "See who's at the bar?"

Kimberly had already taken the initiative and was coming over to their table. "Hey, Mack, how ya doing?" Her American accent seemed totally incongruous in their surroundings, as did her beauty.

"Oh," said Mack. "Kimberly, as I recall."

Jay picked up on the sarcastic tone in his voice. Mack didn't get up or offer her to join them. She dragged a low stool from a nearby table, not bothering to ask the three people sat there if the stool was free or not. There was a half-full pint glass in front of the space where the stool had stood. A moment of awkwardness followed as one of the ladies began to tell Kimberly that the seat was already taken. However, Kimberly simply smiled sweetly at the woman and took the chair anyway, sitting at the table with Mack and Jay and turning her back. The woman began to get up, but her male friend shook his head and beckoned her to sit down, dragging a chair from another table instead. Mack watched them tut and twitter at each other for a moment, before turning to Kimberly.

"What do you want?" he said, flatly.

There was a pregnant pause as Kimberly took a sip of her drink.

Jay looked at him in surprise. "Am I missing something here?" he said to Mack.

"No," said Kimberly, before Mack could speak.

She leaned forward to Jay across the table, and Mack could smell her. It was an intoxicating smell of summer rain showers, of tree sap. Of sex. He tried to remove the image from his mind, but failed.

He had an overwhelming urge to stroke the soft hair on the sides of her face.

"Mack doesn't think he likes me very much," Kimberly said to Jay, conspiratorially. "I think he is worried that he might fall in love with me." Then, leaning back, offering her hand and talking at her normal level again, she introduced herself. "Hello again, Jay."

Kimberly held out her hand with the palm facing downwards, offering Jay the choice of shaking her hand, or taking it. He opted to draw her hand towards him, and kissed it, the curtains of hair falling either side of her hand as he did so. Mack rolled his eyes, folded his arms and crossed his legs.

"Look, Kimberly," he said, retaining the unfriendly tone, "I've already given Al your answer, so I don't know what you expect to achieve by coming here to see me."

Jay looked at Mack, his furrowed brow concealed under his hair. He let go of the hand he had been holding.

"You don't deal with people very often, do you, Mack. You seem like the kind of guy who sits on his own in a room a lot, know what I mean." Kimberly did not phrase this as a question.

"I've been around enough to recognise a chancer when I see one."

"A chancer, eh?" Kimberly leaned forward, resting her folded arms on the table in front of her.

Both Mack and Jay could now see down the middle of her blouse, which revealed her breasts, squashed together on her arms. Mack looked away automatically, not wanting to give her the satisfaction of having some control over him. Jay pretended not to look. Badly.

"Have you people learned nothing from the troubles in Northern Ireland," Kimberly continued, addressing Mack directly. "You have to keep talking. Stay at the table. Even while the Irish and you English keep hitting seven piles of crap out of each other, they still talk. Mark my words, one day they will reach an agreement, and then what once seemed a hopeless cause will have a bright future, and it will all be down to the fact that they didn't give up, they kept on talking, and kept on trying to find a solution. What do you think, Jay?"

Kimberly turned to Jay, catching him off guard. He had drifted off with his arms folded and pint in hand, his gaze directly aiming below Kimberly's chin and following the contours of her breastbone to its natural conclusion. He now jumped slightly, broken suddenly from his vague pubescent daydream.

"Totally, yeah, absolutely," he garbled, then took a pull from his pint of beer, only to smile too soon and have a large percentage of it fall out of the sides of his mouth, down onto his shirt. He continued to smile, ignoring the cold wet feeling spreading across his chest. Mack rolled his eyes once more.

Kimberly turned her gaze back to Mack, who looked her in the eye, refusing to allow his gaze to be drawn downwards. Mack was unaware that, to Jay (who had now put down his pint and was discreetly folding his arms again to cover up the stain down his front), this could be construed as if there was something occurring between them, some sort of connection. They maintained the stare as they spoke, as if daring the other to look away first.

"Why do you think we've got something to talk about?" Mack said.

"Because negotiation is the only way to bring peace," replied Kimberly.

"I don't have a need for peace with you, because I don't have anything to discuss with you. We have no problem because there is no discussion."

"You may have a bigger problem than you think."

"You see, this is what comes from engaging with people you have no interest in. Only they can profit from it. I'm not interested in talking to you."

"Then perhaps I need to capture your attention somehow."

"Al did not write any of the songs. He has no rights to anything."

"That's not what he told us."

"Not my problem."

"It could be."

"No, it's your problem."

Kimberly sat up, straightening her back as if it were stiff, like a cat backing away from danger, arching its back to maintain the readiness to pounce. Jay still didn't speak.

"Has he told you how much?" she asked.

"No. And I'm not interested, because, would you believe…" he paused, leaning forward slightly, "It's. Not. My. Problem."

Kimberly reached into the inside pocket of her red leather jacket. She pulled out a thin envelope which had his name written on the front. She placed it on the table in front of him, then picked up her drink and finished it.

"This may help to explain why this is your problem," she said. "And – because any sensible negotiator should always go to the table with a proposed solution – it will also tell you what you can do to help solve the problem." She smiled, and Mack thought he heard a thousand flowers die. "I'm sure you and I can still be friends. Surely we can *at least* be friends." She turned to Jay, bowed her head very slightly, then turned and walked out of the pub.

Mack didn't pick up the envelope. He continued to look at the door through which Kimberly had just walked, his eyes narrowed, his teeth grinding unconsciously.

"Do you know," said Jay. "I don't think she's a student after all." He turned to Mack. "I take it she's something to do with Al."

Mack didn't answer.

"Hey, you okay, dude?" Jay said, tentatively.

"I'm going to have her," Mack said, under his breath. "One day, I'm going to have her."

Standing up, Jay finished his drink and looked down at his friend. "I think we need a drink. Same again?" he said. Not receiving a reply, he went to the bar and ordered two more pints.

Mack picked up the envelope and opened it, not taking his eyes away from the door to look at the contents until he had actually pulled the piece of paper out. He looked at it for just a moment, and then put the letter back in the envelope. His shoulders sagged slowly, as if he were a giant bean bag. Then he stood, leaving his coat but still holding the letter, and left the pub.

Just a few minutes later, he returned – without the letter.

"Did you catch her?" asked Jay.

"Yes," said Mack.

"And?"

Mack looked at his old friend, and yet he didn't see him. "And I need a whisky chaser," he eventually replied. "Want one?"

Chapter 13

The alarm radio burst into life at 7.30. The DJ entered the room mid-sentence with a forced jollity that gave Mack just enough impetus to reach out of bed and turn it off. He had been awake for a while, rolling recent events around in his mind endlessly, so the alarm provided notice that it was time to move on.

Jude mumbled good morning to him, then, as usual, rolled back over to doze for a while.

Footsteps on the hallway told Mack that Johnny was coming in. The treasured morning ritual that Johnny would get into their bed for a morning cuddle. All the more precious because it was a finite resource. It wouldn't be long now before Johnny would stop appearing round the door, sometimes giving a little wave before running over and climbing into bed beside him, both father and son relishing the opportunity for physical contact.

Mack held the duvet up, and Johnny wordlessly climbed in next to him. They snuggled closer together, Mack lifting his arm up so that Johnny could lie on top of it. Johnny's leg wrapped itself around the leg of his father, and Mack wrapped his other arm around his son's shoulders. He could remember his own father, who was not a tactile man, giving him an occasional arm across the shoulders, perhaps after a football match, and he remembered the feeling of size and strength, of security, that he had always felt. As an adult he would look at his own hands and they seemed perfectly normal, but he could recall his father's hands seeming so big. They represented safety to his younger self. He wanted Johnny to feel safe as well, for him to feel protected by his father both physically and, by extension, mentally. He wanted his son to have the same feeling of a love that makes no demands, a love that his father had managed to give to him.

He could feel his son's body wriggle and relax as his arms enveloped him. How long would he be able to provide such a direct feeling of security for his son? And was that secure feeling sufficiently embedded to last through a lifetime? Even now, Mack could feel his own father's protection, the comfort blanket that had cheated death and lived forever.

This natural urge to protect had been passed to Mack across a yawning generation gap, and he now felt it keenly. But with that urge came the desire to enjoy, to simply *be*. There had been fun in his childhood, but it was despite, not because of his father's approach to parenting. There would certainly not have been cuddling in bed – there simply wasn't the time for that sort of thing in the mornings as his father was always keen to get to work. But holidays, they were different.

His father would take them camping, often to the same campsite near the town of Tenby, in South Wales. To their beach. Mack would always remember that endless expanse of sand.

They had first discovered the secret beach when Mack was nine and still called Michael. They would return many times, just the two of them. There might have been others on the beach, but Mack's memory allowed only for him and his father. Indeed, he mainly remembered his own happy solitude, his father, ever more internal, sitting on a rock for hours at a time reading a book or watching the young Michael playing. Sometimes they would fly a kite together.

The reason the beach seemed to be their little secret was because it could only be accessed through a cave. Michael had discovered this by accident, after having spent an hour in a small cove playing on the rocks. The entrance to the cave was hidden behind some large rocks, and he had gingerly entered. Immediately, he saw that it was not so much a cave as a tunnel, one which sloped downwards for about ten metres. Through the exit on the other side he saw sand. Clambering down the tunnel he saw that the entrance was about two metres above another beach; he could see that he would easily be able to jump down.

He recalled the welling excitement, bubbling over into unbridled joy when he reached the end of the tunnel and looked around. In front of him had been a huge beach stretching hundreds of metres in front of him, the pure, unmarked sand surrounded by high cliffs on three sides and cut off by the incoming sea on the fourth. This tunnel was the only way in and out of the beach – their secret beach.

His father had shared his delight. Every holiday since that shared moment of discovery would include a couple of days on the secret beach, returning just before the tide came in far enough to prevent their exit, allowing them four or five hours of solitary play and fun. Mack would spend the entire day watching the tide creep further up the beach, the thrill of solitude enhanced by the knowledge that if they did not leave in time, there would be no way out.

As he grew older, Mack would enjoy the hidden beach for reasons other than the endless play variations afforded by the sea and the rock pools. One holiday, at the age of thirteen, the first day on the beach had been one of introspection at the troubles life now seemed to be raining down upon him, and he had found himself expressing these musings in words. From that day forward, he had always taken a pen and paper to the beach with him to jot down ideas – not with any thought of organising them but just filling up pages with what came into his head. He did it because he felt he had to – there was no choice. Mack recalled those days so fondly, being with his father even if they weren't actually doing things together.

Johnny nestled his head under his father's shoulder, as if enjoying the strength and love that he could feel coming through the massive arm wrapped around him.

Lying on the other side of the bed, Jude stared at the wall in the half-light of the morning.

Having successfully negotiated her way around her family the following morning with the minimum of conversation, Mary met up with Stretch.

They exchanged nods and grunts of greeting then walked on in silence. Mary had arrived at their meeting place slightly earlier than usual, and was pleased to see that Stretch had the same idea, as if each knew that the other had wanted to talk. A line had been crossed yesterday – they had moved beyond a boundary that separated the usual banter and deeper conversations about others from talking about Mary's family.

Stretch's question had troubled her. Something inside had been poked and it was not happy. So this morning she had studied her father at the breakfast table. He seemed troubled and distant, not his usual bubbly self. However, he and Johnny still chatted, and for the first time Mary had consciously felt left out. It was as if the feeling had been there all along, but she had only just noticed it.

After Johnny had left the table, however, her father had taken her by surprise. Mum had gone up to help Johnny get his bag ready for school and Mary was about to leave the table when Mack had asked her, nicely, to sit down, smiling in a very uncomfortable way.

"You okay, Mary?" he had said.

"Yeah, sure, why?" she replied.

"Well, you seemed upset last night. I gather a lot of kids are very affected by what happened to Kurt."

Mary bridled at this insight, although she was sure she hadn't shown it. He shouldn't call him Kurt, she thought. We can call him Kurt because he's ours, but you shouldn't. It sounds naff; sounds like you're trying to be cool. You don't know him; he's not your generation.

However, all she said was, "Yeah, some girls seem pretty upset by it."

"What about you? What do you think about it?"

Mary just shrugged in response.

Mack continued with his line of questioning. "Are you upset by it?"

Mary shrugged again. She didn't know what to do, how to react. He was breaking all their rules.

"Come on Mary, talk to me. I'm interested. We don't talk enough any more."

And then he did something which totally freaked her out. She had her hands folded on top of each other on the table. He reached out, and placed his hand on top of hers, and smiled at her.

"I do love you, Mary, you know that, don't you? Whatever happens, I always want you to remember that I love you very much."

"Ohhh kayyy," Mary said slowly. She gave him a weak smile, more to get him to stop this mawkishness than from any sort of response mechanism.

He gave her hand a squeeze and then retracted it slowly, as if that would prove how genuine he was. She took the opportunity to escape, trying not to use undue haste but pushing back her chair with a loud scraping noise that her father usually told her off for, before putting her bowl in the sink and leaving the kitchen.

Now, thinking back on the whole episode as she walked to school with Stretch, Mary's mind was a fog of confused thoughts, unable to settle. She was still angry about Kurt – it was like a mass epidemic that she had been affected by even though she didn't want to be, like it was dragging her in. But why would her dad suddenly show her any attention? What was wrong? What was he trying to prove? Even worse, what was he hiding?

"Are we cool?" Stretch asked.

She turned to look at him, her thoughts hauled back to the here and now. She smiled and took his arm, hugging it as her way of giving the answer to his question.

Morning lessons passed uneventfully. Time that they could never reclaim, lost among the detail of learning and living. They met up again at lunchtime, eating with the other students, a few friends that they had in common. They discussed Kurt some more, hearing the latest developments. When they had the chance they left their break time mates behind without a word between them, without seeking each other's agreement – the only real, true friend either of them had. It was as if each of them knew that there was something important that they had to discuss. They sat next to each other on the wall outside the school gym, and, uncharacteristically, Stretch started.

"I've got something I want to tell you," he said.

"Okay. I'm listening."

Mary heard him take a deep breath. It was as if they were in a film, stumbling blindly through the fog of their adolescence, arms outstretched, then bumping into each other and holding on tightly, blind, while the maelstrom roared with ever increasing ferocity around them, until finally it would calm down, and they emerged into a semblance of maturity.

"There's something you don't know about me, Mary. I'm adopted."

Mary looked at him, uncomprehending for a moment. She understood the words, but not their meaning. Nor why he was telling her this now. It was a lot to take in.

"No way."

Stretch smiled at her response.

"You're adopted? Your mum and dad aren't your mum and dad? Who the hell are they then?"

"Well, yeah, they are my mum and dad. They're cool. They're just not my natural parents, that's all." He smiled at her again.

"Shit," she said.

His smile waned.

"Shit," she said again. Her brain seemed to be overloading; she couldn't quite take this in. It seemed to be such big stuff and yet Stretch seemed to be so cool about it. She just couldn't understand why. "When did you find out?"

"Oh, I've known for years. It's never been a big deal."

Mary turned to look at him. She couldn't decide which was freaking her out the most: the fact that he didn't think it was a big deal, or that he'd known for years and never told her. They were supposed to be best friends.

He reached over, put his fingers underneath her jaw, and gently closed her mouth. She hadn't even realised it had been hanging open. Turning back, she leaned her elbows on her legs, her hands supporting her head.

"Shit," she said again, this time a little more quietly, in a more measured way.

"It's cool, you know," said Stretch. "I mean, it's a good thing. I've known all my life, my mum and dad are still great to me and they'll always be my mum and dad. I wanted you to know because, well, I'm not really sure, it just seemed important that you knew. It's probably the most important thing anyone could know about me, and yet it's also something that's really not important. It's just what it is, you know."

Without turning round, Mary said, "When are you allowed to look for your real mum and dad?"

Pausing for a moment, Stretch looked at the side of Mary's head, his own brow furrowed. "Why would I want to do that?" he said.

Now Mary did turn around and look at him. "Don't you want to?"

"Not really. Maybe one day. But Mum and Dad have been great – I wouldn't want to hurt their feelings."

"Don't you want to know what happened to your real parents?"

"What makes you think I don't know?"

Mary realised that she didn't really understand this at all.

She clearly had a host of preconceptions about being adopted and had no idea how they got inside her. She also wasn't used to Stretch knowing something she didn't, and it was making her uncomfortable.

"I don't understand, Stretch. Do you know who your real parents are?"

"Yeah. My birth mother lives in Dudley, near Birmingham. My father was a musician, she didn't actually know his name. Mum gave me up because she was on drugs and didn't want me to be harmed, so she gave me away for my own sake. The ultimate sacrifice, Dad says. I get a Christmas card from her every year. She's off drugs now, but is still not in a great way. Doesn't work or anything, so I could never go and live with her. Dad says she's just not very good at life. I quite like that. I'm not very good at maths, so I kind of know what he means." Stretch smiled at Mary, but the smile soon faded as he saw her jaw had slid downwards again.

"Wow," she said.

"Well, that makes a change from 'shit' I suppose." He paused, giving her time.

"Why are you telling me this now?" It was a mean question, she knew, given the gravitas to which he had already given the secret.

"Because I thought you'd understand. And because it might make you realise that your parents love you because you are their daughter. When my adopted parents took me in, it was because they couldn't have children of their own, so they chose to have me, and in doing so made a commitment to love me. They've told me that. And that takes the pressure off, you know?"

"No," said Mary. "I mean, yes. Sort of." A thought arose from within her like a bubble, reaching for the surface of her mind, a thought that had been waiting patiently for the right moment to appear. "Stretch, I think you might have given me the answer."

"What answer?"

"My dad. Why he's never been that loving towards me." Mary was gazing into the middle distance, as if her eyesight and other senses had switched off, as if her body needed all its energies to process the information that Stretch had given her. Stretch looked concerned, but she didn't notice.

"Why would he tell me he loves me this morning? Why would he do that? What was he trying to prove? He never does that." She turned and looked at Stretch. "I think I know why my dad doesn't really love me." She stood up and walked off towards the school gates. Stretch got up and went after her, running a few paces to catch up, then walking. But Mary was walking with a very determined stride, and Stretch had to run awkwardly, like a palm tree in a gale. Running was not something that came naturally to him – it was more a case of leaning forwards and catching up with himself.

"Where are you going?" he called to her, now only a few paces behind.

"I'm going to find him. I'm going to ask him."

"You can't, it's going to be the end of break soon. And ask him what, anyway? Mary, will you please stop for a second."

She stopped and turned to face him. Stretch was by her side in a moment.

"I'm going to ask him if I'm adopted."

Stretch's face recoiled into his neck in a show of surprise, a physical embodiment of the word he spoke: "What?!"

"It's the only answer. He doesn't give a shit about me because I'm adopted. He's put on a pretty good show over the years, but he's never been very good at being a dad. He's basically been lying to me all this time. Yeah. At least your mum and dad told you early on. Mine never did. And now I'm going to have it out with him." She turned and started walking again.

This time, Stretch didn't follow. "That's not what I said, not what I meant at all," he called after her. Then, as he realised the futility of the situation, "What shall I tell Miss Taylor?"

"Tell her I've got bad period pains and have gone home," Mary called back, as she strode out of the school gates.

Chapter 14

At the same time as Mary and Stretch had been entering school that morning, Mack had been walking Johnny to school. Mack's cheery demeanour may have been a little more forced than usual, but they still played the 'I don't know' game.

Mack had invented the 'I don't know' game, which involved the two of them taking it in turns to ask a question of each other, and if the answer could only be 'I don't know', the questioner won a point. Johnny had proved to be particularly adept at this, asking questions such as 'How many stripes does a zebra have?' and 'How many stars are there in the sky?' Mack, for his part, ended up resorting to song titles, and would win points with questions such as 'How deep is your love?' and 'Why do birds suddenly appear every time you are near?'

Today, however, the game seemed a little harder to play. Johnny had been coming up with some good questions but Mack had been distracted, his thoughts elsewhere. He therefore did not notice a man sitting on his own in a white Peugeot, on the corner of a road which led up to the school. He hadn't bothered to look at the contents of the envelope in detail, a quick glance served to confirm that it was blackmail. Disappointment in his ex-partner had come over him but it hadn't been a difficult decision to reject the threat. He had simply handed the envelope back to Kimberly, without a word, as if to prove that he didn't care what they did with his memories. Every time he closed his eyes he saw the look on her face at that moment.

Because his father was not as much fun as usual, Johnny asked if he could walk up the street to the school by himself. It was one of his 'big boy' things that he liked to do sometimes, and, with the street being devoid of passing traffic, Mack would accede to this infrequent request and watch him from the end of the road. Johnny would give him a wave as he entered the gates, as if to say 'you can go now, stop watching me' as much as to say goodbye.

So today, Mack kissed Johnny goodbye and let him walk the final hundred yards or so to school on his own. They had been a little early and there weren't any other children on the road just yet, but he could see the school, and Johnny started running as soon as he'd kissed his father goodbye for the day. Mack turned before Johnny reached the gates, his mind churning over whether he had done the right thing, and began the walk back home.

As Mack entered the house, he realised that Jude was not already in her shed working, but instead was in the kitchen. As he shut the door behind him and took off his shoes, he heard her flick the switch to boil the kettle. This signified that a conversation was imminent.

The kettle boiled almost immediately. Jude poured the water, stirred, then lifted the teabags out of the cups and into the bin.

"I've just been chatting to Sarah Head," she said, handing the milk back to Mack to put in the fridge.

"Oh?"

"Mmm. She says Jay has come into work with a bit of a headache this morning."

"Yeah, we got stuck into a good chat last night. He's a good man." Mack looked awkwardly at the ground, without yet knowing what he was feeling awkward about.

Jude turned, handed Mack his mug, and leaned back against the work surface, cradling her own mug in her hands. "So what is actually happening here?" she said.

"What do you mean?"

"Oh, come on, you're not telling me everything, are you, I know it." She looked him in the eye and he squirmed. "There's something going on here, and I don't appreciate not being included in it. I heard Al ask you for a share of the royalties on Monday, and you threw him out. Since that time you've been in and out during the day, you've hardly spoken to me, you were out on Wednesday and last night, and we haven't had a chance to talk about it. And I don't know *where* you were on Wednesday night."

"Yes you do, I was at a gig. The open mic night at the Royal Oak, helping to organise it."

"That's what you tell me."

"Well, I was." He raised his voice ever so slightly, raising an eyebrow to indicate that this was not a point he wished to discuss. They both paused, taking stock for a moment. Mack spoke first. "Look, I can handle this, okay."

"Yeah, I'm sure you can. But I don't know what it is you are handling, and I'm not sure I like how you are handling it."

"It's complicated."

"It must be. Tell me what is going on, Mack."

"No."

"Why not?"

"I can't explain."

"Can't, or won't?"

"I can handle it."

They stood opposite each other in silence for a few moments, Mack looking at the ground, Jude looking at him. He felt uncomfortable. Not once in all the time that they had been together had Jude put any ultimatum on him. And not once in their entire relationship had he refused to answer a question. They were in uncharted territory. Mack had no desire to hurt this woman.

"We don't actually seem to talk any more, do we," Jude said.

Mack held back the urge to roll his eyes. "Of course we do," he said.

"Rubbish. We don't go out enough, either."

"What? We go out all the time. Anyway, what about my gig the other day. You didn't even come."

"I want more of us, more things with you and me."

"Christ, I give you opportunities – is it my fault you don't take them?"

"They are not opportunities, they are you, living in your past, living in a dream. Can't you just forget about you for a while and think about us?" Jude's voice was getting ever flatter, her left eyebrow arching ever higher.

Mack felt his hackles rising and tried to fight the overwhelming urge to say what he was thinking. He failed.

"I can't provide you with everything, you know. You can't live through me. You have to create your own reality. I can't be responsible for your life as well as mine, you know…"

Silence. Mack looked at his wife, the woman that he didn't really know, the schoolgirl he had taken for granted. Had he really changed? He had tried so hard to give her what he thought she wanted. And yet it occurred to him now that he had never actually asked her what she wanted.

"Look," he began, but Jude interrupted him.

"Has it got anything to do with that woman?" she said.

"What woman?" He had replied too quickly.

Jude did not speak, but stared at him.

"Oh, for Christ's sake. No it has not. Jude, look, this is complicated, okay? I don't want to worry you with it, I can handle it."

"And who is that woman? Jay told Sarah she is quite a piece."

"She came with Al, kind of like his minder. Please, leave it to me, I will sort this." Mack walked out of the kitchen and went up to the studio, his irritation at not being able to tell the truth increasing with every step.

Jude stood in the kitchen for a long time, staring out of the window but seeing nothing. Something was not right. Things were happening that did not normally happen. When had they started holding secrets from each other?

They might not be as close as they used to be right at the moment, they were too busy dealing with the upbringing of their children to give focus to each other, but they were still open, still honest. If Mack saw an attractive woman, he would tell her. Indeed, she would often be the one to point the woman out to him.

Jude liked order, liked to be in control of her life. It was one of the reasons she kept her life simple, ordered, structured. Like a spot the difference game in a child's picture book, she knew something was wrong, but couldn't yet see what it was. She felt in that limbo land, the in-between place that lies before 'knowing', but after 'not knowing'.

It was the woman that was making her feel so uncomfortable, she knew that. Many women had admired Mack over the years, but for some reason, none of them felt like a threat. There was an intensity about his reaction to this woman's existence that left Jude feeling uneasy. Oh, sure, she knew he had been no saint, particularly in those early years, those Mamal tours. Al had not held back, she knew that. The singer had accepted all offers, which can't have been easy for Mack. But Jude was aware that Mack's sanctimonious posturing about what Al got up to was nothing more than a mask for his own infidelities. Mary's conception had been a genuine accident – in more ways than one – but she was secretly glad that a child had been given to them much earlier than they would have expected, because it meant that Mack had straightened out big time.

Sure, Jude had been no saint either. Poor Mack, she thought to herself. All that time he was out being the pop star, he was so obsessed with himself and his own activities that he failed to notice that Jude had her own needs. He was away for months on end, and so when Spencer came round to keep her company, there was an inevitability in their ending up in each other's arms. Actually, it was more like wrapped around each other's torsos.

In total, she probably only slept with Spencer six or seven times. However, that was enough to get her pregnant. She had lied about the date of conception by a week, in order to make sure the date coincided with Mack being in-between tours. He didn't pay too much attention to the timing anyway, and so Jude was sure that nobody, including Spencer, ever realised the truth that Mary was not Mack's child at all, but that Spencer was her father.

The irony was compounded by that damn song, 'A Bridge of Straw'. She knew that Mack had written it about them from the moment that she had heard the first few lines. It was sent as a demo recording from a tour hotel room, the title of the song reaching out to her, yet admitting the fragility of their relationship. The song simply screamed fidelity, it postured, anguish for a love not present, hope and positivity struggling out of every line. However, Jude suspected it was written in a moment of guilt, and knew that it was received in a blaze of irony.

Spencer happened to be bringing her a cup of tea as she was listening to the song in bed, the lyrics throwing accusations at him like a trembling finger.

The song had worked, but not in the way that Mack had intended. Jude broke off the relationship with Spencer shortly afterwards. He had been deeply upset, and she was worried for a while that he was going to cause trouble for her. He would keep phoning and turning up at the door when Mack was away, as if he somehow knew Mack's movements. Luckily, however, he never turned up when Mack was there, and suddenly his presence in her life stopped. He just didn't make contact with her again.

Jude poured what was left of her cold tea into the sink, made a fresh cup, and went to her shed. She spent the remainder of the morning working on a new idea she had been pondering over, an idea for a bracelet. She assumed that Mack was in his studio but she didn't much feel like going in to see him. Around 1pm, she got up, stretched, and left the shed. As she was crossing the garden she realised that the telephone was ringing, and through the windows at the back of the house she saw Mack running down the stairs from his studio, grabbing the phone in the kitchen. She wondered how many other times it had rung during the morning, and cursed herself once again for not doing something about getting a connection in her shed.

Mack was speaking into the telephone, clearly becoming more and more agitated. He leaned heavily against the wall while talking, as if needing to support himself, then put the phone down abruptly. He ran out of the kitchen into the front of the house.

Jude, concerned and annoyed, ran to the back door of the house, which opened into the utility room. She called for Mack but it was too late. Just as she opened the connecting door to the kitchen, she heard the front door slam shut. She ran through the house, but just as she opened the front door, Mack was driving off, fast.

Chapter 15

Running her hand through her hair firmly and quickly, Mary walked down the road with a purpose she hadn't felt for some time. This was the answer, she just knew it. Her father wasn't really her father. That was why he had always seemed so distant.

Of course, this didn't explain her mother. She had also been distant, but then she'd been distant from everyone, that was just how she was. Her father had always been so affectionate towards Johnny, they had so much fun, yet Mary was just ignored. She had come to feel like a stranger in her own home, focussed on her own issues, no one else seeming to care about them. Now she came to think about it, now that the idea was taking a firm grip inside her head, she realised that over the last few years a creeping, insidious feeling of a lack of love had indeed begun to envelop her.

The realisation felt enlightening, as if she had been staring at the wallpaper in her bedroom and suddenly saw a face among the floral pattern. She turned out of the school gates and onto the pavement alongside the main road towards her home, feeling as if she might finally get some answers to her complicated life.

Bag slung over her shoulder, Mary looked at the ground in front of her as she walked, her mind racing with possibilities. She wondered if she should try and discover who her real parents were, or whether she could accept her new situation. A stone lay at the side of the pavement and still deep in thought, she checked her stride to be able to give the stone a good kick.

Instead of cannoning into the fence and dropping down as she'd hoped, the stone bounced off the fence and jumped up towards the road. Mary's heart lurched for a moment as she realised that there was a car coming and the stone might be about to hit it.

Sitting behind the steering wheel of the car, Mack saw the stone coming from the darkness of his peripheral vision and swerved to avoid it. He was consumed with his thoughts, totally oblivious to his surroundings, and the quick swerve needed to avoid the stone had been entirely automatic, refusing to break his reverie.

She realised it was her father in the car only moments after it had become clear that the stone and car were not going to collide. He hadn't even noticed her, not even accidentally kicking a stone in front of his car. As she stood and looked at the car disappearing down the road, feeling anger boil inside her, she saw an indicator begin to flash and the car slow down to turn right. That's odd, she thought. There's not much down that road. It goes down a lane for half a mile, then out of the village. The only building down there is the hotel.

Then Mary remembered the piece of paper that she had seen. It had a hotel room on it. And shortly after, she had overheard the end of the conversation between her father and the American woman, the one who dressed like an expensive prostitute (or at least, what Mary imagined an expensive prostitute might dress like).

She had only heard a few snatched words. What was it he had said? Something about paying to have sex with her? She had thought it odd at the time, but now her mind raced and she put the pieces together. She thought of Kurt Cobain, of the fragile nature of life, and of time being wasted. There seemed to be so much to do, and yet her father, or the man who had pretended to be her father all this time, was lying with other women, and lying to her mother. Layer upon layer of twisted anger was forming, like magma spewing from a volcano, a confused amalgam of questions and conclusions.

There was only one thing to do, Mary decided, and that was to confront him. She began to walk back the way she had come, then crossed the road and followed the direction that her father went in. If he had indeed been driving towards the hotel then she wanted to know why, and she wanted to know whether he really was her father. They were the two main questions, more than enough to begin with.

It was only half a mile or so to the hotel and the way Mary was walking, with a purpose and with real meaning in her stride, it only took ten minutes to get there.

The Manor Hotel was an old house that had been converted into a hotel some fifty years previously. It was too large to be called a guest house, and yet the phrase hotel seemed to bestow upon it a grandeur that was also not entirely appropriate.

It was on three floors with an additional block of rooms in a converted stable at the back of the car park. The entrance to the main building was up some steps which were covered by a canopy, one which looked as cheap and plastic as it actually was. The canopy had once given the hotel an air of attempted opulence, but now tinged with green algae, it confirmed one's initial suspicions that this was a hotel in a village off the main tourist trail.

The reception desk was unmanned as Mary quickly walked past it and up the wide stairway to the first floor. At the top of the stairs was a door, and she went through onto the landing, out of sight of reception.

The note had said Room 32. Mary quickly went up the stairs to the top floor and through the door at the end of the landing. She continued down to the end of the corridor, to what should have been the highest number possible. However, she cursed under her breath as she saw the number on the final door: 26.

Mary stopped, puzzled. Then she remembered — the converted stables at the back of the car park. Another curse and she ran down the stairs, light on her feet, making little sound. As she arrived in the foyer, her heart stopped suddenly as she realised there was now an elderly lady standing behind the reception. Without breaking stride, Mary said a quick good afternoon and walked past.

"Oh, good afternoon," replied the lady, looking up. She went back to her book, then after a few moments looked up again at the girl's back, realising that she had not seen her before.

Mary skipped hurriedly down the steps underneath the canopy and went over to the car park. The rooms at the end of the car park were actually one long, low building, with a series of doors for each room. As she got nearer, she could see that they started at 27 and ended with 32 at the right-hand side, tucked into the corner of the plot.

Uncertain of what she would find, Mary approached the door with care. Now that she was about to open the door, she was unsure why she was actually there. Confusion ran around her brain, various nebulous concepts and concerns fighting to get her attention. The death of Kurt had seemed to disturb the natural order of things, made

119

ideas possible, freed her thinking, allowing it into areas she had not previously thought open to her. These feelings surrounded her now, all triggered by the death of someone she didn't know. The effect on her seemed to be so much deeper than others at school. Everyone had seemed so upset, and yet superficially so, as if trying to prove that each was more sensitive and upset than the others.

Her own reaction had been anger, and for the first time in her life she had let that anger out, not repressed it or forced it to back down, but let it show itself – she had even managed to explain herself. Thanks to Stretch, because of his belief in her, she allowed herself to feel that her opinions might actually matter, that she might be able to have her own ideas. Could it actually be true that she was adopted?

So much change, so many things not in their right place. Mary did not like change. She felt disorientated. It was about time she had some answers to the questions that prior to today she had not known existed within her.

As she approached the door, Mary could hear voices. One belonged to her father, and she also recognised Kimberly's American accent. She couldn't make out what they were saying to each other.

Mary turned the handle of the door slowly. Wanting to hear what they were saying, she opened the door a little way and put her head through the gap.

The hotel room was large, with a sofa and some tables at the end nearest her. A double bed with a headboard covered much of the wall on the right. There was a dressing table and chair at the end of the bed, against the left wall, and a door at the far end. She didn't take this all in to begin with, but the scene would remain with her for a very long time.

The first person she saw confused her. As the door opened, Al was sitting at the dressing table, facing away from her. She put her head round the door further and saw her father standing on the far side of the bed, looking down. He was bending over, about to pick something up from the bed. Mary realised that she had still not been noticed, and opened the door further, moving into the gap to get a better look into the room.

Then Mary saw that the American woman, Kimberly, was lying on the bed in a dressing gown. From her angle, the dressing gown looked as if it could barely have been covering her breasts. As her father went to pick up the item, Kimberly shuffled down the bed quickly, covering the package with her bottom. She said something to him, too quietly for Mary to hear.

Mary watched on, still unnoticed by the occupants of the room as Kimberly lifted her leg so that her calf rubbed against her father's torso. As she did so, the dressing gown fell away, revealing Kimberly's naked body. Mary stared at her perfect body, the breasts falling either side of her chest, the dark pubic hair.

"Isn't this something you've been wanting to see for a while?" said Kimberly. "Most men do."

Mary's father raised his head and closed his eyes, as if in a moment of ecstasy or temptation. She had no desire to see any more.

"Shit," Mary said, hardly realising that she said it out loud. Three heads jerked towards her. "Shit," she said again, this time her shoulders dropping as if several strings that had been holding her up were now cut. She turned and ran.

Sprinting across the car park, Mary's mind was now completely in turmoil. Her father was one great big lie in every possible way. He didn't love his daughter, had never loved her, but also didn't love her mother either. She didn't even know if he was her father. Christ, what else had he lied about?

Mary kept running, her subconscious mind trying to process this information overload. Unable to come up with answers that could process what she had seen, it instead created the initial fissure of hatred for her father. The scars and wounds that were founded upon assumptions she had begun to form were cemented into place by what she had just seen.

After a while she stopped running and instead walked quickly, not realising that her fists were clenched tight, the knuckles white. She would have to tell her mother. It was the only person she could tell. She would understand.

Part 2 – 2010

The Price of Protection

Chapter 16

Mack put the phone down. So Johnny had managed to get him a really serious break in America. The boy had actually been working hard at it for several years now, and all that time Mack had thought he was messing about on the computer. Now, in order to support his son and repay all that effort, Mack was going to have to leave the safety of his studio.

Leaning back in his chair, Mack stared out of the window and across the courtyard to the fields behind the house, up to the clump of trees in the distance. He didn't particularly see the wood; his focus was elsewhere, his mind racing, trying to catch up with events. Nor did he see the fox, walking low across the far edge of the field, stalking a pheasant. The fox stopped and the pheasant, blissfully unaware of the danger, turned and walked slowly towards the fox, moving closer to the unexpected destiny that fate had bestowed upon it.

Mack would do anything for his son, and Johnny would do anything for his father. The two of them had been dancing around each other ever since Johnny had moved in with him at the age of eleven. Mack had a plan, a goal, to support a child whose parents had divorced when he was still young. Did Johnny act with such awareness, or was his desire to please guided by instinct? Mack smiled, although he would have been surprised if you had told him so. Of course it was instinct, the boy couldn't help himself. He was a fabulous little man when he was a kid. That's why there had been so many sacrifices. To protect and to nurture.

The dance had been going on for all of time, the father and the son trying to please each other, seeking to prove themselves to be worthy of unconditional love.

Rising from his chair, Mack stubbed the cigar out and opened the door, leaving it open to give the small room some aeration. He walked across the yard towards the bungalow, kicking a plastic bread bag into the air and catching it as he went. The rest of the rubbish could wait.

The back door entered straight into the kitchen. He felt the crotch of a favourite pair of jeans that had been placed on the radiator the night before. A little damp maybe, but they would dry on him. A tingle of excitement made its presence felt in his stomach as the conversation with Johnny churned around in his mind. The idea of a tour of America fought with the fear of exposure, but it was the idea of the tour that seemed to be winning.

The black moleskin trousers were removed and draped over the breadbin. Pulling on the jeans, he took the belt from the moleskin trousers, and threaded it round his waist. The forehead and hairline of Joe Strummer poked out of the top of a red lumberjack shirt, a black t-shirt of The Clash hiding underneath.

As he walked into the bedroom, he took off the lumberjack shirt and dropped it where he stood. An index finger moved several shirts along the rack in the wardrobe until it settled on one covered with large blue and yellow flowers. Now, he thought to himself, I am dressed appropriately to assimilate Johnny's news.

Entering the studio once again, Mack sat down at the computer, opened an Internet browser, and typed in 'College Towns'. A tour of America, Johnny had said, focussing on college towns. He spent the next half an hour flicking round the Internet, looking at various cities and bars. He started with New Orleans, the one place he had always wanted to visit.

Jay would have to be told, of course, and Harpo. The trip would be unthinkable without those two. There was a feeling of reward, of return on an investment, of being able to thank Jay for his support in those days around the divorce; days when it seemed that no one else would believe in him. And to thank Harpo for, well, for always turning up on time. This was proof that the more he had learned to ignore the demands of a market and to make music for himself, the more appealing that music became to the market.

He had been forced to crawl into that dark space within himself, the limits and boundaries imposed upon his creativity slowly being attacked, yet other people had been listening all along. The idea rather tickled him. The new voice emerged, blinking into the sunlight as he had slowly uncovered the message that he wanted to impart. He had a pleasant realisation that his true voice was actually a pretty bizarre one, influenced by his loneliness, and by the ongoing act of self-sacrifice that he lived with every day. The bluesy, raw heart of his true musical soul had emerged, and it turned out that people liked it. The irony kept going round in circles in his mind, taking up space and processing power.

Almost on autopilot, Mack sent Jay a text message to meet him in The Feathers that evening instead of coming to his house. Some major news required discussion.

Chapter 17

After Johnny had finished the telephone call to his father, he had been so excited that he had got into his car and just driven, without thinking where he was headed, his mind chewing over the conversation that he had spent such a long time building up to. High up in the Mendip Hills, he parked the car and walked across the fields. To his left was all green, endless fields interspersed with sheep and stone walls. To his right was fifty miles of Somerset, the Tor at Glastonbury sticking proudly out of the ground as if the very earth itself was waving, trying to attract his attention.

He walked quickly with nowhere to go, the bounce in his stride euphoric. That telephone call had been weeks in the making. He had known that he would have to tell his father what he had been up to at some point, but wanted some really good news to give him first. And with the help of one or two of his father's old contacts, he had managed to get some publicity within the industry, which had led, almost unbelievably, to the song 'My Grass is Greener' being chosen for a major new TV series.

It was actually one of his father's old music business mates, a journalist who had originally contacted Johnny to suggest the tour – thought that there would be a demand for it. He had even offered to give it some coverage, do an article on the comeback. Johnny had thought it a great idea, done some research, and discovered that venues were interested in booking. Before long, he had realised he was going to have to reveal all to his father before he took things any further.

Eventually Johnny stopped walking and sat down at the base of a small ancient burial mound. He took out his mobile phone and sent a text to the journalist. It simply read: 'Have told him. Tour is on. Will let you have details.'

Standing, he walked up to the top of the burial mound, honouring an urge to be at the very highest point. He dug his hands into his pockets, clenched his fists tight, closed his eyes, and allowed his head to sink forwards.

Pride, love and relief all welled up inside him. He felt a surge of confidence but didn't know what to do about it, where to place it – emotions like these were such strangers to his psyche. His inner turmoil was fed by a range of irresistible impulses. Desire to prove to his mother that he could be a success like she was, to prove to his father that he could be a success like he had been, and to prove to himself that the something missing from his personal history, the hole he felt in his childhood, was a fakery, and that the future was where everything mattered.

He didn't scream. He didn't shout at the sky, or release a lifetime of frustrations and confusion. He just waited for the rush to pass. There was work to be done.

Chapter 18

"Oh man, I can't wait to see Johnny," said Jay. "I am going to give him a full-on French kiss. What a bloody star!"

Mack placed a beer in front of Jay and sat down next to him, placing his own glass next to his keys, his wallet, and a packet of cigars. They had only been in the pub for twenty minutes and this was already the third pint. Mack had delivered the news after the first. They were now both firmly in the mood for a proper drink.

"I know," replied Mack. "He's done well, has the lad. Crisps?"

Jay put his hand up, palm towards Mack. "Thank you, no," he said.

"Done well? Christ, Mack, he's done more than well. He's my hero, is what he is. Always knew the lad would come good. All that time sat in front of computer screens and I thought he was playing with himself – turns out he was using the Internet for something useful. So do we have a plan yet?"

"I'm leaving it to Johnny to sort it out. He's earned the opportunity to really show us what he can do. He tells me his plan is to get us dates across America, just playing small clubs and stuff, culminating in some party to do with the TV show."

Jay looked at him, mouth agape. "Oh. Em. Gee. Oh My God. Ten minutes ago you told me we had some gigs in the States. That is SO different to 'dates across America'. Man, I can't take this in."

"I know, I felt the same way this morning. It's going to be the trip of a lifetime. Johnny, me, you, and Harpo. An electric guitar, an acoustic guitar, Harpo's bass, and a laptop full of strange noises. How could I do it without your strange noises? Only if you want to come, of course."

Jay ignored the last comment. He was too excited. His right knee was jigging up and down, out of control. "For how long?"

"As long as we want. Johnny reckons he can get us a gig anywhere, as long as we don't expect massive crowds. He says college radio has picked up on the music after students picked it up through the Internet, so we should concentrate on the college towns. There are fifty of them, plus a few other places such as New Orleans and Seattle, so I was thinking if we do two or three shows a week, we can take it easy and take the chance to travel around America. Just the four of us."

Jay just stared, both knees now pounding, fingers drumming the table. Mack thought he could actually see his brain working.

Eventually, Jay said, "You do realise you have just described one of my ultimate dreams, don't you? That and the other one that I can't talk about, revolving around sexual uses for a jar of mango pickle." Jay was so in shock he even failed to smile at his own joke.

"I know," said Mack. "Of course I know! Sounds cool, doesn't it. I reckon we could be over there for about four months in total. Won't earn much, but the shows should pay for all our expenses, so won't cost anything either."

Jay, mouth still open, stared at Mack. Then he turned his gaze to the front and slowly but dramatically allowed his body to move forwards, bending from the hips. He continued until his head landed on the table in front of him with a gentle bump. "I am so happy I could shit," he said into the wood.

Mack paused for a moment, savouring the reaction of his friend. He wondered how he had reacted when Johnny had told him that morning. Had he provided so much pleasure? Probably not. He had reasons for not wanting to be in the public eye that Jay did not. "Reckon you can get the time off work?" he asked.

"Mate, I'd sell the bloody business to do this trip." Jay straightened up, ran his hand through his hair and took a long pull on his fresh pint. He turned at last to look at Mack again. "Seriously, I'm pretty sure that Sarah will be able to handle things at work and the property market is pretty flat at the moment. She'll know how much this trip would mean to me – no one else will even notice that I'm not around. One of the advantages of getting divorced before you have kids. Have you spoken to Harpo yet?"

"Well, as much as one does speak to Harpo. Yes, I filled him in and he's game. He couldn't make it tonight, he's got a private appointment this evening with some rich widow who pays him a fortune to blow-dry her hair at home." They smiled at each other. "You okay with the plan? You, me, Harpo and Johnny?"

"Yeah," said Jay, slightly pensive. "Harpo is a total fruitcake and a miserable bastard, but he does his share, I'll give him that. And he doesn't speak often enough for his overriding negative view of the world to become annoying." He took a very deep breath, and let out a long, happy sigh. Then he looked at Mack, and said, "I need crisps."

The two of them knew each other so well, Mack could not conceive of a better travelling partner. They would stay in good quality hotels. During the day, when not travelling, Mack would visit museums and art galleries. He knew that Jay would lie in late on such days, and have the occasional afternoon drinking beer in a pool hall. After the gigs they would both meet local musicians over more beer and generally tear the place up in a gentle, non-contentious sort of way. Harpo, meanwhile, would do his own thing, either staying in his hotel room or disappearing in the way he did after gigs.

"Seriously, Mack, just think of the opportunities," said Jay, returning to his seat and putting the crisps on the table, unopened. "I mean, the 'opportunities'. It kind of makes me glad I'm single," said Jay. "Know what I mean?" He wiggled his eyebrows.

"Ohhhhh yes," replied Mack. "I know what you mean."

"I can picture the scene now. Groupies, young women, easily impressed, knocking on the door of our dressing room. Me smiling at the best-looking one. 'Excuse me love,' I will say, 'but this isn't going to suck itself, you know.'"

They sat in silence for a while longer, thoughts drifting in a direction that their mothers would most certainly not have approved of. Mack knew that he talked a good game, but it was such a long time since he had spoken with a woman in the presence of desire that he sometimes doubted if such feelings still lurked within him.

Jay had aged the better of the two. Mack had often teased him about his vanity. His image had moved with the times in a way that Mack simply couldn't be bothered with. The floppy fringe was still in place, as were the glasses, but the hair was slightly shorter at the back and the glasses rectangular, allowing him to perch them on the end of his nose and look over them. He remained effortlessly attractive, holding down an image of a suave tennis coach, always willing to put on extra lessons.

Jay had been there for Mack, and Mack had made sure he was around for Jay during his own divorce, although in truth his shoulder had not been leaned on a great deal. Jay had told him that the circumstances behind his separation were actually one big misunderstanding. His wife had gone away for a night one December. She said she was going to visit an old college friend for the weekend. Jay needed to speak to her (he couldn't find the remote control for the television) and so he had called the friend's number. His wife didn't know that Jay even had the number. When he called, the old college friend knew nothing about the visit.

Convinced that his wife was having an affair, Jay had jumped on the opportunity to follow something he'd been thinking about for a while but hadn't had the confidence to go through with. He had telephoned a single lady he knew, a fellow member of the committee of the local tennis club. He gave her the story, and without pausing to consider possible regrets, asked for her company that evening. The request was accepted.

As it turned out, Jay's wife had travelled to Scotland in order to get an extremely rare bottle of whisky for his Christmas present. Staying with her friend had been something she'd thought up at the last moment to hide the real reason for her trip. When she came home the next morning, having started the drive very early in order to get home to her husband, she entered the house to find Jay in bed with another woman. She immediately moved out, deciding to follow her lifelong desire to move to London and study to be a journalist.

"So," said Jay at last, "um, Johnny. He's coming too, is he?"

"Oh yeah," said Mack. "Of course. It's his gig, totally."

"Right."

There was a pause, and Mack turned to look at Jay, his brow showing the early stages of furrowing.

"Is that okay?" he asked. "I mean, why wouldn't he?"

"Oh, no, I mean yeah, of course it's okay. I love Johnny. It's just..." Jay picked up his drink and looked around the bar.

"Just what, Jay?" said Mack.

"Well, you know, just that Johnny's... Look, I love Johnny. He's a great kid, always has been. But he's never been the most confident type, has he. Ever since…well, since he was a kid, he's not been the pushy type. I just wondered what this trip might be like for him, that's all."

"What this trip will be like for him," said Mack, his voice level, with a twinge of irritation, "will be to be the thing that he totally and utterly needs. This could be the confidence-boosting event that defines the rest of his life."

"Yeah," said Jay, smiling, belying a mild nervousness. "Yeah, of course it will. I just wouldn't want him to, you know, well to get his arse kicked, I guess."

Mack leaned forwards. "We'll be there too, don't forget." His voice was now lowered, his tone one of giving an instruction, rather than a request. "And we'll be helping him as much as he needs it. Right? Frankly, that's the reason we're going. It'll be fun, sure, but the main thing is that Johnny takes a major step forward, both in his confidence, and in making contacts to get a career going for him.

"You think I want to go through all this again? Jeez, Jay, I've just spent the last sixteen years keeping my head down and avoiding any form of attention from the outside world whatsoever. I've had a few calls from agents wanting me to join some 1980s reunion tour, and some good money involved too, but I've told them all where to stick it. I don't need the money. But for Johnny I would sacrifice anything, I would do anything. Including tour across America and having a complete and utter blast on the way!" Mack smiled at Jay and lifted his drink to him.

Jay smiled. "Yeah," he said. "Okay. I get it." 'He raised his pint glass and the two men drank.

Mack looked away quickly before Jay could see the moisture building up in his eyes. He didn't want to have to explain the source of those tears.

"So," said Jay, "what are we going to play? We'd better start choosing songs, I suppose, and getting a live act together."

"Actually, I've been working on something new," said Mack.

"At last," said Jay.

Mack continued, ignoring the jibe. "It's a lyric about the difference between G♯ and A♭."

"Okay," said Jay. He lowered his voice and pretended to be

pondering a problem. "Let me think carefully now, where are they on the fretboard…okay, got that. Where are they on the keyboard…"

Mack sat back in his chair and smiled, his lips pursed as he patiently watched his friend fool around

"…okay, got that. Now where do you write them on paper… okay…" Jay looked up and snapped his fingers at Mack. "Got it! They're…the same! You dipshit."

"Have you quite finished?"

"Let me check? Yep, the sarcasm tank is currently empty. Refilling now."

"Then I shall continue. Shut up and listen – you might learn something."

Jay folded his arms, very deliberately.

"Right," continued Mack. "I'm reading Duke Ellington's autobiography at the moment, okay?"

"A bit pretentious, but okay."

"And at one point, he says that the moment he really understood music was the moment when he realised the difference between G♯ and A♭. And that got me to thinking, well, they're the same note on the piano and the guitar, how can they be different?"

"They can't. He was kidding, surely."

"I don't think so. I think it's all about context. Different keys work better for different instruments. The key of F is a good one for piano, but not ideal for guitar. Other instruments sound better in different octaves, which is why the variety within an orchestra works so well. So – and this is getting to the nub of it – each note in a performance has a special place within the piece, lives its own little life within both the written work and the performance. And whether the note is G♯ or A♭ will entirely depend upon the various factors that are at work. In other words, the context within which the note lives."

Mack sat back in his chair, looking pleased with himself. He stared at Jay, as if daring him to disagree.

"But they're still the same note," said Jay, after a few moments' thought. "Sorry. Me no understandi."

"That is the very beauty of it," said Mack. "They are the same note, but played totally differently depending upon the context." His finger jabbed at the table and he spoke with more force. "Like us!"

Point reinforced, he leaned back and drank his pint, largely for effect, but partly because he wanted a drink.

"Like us. Okay, I might regret this," said Jay, "but go on."

"What do you mean, 'go on'? That's it! We're all born basically the same. We all look basically the same: two arms, two legs, mouth, nose, etc. And yet we are all totally different. What makes us different? Our context. Parents, location, economics, friends, DNA. There are millions of little things that mould us to the people that we become, in exactly the same way that G$\sharp$ and A$\flat$ start out as the same note on the piano, but end up totally different depending on the key, the musical approach, the note that is played, the ear of the listener, the acoustics of the room, and so on. Like our music to an American audience. Like a story told by a different person. Like a story told *to* a different person, for that matter. Context."

"Do you know what?" said Jay, lifting his glass and saluting Mack. "I think you might have something there. I like it. Only thing is, how are you going to work it into a song?"

"No idea. But it's a great concept."

Jay laughed, and Mack joined in. "Yeah, thanks for that," said Jay. "Come on, work that up into a song."

"I can't."

"Why not?"

"I'm a concepts man."

"What ever happened to love songs?"

"They need love to inspire them."

The door to the pub opened behind Mack. Jay suddenly stood up and flung his arms open wide. "There is my hero," he said loudly. "Come here you bloody beautiful individual and let me snog you."

"Um, thanks, but no," said Johnny, taking off his coat. "Thanks. Pint?"

Jay stepped around the table, went up to Johnny, grabbed his head in both hands, and gave him a loud kiss on the forehead. Johnny looked an uncomfortable mixture of wanting the earth to swallow him up, and beaming with pride at the same time. The three other people in The Feathers didn't seem to care one way or the other.

"Okay," said Johnny, looking at the floor but smiling, "really, Jay, sit down. Have got a lot to tell you two. Let me get a drink."

"Listen to him," Jay said to Mack, jerking his thumb at Johnny, "offering to get us a pint when all we want to do is make beautiful love to him."

Mack winced.

Jay turned to Johnny. "Listen, my man," he said, "I shall be getting these fresh pints. Then, you can tell us how we are going to take over the world!" Cackling like a Bond villain, Jay went over to the bar and made his order.

Johnny sat down at the table. He picked up the packet of crisps, ripped it open, then placed it on the table, the meagre amount of crisps now bare and obvious. He took a couple and put them in his mouth. "So," he said to Mack, "told him then."

"Don't speak with your mouth full," said Mack, automatically. "Yeah," he said, smiling to himself at his own habits, "and before he comes back, you need to know something, you conniving, sneaky little bastard."

"What's that?"

"I couldn't be more proud of you right now than if you'd just scored the winning run in an Ashes test match and told me you were dating a porn star who had a twin sister." Mack placed his hand on his son's, something he hadn't done since Johnny decided, at the age of eight, that holding his father's hand wasn't cool anymore. "Seriously, mate, wherever this journey is going to take us, I want you to know that I am very proud of you."

"Bloody hell," said Johnny. He looked down at the table, embarrassed, but Mack knew his reddening complexion would belie a swelling heart.

Chapter 19

Taking the clean cotton nappies out of the washing machine, Mary cursed her high moral standards through a fog of hubris. Ever since she had made the decision five years ago not to use disposable nappies, she had been trapped by conscience. The decision was made and would not be changed, but by god there were days when she could just go out to the supermarket and get a pack of disposable nappies, a jar of baby food, and a tub of sleeping tablets.

It had not been so bad first time. David (no rock and roll names for her children, thank you very much) had been a good baby (the concept of 'good' being defined as sleeping through the night almost from day one), and she'd wondered what all the fuss what about. He was now five, and Grace was coming up to two years old – two years of broken nights and red eyes. Grace had not performed her sleeping duties as well as David. Potty training meant she could see a light at the end of the nappy tunnel, thank goodness.

Grace was having her post-lunch nap. That meant an hour to get the washing out, then nap, before collecting David from his school orientation day.

If Phil got home from the hospital at a reasonable time for once, the evening would follow its usual path: eat as a family; put the kids to bed; TV for an hour on the sofa by herself while Phil caught up with some paperwork; then off to bed, before the whole routine started again.

She had been tucking David into bed the previous night. "Mum," he had said, looking up at her and smiling. "I'm happy." He rolled over, then said again, almost to himself, "Yeah, I'm really happy." Mary had kissed him goodnight, gone into the bathroom, locked the door, and cried. Happy. That was not a state of mind that she understood anymore. She had moments of feeling happy, sure, knowing the kids were safe, little kind moments when they might draw something for her. But actually being in a state of happiness? Does that actually happen outside of childhood?

Bed. What a lovely thought. To sleep, perchance to sleep a bit more. Certainly not for any purpose, not these days. There was more than one occasion when she had wondered if Phil's suggestion of separate rooms really was because he didn't want to wake her when returning late from his rounds, or when he got called out in the middle of the night. Truth was, such flexibility suited them both.

Phil was twenty years older than Mary and already a respected surgeon. They had decided to have kids quickly because they wanted to be young enough to enjoy them when they were older. By having David when she was twenty-five, Mary figured that she would only be forty-five when he turned twenty and so she would be young enough to still relate to him. Of course, it was even more relevant to Phil, who would be sixty-five.

Mack hadn't been invited to the wedding.

In fact, there wasn't even a photograph of her father anywhere in Mary's house. As far as she was concerned, he was just the person who had kept her from harm for the first fourteen years of her life. There was, however, a solitary photograph of her brother, Johnny, and of her mother. Separate photographs, next to each other on the windowsill of the conservatory.

Mary put a peg on the last nappy and walked into the living room. Grace was asleep on the sofa, under her Cinderella blanket. Straight blonde hair, cropped into a bob that was growing out, now splayed around her on the cushion.

After a few moments, Mary realised she had stopped staring with an aura of love and was instead simply staring, her tired eyes unfocussed. She sank into an armchair, putting her feet up on the table in the middle of the room. Almost as her eyelids were slamming shut, she took a quick glance at the clock: 13.30. The washing and other chores would wait half an hour.

The factory setting tune on her mobile phone woke her. With a glance at the clock − 13.40, drat, her one chance in the day to catch up on sleep ruined − she grabbed her phone and jabbed at it, trying to stop it ringing before it woke Grace. She just had time to notice that it was her brother calling.

"What?" she said, unable to hide her annoyance.

"Oh. Hello. It's me."

"Yes, I know. It says on my phone. In fact, it's the first thing I saw when I woke up."

"Ah. Sorry. Didn't realise."

Mary blinked heavily, holding her eyes together hard for a few moments. It wasn't his fault. Be patient. There was silence at the other end of the phone, as if he knew the ropes, knew she needed a second to compose herself. He would always be her little brother.

"You okay?" she said, softening her tone.

"Yeah, cool, ta. You?"

"Yeah, I'm fine. Grace is having a nap. So far today we've read eight books, painted, drawn, done three jigsaws and spilt three cups of juice. All while listening to Beethoven and Mozart."

"Cool," Johnny replied. He didn't get it. He didn't understand. But then, why should he? He didn't have kids. He didn't know about the constant panic at the pit of the stomach, the lying in bed at night trying to recall bits from TV programmes in order to block out the fears and worries that were trying to force their way in as you tried to sleep.

"Been talking to Dad," Johnny said.

"And I care because…?" Mary replied.

"Just wanted to tell you. Got some exciting news."

Mary sighed, a loud, conspicuous sigh that seemed to emanate from a dark place in her heart. Once every six months or so, Johnny tried to get her to speak to her father. He just wouldn't accept the fact that she and her father were quite happy not having anything to do with each other. If it's happily broken, don't fix it.

"Go on then," she said. "And it better be good."

"Got one of his songs being used for an American TV show. And am organising a tour of America."

"Wow. Hey, now I am genuinely impressed. How on earth did you manage all that?"

"Website. Been sending stuff out all over the Internet for years now about Dad's music, got quite a following in America. College radio especially. Then someone chose his song. Simple really. Put it out there, see what happens."

"Well, that's cool. For you, I mean. You've worked hard at this, you deserve it."

"Great for Dad too."

"Mm. Listen, Gracie's waking up, I'd better go."

"Okay. Still want to talk to you though. About Dad."

"Leave it, Johnny. I'll speak to you soon."

"Okay. But I want to ask you about something. About why you won't talk to him."

"You know why, Johnny – because of what I saw him getting up to."

"Yeah, okay, but I don't really know what that is. Will you explain it? I want to understand. Can you tell me the story – tell me what you saw him do?"

"Oh, Johnny, not now, okay? Some other time maybe. Grace is waking up, I need to go." Mary said goodbye and hung up. She looked down at Grace, eyes closed, chest barely moving from her shallow, sleep-filled breathing.

Chapter 20

Opening the curtains of his bedroom, Mack stood naked at the window, gazing across the field to the woods. It was very early in the morning, and an orange glow from a sun that had only just woken covered his body and made him look as if he had a tan. He took hold of his penis, semi-erect, leaned back, and waved it to the world.

The fox looked up from the field, distracted briefly from its task, but decided it was not worth further attention. It continued on with trying to drag the carcass of a roast chicken extricated from the bottom of Mack's bin. In order to locate the slightly confusing delicacy, the fox had found it necessary to topple the bin, rip open the sacks within and spread the rubbish around the courtyard.

Mack turned to look at the Beatles bedside clock. The big hand was pointing at John, the little hand at Ringo. 6.15. Two hours before the taxi was due to arrive, but he couldn't get back to sleep. The last few weeks had been something of a blur as final arrangements had been made for the trip. It would last several months, starting from New York and travelling across America, with a showcase gig for the TV company in Los Angeles to finish.

Harpo had been able to get someone to sub for him in his hairdressing studio (he referred to them as a locum, which Mack felt was a little pretentious for a barber shop, but didn't say anything). Sarah Head was actually quite happy to have Jay out of her way, and Mack didn't need to check anything with anyone. The three of them had rehearsed almost all day, every day, ever since, getting a bunch of songs into the sort of shape they hoped would entertain an audience of mainly students for anything up to two hours, depending on whether they were the only act on the bill that night.

Johnny had also been busy, and Mack had strict instructions covering the practical details of the next few weeks in a moleskin-covered book that he and Jay were told to refer to constantly. Mack appreciated the classy touch. Johnny said he would catch up with them later as he had further arrangements to cement for later in the tour.

Two hours and fifteen minutes later, Mack felt a twist in his stomach when he heard the taxi beep its horn outside. He still wasn't sure whether the twist was excitement or apprehension. Mack smiled to himself as he looked up at the line of people queuing to board the plane to New York. He took out his boarding pass. Yep, the ticket definitely showed a seat number. So why were these people queuing? Surely he could just wait until everyone else had got onto the plane, then stroll on, and calmly take his seat. No wonder he had barely ventured out of a five mile radius of his bungalow for the last fifteen years, he thought to himself. People out there seemed to be, at a very basic and intrinsic level, deeply stupid.

Harpo was sat next to him, reading a dictionary. Mack hadn't asked why. Jay would be back from the toilet shortly – he was not a good flyer, and seemed to have some pre-flight nerves.

Mack opened up the moleskin book. Jay had glued a map of the USA into the inside cover, and Mack looked again at the zig-zagging yellow line that that moved from New York to Los Angeles like a sales chart. To give them a sense of perspective, Jay had worked out that it was around 1,800 miles from the top of America to the bottom, and around 3,600 across (which he had written next to arrows at the top and side of the map). He had then drawn a scaled picture of Great Britain next to the map, to help them gauge distances. Mack smiled to himself at his best friend. He knew there were going to be moments when his attention to detail was going to drive them all mad, but he was so glad that Jay was going on this trip with them.

A small oblong cardboard box sat on his lap. Mack opened the box and took out a mobile phone that Johnny had bought for him. Johnny had only taught him two functions, and he followed one of them now. He pressed and held the number 1 on the keypad. The pre-programmed speed setting dialled Johnny's mobile number.

"Dad," said Johnny, across the airwaves.

"Hey, bub, how you doing?" said Mack. Then, not waiting for an answer, "Just thought I'd call in. We're going to be boarding in a minute, so next time I talk to you it'll be from the States! The three of us are so excited, we're like a bunch of school kids." Mack looked across at Harpo. "Well, me and Jay are, at least. Harpo is more like the teacher that all the kids suspect likes to play with himself during games lesson."

Harpo gave Mack the single finger salute without looking up from his dictionary.

"Anyway, I've got a newspaper, also bought *Rolling Stone* magazine, you know, thought I'd try and get up with the latest scenes in America, and Jay has gone to the toilet, so I'm…"

"Dad," Johnny interjected. "Dad," he said again, as Mack continued rambling on. Johnny said again "Dad, okay, got the message."

"Oh. Ha, sorry, mate, just excited. Am I gabbling? Sorry."

"No problem."

"So, we all set? Everything in order?"

"Yep, as I told you. Nothing's changed since we last spoke two hours ago."

"Okay, alright already, I'm just so excited. Did I mention that? Mate, I've hardly been out of the village in years, let alone out of the country, let alone to the States, let alone to play gigs, let alone… oh, well, you get the idea."

"Yeah," said Johnny, laughing, "I get the idea. Hey, got some news. Cool development."

"Yeah, what's that?"

"Journalist. Might do a piece on you. Wants to meet up. Watch a few gigs, spend a bit of time on the tour. You into that?"

"Not sure. It's been a long time, mate, and I wasn't too keen on journalists at the best of times. I've been reading this newspaper. You know I haven't read a paper in years. Now I know why. Jeez there's a lot of crap in there. Whole load of stuff that doesn't matter about people I've never heard of. Two footballers arguing about a tackle, scuzzy looking women boasting who they've had sex with…oh man, it makes you wonder for humanity. If this is the boat we're travelling on together, I think I'll break out the life rafts."

"Had your head down for a long time, Dad. They're not all like that."

"Hmmm. I guess not. I had my own fill of the press too, mind you. I don't really want to stick my head out of the hole I crawled into, just to get it bitten off again."

"This guy's cool. He's been really helpful in promoting your stuff over the last few years. It was him that put your song forward for the TV programme. You might even know him. His name is Kent Nicholls."

The phone went silent.

"Dad?"

"Yeah."

"You okay? What's up?"

"Nothing mate, it's fine." All the excitement had left his voice. "When are we going to meet Kent?"

"Not sure. He's got your itinerary, so will catch up with you. That okay? You don't sound too chuffed."

"No problem. You've done your job. Top man. I'll call you on the other side of the pond." His voice was hollow, no matter how much he tried to fake enthusiasm.

"Okay."

"Oh, and Johnny?"

"Yeah?"

"Be careful, okay? These people, the journalists, the hangers-on – they might act like they're your best friend, but they're just out to make money out of you. I've been there before, don't forget that. Don't trust anyone, alright?"

"Got it, Dad."

"I'm not kidding. They will say one thing and do another. Do not believe anything they say. You're not dealing with local promoters now. Some of these fuckers are bad news and you won't know the good from the bad until it's too late."

"Okay, Dad, I've got it."

"I'll speak to you on the other side."

"Okay, Dad. Have a good flight."

Mack put the phone back into the protective bag, put the bag into the cardboard box, and the box into his holdall. Each action was undertaken with a little more aggression than was necessary.

Jay came out of the toilet, walked across the waiting area and stopped. He looked at the queues, then took his ticket out of his pocket and studied it. Then he shrugged, put the ticket back in his pocket and sat down next to Harpo, who continued to read his dictionary.

145

"What you doing, Harpo?"

"Reading," Harpo responded.

"Yeah, I kind of guessed that. *What* are you reading?" Jay leaned forward and looked at the cover. Sitting back, Jay rolled his eyes, as if he knew he shouldn't ask, but had to. "Come on then," he said. "I'll play. Why are you reading a dictionary?"

"I'm looking up 'omniscient', to see if I am," Harpo replied.

The aeroplane was boarded without incident, squeezing past middle-aged ladies rummaging in small suitcases which doubled as hand luggage. They sat together, three in a row: Harpo sitting by the window and Jay in the middle. Mack had insisted on sitting on the outside, in expectation of requiring the toilet more than the others. Harpo spent most of the flight with his nose pressed against the window, only turning round to accept offerings of free peanuts and wine. He seemed to make it a point of personal achievement to not empty his bladder until Mack had been at least three times.

At the very first opportunity, Mack and Jay ordered two mini bottles of red wine each. The flight to New York was due to take around eight hours, and they intended to get drunk in the first hour and sleep for as much of the remaining journey as they could. This plan had been hatched to try and combat Jay's fear of flying and Mack's fear of boredom. They certainly weren't going to rely on Harpo to entertain them.

With wine and nuts safely opened and attacked, they settled back into their chairs. Jay had noticed that Mack seemed pensive in the departure lounge, but had not quizzed him immediately. He knew his old friend well enough to wait for the right moment, such as when he'd relaxed with wine and peanuts.

"You okay, mate?" He spoke in a low voice, helped by the fact he was facing away from Harpo. The bass player would not have been interested in the conversation if he had heard it, but Jay was conscious of not wanting to make Mack feel uncomfortable.

Mack looked at his companion and smiled. It seemed a pretty poor effort to Jay. "Yeah, I'm fine." Then, as if realising he was bringing the mood down, he sat up in his seat and said, "Hey, come on, what are we going to do first then, eh? Statue of Liberty, or a pool bar?"

"Ha!" replied Jay. "Got to be the pool bar. Do you know American rules?"

"Sure, can't be any different, can it? Do you think they give two free shots for a foul?"

"Blimey," said Jay, "I don't have the foggiest, mate." He paused for a moment, thinking. "Do you reckon there will be a language barrier?"

"I dunno," replied Mack. "Shouldn't think so. Main thing to remember is not to ask anyone for a fag!"

"Oooohhh, yeah," laughed Jay. "Day one of 'things not to say in America' school, that is. No, I suspect Americans might not use the phrase 'don't have the foggiest' very often either."

"Jay," said Mack, "I don't know anyone other than you who would ever use that phrase."

"Yeah, but then you don't actually know anyone other than me, do you."

Now it was Mack's turn to laugh. "Harsh, but with a grain of truth," he said.

"You nervous about this trip?" asked Jay.

"Not really. Not sure what to expect, so nothing to be nervous about. I only get nervous when I know what might go wrong. This trip is a complete leap into the unknown, especially when you've barely been outside your back yard for a decade. You?"

Jay was quiet for a moment. Then he said, "Did you know my mum died when I was six years old?"

Mack turned in his seat to look at Jay. "No," he said eventually. "No, I don't think we'd ever talked about that."

Jay looked at his wine, his fingers fiddling with the stem of the glass. "I can't say I missed her as a kid because I didn't really know her. I wish I had known her, obviously. And yet as an adult I kind of realise that her dying gave me something else, something that replaced her not being there. It gave me the love of a whole load of other people instead. Couldn't replace her, of course, but there were a lot of people looking out for me. There were the obvious ones – aunties, uncles, even friends at school for a while – but it was the others that really struck a chord, like parents of my mates who would make sure I was invited to parties, or to play at their house. I remember one guy, he taught me how to play rugby. He ran the local youth team and he made sure that I got a lift to practice, and then to games, and instilled in me the love of the game that I have today. He didn't need to do it, I don't suppose he even realised how kind he was being, it was just natural for him to look out for me. But I noticed it."

Jay paused for a moment. Mack didn't fill the silence. Eventually, Jay continued. "It made me feel that I have people out there looking out for me. In a strange way, my mum dying made me an optimist. I saw the best in people, and I still do. I still assume people are good." He looked across at Mack and smiled. "So I'm not nervous about this trip either. Because deep down I really believe that people will want the best for us."

"Thanks, Jay," said Mack. "I take your point. And I'm glad you're here looking out for me."

Jay smiled bashfully.

Then Mack lifted his glass and banged it heavily against Jay's, the clash of plastic on plastic resonating unsatisfactorily. "To your mother."

They both took a long drink. Jay looked around him, trying to judge when it would be safe to continue without making it obvious.

"So what was the news from Johnny?" he asked eventually.

The smile on Mack's face changed. Instead of both sides of his mouth going up, the left side dropped, leaving the right side high, turning his mouth into a grimacing line which ran diagonally across his face.

"Well, it's a bit of a blast from the past. And to be honest, not a very welcome one."

"Oh, really?"

"Yeah. He's managed to get a journalist involved. Wants to do an article on us."

"Cool! Wow, I knew being your mate would get me into the papers, although I confess I did wonder sometimes if it would be more likely in the news section rather than the entertainment section." Jay chuckled, but noticed quickly that Mack wasn't laughing with him. "Do I detect the idea that you're not so keen on this then?" he asked.

"I've spent a long time avoiding these sort of people," Mack said, staring at the laminated emergency landing instructions tucked into the seat in front of him. "You haven't dealt with them – the music journalists and the other leeches and talentless hangers-on that surround this industry. They want to be your friend. They are usually people who want to be doing what you are doing, but don't have the ability, or any other ability for that matter, so instead they follow you around and somehow live a vicarious rock and roll lifestyle through you. And, if you fall for it and let them become your friend, they suck out the best bits for themselves and leave you to pick up the crap."

"Blimey. What happened with this guy, Mack?"

"His name is Kent Nicholls. I used to think he was cool because he'd been in the game longer than I had. Then I realised he was even worse than the rest of them. A leeching, fucking bastard."

"Did he do something to you?"

"No. Yes. Well, yes. One thing in particular that he shall never, ever be forgiven for. Ever. Plus he wrote an article that basically split up the band. He is a nasty piece of work."

"You worried about Johnny?"

"Of course," replied Mack, not smiling. "You may as well ask a ballet dancer, 'do you have any pain in your feet?' Worrying about Johnny is what I do. It's what I have always done. I've been protecting this boy since…since his mother and I split up. But the fact that he's going to be exposed to people like Kent Nicholls is what made me so reticent about even coming on this trip. Now change the subject please – even thinking about that malodorous little prick is getting me agitated."

Mack reached into the pouch in front of him and took out the copy of *Rolling Stone* that he had bought at the airport. He started flicking through, making it clear to Jay that the conversation was finished.

Settling back into his seat, Jay looked past Harpo's right ear and out onto the blinding whiteness of the clouds below. As he always did at some point when on a plane, he thought of Joni Mitchell's song, 'Both Sides Now'. It seemed somehow appropriate. "I've looked at clouds from both sides now," he sang quietly to himself. "I really don't know clouds at all."

Harpo turned round to look at him. "You're singing Joni Mitchell," he said curtly. "Stop it."

Chapter 21

"Okay, thanks Paula. Tell him to come straight in." Jude put the phone down and waited for Johnny to enter her office.

The main studio and administrative hub for Jude's jewellery business was situated in an old factory site that had been converted into a series of individual units and sold in a targeted way to creative businesses. Graphic design companies, sculpture artists, website designers, recording studios, architects, photographers and TV post-production companies all rubbed shoulders with PR, marketing agencies and advertising companies.

Poppy, the company that Jude had formed to sell her jewellery, now had fifteen shops throughout the UK and one in Bordeaux. The company also owned a small house near the French outlet, the shop really just an excuse for Jude to treat her excursions as business trips, and so have the company pay for the expenses. There were plans to open the next shop near Sienna. The jewellery was designed and handmade out of the studio at the Flowerworks, and then shipped around the country, with Jude taking the French stock personally when she visited once every six weeks or so.

Prices were kept high and stock in the shops was low. Upon entering a Poppy shop, you had a feeling of space and of light. Each item carried an air of exclusivity, and was very profitable. The shops were opened in areas of towns and cities that were just a short walk from the major shopping centres. Going to buy jewellery from Poppy felt like being included in a well-kept secret.

One particular item had been the catalyst for the success and growth of the company: the Kowtow bracelet. The word kowtow descended from the Chinese expression meaning to bow so deeply that one's head would touch the floor, thereby showing ultimate respect. Jude had made a simple yet elegant bracelet which was rather gorgeous on its own. However, she had then designed a series of symbols out of either silver or gold. Each symbol could be attached to the bracelet and came with a brief explanation of what it meant and how it embodied certain personality traits. This meant that the wearer could build up a series of statements they felt were representative of themselves, or what they wanted to say to the world.

The idea had quickly caught on and Jude began engraving names onto small plaques to hang alongside the charms. Over the next few years, she had taken a small loan from her bank (she could have easily asked Mack, but hadn't even considered it as a possibility), opened a shop, and sold other kinds of jewellery too. However, it was the Kowtow bracelet that had customers continually coming back to see her in order to update their personal statement. At which point they would often see other items that they liked... And so the business had grown.

Now nearing fifty, Jude Finn (she had reverted to her maiden name not long after the divorce was settled) was ageing well. She kept herself in shape, for health reasons. She was five foot eight with granite-grey eyes, her long dark hair now streaked with silver and tied permanently into a loose ponytail. Her cheekbones remained on show, sculptured and defined, giving her a somewhat intimidating look that she really quite enjoyed. Certain men found it highly attractive but they tended to be the type of men that Jude wasn't interested in.

Jude put down the portfolio she had been perusing as part of her role as mentor to design students at the local College of Art. She stood up and walked around her large desk towards the door, greeting Johnny with a gentle hug.

"How are you, darling," she opened, guiding him by the arm to one of the two brown soft leather sofas that were set up to face each other.

"Yeah, good, Mum, ta." Johnny said. He stood for a few moments, until Jude indicated by waving her arm in the general direction of the sofa that he should sit. He did so, leaning back in the sofa awkwardly, crossing his legs by lodging his right foot onto his left knee. This made his right knee higher than his head, and he shifted position slightly so that he could look at his mother when he was talking to her.

"Have you told your father about the trip?" asked Jude, sitting upright at the edge of the other sofa.

"Yeah. Delighted. Jay too. Been finalising plans last few weeks. Been rehearsing loads. They fly out today."

"'They'? Not 'we'?"

"Yeah. Got a few things still to sort. Late preparations. Joining them later."

It was never a relaxing pastime talking to her son, not easy getting him to elaborate. Of course, that was the way of the teenager and twas ever thus, but now he had matured his stilted delivery and awkward manner seemed to have embedded itself. A fleeting concern flickered through her mind yet again – had she done the right thing letting Mack take such a dominant role in his teenage years? It went the same way as the thought had gone so many times before, into the drawer in her mind marked 'Reconciled'. It was a real thing, this drawer; she knew it was there, along with many others – it was her way of dealing with things. She and Mack had talked about such ideas when Mamal was starting to create stress and pressure: how to cope late at night, where to put those thoughts that kept jumping out from behind the promise of sleep. For Mack, such a drawer would have been labelled '*Que Sera Sera*'. It was one of the things that had annoyed her about him.

"Well done, Johnny," said Jude, adopting a different tactic. "What you've done for your father is really rather fabulous."

Her son produced an involuntary smile of cautious delight. "Wow. High praise. From you."

"You've done well," she shrugged. "I'm proud of you."

Johnny's face now pulled a strange expression. If a photograph had been taken and an independent witness had been asked to describe what the owner of the expression had been thinking at the time, they would have paused for a while before answering. Perhaps, they might guess, the person had been given some shocking news but they weren't sure if it was good or bad. Or maybe, they would say, the individual had been told they had won first prize, but they knew the person telling them had deserved the prize more than they had. Or maybe they were suffering from trapped wind.

After a few seconds, Johnny seemed to regain his composure.

"Um, blimey, uh, thanks, Mum. That means a lot." Now he beamed at her. "Thanks."

"So what did you want to see me about?" said Jude, in a more businesslike tone. Time to move on.

"Want to ask you a question."

Jude looked at him expectantly for a few moments. When he didn't speak further, she said, "Well, as you haven't yet asked me anything, and since you seem to think you need to prepare me for it, I assume it's going to be a question you don't think I'm going to want to answer. Correct?" Jude had once overheard one of her staff saying that their boss would have made a very good schoolteacher – in the nineteenth century. Jude had rather enjoyed the comment and congratulated the individual on their perceptive powers.

Johnny got to the point. "What was going on when Dad got caught in that hotel room?"

Jude's face remained in situ in every way except for one. Her left eyebrow flicked upwards.

"And why, pray, do you want to know that?"

"Things aren't right. You're long past sorting out, but Mary still won't talk to him. Why not?"

"Well, thank you for your concern."

It was Johnny's turn to shrug. "Don't expect you two to get back together, way too long ago. But Mary and him should talk."

"What Mary chooses to do is up to her, and is not for you or me to try and correct."

"You can't choose your family but you can choose your moments. And this is a good moment."

"Is that one of your father's lines? Sounds like the sort of rubbish he'd come out with."

Johnny didn't answer but continued to stare at the table in front of his mother. As she glared at his forehead, it occurred to her that he was steeling himself.

Without looking up, he said, "He's her father. She's his daughter. They should have a relationship."

Jude studied him for a moment, with his shaven head and small movements. He had definitely calmed down since she last saw him, as if he had gained confidence in himself, but he was, and always had

153

been, a nervous character. It had started around the time of her and Mack separating and she had always felt guilty that their divorce had seemed to affect him so deeply. She could understand that he wanted to make sense of it all somehow. But still…

"I don't think that's anything to do with you, Johnny."

His head moved up and he looked his mother in the eye. "It is. My sister, my dad – my family."

This time the right eyebrow joined the left. The confidence in his voice and in his attitude towards her was new. Jude wasn't entirely sure if she liked it. She stood up and walked around her desk to look out of the window, turning her back to him to indicate that she was thinking.

"You know, Johnny. There are times when I wonder if I was right to have children. I'm not entirely convinced that I was the right personality type to be a mother."

Behind her, Johnny's ears went red. He looked at the back of his hands.

"Not about you, or me," he said. "Well, a *bit* about me. There's stuff up there…" He pointed to his head. "Stuff I can't make sense of. I was only six, but I've got strange memories, fuzzy stuff, Dad holding me, crying." He was squeezing his hands now, fingers interlocked, knuckles white with the pressure. "But main thing is Mary and Dad." He unwound his legs and sat forward on the sofa, putting his arms on his knees to better express himself with waving hands. "Mum, look. I know it was his fault, okay – not suggesting it wasn't. But I'm on a roll. I'm doing stuff. Things are good. I can help. I *want* to help. Make stuff better."

She turned and looked at her son, assessing him afresh. In the past when she had challenged him, there would have been a mumbled apology. He even looked as if the word 'sorry' was bursting to come out. But he had a purpose now. To help his father. To help Mary too, although that was probably a happy by-product.

"Just tell me your side, would you?" Johnny said.

"There's really nothing to tell," said Jude, still stood by the window. "He had sex with another woman. He forfeited the right to have me as his wife by doing so. End of story."

There was no answer from Johnny. He was focussing on her,

expectantly, and she returned the look. It was as if he was daring her to speak next, taking her on. She felt the flush in her cheeks as the level of awkwardness rose. She knew that the next person to speak would immediately be on the defensive – it was a technique she had used in sales meetings many times, but now, being taken on by her son, it felt wrong and uncomfortable.

She moved her stare from the bridge of his nose, choosing instead just one eye, the right one, and stared straight into it. She held her gaze there for a few more seconds, her cheeks feeling hot now, indignancy rising inside her. Eventually, knowing that if she allowed this to continue she would run the danger of getting properly angry, she spoke.

"I don't 'cultivate' this image of a tough, hard businesswoman, son. It's an image that sticks to me, presumably because that is the person that I am." She pulled back her black leather chair and sat down, placing her hands deliberately in front of her. Her voice was even, emotionless.

She looked at Johnny and waited. To her surprise, he did something he had never done before. He did not apologise.

"What happened, Mum? Please just tell me. The whole story. I want to know."

Cocking her head slightly, Jude looked at her son; not exactly with fresh eyes but eyes that knew something had changed between them. She wasn't certain if it was a good change. She allowed that possibility to exist for a moment, and found that she liked it. Maybe it was time. If he wanted facts, why not let him have the responsibility of knowing them.

"Okay," she said. "If you want to know that badly, then I'll tell you. Not that there is a great deal to know."

She leaned forward, putting her folded arms on the desk in front of her, buying a few moments to compose herself. "Al was around at the time," she said. "You probably remember Al was his old music partner in their band, Mamal. An idiot of the highest order. I never liked him, even in those days. I always thought he was a bad influence on Mack. Goodness knows what they got up to when they were on tour. Mack always pretended that Al got up to no good, groupies and all that, while Mack had nothing to do with it. I never believed it. I always reckoned your father was just as bad as Al was."

She paused momentarily, studying her son's face. It gave nothing away. Maybe he had learned something from her after all. "Anyway, Al turns up again all these years later, out of the blue. He came round the house and talked with your father, asked him for money. Al seemed to be hard up, suggested there were some people who wanted money from him, so he wanted some from Mack, to be able to give it to them. Threatened him with legal action over who actually wrote their music."

"And did he have a point?" asked Johnny.

"Not as far as I'm aware," said Jude. "I saw Mack at work on many an occasion. Boy did I ever see him at work. I made a lot of sacrifices in my young life, you know, for your father to enjoy the freedom he had. I backed him a lot in the early days, when we'd be in transit vans, driving around to gigs. I'd be arranging the food, making sandwiches and stuff, while he never gave a thought to where it came from, who paid for it. Just him writing lyrics, strumming his guitar, or him and Al playing around. I was something of a rock and roll widow. Never again."

A shadow seemed to have appeared over her face. For a moment, Johnny almost felt sorry for any man that tried to have a relationship with his mother.

"What did Dad say to Al?"

"Kicked him out. Then over the next few days he became very insular. Maybe it's because my own antennae were out and knew something wasn't right, but I noticed him becoming more withdrawn. He wouldn't tell me what was going on, just kept saying that he could handle it."

"Odd," said Johnny. "Almost as if he didn't want you to know something."

"Well, I soon found out what that something was."

"What?"

"Well, let's just say she was six foot tall, with dark hair and pert tits. And called Kimberly."

"Why would Dad have an affair because Al had asked him for money?"

"I've no idea. The two things might not even be connected. All I know is that Mary saw them."

156

"What happened?"

"Oh, Mary was going through a difficult time. She had this friend, Stretch his name was. He was from, shall we say, a difficult background. Do you remember Stretch?"

"Vaguely."

"Well, he kind of came from a difficult family. Nice lad, gentle. He was adopted, and told Mary about it. I, uh, seem to recall Mary became pretty obsessed with the whole adoption thing at the same time." Jude paused to move a piece of paper from one side of her desk to the other.

"Why?" asked Johnny.

"No idea," replied Jude quickly. "Anyway," she said leaning back in her chair, "Mary had seen some note with a hotel room written on it, so she told me afterwards. It was one of those cottage-type rooms at The Manor Hotel. She went to see your father, opened the door of the room, and saw him with this Kimberly woman. End of story. End of quite a few stories, actually."

"When you say 'with'...?" asked Johnny.

"Oh, Johnny, for goodness' sake, do I really have to get into the details?" She paused, then said, "I didn't really discuss it with Mary. I didn't want to upset her even more. She came running into the house and told me that she'd seen her father with that woman and she was naked. When I challenged Mack with it, he immediately admitted that he'd been having an affair. That was that."

"What about Al?"

"What *about* Al", responded Jude, coolly.

"Well, where was he at this time? Thought he was part of the story."

"No idea. To be honest, I didn't stick around in your father's life long enough to find any more out. Your father admitted to having an affair with this woman, and my concern was to make sure Mary was as untroubled by what she'd seen as possible. Given what happened, I think you've both turned out pretty well."

"And where was I?" asked Johnny.

"Well it happened during the day, so you must have been at school. Your father used to get you to and from school and I did food – that was kind of our split of jobs. As I recall, you came home with your father. I think you'd fallen asleep in the car so he put you straight to bed. I presume he knew that he and I were going to have something of a 'discussion'."

"What did he say to you?"

"Nothing, really. No explanations, other than simply that he had an affair with this woman. He was quite happy to admit to that but wouldn't say why, or what was wrong between him and me. Over the next few weeks I tried to get him to talk to me, to see if we could save our marriage, but it's like he just put up the shutters emotionally. He became sullen and withdrawn. Eventually, I gave up and began my new life. There didn't seem to be any other alternative, given that he didn't seem to want to work things out."

"And that's why Mary won't speak to him? She hasn't forgiven him."

"I guess so." Jude looked at her son and saw the disapproval on his face. "Look, if he wanted to repair his relationship with his daughter, that was something he should have spent more time on. It wasn't for me to tell your father what to do. I didn't exactly have his ear at the time anyway. Nor did anyone else for that matter, apart from Jay perhaps, but even then I don't think they spoke much about what had happened."

The two of them sat in silence for a few moments, Johnny staring at the floor. Jude gave him silence in which to think. It was Johnny who eventually broke the quiet contemplation.

"So, *was* Mary adopted?" he said.

Jude sat up straight. "No," she said, her face impassive, her words clipped. "No, she is not. And might I request that you do not ask that question of Mary? It has taken me a very long time to make that woman accept that she has a mother in her life. Rejecting her father was one thing, it's important for her that she knows she has a mother. I do not want you undoing that good work. Got it?"

"Yeah," replied Johnny, not as scared as he might have been once, but by no means missing the message either. "Yeah, okay, Mum. I think I've got it."

Chapter 22

The first few dates of the tour were deliberately low-key. They stayed a few nights in New York, just for the experience, and Jay and Mack acted unashamedly like tourists. Harpo came with them to the Statue of Liberty but at night went out on his own to visit some 'old friends'.

The moleskin diary told them to drive down routes 78 and 81 to Winchester. There they had a support gig in a club called Sweet Caroline. The performance was predictably stilted and nervy for such an early stage of the tour. However, the small crowd who had arrived early were appreciative enough for the experience to leave them more confident, not less. With a pleasure that surprised him, Mack welcomed the feeling of starting over, of being a struggling artist again.

The car was huge in comparison to anything they had been used to: a classic 1955 Dodge Coronet. It was a bus compared to European cars, but once out on the freeways it felt like you could just sit back and let the car take you where it wanted to.

They took it in turns to drive to begin with. Jay was unmoved by the experience but both he and Mack noticed how excited Harpo had become as soon as the vehicle stopped in front of them. His usual negativity seemed to leave him for a moment – could they have finally found something that would make him smile? Once behind the wheel, however, Harpo's face reverted to the intense concentration that it held when he was cutting hair.

While Harpo drove, Jay and Mack chatted – incessantly. Their conversation would be cheerfully inane, almost as if it were specifically designed to irritate Harpo, far removed from the comfort of his virtually silent salon.

They would stop off at roadside cafes as much as possible, immersing themselves in their perception of the American road trip.

The next gig was in Lexington, down Route 64 from Charleston as it wound through the Daniel Boone National Forest. They stopped for some waffles and Mack went outside to call Johnny, chatting excitedly as he walked round the parking lot.

"Okay Dad," said Johnny, "think that's everything covered. Kent Nicholls will join you in Lexington, and you've got the hotel details. How's Jay? Enjoying himself?"

"Oh crap, yeah!" said Mack. "I think we're just starting to get warmed up."

"Cool. Can I have a chat with him?"

"Sure, no problem," said Mack. He resisted the temptation to tell his son to have a nice day and instead went over to the window, the other side of which sat Jay and Harpo finishing off a huge stack of waffles. He banged on the window and gestured to Jay, who came out and took the phone from Mack. Jay now started to walk around the parking lot with the phone held to his ear, while Mack began a frontal attack on his own waffles.

"Hi, Jay," said Johnny.

"Hello, mate. This is so cool, I'm like a big kid. I still haven't calmed down yet."

"That's great," said Johnny. "Enjoying the car?"

"Oh yeah, it's awesome! Me and your Dad are letting Harpo do all the driving – he loves it and it keeps him from being miserable at us. I'm just spending my time staring out the window going 'Look at that!' to your Dad every mile or so."

"That's great," said Johnny. "Jay, want to ask you something. About Dad. Can you tell me what happened when Dad and Mum got divorced."

"Oh, jeez, Johnny, my man, you really don't want to go raking that up again. Why do you want to know that for?"

"Pissed off at my family. They never talk. I'm the only one who opens up. Want to bang their silly heads together. Come on, what's your view."

Jay couldn't help but smile at the irony that Johnny thought he was the only one in his family who could express themselves. Johnny's clipped and rather nervous mannerisms had been present ever since Jay had known him. He could picture Johnny now, with his piercing blue

160

eyes and shaved head, moving the phone from ear to ear, one moment clasping his hands together on his knees, then, unable to hold that position for long, folding his arms, then unfolding them and linking his fingers once again. Jay always thought he looked like a squirrel, unable to sit still or contain itself, constantly on the lookout, jerking from one position to the next.

"Johnny," replied Jay, "this isn't stuff I have the right to talk about. Let's wait until you get over here and perhaps we can talk it over with Mack."

"Can't wait," said Johnny. "Don't want to talk about it with Dad, not yet. I've got some ideas. What do you remember, Jay? Come on."

"Well," Jay began, "as far as I can tell, your Dad was caught by Mary in the act of having an affair with an American woman in a hotel. Mary was left pretty traumatised by what she saw. Your mother was never the one to stand on ceremony, so she kicked him out. He came to live with me for a while but he didn't get much sympathy from my wife, so he moved into his own place."

"I know all that. But what happened? Why did he do that?"

"Oh, bloody hell, Johnny, why does any man? He followed his cock. She was pretty bloody gorgeous, I have to tell you."

"Something's not right," said Johnny.

"What do you mean?"

"I want to help, want to sort it out."

"What makes you think there is something that needs sorting out, Johnny?"

"Mary told me once that it was a bit weird. What she saw, I mean."

"Johnny, I'm really not sure I want to know about this. This is your family, not mine. Your dad and me don't really have this kind of conversation. We usually just talk bollocks about music or women."

"I'm going to ask her."

Jay stopped pacing the parking lot. "That will go down well," he said at last. "Johnny, why do you want to start digging around here? Seriously, mate, this is something best left alone."

"Can't. Something in my head. I was only eight, or something. I seem to remember meeting Al. I think. Can't really remember. It's like there's something missing, Jay. Something not right."

Jay noticed the crack in the last word. He realised that Johnny was crying. He allowed the silence for a few moments, to let Johnny find his own words – if he chose to.

After a few moments Johnny continued in a more even voice. "It's like there's something wrong. With me. Don't know why. It's like I can remember, but then can't. I'm sure I met Al. But Dad says I didn't. So does Mum. Dad and Mary don't talk. That's not right. Not fair on Dad. Need to get this sorted."

"Okay, Johnny. Okay." said Jay.

"I want to find Al. Find out what happened."

Jay narrowed his eyes. A thought had occurred to him. "Is that why you've arranged this tour, Johnny?"

"Wouldn't go that far. Kent Nicholls kind of set this up. But it's perfect, isn't it? Gives the ideal opportunity. So yeah, in a way it is, I suppose. Will you help me?"

"Oh crap. Johnny, this is *so* not a good idea. It's one thing wanting to help your dad, but find Al? Who knows what you might uncover. Just leave it, Johnny, eh?"

"Can't. Sorry. Mary doesn't talk to Dad. That's stupid. Mum and Dad, okay, forget that, can't mend that one. But for me. Something's not right. In my head. It's just not fair on Dad."

Jay tilted his head back and looked into the blue sky. He raised his shoulders as he gently arched his back, then his entire body sagged back downwards as he gave in to the young man's determination. "What do you want me to do?"

"Not much," said Johnny, "don't want you to do anything special, just make sure Dad stays off my back. Party hard, enjoy the trip. I'll be off doing stuff and will catch up with you. Agreed?"

"Okay. Agreed. Call me on my mobile number, not Mack's. What sort of stuff are you going to do, Johnny?"

"I'm going to find Al. Get his side of the story. But one thing I want to clear up first."

Chapter 23

Arriving at the garden centre cafe an hour before she was due to meet Johnny, Mary had spent the extra time preparing the children. Timing was everything with toddlers – an art and a science. This being a Saturday, Grace had been to her Trapeze Tots class and David had been to judo club and his piano lesson. Now, a salami sandwich for David while she fed Grace her plum snacks, coated in mild pecorino cheese and dipped in pomegranate puree. David shouted "Finished!" then jumped down and ran to the giant wooden pirate ship surrounded by soft bark.

As she placed the last sticky morsel into Grace's open mouth, Mary noticed the slices of cucumber lying guiltily on the floor where David had picked them out of his sandwich. As Grace chewed noisily, Mary opened her rucksack and rummaged for a few moments, eventually emerging with her diary. She made a note about the cucumber, then put the diary back in the bag.

After wiping the little girl's mouth, cheeks, hands and part of her hair, Mary lifted Grace into the pushchair, bringing the cover forward slightly to provide a shield from the sunshine. With a smile to the retreating face of her mummy, Grace closed her eyes. Mary stared at the dozing child and tried to collect her thoughts.

What was Johnny so eager to talk about? He was due to fly out to America and said he wanted to see Mary and the kids before he went. Showing such concern for David and Grace was rather out of character and Mary was suspicious. That *she* was the reason for meeting would not have occurred to her.

Mary caught sight of her reflection in the window of the cafe. Her hair was cut extremely straight, almost shaved at the back, with a side parting on top. It was a functional hairstyle, one which had no interest in the eye of the beholder whatsoever. Motherhood had embedded an attitude in her that her looks had done their job, thank you very much, and could now stand easy. Her marriage with Phil wasn't exactly loveless, but it was pretty much sexless.

Sitting back, Mary allowed herself a moment to relax. Not relaxing in the sense of losing tension or breathing deeply, more a question of briefly regrouping.

Johnny tapped her on the shoulder from behind. "Hello, Mary," he said.

He walked in front of her and leaned forward to kiss her on the cheek. Mary turned her head awkwardly to receive him and Johnny's kiss landed just behind her ear.

"Hello, Johnny. You okay?" she asked, in a voice that let slip the fact that she wasn't overly concerned in the answer.

"Yes, thanks," he responded, in a voice that showed he knew.

Johnny leaned over to look into the pushchair. His demeanour towards the sleeping child was as if he was dealing with the Mafia: one must pay respect to the boss of the family before moving onto a conversation with anyone else in the room.

"Ahh," said Johnny, "she just gone down? And where's David?" He looked around and sat down as he spoke.

What Mary heard in his question was, 'Do we have twenty minutes to talk?'

"Yes, she has, bless her. And David's having fun on the pirate ship. He'll be starting school full-time next term."

"Phil at work?"

"He's at the hospital, yes."

Mary shifted her position to make sure she could see David climbing out of the back of the pirate ship and running round to another entrance at the side. The boy hadn't realised that Johnny had arrived, or looked over towards his mother at all. Finally she focussed her eyes on Johnny. He looked different, but she couldn't quite place how. "Are you well then, Johnny? Enjoying yourself, I should imagine."

"Uh, yeah, guess so." He paused. "What do you mean, enjoying myself?"

"Well, you know, you've really got something going with Dad's career, haven't you. I bet he's really pleased."

"Yeah. Get him out of the house." He smiled at Mary, as if trying to draw her into her father's world.

"Are you going on the trip as well?"

"Yeah. Meeting them somewhere." Johnny was nodding as he spoke, his eyes widening as if in surprise each time he replied to her, one of the nervous twitches that Mary had become oblivious to over the years.

She looked over his shoulder at David talking to another boy on the ship deck.

"Got a gig lined up in New Orleans. Dad's always wanted to go there."

"Brilliant," said Mary, still looking at David. What was that other boy holding in his hand?

"Mary," said Johnny, "why I'm here. There's a reason. Not just to see the kids." His smile went unnoticed. "Want to ask you something. About Dad."

Mary turned now to look at her younger brother. Her much younger brother.

"Why would you want to ask me something about Dad, Johnny?" she asked.

"I'll be honest with you, Mary. Bugs me that you and him don't speak. It's not right. He hates it, you know."

"What's it got to do with you?" Her tone was a little bit to the left of welcoming. The sun hid its light behind a cloud and Mary folded her arms, feeling cold all of a sudden.

"Family," said Johnny, finally. "Family. You should have a relationship. I know you saw something, but you've all kept me away from what happened. No one's ever told me anything. What's the great secret? What actually happened? If I knew, I might be able to help you and Dad in some way."

"What makes you think we want helping?" Mary replied. Then, before Johnny had a chance to answer, she said, "Johnny, I'm eight years older than you."

"I know," said Johnny. "You've *always* been eight years older than me."

"Right," said Mary, missing her brother's sarcastic tone. "And whatever the family has done for you over the years has been with your best interests in mind. Agreed?"

A moment of silence spoke to them both but in a different voice.

Then Johnny said, "Family is everything, Mary."

Mary looked over his shoulder again and saw David and the other boy taking turns to slide down the pole at the side of the ship. They were laughing. Whatever they had been discussing was sorted out now.

"I know, Johnny. But we may be talking about different families." Whether it was defeat or acceptance she couldn't tell, and at that moment she wasn't sure that she cared. Mary came to a decision.

"Okay. Maybe it's time to let you make your own mistakes. I'll tell you. But don't get any big ideas that you're going to get me and Dad to be best of friends."

"Okay, thanks, sis." He was nodding his head vigorously. "I heard a great quote on the radio, made me think of you. 'Older sisters love younger brothers, until they become bigger than they are'."

Mary narrowed her eyes. "Don't push it, mate," she said. Then smiled, to show that she had been joking. The smile was necessary but unexpected, taking Johnny by surprise. The effect on her face was like seeing a crocodile crunching on a pelican, and he recoiled ever so slightly.

"If you want to know what happened, I'll tell you," said Mary. "There's no reason why you shouldn't know. I'm surprised Dad never told you."

"No. Always changes the subject."

"Hmm. Well, I caught our father in the middle of having sex with another woman. That's it. I was so angry at him, and I still am. He's never apologised for it, or shown any contrition, so I don't see why I should try and be nice to him if he can't take a step towards me first."

"Why were you there?"

Mary took a deep sigh. To give a full answer meant going into so many issues from her teenage years that she really didn't feel like opening up. How she had become convinced that Mack wasn't actually her father, a fact that her mother had told her in no uncertain terms over the years was not true; foolish teenage emotions around Kurt Cobain killing himself; the fact that she had been so in love with Stretch at the time that it hurt, but that he had no idea and had done nothing about it. She had been so confused at the time, how could she explain all of this to Johnny all these years later?

"Let's just say I was having a bit of a teenage moment," she said.

"I...well, I just felt that I wanted to see Dad, urgently."

"Was that when you thought he was not your Dad?"

She looked at her younger brother with her eyes narrowed. "What do you know about that?"

"Obvious. You and Mum used to argue about it. Thought I wasn't listening."

"Humph. Okay, well, anyway, yes, that's kind of what it was about. And a few other things. Anyway, I just wanted to see him, then as I was walking home from school, I saw him driving the other way. I had seen some note about a hotel, he'd had a call from a woman, and his old music buddy was around, Al."

"Odd coincidence."

"Coincidence?" said Mary. "No. No, he was part of it." Johnny furrowed his brow, confused, but Mary continued, not noticing. "Anyway, I went to his hotel and they were in the room, having sex."

"Actually having sex? You interrupted them?"

"Oh, God, look, do I have to describe it for you? Johnny, they were in the hotel room, she was naked. Yes, they were having sex."

"Describe it please. I want to know."

"Okay. If I must. I was about to go in the room, but stopped because I heard voices."

"Whose voices?" Johnny was leaning forward in his seat now.

"I couldn't tell at first, so I opened the door. Then I saw Dad and that American woman. And Al."

"Woooooaaah, wait a sec," said Johnny, raising his hands, palms facing towards Mary. "Second time you've said that. Al was in the room?"

"Well, yes. What's the big deal about that?"

"Carry on."

Mary bristled. No one talked to her in that way. And yet... She looked at her brother; his eyes were shining brightly as he rocked slightly on the chair, hands tucked between his knees. She reminded herself to see him as an adult and not as a younger brother.

"Okay. I stood outside the room with my head round the door." She was speaking matter-of-factly, as if giving a statement to the police, trying to remember any small details. "It was dark in there so it took a few seconds for my eyes to get used it, but then I could see the woman on the bed, naked, and Dad standing over her."

"Was Dad naked?"

"No, he had his clothes on. Al was sat on the left, at the dressing table, watching them."

"Watching them sexually, or just looking at them?"

"Christ, I don't know, Johnny. It was a long time ago and it was only for a few moments."

"Okay. Go on."

"Dad went to pick something up off the bed, she put her leg up on his chest, and I ran away. That's it. What's the point of this, Johnny? He had an affair with another woman. He admitted it. What's with the Miss Marple stuff?"

"Why was Al there?" he said, almost to himself, now looking at the ground, thinking. "And why was Dad dressed?"

Mary looked at him through narrow eyes and spoke with a firm voice. "Johnny, what's going on?"

Johnny sat upright, as if called to attention. "Something's not right. Dad won't tell me anything. Doesn't make sense. Mum didn't know that Al was in the room. She thought he was somewhere else."

"So? What's the big deal? And why go raking it up now?"

"It's not right. You won't speak to Dad. He's been a hermit for ten years. Might not have been his fault."

Again, Mary narrowed her eyes. "Johnny, listen to me. He did wrong. He had an affair. He cheated on Mum. I know, I was there, I saw it. And he knows he was wrong, otherwise he would have told us, wouldn't he. Set the record straight."

"Guess so. But it doesn't fit right. What if something stopped him from being able to tell the truth?"

"Then what exactly do you think I saw?" Her words were clipped and she spoke slowly.

"Don't know. But why would Al have been in the room? Why was he around at all? Why didn't Mum know he was there? And who was that woman?" He looked at Mary. "If I get to the bottom of this, and Dad wasn't as much to blame as you thought, will you talk to him again?"

"What?" replied Mary, recoiling. "I'm not making deals with you, Johnny. I know what I saw." Her tone was final.

Johnny pressed on. "But what if things were not as they seemed. If he was not actually having an affair, or something else was happening that wasn't his fault. Would you speak to him again?"

"Well yes, I suppose so," Mary replied. "But Johnny, have you thought of this. It might be exactly as I saw it. It might be that our father really is a bastard, and isn't rose-tinted after all."

But Johnny wasn't listening. He stood up and turned round, deep in thought. As he did so, Mary saw David running away from the other boy, crying. Mary cursed and stood, poised to get David away from the other child, her face angry that David was so often susceptible to being bullied by other boys.

Instead Johnny shouted, "David! Hello, mate!"

The boy saw his uncle. Forgetting the other boy, he ran over to Johnny, who lifted him high up into the air.

Chapter 24

The road into Lexington was surrounded by references to horses, with every fifth car seemingly towing a horse trailer. As the car worked its way towards the centre of town, Harpo refused to slow down, even when Jay and Mack shouted that there was something they wanted to look at. He wouldn't argue with them or tell them to grow up and stop behaving like excited school kids. He would just ignore them and keep driving.

The hotel Johnny had chosen for them was large enough to offer a glimpse of luxury but small enough to feel homely. It was now late afternoon, after an early start followed by a leisurely drive through the Olympia State Forest. They agreed to meet in the bar at 6.30pm. Jay said he was going for a walk to stretch his legs and take a look at the town. Harpo didn't even take his bags out of the car, just walked out of the hotel and into the street without another word.

Mack put his bags on the double bed which dominated his room, then laid the guitar case next to them and flicked open the catches. He had been brooding for much of the day, trying to keep his focus on a new song that had been vying for his attention, a melody floating down to him from some unknown source.

Travelling between gigs left so much time for the mind to wander. Straight after the gig itself, when the adrenaline was still pumping, he felt like he could write a song every night. Sometimes on Mamal tours he had attempted to, inspired by the David Bowie album, *Aladdin Sane*, where the towns in which he had written the songs while on the Ziggy Stardust tour were written on the record label. It was reading that label as an 'almost teenager' which first planted the romantic notion of being 'on the road' as a fertile and imaginative place.

Taking the handmade acoustic guitar out of the case, Mack strummed a few chords: G to C to A minor seventh, helping his fingers to loosen up. He felt as if he was performing a ritual, attempting to summon the demons of inspiration.

He started a fresh rhythm with his right hand, the left held across the strings, dampening the sound so that he developed a scratching beat, mid-tempo. The tune had been buzzing round his mind all day, shouting for his attention like an irritating friend with his best interests at heart. Now he wanted to release the idea, to open the lid of the jar and catch as much as he could of whatever was in there before the rest managed to escape. This process had been navigated many times before and Mack relaxed into the rhythm, allowing his mind to empty.

Concerns about Johnny, where he was or what he was doing, tried to knock their way back in, but Mack focussed on the symbiosis between his hands and the something that was peering up from his subconscious, wondering whether it was safe to come out. The left hand formed a G chord and the right hand kept consistency of the strokes: three down, two quickly up, trying to ensure the mid-tempo groove didn't lapse into a plod. He settled into a rhythm and closed his eyes, just playing the G chord to the conga drum that could only be heard in his head, now with more of a beat, a slow groove instead of a dirge.

The melody flitted around his mind. Edging in from the periphery of his consciousness, he felt the next chord was naturally going to be A minor seventh. It needed something more, so his little finger danced on and off the third fret of the B string, adding a D note into the A minor seventh chord, and the cloud around the melody started to dissipate, this first part of the tune becoming clearer and more consistent each time he hummed it.

A third chord was needed. The next part of the melody was only a suggestion, revealing itself coyly like a Victorian lady in an old peepshow film at a seaside pier. The melody must spring naturally from the first part, knitting together the various pieces, chords, energy, emotion and cold hard notes, drawn together in an implosion of musical matter in order to create a simple song.

He practised the change between G and A minor seventh a few times, allowing the little finger to find the correct moments to add the D. His mind was now functioning in a way that wasn't conducive to anything other than what he was doing: writing a song. Delicate and fragile, a focus that could be snatched away in a moment by outside distraction.

Mack's fingers formed the C major seventh chord without knowing why, without being placed there, and as they did so, Mack started humming a melody, a melody that had been there all along just waiting to be found.

Next he sang whatever words decided to come out of his mouth. Ensnaring the melody was the important thing now; the words could be whatever they wanted to be for the moment, creating an almost direct line into his subconscious. They would be changed later, disguised from the first raw state they appeared in. Only he knew what really came out that first time.

In the base of the guitar case was a flap which he lifted to reveal a small chamber containing guitar periphery, such as strings, an electronic tuner, plectrums, plasters and wire cutters. He took out a small recording machine, placed it on the bed and pressed record. He sang through the chords a few times, humming the melody. Another melody popped out, a counter melody suitable for a lead guitar part. Now safe in the knowledge that two integral parts to this new song were safely banked, he returned to the words and sang, just sang, not caring what came out, now totally in the moment, in the feel of the song, in the mood of the notes that were created by the movement of his own fingers.

The rest of the words came out of him, as if they were being gently teased out of his very soul.

The more I see, the more I learn
About stupid lies, and wicked games
Your healthy mind is my only concern
Keep the devil in his bitter cage

He grabbed a pen and paper and quickly scribbled down the words, leaning over the deep bowl of the guitar. His fingers returned to the chords with the additional melody that just a small movement of the finger could pick out, and played it a few more times. He paused and looked at the pad again. The meaning of the words had hardly registered as they were released and yet now, as he looked at them on the piece of paper, he was surprised. So that's what I was really thinking, he thought to himself.

The release seemed to be complete. When he tried to empty his mind to allow new ideas into the vacuum, nothing came. It was as if a fog had descended over his eyes. Five minutes later, he realised that he was staring blankly at the wall.

Showered and refreshed, the three men met in the bar of the hotel then walked the short distance to the club where they would be playing that night, Bobby's Billiards and Backroom. The soundcheck was swift as there were only three instruments and two microphones to balance. They chatted with the manager about other bands that had played recently while waiting for their complimentary food to arrive. Jay and Mack nodded politely at the list of bands they had never heard of; Harpo, being the only one able to join in the conversation, chose to simply nod appreciatively at every third band the manager mentioned.

Ticket sales had been pretty good, they were relieved to hear. The locals were a hip, young, college-type crowd, and the manager told them there was always an appetite for hearing something interesting. Local college radio had been plugging the gig, and there would be plenty of people eager to experience an ex-minor pop star now ploughing his own furrow.

"Seems like a decent guy," said Mack, as the manager left them to their food.

"Huh, yeah, better than that tosser in Huntingdon. Don't think I'm ever going to forget him," said Jay.

"Hmm," replied Mack, "and I don't think he'll forget Harpo in a hurry, either." They both looked at their bass player but could only see the fuzzy clouds of hair pointing back at them, as he kept his head down and attacked his ribs in a frenzy. "I don't suppose he's ever been bitten on the leg by a bass player before."

"Well, at least we got paid," said Jay.

Harpo looked up, wiping meat juice and sauce from his moustache with a napkin. "Isn't that Johnny's job? Where is he, anyway?" he said, before lowering his head again and attacking his food like a lion after a long and particularly drawn-out stalking.

"Last I heard," replied Mack, "he said he had something to sort out, and hoped to join us down south somewhere, probably Baton Rouge, in a week or so."

Jay looked around, rather self-consciously. Mack was staring at him.

"I like this place," said Jay. "Totally American, got a really good vibe. If the gigs keep going like the last few have been, should be a good night."

Mack looked at Harpo. "How are the ribs, Harpo?" he asked.

The grey frizz bobbed upwards once again. "Fucking gorgeous," Harpo replied. "Absolutely, uncontrollably, gorgeous. They are so good, they taste like sex."

"Oh," said Mack, "a bit too much salt then."

Jay laughed hard, and even Harpo grinned, before putting his head back down to the plate.

"How was town, Jay?" asked Mack.

"You know something?" Jay replied. "It's only when you've been walking around a new town for an hour that you realise just how many women there are in the world that you'd like to have sex with." Jay and Mack clinked their beer glasses, smiled at each other, then continued munching on their burgers.

Harpo belched loudly, pushed his plate away and sat back in his chair. He went to fetch some more beers for the three of them, then returned to the table just as Mack and Jay took the last mouthful of their meal. Jay's gaze went past Harpo as he put down the fresh beer, and over Mack's shoulder. His brow furrowed. The bar was still pretty empty, with just a few after-work customers playing pool. Noticing Jay's expression, Mack turned round.

Walking across the wide room was a middle-aged man, with shoulder-length hair and a stoop. The hair was unfeasibly black. He half shuffled, half walked, as if he was carrying the weight of a thousand syringes on his shoulders. He was tall, well over six foot, slight if not skinny. His hair was not greasy and straight in the English rocker style, but fluffy and large, as if he belonged to a 1980s soft rock band from Los Angeles. And yet there was something English about him, something that made him seem out of place surrounded by the Americana of the bar. He wore dirty black jeans and New York Dolls t-shirt, which could be glimpsed through the open front of a long black leather coat which seemed to almost sweep along the floor behind him.

The image was very rock and roll; very casual and yet very deliberate. As he lounged his way towards their table, the aura presented was one of a studied and experienced cool. Dark wraparound sunglasses hid his eyes so naturally that they seemed to be part of his face. The t-shirt and jeans seemed fused to his skin, creating the appearance that he slept in the same clothes that he walked around in – including the sunglasses.

Mack turned back round and muttered "Fuck" under his breath. Jay didn't notice as he was studying the man who was approaching them, his face beginning to change from puzzlement to one of a small child meeting someone off the telly. Had he looked round, he would have noticed Harpo still slouched in his chair, his eyes trained on Mack, not moving, waiting to see his reaction, as if he was ready to jump in at any moment if needed.

"I know that guy," said Jay.

"No," said Mack, crisply, "you don't know him. You just recognise him." He stood up and turned to greet the man. There was no question now that he was walking towards their table.

"Hello, Kent," said Mack, deliberately keeping his hands in his pockets. "My son told me you might show up."

Kent Nicholls walked round the table and stood behind Harpo, who – still slouching, still with his eyes on Mack – slowly lifted his hand and offered it over his shoulder.

"Mack," replied Kent, his voice low and croaky; a flat London brogue tinged with New York melodrama. It was a confused accent, adaptable. He grabbed Harpo's proffered hand and squeezed it. "Harpo, dude." It was like one great hairstyle greeting another. He let go of Harpo's hand, then wiped his own hand on his jeans to remove the barbecue sauce. The jeans didn't look like they'd notice the difference. "I could do with a trim, Harpo," he said, turning his head slightly. It probably meant he was now looking at Jay, but with the sunglasses in occupancy it was impossible to be certain. "Quite fancy a snip from the master. Got ya kit with you?"

"Sure," replied Harpo. "Looks like you could do with the thinning scissors."

175

"Yeah," said Kent, with a drawl. "Perhaps get the 6.3 mil on the back, and use the offset thinners on the top. You still using the Tondeo Spider?"

"Course," said Harpo. "Best scissors around. Always were, always will be."

"Humph," said Kent, "I'm more of a Suvorna man, you know that. A classy set of scissors."

"Yeah, that's cuz you're a flash git. Tondeo will be your friend forever."

Still standing behind Harpo, Kent Nicholls put both hands on the bass player's shoulders. Harpo visibly flinched.

"Hey, Kent, my man," said Harpo, seeming to choose his words carefully. "Prefer if you wouldn't touch the merchandise, know what I mean?" His voice was strained, and he laughed unconvincingly.

"Oh yeah," said Kent, keeping his hand on the left shoulder and patting Harpo hard on the right shoulder with his other hand, a skinny wrist revealing itself briefly from the leather jacket sleeve. "Sorry, dude. I forgot you've got some hang-ups about that sort of thing." He took his hands off Harpo's shoulders, and made as if to move away. He then stopped, turned back to Harpo, and put one hand in the huge mound of grey frizzy hair, giving it a ruffle. Harpo's teeth were grinding audibly, but still he remained in his seat.

Jay watched Harpo, who was still watching Mack, despite his clear agitation. Mack hadn't taken his eyes off Kent, and Kent was probably looking at Jay.

Eventually, Kent moved around the table towards Jay and thrust out his hand. "Hi," he said to Jay, "Kent Nicholls. How ya doin'?"

Jay stood up and shook his hand enthusiastically. "Hi, Jay, yeah, great thanks, Kent Nicholls, hah, well I used to read your stuff all the time."

"Thanks," said Kent, trying to remove his hand from Jay's, eventually retracting it with a jolt. "That's several insults in one. Can't decide which is worse, the fact that you *used* to read me making me feel seriously old, or the fact that you don't read me any more *at all.*"

"Oh no, no, I didn't mean it like that," said Jay, "sorry, it's just, well, you know, I read lots of your stuff, I mean I *have* read lots of your stuff over the years, and…"

"Jay, shut up, eh?" said Mack.

"Oh, sorry," Jay replied, sitting down again. "Sorry. It's just, well, you know, well let's be honest, he's a bit of a star, and I haven't met a rock journalist hero before, and…"

"Christ, Jay," said Mack, raising his eyebrows without taking his eyes off Kent, "what are you going to be like when we meet someone *properly* famous. Someone who has actually done something of interest."

Kent smiled. "Good to see you too, Mack. Been a while, ain't it."

"I see that fake American accent you always put on hasn't improved much," said Mack. His words were in the same tone of voice as a surgeon who had just been asked to do his own paperwork.

"Ah," replied Kent, "that's a shame. I guess living in America among the rich and famous for the last twenty years hasn't rubbed off on me as much as I'd hoped."

"Still getting wealthy off other people's creativity then?"

"Hey," said Kent, holding his arms out, "can I help it if I'm good at what I do?"

"Yeah. You always were good at what you do. You always did try and be the best at being you. And I'd say you succeeded. You seem to have managed to become a complete Kent."

"Hey, Mack," said Jay, leaning forward and turning his head away from Kent Nicholls. "Cool it. What is with you?" He looked at his friend and raised his eyebrows, as if to encourage him to shut up.

"Let's just say," said Mack, addressing Jay but looking at Kent Nicholls, "that the man in front of you wrote some things about me that I'd rather he hadn't written."

"Well," said Kent, leaning forward to emphasise his point, "there were also plenty of things that I didn't write about you that I could have. Doesn't that balance it out?"

Mack leaned forward, his voice now slower and more deliberate. "You're not funny, and I'm not laughing."

Kent leaned back and smiled with one half of his mouth. He took a large, white plastic tube out of his pocket and put it in his mouth. Then, turning to Jay, he said, "So you're Jay Golding. I've been listening to a lot of the stuff you guys have been making and I like it. I like it a lot. What's your part in this caper, Jay? You can't just be here for your

177

looks. I gather you make 'noises' on the tracks."

Jay started to eagerly tell Kent Nicholls all about himself, oblivious to the double-edged compliment that had just been delivered. Mack sat back in his chair, slouching again, and looked at Harpo, who was still watching him carefully. Harpo raised his eyebrows slightly, without any other part of his face or body moving. Mack winked at him, just a half wink with no smile or other expression, as if to say, 'It's okay, I'm not going to do anything stupid.' Harpo relaxed, but just a little.

Jay was still talking. Kent Nicholls was so still that it was possible he had actually fallen asleep behind the sunglasses.

"...and then once Harpo has added his bassline, I go back into the track, and..."

Kent Nicholls moved suddenly, turning his head towards Mack, cutting Jay off mid-sentence. "So, where's Johnny?" he asked.

Mack pursed his lips. "Made yourself a friend there, haven't you," replied Mack. "Very clever."

"Nothing clever about it. Just been trying to help him out. He's a bright lad. Lots of energy, ambition, eager to please. Clearly takes after his mother."

"How long are you with us for, Kent," said Mack, without enthusiasm.

"Just a few days, on and off," he replied, stretching his back and moving the white plastic tube to the other side of his mouth. "Got a photographer coming to join us for a few days too."

Mack muttered, "Oh bloody great," rather loudly, then added, "cameras shoved in my face every ten minutes, trying to get 'natural' shots. Just what I need."

"Don't worry, it won't be for long," Kent Nicholls continued. "I'm afraid you're not so interesting anymore, so it's just a short article."

"Then we'll both be happy," said Mack. "You don't have to spend long writing about me, and I don't have to spend long in your company."

The journalist leaned deliberately towards Mack across the table. "I can still make someone's career, you know," he said, quietly.

"What, like you did for Al?"

Leaning back again, Kent Nicholls said, "He had to do *something* to move his career along. Being with you wasn't helping him any."

"Being with me got him further than he was ever likely to get on his own."

"Standing on the bottom rung of a ladder doesn't make you a window cleaner."

"Very good. Did you make that one up yourself or get it from a Christmas cracker?"

"Johnny seems curious to know why you became a recluse. I agree with him. It would be a good starting point for the article. 'The man who gave it all up then realised that it was too much of a sacrifice'. So, what can you tell us all, Mack?"

There was a silence, the kind of silence that was so much more than a simple lack of noise. Eventually, Mack spoke in an even, calm voice. So calm that the hint of menace became a clear threat.

"My son is old enough to look after himself. But if you fucking mess with him, I will finish off what I started thirty odd years ago. Understand?" His face had paled, and the hint of a smirk on the journalist's face suggested that he had managed what he had set out to achieve.

Kent Nicholls chuckled then stood up. "Guys," he said, "it's been a pleasure. Don't think it hasn't." He turned and walked slowly away from them.

The three men watched his black back as he shuffled across the bar and out of the room. Harpo's eyes flicked back and forth to Mack.

After a few moments, Jay turned to Mack and said, "Well, that was an experience. You do hold a grudge don't you."

"Yes," replied Mack. "When the cause is sufficient, yes."

Jay waited for more. When nothing was forthcoming he said, "Well this is going to make for an interesting few days. I hope you're going to be a bit more civil to each other."

"Ah, give our man some credit," said Harpo. "That 'complete Kent' line was good. I was pissing meself inside to that one!"

Mack raised his glass. "That, my hirsute friend, is a line that I've waited twenty years to deliver." He drained his glass, smiled, and stood up. "I feel unclean after that. I'm going to have a quick smoke outside, then I'm going for a nap. See you back here at 8.30." It was an instruction.

Jay turned to Harpo, who was still watching Mack as he walked out of the bar. Harpo's face, usually totally impassive, was showing some concern.

"What the hell was all that about?" Jay asked.

"Some bad blood," Harpo replied.

"No shit, Sherlock," said Jay. He picked up his beer and leaned back in his chair. "Care to elaborate? How do you know Kent Nicholls so well, for example?"

"We go back," Harpo replied, simply.

"Yeah, I know you do, Harpo, I wouldn't be asking otherwise. Can I get a bit more please? Hmm? What was all that business with the scissors, for example?"

Harpo turned his head slowly. It looked to Jay like a robot turning to look at him, the straight back and minimal movement below the neck.

"Kent came on tour with us," said Harpo. "He was a bit of a knob. He and I talked about hairstyling one night. It's a passion for us both. We had an argument about makes of scissors. It got heated. I threatened him with my curling tongs. He kind of respected more after that. But only a bit. After the tour we kept in touch. Occasional phone calls, Facebook. Asking for hair tips, keeping up to date with stuff."

"What 'stuff' was he keeping up to date with, Harpo?" asked Jay, his fingers miming the inverted commas in the air.

Harpo had his hands in his hair now, rubbing his scalp as if trying to wash away the feeling of someone else touching him.

Jay put the beer back on the table. "Oh, Harpo," he said after a moment, "how could you?"

The other man shifted nervously in his seat. Jay's hand now dropped back onto the table, leaving his face in a state of realisation. "Is that how Kent got in touch with Johnny? Through you? Did you give Johnny's number to Kent Nicholls?"

Harpo didn't speak, but Jay could see a small red patch appear on the side of his neck. He had seen it before, usually just before Harpo lost his temper and did something that was often rather disturbing. This time, however, Jay felt a more important calling and pressed on.

"Harpo, tell me. Did you put Kent Nicholls and Johnny together?"

"Not exactly," said Harpo, through pursed lips. "Just confirmed something he already knew. Said he wanted to get back in touch with Mack. Patch things up."

"Is that right," said Jay. "So if he was so keen to get back in touch with Mack, why didn't he just pick the phone up and speak to him? Why go through Johnny?"

"I don't know," said Harpo in frustration. "All I know is that he'd seen that Mack's music was getting popular and wanted to get involved. He knew that Johnny was behind it. I told you, he has a way of knowing things about people."

"And you knew about the bad blood between Kent and Mack?"

Harpo continued to stare straight ahead. The red patch flared up again.

"Let me guess," continued Jay. "You thought it was all over. You believed Kent Nicholls when he said he wanted to make things right with Mack. And you gave him Johnny's number."

No answer from Harpo.

"Tell me this, Harpo. What happened between those two? Was it really just this article that Kent Nicholls wrote? Was there anything else?"

Harpo still didn't say anything. The silence confirmed to Jay that he wasn't going to find out anything more from Harpo tonight.

Chapter 25

Johnny stood in his hotel room looking across Galway Bay, the Aran Islands appearing as if they were lying softly on the surface of the Atlantic Ocean in the distance. There was still some mist hovering over the bay at this early hour of the morning, and the rocks in front of the beach framed an idyllic vista that he would still be able to picture clearly in his mind many years later.

Moving to the small writing desk that the hotel provided in each room, he pressed the power button on his laptop and returned to the window to soak in the view while it booted up.

Johnny had come to Galway to find Al. He had been given an address and wanted to turn up on the doorstep in order to surprise his father's old partner. He had a few questions to ask, and he had been warned that Al might not necessarily be too keen on answering them.

Galway time was five hours ahead of where the tour had reached, Lexington, and he and Mack had chatted for a while before Johnny went to sleep the previous night. Mack seemed in good spirits, telling Johnny that Kent Nicholls had arrived. He had reeled off a series of pithy insults about Kent that had made Johnny feel his father was really coming alive again, enjoying the new experiences and intellectual rigours of dealing with life on tour. There was such a spirit of the new world about him, Johnny felt; he was really enjoying the sparring with his old journalist mate. It was exactly as Kent Nicholls had told him it would be.

The Galway Bay Hotel had been selected in a moment of indulgence – he was only staying for one night, after all – but he hadn't realised the hotel would be a little way out of the town. It was mainly occupied by people who preferred a slightly more subdued Galway experience. And Americans. Lots of Americans.

He checked through a small list of unread emails, eating the bacon and scrambled eggs with potato bread that room service had brought him as he did so. The email with Al's current address on it was already printed and tucked into his back pocket.

He then typed Al's name into Google. Al Smart did not bring up many entries these days – at least not any of the sort that Johnny was looking for. He had looked through all the old film reviews and the Wikipedia entry, but everything about Al Smart stopped in 1994. It was as if he'd jumped off the planet.

The article that Kent Nicholls had written about Mamal for *NME* appeared on the search results list, reproduced on a 1980s tribute website. Although he had read it before, Johnny skimmed through again. It was well written, he had to admit; albeit in the florid, self-conscious style of the time.

Shutting down the laptop and wiping his mouth with the napkin from the tray, Johnny took one last slurp from his coffee and left the hotel.

The Seapoint Promenade took him a slightly longer route, but with bright sunshine and the morning sea air easing across his head it was worth the extra yards. Al, so Kent had told him, was staying in a rundown house in the Westside area of the town. He was driven by the determination to discover why Al had been in that hotel room and what had really happened. It was time to get things out in the open, so that his father could stop being such a damn recluse and show the world what a brilliant musician, hell, what a brilliant person he was.

With a last look across the bay, Johnny turned inland. After twenty minutes of walking through pleasant suburbs, he found 32 Spiddal Street. It was a house that looked similar to the others from a distance, but close up the ripped and soiled curtains gave away the fact that this house might not be quite as cared for as some of the others.

Johnny felt a sudden twinge of nervousness in his stomach. It had occurred to him that Al might not necessarily be living in happy domestic bliss, but he hadn't gone as far as to imagine the depths he might have reached. What if he was a heroin addict? What if he was violent?

Steeling himself, Johnny walked up the path and pressed the doorbell. There was no sound, no chime from within. He peered through the frosted glass, seeing daylight through what was presumably the kitchen at the end of the hall. Unsure whether the bell wasn't working or if it was just somewhere within the house that he couldn't hear it, he knocked on the front door. Inside, he could hear someone – a gruff male voice with a thick Irish accent shouted "Door!" Still no one came.

After a few more minutes, he knocked again. This time the same voice shouted, "For fuck's sakes!" and then he heard movement. A shape began to come into focus through the glass, looming larger and larger as it came closer to the door, until it blocked out the daylight completely.

The door opened, revealing a man who was huge in every conceivable way. Johnny's first impression was of a bear that had grown old and grey, woven beads into the fur on its chin, and stuck a tea cosy on its head. The ageing hippy who stood in the doorway had a belly that pushed proudly at a suede waistcoat which was attempting valiantly to contain it; that same belly made its presence felt by protruding between the top of the brightly coloured cotton trousers and the bottom of a tie-dyed t-shirt. The head seemed to be smothered in hair, grey locks falling down from the floppy woollen hat like a waterfall. The eyes were half hidden by bushy grey eyebrows.

Even more overpowering was the smell that leaked out of the house, crawling its way past the man blocking most of the doorway. It was a smell heavily influenced by marijuana, but also held traces of body odour, Indian cuisine and cats. It was a smell that Johnny would never forget, and for the rest of his life, every time he would experience those four smells combined, he would be immediately taken back to Galway. As he looked at the man, there was only one certainty to his identity. This was not Al Smart.

"Hello?" said the man, and not in a kindly or welcoming way. It was a neutral hello: inquisitive, and yet making it plain that he was not happy to have been forced up from whatever reclining position he had been enjoying. Also spilling out from behind the man was the sound of the television, but Johnny couldn't quite place what was currently showing. There was silence, then the burble of voices, then silence again, followed by applause. It was a familiar sound.

"Um, hi," said Johnny, more confidently than he felt. "Wonder if you can help me. I'm looking for Al Smart."

"Why?" replied the man, in a thick Galway accent. He sounded non-committal, as if he had people coming to his door and asking to speak to Al Smart every day.

"Long story," said Johnny, smiling, unsure of himself. He hadn't expected to be quizzed, and he suddenly realised how unprepared he was.

"Is it," said the hippy, looking straight at Johnny, his own face still giving no clues as to his thoughts. He wasn't imposing, he was just *there*. His silent glare made it clear to Johnny that he was going to have to give a little more away if he wanted to go through that door and find Al.

"I'm an old friend of his," said Johnny, smiling hard now.

"No yer not," said the man.

"Well," replied Johnny, quickly, "I say friend, actually it's my dad he's friends with. They were at school together."

The silent, violent staring continued. Johnny wondered how he could be so intimidated by someone wearing sandals.

"I just want a word," Johnny said. "Something to do with my dad he can help me with." No movement from the doorway. "So…can I speak to him?"

"No," said the man.

Johnny felt himself getting a little impatient. He checked himself, and took a slightly deeper breath than normal. The man continued not to move.

"May I ask why not?" asked Johnny, suddenly feeling extremely English.

"Cuz he's not here," replied the man.

"Oh," said Johnny. "That's fair enough then. When will he be back?"

"No fecking idea," said the grey bear.

"Do you know where he's gone?"

"Yes."

There was a pause, but the man didn't say anything further. My God, thought Johnny, he has absolutely no fear of silence. That makes him extremely powerful.

He tried a new tack. "Where?" he asked.

"America," came the answer.

Johnny stopped for a moment. So it was possible to get information out of this person. He wasn't being difficult. You just had to ask the right question. It was like interrogating a child who had done something naughty, didn't want to admit it, but didn't want to lie either.

"Why?"

The man stared at him. Underneath the shaggy eyebrows, Johnny thought he saw a flicker. An open question – one that required a careful answer and couldn't be batted away quite so simply. A slightly pained expression crossed the hippy's brow, as if he was reaching down, deep down, through a fog of dope smoke.

Johnny heard a quiet roar from the television set and the man's head turned, his face confused, as if he didn't know what to do. All of a sudden, Johnny understood the man's reticence. He had been watching cricket and was just trying to listen to the commentary. Now a wicket had fallen and he was desperate to see what was happening.

"Look," the man said quickly, "he got a call from someone late last night. I don't know who it was but he said he'd got to leave so he left early this morning, saying he was going to New York. I don't know how he's managing it, he's got no money and owes me fecking rent, but there ye are, now can I please go?"

"Is he coming back?"

"He didn't say. He's left some stuff here but that means nutin', he hasn't got much anyway. He just bought a fecking great big rucksack and filled it full of stuff then went. Okay? Are ye done now?" He was hopping up and down now, as if he wanted to go to the toilet.

"Thank you," said Johnny, absently.

The man muttered, "No worries," then shut the door.

Johnny could see him running clumsily back into the front room, trying to get back in front of the television before the replays had finished.

He walked back to his hotel slowly. So Al had received a telephone call. Someone had tipped him off that Johnny was coming to find him. But who knew that he was coming to Galway? Only Kent Nicholls and Jay.

Somebody didn't want him to meet with Al, someone who knew that Al had been in the hotel room the day that Mary had walked in on them. Someone with something to hide.

Who knew that Al had been present? His sister had told him, and obviously his father knew. But his mother hadn't known. And he had told Jay. He furrowed his brow in annoyance at himself for not having been more careful. And yet Jay was harmless, wasn't he?

Now he was more certain than ever that there was some sort of secret. The fact that Al had received a telephone call shortly before Johnny arrived, then moved out of his rented dump at extremely short notice and flown to America using money he undoubtedly didn't have – all this meant that someone else was moving him.

Chapter 26

Sliding into a semi-circular padded booth behind a table in The Melting Pot nightclub, Mack watched Jay and Kent Nicholls standing at the bar, talking to a third person he didn't know. Earlier that evening they had played a really solid gig – one of the best of the tour so far – and Mack's confidence in the music was growing. Leading up to the tour he'd had concerns about how the music would be accepted, but now the belief was growing that they might actually get away with it.

The tour had reached Athens, Georgia. This was one of the towns he had most been looking forward to playing: a happy combination of a large student population from the University of Georgia, plus a rich musical heritage through bands such as REM and The B-52s.

The audience had been appreciative, the relatively low level of background chat and generous applause conveying an understanding of the chances that the music took. The three band members had responded by really connecting for the first time in ages. There had been moments when Mack had totally forgotten about the audience, or worrying about Johnny, and just found himself listening to the sound the three of them were making coming back at him through the foldback speakers.

Johnny had done his homework in selecting this venue. The Melting Pot, with its slogan 'Eat, Drink, Listen Closely', was a great place to play. They'd been treated well, fed well, and now Mack was able to relax with a Sweet Georgia Brown cocktail, a mixture that seemed to include a generous portion of Southern Comfort. What else it contained was really no concern of his.

He was sat at a corner table by himself. The bar was spacious but still pleasantly busy, affording Mack the feeling of being private in such a public place, alone with his thoughts. A warm, post-gig feeling was nestling in and things felt okay, if a little bit fuzzy in the head. Was that from the cocktail or from constantly worrying about Johnny? He took a rueful glance at his drink. No easy feat, happiness. Feeling happy for a fleeting moment is attainable, but maintaining a state of happiness is rather like trying to balance a chicken on your nose.

The fuzzy feeling in his head had been around for a while, but he'd been able to associate it with events, such as being hung-over. However, it had returned this afternoon during total sobriety, a sort of dullness of the mind. He struggled to concentrate at times, and found himself drifting off. Nothing to be concerned about, he thought to himself, just not used to working this hard.

"Hi."

Mack looked up and saw a woman, probably in her mid- to late-twenties. It was a warm evening, and yet she was wearing a black polo neck jumper and faded denim jeans. Her head was covered with a swathe of black, frizzy hair, which was desperately trying to force its way out of being confined by a large butterfly clip. The hair imposed itself on her overall image, its dominance only threatened by a large smile that instantly gave him the feeling that things would somehow be okay. Above the smile was a nose that, at best, did not draw attention to itself, but sitting above the nose was a pair of green eyes, framed by the black hair, that Mack immediately found himself falling into.

"Hi," he replied.

"Julia," she said, expectantly.

He smiled back at her, somewhat vacantly. "The photographer? I'm with Kent?" She lifted the camera that had been around her neck all that time to show him. He hadn't noticed it before.

"Oh," said Mack, standing up quickly. "Sorry, of course." He offered his hand and she grabbed it with a firm grip. "Please," said Mack, "take a seat. Kent is over at the bar, talking to Jay, my mate, the other one in the band. With Harpo. Not that he's with Harpo now, he's with Kent, obviously, but he's in the band with Harpo. And me. Can I get you a drink? The cocktails are pretty good." He pointed at the glass on the table.

"Please," she said. "That would be nice, thank you." That smile again. She sat down, and Mack hovered for a moment. A puzzled look scurried across his face as he struggled momentarily to remember what he was about to do. As if by magic, a waiter appeared at the table; a tall young man with shiny, ink-black hair and a jaw that would have had a very good chance of winning a jutting competition.

"May I just say, sir, that I absolutely loved your set tonight," the waiter said to Mack, with impeccable manners. "Can I get you another Sweet G?"

"Oh, thanks. Yeah, that's very kind, thank you." He turned to Julia. "You want one of these?" he asked her, offering the glass to her to try a sip first.

She smiled gently at him, lips together, and leaned forward slightly. "It's okay," she whispered, "I know what they taste like." Then her smile broadened to show her fine white teeth as she turned to the waiter. "Please make that two Sweet Georgias, thank you," she said, and in doing so Mack felt that the smile seemed to lose some of its charm. A momentary feeling of annoyance surprised him as he watched the waiter flash a smile back at her.

Mack sat back down in his seat opposite her. "So," said Mack, "what do you want to ask me, fire away."

That smile again – he couldn't take his eyes away. It was perfect. When in repose, her mouth went down at the sides, and could have had the effect of making her look grumpy. But when she smiled at him, her knowing smile, the one that showed she was thinking about or absorbing what he'd said, her lips stayed together but her cheeks raised. The edge of her mouth pushed her left cheek back slightly further than the right, making a frame for the lips. Her eyes narrowed at the same time, as if they were sharing a joke together. It was a fascinating face.

"Why would I want to ask you something?" she said, shaking her head slightly. "I'm the photographer, remember? Kent is the journalist."

"Oh, yeah, sorry, of course," said Mack. "Photographer, yeah."

"I'll try not to get in your way," she said. "I prefer to take pictures of people candidly, as they relax or talk, you know, rather than setting up a pose. Is that okay with you?"

"No problem, sounds great."

They sat in silence for a few moments. Then Julia spoke. "So, how's the tour going?"

"Really good," said Mack. The tip of her nose moved up and down when she talked.

"Greeeeaaaat," said Julia, slowly. She looked round the bar, then turned back to Mack and asked, "Written any new stuff? That's what you musicians do on tour, don't you? Among the other things." The last line was said with a suggestive raising of the eyebrows.

"I'm a little long in the tooth for the 'other things'," Mack said. "Yeah, I've written a little, but we've been moving around quite a bit. No tour bus for us. Hey, that could be a lyric!" He laughed, awkwardly.

Mack reminded himself that she was a rock photographer. She would be as bored talking to musicians as he would be talking to journalists. The waiter brought over the cocktails, and this time Julia gave him only a brief thank you before turning back to Mack. For a moment he felt guilty at enjoying the flash of irritation on the young man's face. But only for a moment.

"So, have you played any of your new stuff to Kent?" she asked him. "He loves that, being the first to hear it, makes him feel important."

"No," said Mack, and felt his stomach muscles involuntarily tighten at the sound of the journalist's name.

"He wasn't a great fan of your old songs, was he?" she said. The tone was engaged, the verbal equivalent of poking around an old shoebox that she'd found in her loft. For some reason this annoyed Mack more, now that she had mentioned Kent Nicholls.

"What Kent Nicholls thinks doesn't interest me," said Mack. "I didn't write those songs for him."

"Really. Who did you write them for then?"

"Well, um, ah, I don't know, not really thought of it like that. They just kind of happen. Ultimately I wrote them for me, I suppose."

"So why didn't you keep them to yourself then?" She took a long suck on the straw and looked at him over the top of the glass.

Mack opened his mouth to speak but nothing came out.

"Seriously," Julia said again, this time taking hold of her camera with both hands. "I take lots of photographs that I don't show anyone. Why do you musicians think that your music is only valid if other people hear it? Why not keep it for yourselves. Record it if you must, then move on."

The expression now passing across Mack's face was a mixture of confusion and intrigue. Before he had a chance to change it, Julia had looked down into her camera through the viewfinder and pressed the shutter.

"What…" said Mack, taken aback. "Was that… Flip me, you cheeky cow," he said, a smile starting to form, despite himself.

"Sorry," said Julia, taking the camera from over her shoulder and placing it on the table. "Bit of a cheap trick, that. There's one thing I know about you – that you've spent the last fourteen years recording music that your son put out without you knowing. So I thought the one way I could get a natural face out of you would be to contradict that one fact. Worked like a charm, too."

"Are you going to use that photo?"

"Up to Kent. It also depends what other reactions I can get from you over the next couple of days. I don't *have* to show him every picture I take. I sometimes keep some for myself." That smile. It's almost like she knew what effect it was having on him…

"Okay," said Mack, attempting to locate his composure and haul it back to him. "Okay. Now that is the sort of trick that used to really get my back up when, well, when I was a bit of a pop star. So why is it my reaction to you now is to find it rather amusing?"

"Can only be one of two things," said Julia. "Either you have mellowed. However, I doubt that. You don't seem the mellowing type to me."

"What type do I seem then?"

"Well, you've been sat at home sulking over your divorce for the last fourteen years. I suspect that's made you more…entrenched in your view of the world."

"How on earth do you know so much about me?"

"Well the facts aren't too difficult to find. And for the stuff between the lines, there are your lyrics. You don't like to think they reveal much about you, you try very hard to keep them obtuse. But you do come across. If you listen to them enough times, the real Mack comes careering through."

"And you've listened to them enough times, have you?"

Julia simply smiled back.

"And what's the other thing?"

"Well, I don't suppose in those years sitting at home you came across a woman who was as attractive as me."

Mack laughed, a barking laugh that he instantly wasn't proud of. "Wow," he said. "You're not short of confidence are you."

"I have eyes," she replied, looking directly into his right eye. "Listen, I'm not classically good-looking, but I know I'm striking. Not all men go for me, but when they do, they really do." It was as if she was daring him not to fall in love with her.

Mack looked at her afresh, assessed her beyond the smile and the hair.

"Really, how *do* you know so much about me?" he asked her again. "You may – or may not – have got some notions through my lyrics. I'm not admitting anything at this point. But you didn't find out that my son had been putting my music out through listening to my songs."

"Kent Nicholls briefed me."

"Of course he did. And I assume he got the information directly from my son."

"I guess so. I didn't ask. He just, well, knew." She looked flustered for the first time. "Where is Johnny, by the way? I was hoping to meet him, he seems like a remarkable young man."

"He's... he's doing stuff. To do with the tour. Organising."

The two of them looked at each other, and Mack reminded himself once again that they had only just met. In just a few short minutes it seemed as if they had covered a lot of ground. Tread carefully. After all, she is currently employed by Kent Nicholls.

"Kent speaks very highly of Johnny," said Julia.

"Do you always work with Kent?" Mack asked.

"If I'm honest, I actually try not to. But I need the job at the moment – things have been a bit quiet. He rather creeps me out, in truth." She shuffled herself closer to the table and leaned on her elbows, putting her chin on her fingers. "He's got an amazing reputation as a journalist, but he's got other reputations too, know what I mean?"

"Not really," said Mack, leaning forward conspiratorially. "Tell me more."

"Hi," said Jay, approaching the table, seemingly unaware that he had interrupted them. He walked over to where Julia was sitting. "You'll be Julia, I take it. Jay Golding. Hi." They shook hands. "Kent pointed you out to me."

Julia shook his hand and Jay sat down on a chair opposite Mack, next to Julia. Mack looked at Jay for signs that his friend would be hit by the same first impression as had overwhelmed him not so long ago. But Jay seemed not to notice the smile, the frame of the hair, the poise, the easy grace.

"Is he still here?" Julia said to Jay. "I need to check in with him."

"No, he's gone for a slash," Jay replied.

"I beg your pardon?" said Julia. "What the hell is a slash? I'm assuming you don't mean the Guns N' Roses guitarist."

"Sorry. To the bathroom. 'Slash' is, well, I suppose it's a Britishism." He looked at Mack. "Is that a word?"

"It'll do," smiled Mack.

Jay turned his entire body to face his friend. He was obviously excited about telling Mack something, and put both hands up in front of himself as he spoke. "Oh. My. Giddy. Fanny. Do you know who I was just talking to? Mike Mills and his wife. Mike Mills!"

"Cool," said Mack, in the manner of a teacher who's just been told by one of his pupils that they ate all of their omelette for tea last night.

"Oh, come on, Mack," said Jay. "You do know who Mike Mills is, don't you?"

"Honestly? Not a clue."

"Argh!" said Jay, throwing his arms in the air in exasperation. "You really are a cultural vacuum. Mike Mills is the bass player for REM!"

Mack raised his eyebrows. "Okay. Now I can agree that is pretty cool."

"Sorry I didn't bring him over," said Jay, "but, well, I just couldn't quite believe I was talking to the guy."

"No worries. I've been enjoying Julia's company." He smiled at her, and felt slightly embarrassed by the tickle he felt in his tummy when she smiled back.

Slinking back in his chair, Jay took a large swig from his bottle. "Mike fucking Mills," he said, mainly to himself.

"That's an interesting choice for a middle name," said Mack. "His parents must have had quite a sense of humour."

Julia laughed.

The sound of clicking heels and swishing leather from behind him told Mack that Kent Nicholls was approaching. He felt the muscles in his neck tighten. Jay stood up, excitedly.

"Kent and I are going to a party," he said. "A guitarist he knows from way back. I'll see you in the morning, Mack, okay?"

"Okay," said Mack, quickly, happy to not be invited for two very different reasons.

He watched Julia. She was looking at Kent Nicholls, who was now stood behind Mack.

"Do you, uh, need me?" she asked the journalist, and Mack thought he detected a slightly hopeful note in her voice.

Kent Nicholls walked around the table, as if he wanted Mack to be able to see him. His head – and therefore his sunglasses and, presumably, his eyes – was pointed towards Julia.

"Why?" he said. "You got someone better to do?"

Julia looked back up at him, her cheeks flushing. "I just thought I'd stay here," she said. "Those parties can get pretty wild, and they're not really my scene. Besides, it would be better for the brief if I got to know Mack a bit better." She turned to Mack. "That is, if you're okay with that?"

"Of course," said Mack.

"Okay with me, you're a big girl now," said Kent Nicholls. "Just be careful. You know how these rock wannabes can be. You of all people should know that." He turned and walked off towards the exit.

"Tsk," said Jay, smiling awkwardly. "He speaks his mind, doesn't he! Guess you've got to in the world he lives in. See you in the morning, guys."

Jay got up and walked after Kent Nicholls, easily catching him up and then having to slow his pace to match the journalist's languid stride. Jay's arms were waving excitedly as he was talking, walking alongside, then in front, then turning around, then getting back in line again. All the while Kent Nicholls sauntered across the floor, his long leather coat fanning out behind him.

"It seems Jay has rather taken to your colleague," said Mack, with no attempt to hide the annoyance in his voice. He turned back to Julia. "What was that comment all about? 'You of all people should know that.'"

"I don't know," she replied, looking at the back of Kent Nicholls as he allowed Jay to open the door to the street for him. She was clearly agitated. "Well, I do, but I don't see how the hell he knew about it."

She paused, then turned back to Mack, smiled with great effort and effect, then said, "Can I ask you a question? What the hell did you do to piss Kent Nicholls off so much?"

"You know," said Mack, "that's the first thing you've said that's really made me feel happy inside. You and him not friends then?"

"Not exactly. We had a bit of a disagreement once. Well, to be fair, there aren't many people in the business who haven't. To be honest, I wouldn't be doing this job if I hadn't been asked to by a friend of mine who had to drop out at the last minute because her child is sickly. What's your story?"

"I can't tell you."

"Can't, or won't? Okay, let me guess. He got you involved in some dodgy activity, but he was prepared to take it much further than you were. Nevertheless, you're still embarrassed about what you did actually do, therefore you don't want to admit to anything. Close?"

"Too much for comfort. But I'm still not telling you."

"Don't worry. You won't be the first to be caught out. I told you he had other reputations. Let's just say the man has a rap sheet as long as his pretentious coat. But why does he seem so agin you? You seem pretty harmless to me."

I like that twinkle in her eye, Mack thought to himself. I could get used to that. "Agin? Is that really a word?"

"It is around here. And don't change the subject."

"I'm sorry, Julia. I like you. I think I'd like to get to like you a lot more. But I've only just met you, and I can't start handing over the family secrets. Not on the first date. All I'll say is, when we had our – what did you call it – dodgy activity, I ended up giving him that gold tooth."

"Holy shit," said Julia, her green eyes widening. "That was you? And the jaw? You gave him the jaw?"

"Uh, now, I'm not entirely sure what that means."

"He has a dodgy jaw. Everyone in the business knows that. It causes him pain almost all the time. It's why he mumbles a bit, he doesn't open his mouth when he talks, it hurts him too much. The rumour was that someone punched him at a party so hard that he had to have three teeth replaced and his jaw rewired. Was that really you?"

Mack smiled broadly. "Now, I did not know that. Ha! I really did not know that. Oh, wow, what fantastic news. Julia, I am so glad I met you. You have made my night." He chuckled, and a tear actually formed in his eye. He did not try to hide it from Julia, but lifted his glass, finished his Sweet Georgia Brown, and waved over the waiter to bring them another.

Chapter 27

Sitting on the park bench, Mary mechanically moved the pushchair forwards, then pulled it back. She had been repeating the process for ten minutes, despite the fact that Grace had fallen asleep five minutes earlier. So tired, so very tired. Grace had been up in the night, wanting to come into her bed to sleep with her, which Mary had not allowed. It would have been much easier to let Grace climb in with her, but she knew it was best for the child to get used to sleeping in her own room. Grace, of course, didn't have the benefit of having read innumerable 'How to be a Good Parent' books, and kept returning for another attempt.

A fog of tiredness seemed to have settled in front of Mary's eyes. Grace could catch up with sleep during the day, but her mother did not have that luxury. And yet the girl was just so beautiful when she was asleep. With a slowness caused partly by tiredness and partly by the enjoyment she felt in staring at her sleeping child, Mary tore her gaze away to watch David. He was playing on the climbing frame in the park and was shouting at her to look at him while he jumped from the second bar. She waved at him, and felt a moment of panic as he flew through the air in case he twisted an ankle.

A rare idle moment. Her thoughts were one-directional, down the family tree towards her own children rather than upwards towards her parents. She spent almost all her time thinking about David and Grace, either planning or worrying. Before children, she had spent her time obsessing about Phil. Before Phil, she had spent her time obsessing about herself. And there *was* nothing before herself.

But since Johnny had visited, a nagging thought had wormed its way past her usually stout defences. There *was* something not quite right about the whole episode from so many years ago, something inconsistent. It was as if her father had never tried to sort things out with her mother; simply accepted his guilt, and accepted the consequences. Presumably her parents had never discussed what happened, otherwise her mother would have known about Al being in the room. *Had* she told her mother about Al? She had been in such emotional turmoil following what she saw in that hotel room, maybe she hadn't; maybe they had all just accepted her father's guilt as easily as he had allowed them to.

However, that would suggest he was hiding something. Something he was prepared to sacrifice his entire family – his entire life – for. And that simply didn't fit with the arrogant, selfish man that Mary remembered him to be when she last spoke to him at the age of fourteen. Something didn't fit. Something was out of place.

She telephoned her mother, speaking quietly so as not to wake Grace. Their relationship was a functional one, not without warmth, but it mainly revolved around the well-being of Grace and David. Jude would have been happy to babysit, but as Mary hardly ever left the house after dark, Grandma was rarely called upon. Jude therefore simply invited herself over if she wanted to see her grandchildren. It wasn't as if she was being excluded, it's just that Mary rarely thought of her.

After a lengthy update on the welfare of her grandchildren, Mary broached the subject with a typically direct question.

"Did you know that Al was in the room when I saw Dad with that woman?" she asked.

Her mother paused, then replied, "No. That is rather odd."

"Yes, Johnny seemed to think so too."

"Ah, you've been talking have you. He came to see me as well. I'm not sure what he's up to, but it's probably some sort of well-meaning interference which will make everything worse."

"But it is odd though, Mum. Why would you not have known about Al being there? Did I not tell you?"

"Darling, the days after it happened were very complicated. Your father basically fell on his sword, did the right thing, and just left. He and I didn't talk about it much, we didn't need to – he had done wrong, he knew it, and didn't try to explain. And frankly I had my hands full with you at the time, that was my number one priority. You were rather…complicated."

"Hmmm," said Mary. It didn't occur to her that she should have

199

thanked her mother for her devotion; motherhood is an unconditional arrangement as far as she was concerned, and thanks were therefore not necessary. She didn't expect any from her own children, and she didn't think of giving any to her own mother.

"Mary, are you absolutely sure that Al was there as well? In that room, I mean? It's just very…well, strange. I can't think why he would have been."

"Mum," said Mary, ignoring the question. "Dad is my real dad, isn't he?"

"Yes," Jude had said, firmly, almost angrily. "You know he is. We've been through this many times." She sighed loudly, making a point. "Christ, I knew Johnny raking this stuff up would be bad news. Where is he? I've left a message on his mobile phone."

"He's flying to New Orleans to meet Dad, he sent me a text. I can't understand why Dad would not have bothered to explain himself. It's like he's covering something up, and I'm worried that it's about me."

"It's not about you, darling," Jude replied, in a softer, kinder tone. "It's about him. It always was, and it always will be." She then asked about David's piano lessons, in a brazen and highly successful attempt to change the subject.

Chapter 28

At around 2am, Mack got up from his chair in the hotel bar. He had hoped that he would bump into Jay there, but instead had sat on his own for the last half an hour. He went to the bar and signed the piece of paper which meant his drinks would be added to the room bill, then went out into the lobby and began up the stairs.

The hotel was next door to the venue, and was definitely one of the classier ones they had stayed in. The decor was all pot plants and armchairs in the corridors. Mack had once argued at a dinner party with someone who suggested that interior design was an art form in the same way that architecture was. Jude had been furious with him afterwards. As he reached the first floor, where his and Jay's rooms were situated, he smiled at the attention to detail in the hallways and wondered if he may have been wrong after all.

The evening with Julia had set his mind whirring. She was the most entrancing person Mack had met for a very long time. Although given that he had hardly met any new people in the last decade or more that wasn't difficult. He had found her bright, intelligent, and unwilling to accept any bullshit. They had stayed in The Melting Pot for the next two hours, just talking; about everything, about nothing, and about most points in-between.

It had been a very long time since Mack had spent such a long time with another person, let alone someone he had also felt so physically attracted to. At first they had sparred a little, each used to enquiring about the other person in a conversation and automatically deflecting questions that would involve talking about themselves. Each had adopted their own default approach to social etiquette, which happened to coincide with the approach taken by the other, seeking knowledge about the background of the other as a way of shielding against enquiry into their own lives. Julia had quickly offered the information that she was currently single, although she had several offers on the table. Mack had countered that it might be time for her to move to another table. She seemed to enjoy the flirting, but he quickly reverted to more honest lines of enquiry, momentarily uncomfortable with the reality of what he hoped was developing between them.

Soon they found common interests, and had talked about Peter Cook; The Specials; the effect that the Two Tone and Ska music movement had on racial relations in the UK; the photographer, Philippe Halsman, and the quadriplegic cartoonist, John Callahan. They discovered they both enjoyed making their own bread, and swapped tips and recipes. Neither had much interest in politics, and Julia laughed when Mack suggested the principle that anyone interested in being a politician should be prevented from being one. It was as if they had silently agreed on a test, a first hurdle, an almost scientific analysis to identify if they were compatible: if they had sufficient interests in common. And, without realising it, the fact that they had both adopted this tack had, in itself, registered at a subconscious level that this was a relationship worth considering.

Around 12.45am, Julia had announced that she needed to be up in the morning. She was staying at a friend's house in town and needed to get back. Mack had asked her about the friend and they ended up talking for a further half an hour. Eventually, Julia rose to go, and Mack got up out of his chair too. There was an awkward moment as Mack began to speak, but Julia firmly held out her hand and thanked him for a beguiling evening; an action which Mack felt contained the perfect mix of strength of purpose, taking control of a situation, and flattery. He shook her hand, an act which felt insufficient. From now on, he hoped, it would be kisses on the cheek for greetings and farewells.

Unable to sleep, he felt elated, buzzing, but he was also getting a little drunk. He had decided to push the process on a little further, almost as a sort of celebration for meeting Julia, and so ordered a local bourbon in the hotel bar. The barman had been professional, reminding Mack of a time when he had been in Edinburgh on tour with Mamal – he and Kent Nicholls had sampled eight different single malt whiskies that the barman had recommended to them, not realising they cost five pounds per shot.

Having walked confidently down the corridor towards his room, Mack now realised that he had sat in one of the occasional pointless armchairs. The bourbon had been 'a large one', and it occurred to him that it might have been one more drink than he actually needed. Perhaps these armchairs served a purpose after all.

Struggling to his feet, Mack strode on down the hall, kicking the leg of a table as he did so. It was only a glancing blow; the potpourri and lamp tottered slightly but stayed in place. He turned the corridor and reached the door to his room, which was situated directly opposite the room that Jay was staying in. He took out his plastic key card, opened the door, and went inside.

The door shut automatically. He let his coat slip off his arms and drop to the floor, then slowly leaned forwards until his head rested against the wall.

The sound of a door handle being carefully turned across the corridor seeped into his consciousness. So Jay was back before him. He hadn't thought of that possibility; him and Kent seemed to be planning on making a night of it when they had left the bar earlier. Why would he be going out again now? There could be only one explanation. He had been successful with some girl, and it was her that was leaving. Drunkenly giggling to himself, Mack put his eye to the peephole that was in the middle of his door. I've got to get a look at this, he thought to himself. I'm either going to be congratulating him in the morning, or I'm going to be taking the piss out of him.

Through the small fisheye lens, Mack saw Jay's head gingerly poke round the door, looking up and down the corridor. Oh dear, thought Mack, this doesn't bode well. She can't be too good-looking if he's being this careful to make sure she's not spotted leaving his room. It could only be Mack that Jay was worried might see – Harpo's room was on a different floor, something he had insisted upon from the very first night of the tour.

He saw Jay turn and talk to the person behind him. Then the door opened and Mack saw Kent Nicholls stride out of the room with his usual arrogant swagger, walking casually past Jay down the corridor.

Mack jerked his eye away from the peephole as if it had suddenly become red hot. Kent Nicholls? What in hell's name was he doing there? And why was Jay being so careful about it? What was Jay hiding?

Okay, he thought to himself, okay, calm down. Kent Nicholls is starting to infect me – I'm seeing plots and motives everywhere. All that has happened is that the two of them went to a party, then Kent Nicholls came back for a nightcap, for another drink, maybe something stronger. No big deal.

Then why the subterfuge? That furtive peek up and down the corridor had been a dead giveaway. It can only have been Mack that he had been looking out for; there was no one else likely to be walking past their door that would matter to him. Kent Nicholls was unconcerned, but then he always was. But Jay clearly didn't want Mack to know that Kent Nicholls had been in his room. Why?

There was only one obvious conclusion. They must have been talking about him. Kent Nicholls must have been doing research, and was pumping Jay, getting everything out of him that he could.

Mack went to the window, carefully opened the wooden shutters, and stared out past the bushes and trees which were lit up orange by the streetlights. What did Jay know? What had he told Kent Nicholls that he knew Mack wouldn't have wanted him to divulge?

Jay didn't know everything. He had been such a big part of Mack's life, especially after that impossible period leading up to the divorce, and Mack had needed to be so careful. Indeed, Jay and Johnny were so close that Jay was the very last person who should know his motives for being in that hotel room. That boy was so special, he had to be protected from that particular truth at all costs.

Then there was Kent Nicholls. That bastard was out to get him somehow, but Jay didn't know enough to give him the ammunition he would have so dearly loved to get his hands on. But Kent Nicholls knew stuff about Mack. Is that why Jay was looking so worried? Had Jay been told something? Had Kent Nicholls told him some lies, half-truths, embellishments?

The point was that Jay didn't want Mack to know that they were talking. Which meant it must have been something about him. Which meant he had a right to know. He wasn't going to find out by reading it in print, oh no. There's no way Kent Nicholls was going to write another article to ruin his life. It would come out now, or not at all.

He rubbed the bridge of his nose as if unable to concentrate on two things at once. He was struggling to differentiate between the muzziness in his head from earlier and the effects of the variety of cocktails and other drinks he had consumed throughout the evening. It was as though something was just out of sight, but he could feel it was there; something oppressive, as if pieces were falling into place, but behind a closed door. He knew there was an answer to the last fifteen or so years of his life, but it remained just out of reach.

Mack made his mind up. He was going to get to the bottom of this sordid business. Hang the consequences.

He opened his door, not so worried about the noise he made this time, and tried Jay's door. It was locked. He knocked, quietly, feeling angry, straining to retain his manners and composure.

Jay opened the door, rubbing his eyes in a hackneyed and comedic attempt to appear as if he'd just woken up. "Oh, hello, mate," he said, yawning and stretching his arms. It reminded Mack of watching some bad children's television, as if Jay was trying to act like he was a tree.

"Fuck off," said Mack, and walked past him into the room. It was identical to his own, except in reverse, which disorientated him for a moment. He stood, slightly swaying, then chose a stiff-backed chair and sat down.

Jay walked into the room after him, looking nervous. "Mack?" he said, carefully. "Are you okay? How did you get on with Julia?"

"Fuck Julia," said Mack, and then didn't bother to correct himself. His tendency towards verbosity increased as he drank more, then he would usually topple over the edge of inebriation and into sullen silence, punctuated by abuse. Right now, that fall had been aided by the shock of betrayal that he currently felt. He didn't feel like being polite or subtle, he wasn't in the mood. He just wanted to get to the point.

"What the fuck were you and Kent Nicholls talking about?"

"Kent?" said Jay, feigning surprise, and Mack almost laughed at his friend. He seemed rather drunk himself, as the two bottles of Verve Clicquot sitting on the writing table testified to: one empty, one mainly full. Two glasses stood next to them. He smiled rather pathetically, with his eyebrows raised as high as they could go without actually reaching his hairline.

Mack looked him in the eye. "Yes, Kent Nicholls. Don't dick about, Jay. I just saw him leave your room. Furtively. Which can only

205

mean one thing – you were talking about me. He's a journalist, for Christ's sake, Jay. What have I been telling you for the past few weeks, over and over again? You have to be careful who you talk to, especially that sodding bastard. So what was it? What do you know? What did he tell you?"

Jay sat down on the other chair, leaned forward in his seat, and put his head in his hands. Neither of them spoke for a minute, until eventually Jay got up and walked over to the bottle of champagne. He poured two glasses and handed one to Mack.

"No, thank you," said Mack, aggressively, trying to keep his focus on his anger.

"Take it," said Jay. "You might need it."

Mack took the glass and put it on the table next to his chair.

Jay sat down opposite him again. Mack noticed that he looked tired all of a sudden. For a moment his anger dropped and he felt worried for his old friend. "What have you done, Jay," he said, in a calmer voice. "What have you done?"

"Something I enjoy doing, and have done for quite a long time now," said Jay.

"Eh?" said Mack, confused.

"Mack. It's pretty simple, mate. I'm gay."

Mack looked at him. Then looked at him some more. His brain seemed to have stopped. No thought crossed his mind for at least ten seconds, while his subconscious worked away, feverishly trying to sort all his previous memories, preconceptions, prejudices and fears into a new order. Eventually, all he could do was repeat back to Jay, "You're gay."

"Yes. And this evening I had sex with Kent Nicholls."

"Oh, Christ." Mack continued to stare at him, open-mouthed, his mind now totally blank. It was as if his body had suffered a shock and had shut down all unnecessary activities while it sent all resources to the deal with the issue. They hadn't been talking about him. They had been having sex. This wasn't about him. It was about them. "Just give me a moment here, would you," he said, eventually. Jay hadn't spoken.

After a few moments, Mack got up out of his chair, took his glass, and walked to the window. This room overlooked the car park, and Mack looked down, not actually seeing anything. After a few minutes, during which time Jay sat quietly but anxiously, Mack turned round and addressed him.

"Okay. We've got two things here. You're gay. Right?"

"Yes. Well, I'm actually bisexual."

Mack's mouth worked before his brain had a chance to stop him. "Isn't that having it both ways?" he said.

Jay laughed a little too loudly. "You just can't help but make a gag, can you," he blurted. After another awkward chuckle, he said. "Yes, I have sex with men. And this evening I had sex with Kent Nicholls."

"Right," said Mack, his brow now starting to furrow.

"Yes," said Jay.

"Why?"

"Why?" Jay repeated.

"Yes, why. Whose idea was it? What did he get you to talk about?"

"No." said Jay, shaking his head. "That's not it. I had sex with Kent Nicholls because we got on really well tonight – he's a very charismatic guy. We both had a bit to drink, and he told me some of his tales of being on the road with bands over the years. He's done some pretty wild things, and he admitted that he's had sex with both men and women. Then he asked if I wanted to have sex with him. We came straight here from the bar – there was no party, that was just a cover story – and we've been at it ever since. Simple as that."

Mack winced slightly at his friend's terminology, despite himself. "Yeah. Simple as that. Of course." Mack smiled weakly and downed the glass of Verve Clicquot in one gulp. Wordlessly, he stuck his arm out with the glass at the end of it. Jay got up and refilled the glass. "Are those sandwiches fresh?" Mack asked, pointing to a plate on the table.

"Not really," said Jay, handing him the plate.

Mack grabbed a ham sandwich and took a large bite. The bread was crunchy on the outside, soft just beneath. "Good enough," he said, and shoved the rest of the sandwich into his mouth.

"So that's it?" he said, swallowing.

"That's it." Jay smiled nervously at Mack. "Bit of a shock, eh?"

"A bit?!" exclaimed Mack. Something was still bothering him. "So come on," he continued, painting an air of insouciance, "what happened? I confess I'm slightly struggling to take this on board just at the moment, given that the majority of discussions you and I have had over gawd knows how many years have been focussed on the female form. What was it that turned a happily married man into a happily divorced, gay man?"

"Do you know, that's something I've thought about long and hard," said Jay, and took a sip from his glass, collecting his thoughts.

"Is it just me," said Mack, "or is it common that when a straight man talks to a gay man he hears double entendres in everything that is said?"

"Probably just your paranoia that I might be sitting here thinking about having sex with *you*," said Jay. His laugh cut short when he noticed the look on Mack's face. "Oh, sorry, bit too soon for that kind of joke is it?"

Mack smiled. "Well," he said, moving swiftly on, "what happened?"

"You know that story I gave you?" said Jay. "About my wife going to Scotland and returning to find me in bed with another woman?"

"Of course. Wasn't that true?"

"Partly. The other woman was Sarah."

"Your business partner?"

"Yes. And another man."

"Bloody hell. All those smutty comments, I always thought you were all talk, like me!"

"I was, honest! In fact I still am. But Sarah and I were talking that night, after the staff had gone home. I think I'd made some crack and she took me seriously. She'd been single for a while and seemed to want to talk about sex. So we did – I thought we were just chewing the fat."

"Stop it."

Jay smiled. "Anyway, after a while she said that she'd always wanted to have a three-way. I think that's what she'd been building up to all along."

"Jeez, Jay."

"Yeah, I know, how lucky was I! Me and two women!" Jay saw the look of disapproval on Mack's face, and quickly got back to the story. "Anyway, so she fixed it up for later that night at her house. I turned up expecting another woman. But that's not what she had in mind. By three-way, she had meant with two blokes. Well, having made the trip, I thought, why not? Thing was, I didn't really know the rules of a three-way. I kind of assumed that he and I would, well, you know, be at separate ends, shall we say. But it turned out that he was bisexual. I didn't think it counted as 'gay' if there were three of us, so I kind of went with the flow."

"And that gave you a taste for it? Oh Christ, now I'm at it."

"Yeah, I enjoyed it. So I sought out a bit more. And I came to a very important conclusion."

"What was that?"

"I realised that the only person who can truly understand how much a man's cock means to him is another man."

Mack sat for a moment, looking into the landscape picture on the wall. It was a fairly bland picture – the hotel took no chances in its choice of art. He didn't particularly see the picture, his mental energies were still being used in directions that more than five minutes ago he never thought would have been necessary. After a few moments, he started to laugh. And laugh.

Jay laughed too, a little more cautiously. "Do you like that line?" he said. "I've had it knocking around my head for a while now."

Mack slid off the front of his chair and onto his knees; he was holding his sides, laughing as a release, laughing out of relief, laughing out his tension, and laughing because it was just so damn funny. After a minute or two he took a deep breath, sat back down, and looked at the man who had been by his side for such a long time now.

"Mate, I get that. Actually, I do get that." He paused, catching his breath, still smiling. "So, all that chat about women and girls that you'd indulged me in over the years, all a front?"

"Actually, no, I do still like women. You'd probably define me as bisexual, although I don't really think of it that way. Actually I prefer to think of it as multi-sexual! As much as possible!"

Mack looked at his oldest friend, buzzing and so alive with energy, and suddenly felt tired. It was as if he was staring out from behind a thick transparent mask, watching Jay laughing and gesticulating at him. He was involved in the action, he was there, in the middle of it all, and yet everything seemed to be muffled. He suddenly felt exhausted through every ounce of his body. The weight of years of solitude and reliance, of worry and silence, pressed against the inside of his skull.

Years of having to put on a front and make sure there was as few people around him to see it as possible. Jay had lived a lie to him, and he could only love his friend all the more for it. He was finally not alone; finally he felt as if he had not been the only one carrying a burden by himself. To know that his buddy was carrying his own sack of issues alongside him all this time made him feel exhausted, but content. He closed his eyes, and felt himself relax. Perhaps for the first time in sixteen years, he felt his shoulders unclench themselves.

"Dude. You okay?"

Mack opened his eyes, and saw Jay, still sat opposite him, leaning forwards on his knees with a concerned expression on his face.

"You alright?"

Mack smiled. "Yeah. Yeah, I'm okay, mate. It's just been quite an evening, you know?" Mack got up and walked towards the door, then stopped. A thought occurred. He turned, as if in thought, but actually trying to find the right words. "How did Kent Nicholls know you were gay?"

"What do you mean?" said Jay.

"You said he asked you if you wanted to have sex with him. How did he know you were gay?"

Jay thought for a moment. "I don't know. Never occurred to me. He just asked me."

"And did Kent Nicholls ask you anything about me?"

Jay laughed. "It was a bit difficult for him, what with my cock in his…"

"Too soon!" said Mack, quickly, putting his hand up. "Still way too soon."

"Sorry," said Jay, "I think I'm still on a bit of a high." He laughed and put on a Southern drawl, flourishing his hands dramatically as he spoke. "This poor girl's head is all in a whirl."

"Jay. Did Kent ask you anything about me?"

"Yeah. Of course we talked about you. We talked about everything, it seems. After we'd, well, you know, 'finished', we chatted for a bit. Kent wanted to know a bit more about me. He's actually very sweet, you know."

Mack sighed. "Well," he said, a little impatiently. "What did he want to know?"

"Oh, lots of things. About Johnny. About your divorce. Asking how I had helped you. You know, after what you had done."

"Did he ask about Al?"

"Al? No, he never came up. Why do you ask?"

"The dog that didn't bark," replied Mack.

"Huh?" said Jay. "Say what?"

"Never mind. Goodnight, my old mate," said Mack, opening the door. "I am going to hang out of my bedroom window and have a last, totally unnecessary cigar. But tomorrow, on the way to New Orleans, I want you to tell me all about what it's like to have sex with another man."

Chapter 29

Johnny stood in front of the door and waited, having just rung the ancient-looking iron bell. The house was on the end of a terrace, formerly a corner plot on a crossroads, and was typical of those in the French Quarter of New Orleans, where he now stood. The intricate ironwork went from the floor to the roof, with a balcony on the first floor. The steps up to the wooden front door had frosted patterned glass in the panels and more ironwork on the surround of the door; the bell was an ancient pull system. Johnny had heard the bell clang from somewhere deep inside the house.

He had arrived in New Orleans a few hours ago, and had checked into the hotel at the bottom of Canal Street. It was filled with conference attendees, each in their identikit outfits of polo shirt, khaki shorts, knee-length socks and sensible sandals. He had put in a quick call to his father, agreeing where to meet them all that evening, and then jumped into a cab to take him to the other side of the historic French Quarter.

There was no answer for around a minute, so he took out his mobile phone and checked the address that had been texted to him. This was certainly the right house. He was reaching to pull the bell again, when the door opened and a woman greeted him.

"Hi!" she said, in an overly friendly way. She was aged around fifty, he guessed. Her skin was pale and freckled and she had frizzy blonde hair that seemed to hover over her head as if held up by a static charge. A huge white dress shirt made a decent attempt at covering her large frame, with a pair of dark blue jeans poking apologetically out underneath. The shirt was splattered with paint, and yet her hands and face were clean.

"Hi," replied Johnny. "I'm looking for Al Smart. Is he here?"

"Al Smart?" the woman replied. Her accent, to Johnny's ears, did not sound like it came from the Deep South, but more likely from New York. She seemed unsure as to how to answer, like a bad actor forgetting their lines. "Oh, Al Smart. Yeah, Al, well he's, um, probably not going to be here. He's left, yeah, he's left, I'm sorry about that." She glanced over her shoulder just slightly, then smiled at Johnny.

"Okay, thanks," said Johnny, and walked away quickly. As soon as he heard the door shut behind him, he ran around the corner of the building, just in time to see Al Smart dive through the open passenger door of a black Pontiac G5. The car was no more than twenty metres away from him, but it immediately drove away in the opposite direction. Johnny could tell that it was a hired car; he had seen rows upon rows of them at the airport.

He stared intently at the back of the heads of Al and the driver, trying to remember any detail possible. What remained of his hair was dyed black and kept very short. There was an outside chance he might recognise the back of Al's head in the future.

The driver, however, was wearing a black fedora hat, a style Johnny recognised from old Humphrey Bogart movies of Raymond Chandler books that he had watched with his father as a teenager.

With no other way of getting a visual clue as to his identity, Johnny clenched his fists in frustration and began the walk back to his hotel.

Chapter 30

The morning had been a busy one, and Mary didn't feel she really had anything to show for it. She had read three picture books to David and Grace, got them started on making a collage with paints and glue, and made a den out of sheets and chairs which they had played in while Mary prepared lunch. And now they were both asleep for an afternoon nap, toe-to-toe with heads at either end of the sofa. Baby Mozart was playing softly from the stereo as they slept, and Mary sat in the single chair and looked at them.

It was the first time in a week or so that Mary had found time for her own thoughts. The gnawing feeling that something wasn't right had been eating away at her, but she hadn't wanted to allow the thoughts to come forward because she was either thinking of the children, cooking food, or trying to get to sleep. Now, however, she unbolted the iron gates in her mind and allowed those thoughts to come tearing out towards her.

Ideas had been sifted and sorted since she last allowed herself thinking time. The image of what she saw in the hotel room that day was still clear to her. The woman had been naked on the bed, or perhaps had a towel or a dressing gown or something like that underneath her. She had been rubbing her leg on her father. And Al had been watching. All these things were facts.

However, her father had been fully dressed. That was a fact as well. Why? Why would he have been dressed if he had been having sex? At the age of fourteen such things hadn't entered her mind, and she doubted if she'd given this level of detail to her mother, who had been the only person she had talked to about what she had seen. All she had really assimilated at the time was the naked woman and the presence of her father.

The facts, what she had seen, clearly pointed to her father intending to have sex with this woman. He had admitted it. He had lost his marriage because of it. He had lost his daughter because of it. So either this was true, or something else was going on that her father didn't want anyone to find out about. Something that he would sacrifice his marriage for. He would have known that possibility existed beforehand if it had been sex. But something he would risk losing his daughter for? He couldn't have known that it would be his daughter that caught him red-handed, so that possibility was just an unfortunate happenstance. And yet he had not made a great deal of effort with her over the years. It was as if he just accepted his fate. As if by trying to undo any of the damage, the secret would be out. So perhaps the secret was about her after all.

A sudden thought hit Mary. She had often questioned whether her father was her real father. But what if both her parents were not real? What if she actually *was* adopted? Oh my god, she thought. What if Al Smart and this woman were her real parents? Was that why they had come back − is that what they were arguing about? But that wouldn't explain why the woman had been naked. And Mary didn't look like either the woman or Al Smart. Not that she was the spitting image of her mother or father, mind you, but no, it just didn't feel right. And yet something was wrong; something was missing.

David and Grace snored gently on, oblivious to the mangled logic and befuddled conclusions that were being drawn just a few feet away. All the time Mary was ruminating and turning round the ideas and thoughts, she never once took her eyes off her children.

So she was looking for a secret that was about her, and which was so monumental that her father would risk his marriage over it. There simply was nothing she could think of that would be so massive that didn't involve the true nature of her parentage.

But one possibility was starting to creep up − perhaps her father hadn't been quite such a terrible person after all. Maybe, just maybe, she had been a little hard on him over the years. Events had unfolded so quickly at the time − the way he had just accepted the blame and moved out of their house − that Mary had been happy to accept his explanation. But now Johnny had brought a view of those events from a completely different angle.

She stood up slowly from her chair, ensuring that she did not wake the children. Walking into the kitchen, she took her mobile phone from where it had been plugged into the electric socket to charge, and sent her brother a text. It read: 'Been thinking. Lots. Can you send me Dad's tel no, ta.'

Chapter 31

That evening, Johnny joined up with his father, Jay and Harpo at their hotel. The four of them had taken a taxi to the Maple Leaf, a small club in a district of New Orleans some distance from the tourist orientated French Quarter.

The Maple Leaf was the one venue that Mack had insisted upon when Johnny had been putting the tour itinerary together. Not much to look at from the outside, it was a traditional New Orleans town house, with a wooden panelled front painted yellow and white and wooden railings on a first floor terrace. It seemed to Mack to signify everything that was mysterious about the city. It looked like a small house from the front, detached from the other houses on the street, but it actually went back a considerable distance. The bar was in a long, thin room, and was the first room you entered. The main part of the venue, where the music took place, was another long, thin room; the ornate decoration shiny and dark brown where the nicotine stains had been covered in lacquer. At one end, nearest the entrance, was a slightly raised area which constituted the stage.

Lighting was sparse, and in order to put the lights down, the MC or a band member would simply reach up and unscrew the light bulb over the stage area. Recently, extra touches had been added; in particular a string of fairy lights around the walls and ceiling in front of the stage, so that when the bulb was unscrewed, the musicians could at least still see what they were doing.

Mack owned a scratched vinyl album called *The Main Event: Live at the Maple Leaf*, which had been played countless times. He had built the club into a mysterious wonderland of music, smoke and happiness. The album was by the Rebirth Brass Band, a second line marching band traditional in New Orleans, but one which had taken that tradition into uncharted musical waters. Aside from a drummer who stood while playing and had only a snare drum and a cymbal, all the other instruments were brass, with a huge tuba playing the basslines, and lots of calling and cheering from the band. It sounded like the biggest party ever, and Mack wanted to see it, in locale.

So Johnny had pulled off his biggest coup of the tour. He had arranged for the band to play as a support act for the Rebirth Brass Band at the Maple Leaf. They would go on at about 11pm and the Rebirth would turn up through the evening, as they all got back from the various other gigs that they had been playing that night. It would not be a huge crowd, but it would increase in size as they played and people turned up for the main event. Mack didn't care, he was just so thrilled to be in the middle of everything he loved about America: great food, wonderful music, and a party.

The walls almost dripped with memories of some of the greatest musicians New Orleans had ever produced: Dr. John, Professor Longhair, the Wild Magnolias, James Booker, the Dirty Dozen Brass Band. The set that the three of them played that evening had been one of the best on tour, the atmosphere soaking into their veins as the swampy, Cajun aspect of their music reverberated, as if feeding off the history around them. The room had been fairly full, as those arriving to sit at the bar in the other room before the Rebirth came on were instead attracted by what they could hear: the unusual mixture of guitar, bass, and Jay's unusual noises and beats complementing Mack's voice, which had been more soulful that night than it had been for many years.

Johnny watched the performance from a position by the mixing desk, as he always did, so that he could hear what the sound mixer heard. To him, his father's singing – which he had heard thousands, probably tens of thousands of times before – sounded as though it had found a deeper resonance. He incorrectly assumed it was because of the enjoyment his father was taking from the experience of finally being back and part of the outside world.

Towards the end of the set, Johnny spied Kent Nicholls. The journalist put his head through the door and pulled it back out again, presumably to go into the bar. There were enough people in the room by that time for Johnny to leave and go into the bar without being noticed by the band. He picked his way through the crowd, now thick enough to mean he had to gently squeeze his way through, and saw Kent Nicholls sitting at the bar ordering a Bloody Mary. The Maple Leaf made it the Creole way, with lots of Tabasco and Worcestershire sauce.

He still had on his sunglasses and long coat, the tails of which draped down the sides of the high bar stool that he was sat on. It gave the impression that he was floating in mid-air.

"Make that two," Johnny said to the bartender, as he took his seat next to Kent Nicholls.

"My man," said Kent, offering his hand, fingers up so that they would lock thumbs, giving each other half a high five, half a handshake. "Nice work, getting the guys a gig at the Leaf."

"Seriously cool place," replied Johnny, watching the bartender go to work, a slight nervousness entering him as he watched the amount of Tabasco being added.

"How long are the boys on for?" Kent asked, now back in his previous position of arms on the bar, leaning heavily forwards.

"Three more songs."

"Okay. So." Kent Nicholls picked up the tall glass that had been put in front of him, moved the celery to the side of the glass, and took a long drink.

The bartender stood in front of them, looking at them both. At first Johnny thought it was because he was waiting for a response to his creation. Then he realised with a start that it was because they hadn't paid for the drinks yet. He looked at the receipt on the small metal tray that had been carefully placed between the two of them. Kent Nicholls made no motion to reach for his wallet, and so Johnny, now understanding the relationship between the three men around the bar, took out a twenty dollar note and put it on the tray. The bartender nodded his head forwards slightly, and took the tray away.

Kent Nicholls put down his glass, and, to Johnny's mind, consciously failed to thank him, as if making a point of it; as though thanking was not cool. He found himself realising that there was something about this man that irritated him. Something he had only noticed since he had told his father. All the time he had known the journalist, he had been courteous, going out of his way to be helpful. But there was something about his demeanour today that was somehow less respectful. Johnny wondered if Kent Nicholls had got all he needed, and was turning off the charm.

Slowly and self-consciously turning to Johnny, Kent Nicholls said, "Well, how did you get on? Did you find him?"

Johnny put his glass down, started to speak, then had to pause for a moment, while his throat tried to regain its previous balance. "Whoah," he said. "That's one spicy Bloody Mary."

"Yep. That's the N'Orleans way." He pronounced the name of the city as if it was one word.

"Not had the best of days. Same as Galway. He had just left when I got there."

"Shit," said Kent Nicholls impassionedly. It sounded more like 'shee-it'.

"Yeah. Your information is good, but your timing is not." Johnny didn't say anything about seeing Al driven away by the man in the fedora hat. It occurred to him that the journalist was helping for his own reasons, and decided to keep some information to himself.

The two of them sat for a moment, drinking. After a few large sips, it was Johnny that spoke next.

"Someone is telling him, Kent. The only logical conclusion. Who?"

"Dunno. I've got my sources, and lots of them. There ain't much love lost out there for Al Smart. He's pissed off too many people over the years. I can't think of a single person who would piss on him if he were on fire. Believe me, there's no shortage of people happy to tell me where he is. All I'm doing is passing on that information to you."

"Making me more and more determined," said Johnny. "Someone is trying to stop me from finding him. So someone is trying to hide something. Whatever that something is, affects Mack. My dad. I want to know what it is. Clear his name."

"Why don't you just ask him?" said Kent Nicholls, his tone unchanging. "Straight out. What happened in that hotel room, Dad? Why did you dump on Mum, Dad?"

Johnny continued looking into his drink. This man seemed to be enjoying himself, perhaps a little too much. He was helping Johnny to find Al, to find the man who had been in that hotel room, watching his father having sex with another woman, and yet whose presence had been covered up, or, at best, ignored. Johnny suddenly had a feeling of being manipulated, of being used to unearth a story for the journalist.

"Why are you helping me?" he said, still looking into his drink.

"Cos you asked me to," Kent Nicholls replied.

Johnny looked at their reflection in the mirror behind the bar. Kent Nicholls' head was angled slightly down and facing forwards, but with his sunglasses in place. Johnny had no idea where he was looking.

"And cos I'm such a nice guy."

"Dad was not happy when I told him you were coming on the tour. Why?"

The journalist turned in his seat to face the younger man. Johnny felt pretty certain he was being looked at now, but continued to face forwards.

"Let's just say the two of us got history," said Kent Nicholls. As if driven by a reflex, he moved his jaw, and winced slightly.

Johnny turned to stare into the sunglasses. "Mack doesn't want me to find Al. But you are helping me. Mack doesn't like you." He paused. "Maybe you are helping me to annoy Mack. Okay, I can live with that, perhaps you're not a very nice person, that's okay."

Pushing his glass away from him by a few centimetres, Johnny swivelled on his bar stool to face the other man. He had come to a decision.

"Did you know Al Smart was blackmailing my father for royalties to his songs," he said, making a statement more than asking a question. "That's why he came back. But why was he in the hotel room that day? Who was that woman? And why does my father not want me to find out?" There was a longer pause, as if Johnny was waiting for an answer to a question he had not yet asked. When he received no reply, he asked it. "And what do you care?"

Kent Nicholls lifted his right arm. His index finger hooked gently behind the sunglasses and lowered them slowly down his nose. Johnny had never seen this man do anything with his sunglasses except wear them. He half expected to see red, bloodshot eyes; swollen and sunken after years of partying and drug abuse. But instead he saw piercing blue eyes, with a stare that seemed to bore through his head and down into his soul. After a few additional moments to increase the drama, Kent Nicholls spoke.

"Tell me, Johnny. Do you ever have those moments when you look at yourself in the mirror, and think to yourself, 'Why do I have friends? Why do people like me?'"

Johnny looked down for a moment, his face impassive. A slight sigh slipped from his lips. "Yes," he said, looking back up at Kent. "Yes, I do."

Kent Nicholls leaned forwards, increasing the intensity of his glare. "I don't," he said, and he pushed the bridge of his sunglasses softly so that they slowly slipped back into place, his eyes slinking back into their hiding place to await the next unsuspecting victim. He turned back to his drink and continued talking, quietly, with a level voice, as if explaining to a small boy why he could not stay up late.

"Me and your dad got history, son. And I don't just bear a grudge. I wear it. I become it. I live it. I AM the grudge." He lifted back his head and drained the glass.

"Know what?" he continued. "When you've got somebody by the balls, you don't stop squeezing. You might pause for a while. Perhaps you might just loosen the grip slightly, to give them hope. Because hope is the greatest tormentor of them all. Hope that you might be about to stop, hope that you will finally leave them alone. But you don't let go. Oh no. What you do is you give those little round balls a gentle little stroke, just so that they know you are still there. And then you start to squeeze again."

Kent Nicholls slipped off the chair and put the glass back on the bar. As he stood up he actually became lower than when he was sitting down. "You wanted to find Al. It suits me that you want to go snooping round your father's past – anything to wind that old bastard up is good for me. You want to know what happened in that hotel room. But you didn't want your father to know that you were trying to help him, because your father doesn't want to be helped. He never did. The two of you are like two peas scraped out of the same fucking pod."

If Johnny could see those eyes again now, he knew that they would be burning brightly.

"Let me tell you a few home truths, little boy. Your father has secrets in his closet. They ain't always very nice secrets. You think that asshole can do no wrong. Well, he's your father, I can understand that. You know what I say to my father? Nothing. He's almost as big a prick as your father is. Difference between you and me is that I recognised it. Did something about it. He wouldn't let me borrow his car when I was nineteen years old, for the biggest date of my life, spiteful old bastard. So I torched his car and left home that same evening. Didn't leave a note. Didn't need to. We've not spoken since.

"I'm going to get you one more address. And it's up to you whether you go searching for Al Smart. But when you do, just make sure you have the right questions ready for him.

"You think I'm on your side? I'm not on anyone's side, boy. I've helped you out because it suits me, not because I like you. I don't like you. But don't take it personally. I don't like anyone.

"You want some information from me? Okay. I know why Al Smart was in your home town at that time. He had debts. He was being forced to blackmail your father, to try and get some of his royalties from that mindless bit of pop music he wrote. Your mother knew about that. So why did she still divorce him? Maybe she just came to the same conclusion I did about him.

"Don't blame Al. He was an egotistical little shit, always was. But think on this. Your father has never pretended he wasn't having an affair with another woman. He's never protested his innocence. Ask yourself why. Even better, just ask him."

Kent Nicholls continued to glare from behind his sunglasses for a moment, then turned and walked out of the establishment.

Johnny stared at the back of the black leather coat for a moment, as it swaggered away. He continued to stare, even after Kent Nicholls had turned right out of the bar and out of sight.

So Al Smart had been blackmailing his father. Which must surely mean that there were other people involved. It seemed so obvious now. It was the woman. Did Al have photographs of his father with the woman and used them to blackmail him; threatened to show them to his mother?

And yet… something wasn't sitting right. Why would his father have agreed to be in the room? Al was sat *with* them, not hiding. And once he had been found out, why didn't he tell his mother what had happened? Surely he could have spoken to her – she would have understood. The sex with the woman angle didn't work. There must have been something else. In fact was there some*one* else – were Al and the woman doing somebody else's dirty work?

The conclusion he reached was the same one that he had reached weeks ago. He needed to find Al Smart and ask him what happened.

Loud applause and an occasional whistle from the other room signified that the set had come to an end. People started coming into the bar, so Johnny picked up his own drink and fought against the tide. As he entered the room, he could see his father sitting at the front of the stage, with a short line of people waiting for him; several of them were ladies only a little more than half his age, all of whom seemed eager to speak to him.

Johnny spoke with Harpo and Jay briefly, making sure they had everything they needed. He handed some money to Harpo, then went over to his father, who was now talking to a woman with a slightly disturbing amount of black curly hair. He was still sitting on the stage, and she was sitting next to him. Something about how they had arranged themselves gave Johnny the feeling that they had known each other for a long time, although he knew they hadn't.

"Hey, Johnny," said Mack. "Meet Julia. She's the photographer who's working with us." He and Julia both stood up.

"Hi," said Julia, holding out her hand.

Johnny shook her hand and smiled at her, cautiously. "Hi," he said, "are you with Kent?"

Julia laughed. "Why do I think you sounded a wee bit nervous when you said that! Don't worry, I think he's a creep too. I was a late draft into the team for a friend of mine."

"Ah," said Johnny. "You two old buddies?" He pointed at the two of them. Julia laughed, slightly embarrassed.

"No," she said. "But your father is a very charming man, one who has been assiduously applying that charm to me. Not without some success, I may add."

Mack positively beamed with delight. "Wow," he said. "That's the first time you've said that."

"Well," said Julia, "you've clearly been on your best behaviour. I thought it deserved acknowledging." She turned to Johnny. "Did I see you talking with Kent at the bar?"

"Yes," said Johnny, not failing to notice the instant change in his father's expression at the thought that Kent Nicholls was still in the building. "Getting to know each other better. He's just left, Dad, don't worry."

"Ah," said Julia, "I'd best be careful. I, uh, got told off this morning by him. Told me to…" She looked at Mack and smiled sheepishly. "Well, let's just say he didn't approve of me fraternising with a client. Said it might compromise the article."

"You know what," said Mack. "That's the second time you've told me about things I've done to hurt or anger Kent Nicholls. And I get the same feeling of deep pleasure every time it happens." He looked at Johnny. "Sorry, mate. Maybe I should have said before. Kent Nicholls and I just don't get on."

"Yeah," said Johnny, "I'm getting that idea."

A man excused himself into their conversation and spoke a few words to Mack, congratulating him on the performance that night. The man was a musician himself; he had already played for three different bands in three different bars that night: two for tourists, one for fun. They spoke for a few minutes about New Orleans, the man passing on some tips of the best venues and artists in town. Johnny and Julia stood awkwardly either side of the two men, exchanging the occasional smile, waiting for Mack to finish his conversation.

The man gave Mack the customary vertical handshake, and Mack looked up at Johnny, who couldn't help but feel happy that his father had chosen him to share his excitement with first. His father having a girlfriend would be a wonderful thing, of course, and in many ways it would have been the ultimate conclusion of the project Johnny had embarked upon when he had first set up the website to publicise his father's music: to reintegrate his father into the outside world. But it would not be easy letting go when his father did finally move on. The irony of this was lost on him.

"Bit of a star, Dad", he said.

Mack looked up at his son and smiled. "Thanks, mate. This gig is your finest hour. No question about that. And I get to see the Rebirth next. Man, this is the tour highlight – don't see how anything can beat this."

"Well, the final show in LA might give it a challenge."

"Is that definitely on?"

"Yeah. It's part of the launch party for the TV show. Gonna be a big deal."

"I am so going to be there for that," said Julia. "Wow, Johnny, that's amazing, you have really pulled it off."

Johnny looked down at the ground and didn't speak. His head wobbled and his shoulders shrugged.

"Yeah," said Mack, "honestly, son, I could not be prouder if you'd just told me you'd been sleeping with Miss Jamaica and just discovered she has an older sister."

"Okay," said Julia, "if that's the quality of the conversation, I'm going to the bar. Beer?"

"Sorry, force of habit," said Mack, rather more meekly than Johnny had heard in his voice before.

Julia walked to the bar, with both sets of their eyes on her back.

"Seriously," said Mack, turning back to Johnny, "you've done an extraordinary job. My only complaint, if I had to have one, would be that you've not been with us for much of it."

"Sorry," said Johnny. "Got stuff to sort. Have to go again tomorrow. Something else going on. Something you'll be pleased with, if I can pull it off."

"What is it?"

"I can't tell you."

"Why not?" Mack's tone of voice had become fatherly and firm again, slipping back into his role of parent.

"A surprise. Don't want you disappointed if I can't sort it. Anyway, everything's going smoothly, that's important. Just want you to be happy."

"Oh, I am." Mack smiled, more in order to give his son encouragement than because he felt like smiling. It showed in the quality of the smile. "I am enjoying it. I've just....well, I've just got a few more things on my mind than I thought I would have. Like a mysterious son." He stared at Johnny, looking him directly in the eye. Johnny didn't return his stare, choosing the wooden floor instead.

"I am now going to do something that I really should do more often," said Mack. He took a step towards Johnny, opened his arms, and pulled his son close towards him. Johnny slowly allowed himself to sink into his father's shoulders. Mack whispered into his ear. "Just be careful, my love."

Chapter 32

Taking his beers from the bar, Mack pointed out their table to the waitress so that their nachos could be brought over. He then went back into the main room to rejoin Jay. Harpo had disappeared some time towards the end of the Rebirth Brass Band set, and Johnny had gone back to the hotel after the band finished. Julia was talking to some of the band, making contacts, networking, leaving him and Jay to wind down with a final beer before heading back to the hotel.

It was 3am and a DJ was playing jazz, albeit at a lower level than the Rebirth had managed with their set. They had needed no amplification, just a wall of brass powering out funky rhythms. There were still a few people dancing, and the club didn't look like it had any intention of going to sleep for some time yet.

As he walked through the long, thin room, Mack stopped to admire the painting that had been completed during the set. An easel had been set up on top of a table and during the performance a young enigmatic man had been enthusiastically covering the blank canvas with an array of bright colours, depicting the scene in front of him. Mack recognised the style from the cover of the album by the Rebirth that had made him fall in love with this venue from across the Atlantic.

The artist was putting away his equipment, the painting finished. Mack stopped and admired his work for a few moments. It was a jumble of people, horn instruments, angles and colours, and totally captured the exhilaration the exhilaration that Mack had felt when watching the band play. Each song had started with an impossibly happy rhythm from the tuba and drummer, then a melody would be stabbed on top by the line of horn players; the strength and personality of the song almost hit Mack in the face. Each player would take his turn to solo, melodies jumping in and out of his awareness, then suddenly all the players would return to the main melody at once, seemingly out of nowhere, as if they had a sixth sense connecting them all, keeping them syncopated. It had been the funkiest, most exciting music he had ever seen played, and the painting in front of him, with its wild use of yellows and ochres, seemed to sum it all up perfectly.

Mack spoke to the artist, shaking his hand and chatting for a few minutes, holding the two bottles of beer in the other hand. He then went over to Jay and handed him one.

"Cheers, dude," said Jay. "What was that about?"

"I just agreed to buy that painting," Mack replied.

"Cool!"

"Yeah, and how. It's not cheap, but he just seems to have captured everything about tonight that I really want to remember." Mack turned his seat sideways and leaned his back against the wall. His eyes went to the ceiling, and his shoulders dropped for a moment.

"That band," said Jay, not looking at Mack, "was awesome. Seriously, I don't think I've ever enjoyed something more. I know you've played me their stuff, but it didn't prepare me for the live experience. Man, such energy, and for lots of them this was their second gig of the evening. How do they do it?"

When Mack didn't answer, Jay looked at him. For a moment it occurred to Jay that his friend looked old. It was as if he had stopped for a moment, his batteries run down, or something in his mechanism had broken. Eyes slightly glazed over, Mack was looking at the ground, and yet not looking at all, the expression on his face showing not so much that he was deep in thought, but more that he had no thoughts at all.

"Mack?" said Jay. "Mack, you alright, mate?"

Mack blinked rapidly, then looked up at Jay. "Hmm? Yeah, yeah fine," he said, quickly, smiling unconvincingly.

Jay didn't speak. He watched Mack carefully, worriedly, giving him time to gather himself, which it seemed he needed to do.

"I'm tired, mate," said Mack, after a few moments. "Just tired. We've been partying pretty hard."

"Mack?" said Jay.

"Yeah?" Mack replied.

"Do me favour, and fuck right off, would you."

Putting his hand into his pocket, Mack pulled out a packet of cigars. They were slim, just a bit larger than a cigarette; a local brand that Mack had discovered. He took one, and lit it with a cheap plastic lighter. Jay breathed in the sweet smell.

"A pleasant, if unexpected aspect of this trip is once again being allowed to smoke indoors. Just my luck to have started smoking just after the British government decided to introduce a smoking ban." Mack smiled at Jay, who didn't smile back, but just continued to look at him expectantly. "Oh, alright. I've not been feeling great, to be honest, mate."

"In what way?" asked Jay.

Running his hand through his hair, Mack said, "It's not easy to describe. It's like a blankness, a fuzziness in the head. It's been around for a wee while and I've always put it down to a late night, but since Johnny told me about the tour, it's been happening more often. It's like I am not in control. It can last for a few hours, or it can be all day. I try to say the sort of things that Mack usually says, but I just know that if anyone watched me carefully, I'd seem distant. It's like I am both on the inside looking out, and at the same time on the outside looking in. It's like I'm in a glass cage dressed in a spacesuit, watching myself on closed-circuit television."

He paused, and for once Jay did not jump into the silence. "I will forget myself for a few moments, drift off and stop pretending to be me. Then someone will engage with me, and I'll be back, being me again. I must do an excellent impression of myself, because I am carrying off this impersonation on a daily basis. I seem to be able to keep up such a good illusion. But I'm telling you, Jay, I'm not sure how much longer I can keep this up for. At some point I'm going to have to admit that things are not right, that I am not who people think I am, and that I am not a well man."

Mack leaned forward and brought his hands to his face, rubbing his eyes and cheeks; he didn't make eye contact with Jay, as if he was within a bubble of his own existence. For a moment Jay wondered if his friend was actually crying, but then he continued.

"I just can't seem to let my mind wander anymore. I can remember, as a boy, rejoicing in my own imaginative powers. Friends would join with me in the adventures that I would make up. Once, at school, we were going back into class after playtime. I was probably about ten. We'd spent the entire time defending the school from an attack by a giant mole – a game I had invented. We were walking back into the school when a dinner lady said to me, 'Michael, you are undoubtedly the weirdest child I have ever clapped eyes on.' I said thank you to her, then walked into class smiling my head off. It was like the biggest compliment she could have given me.

"But I just can't seem to find that place any more. I try to. I switch off a little, and allow myself to float, to dream, to let my mind travel to places that it wishes to find. But nothing happens. I just end up with the last song I heard on the radio entering my head instead, and going round and round. Often, I can feel an idea living in there." Mack tapped the side of his head, aggressively, as if he was angry at himself. "I can even get the gist of what it is trying to say to me. But when I try and focus on it, the idea backs away, and the radio song just starts round again. It's as if new thoughts are scared to come out, as though I have spent so long hiding things in the back of my mind that new ideas have decided to take refuge back there as well. I think I must have created a space in my mind which I have bricked off. The purpose was to stop a memory from getting out and infecting my conscious, but I fear I may have created a bigger space than I meant to, and now ideas can't get in or out."

It was a long time since Jay had seen Mack looking and sounding so morose; not since those weeks and months after Jude had kicked him out all those years ago. He remained silent for a moment, as much unsure of what to say as feeling that it was what his friend needed.

The waitress came over to their table and placed a large bowl of nachos covered in cheese, guacamole and salsa in the middle of the table. They both took a few and munched in silence for a few moments. She asked if they wanted more drinks. "Thank you, no," Jay replied, holding up a hand, and the waitress left them alone again.

Eventually Jay spoke, gently. "I know what this might be, mate. May I offer you an opinion?"

"Sure."

"It's stress. Delayed stress. From the divorce. You've blocked everything out, and now it's coming back to you again. Probably the change of scenery – going from virtual recluse to all this," Jay swept his arm around him, "is allowing out all those emotions that you've been suppressing all this time. A mate had a similar thing, I've seen it before."

Mack put his hand briefly on his friend's knee. He left it there only a moment, but it was enough to pass on the required message that he appreciated the sentiment. "Thank you, mate," he said. "You may well be right. Although," Mack wagged his finger at his friend, "just because it turns out you like a bit of cock, doesn't mean you're allowed to act like a sodding psychologist."

"Mack," said Jay, straightening in his chair a little. "I've got a question for you. It's been bugging me for a long time now."

"Okay", said Mack, "fire away." He took a nacho, using it to scoop up extra guacamole.

"What actually happened in that hotel room with you and that American woman?"

Mack looked at him for a moment, his face impassive, then said, "Ask me one about sport."

Jay laughed, deliberately ignoring the implied warning in the joke. "I'm serious," he said. "Come on, I've opened up to you about my sexuality."

"Pal, the only reason you 'opened up' to me, as you put it, is because I caught you bang to rights. Oh bloody hell, here we go again."

"Firstly," said Jay, "I'm not sure 'bang to rights' has any innuendo in it whatsoever. You're just getting yourself a little bit paranoid. And secondly, just tell me, you miserable bastard. Why did you have sex with that woman?"

"Because Jude had seen my cock many times before. That woman hadn't."

Jay laughed, then stopped laughing abruptly and dramatically, for effect. "Come on. Tell me, why? What was it all about?"

Mack looked up at the roof and rolled his eyes. "Why do you want to know?" he said.

"I don't have a reason. Except for the fact that it is out of character for my best mate to do something that, on the face of it, seems to be a complete bastard-type thing to do. So I thought I'd get your side of the story."

"I already told you, at the time."

"Not really. I pieced together what had happened from various hysterical women, but you and I never actually talked about it. And you also never speak about Mary, and why she won't talk to you."

"Oh, that's easy. Because she thinks I'm an arrogant selfish bastard. And she's two-thirds right."

"So, what happened?"

Mack held up an empty beer bottle. "Get me another one of those and I'll tell you," he said, grabbing more nachos.

Jay jumped out of his seat and walked quickly to the bar. He came back a few minutes later with four bottles of beer. "In case you run out," he said. "I don't want this to be interrupted for anything."

"There's not much to tell," Mack began. "Al Smart had come over to England to see me, and he'd brought this woman with him. She was absolutely gorgeous."

"Oh, I remember," said Jay.

"Well, we just seemed to hit it off, and well, you know. And Mary caught us in the act. That's it."

"That's not two beers' worth of information," said Jay. "So if you're not going to tell me straight, I'll have to prise it out of you. For starters, what did Al want to see you about?"

"Mamal business. And none of yours."

"Come on, just give me a flavour. What was he after. I mean, he was obviously after something, otherwise he wouldn't have come all that way over. And why was she with him?"

"Okay, if you must know, he wanted to talk to me about rereleasing some of Mamal's songs. Putting together a compilation. She worked for the record company – a lawyer."

"Hmmm," said Jay. It didn't sound very plausible, but he did remember a compilation album being out around that time. "Okay, suppose I buy that. It's not easy to swallow, because it stinks, frankly, but I'll run with it."

"Jay," said Mack, "I think you get the award for putting the most amount of conflicting clichés into one sentence. Not an easy thing to do, and not a particularly easy thing to say either."

"So why did Mary come to the hotel?"

"She was upset about something. Teenage issues. From what little Jude has told me, I think she was emotional because Kurt Cobain had shot himself around that time, plus she fancied her best mate, and she found out that he was adopted. She's been unsure if I'm her dad ever since."

"And are you?"

Mack looked at Jay with narrow eyes. "Would you care to *not* repeat that question?" he said, through gritted teeth.

"Okay, sorry, sorry, I wasn't thinking," said Jay. "But that doesn't explain why Mary was at the hotel."

"No. It doesn't, does it. I guess I've always assumed she saw me go there. I've never asked that question myself. Didn't really get the chance to. The retribution for my transgression began pretty much instantly."

"Okay, the big question." Jay leaned on the table across from Mack. "Why was Al in the room with you and Kimberly?"

"Right, you can fuck off properly now," said Mack, folding his arms and crossing his legs.

"What?!" said Jay, putting his hands out, palms facing upwards, as if protesting his innocence. "Come on, Mary told Johnny Al was there too, sitting at the table, watching. Was it a threesome?"

"Given that I was also there at the time, I think I might have some authority on this subject." Mack was properly angry now. "I had a thing with Kimberly, and Mary caught us at it. That's it. That's all. And you can stick any other questions up your arse. And I don't care if that is a double en-fucking-tendre."

Jay pressed on. He was asking for Johnny now. "Mack, are you seriously telling me that Al was not in the room?"

"Correct. I am telling you that Al was not in the room. Okay? Now you've got your story. I was an idiot, I was taken in by a very beautiful woman, and I've paid a very high price. End of, as I think they say over here. And if any of this gets to Kent I'm-So-Cool Nicholls, I will personally rip your larynx from your throat."

"I'm not asking for him. So don't worry." Jay sat back.

Mack stood up and went back to talk to the painter, who was putting away the last of his materials. Jay cursed his own lack of tact and skill. He had told Johnny he wouldn't get involved, but in the end the temptation was too great. And yet he knew now that Mack was lying. Johnny was right – there was something wrong here.

Chapter 33

Two large brown leather sofas facing each other, separated by a low table, dominated the small lobby of the New Orleans hotel. One of the sofas squeaked in compliance as Mack sat on it. His back was stiff, presumably from all the dancing with Jay and Julia to the Rebirth Brass band the night before. He had felt it the previous evening while talking to Jay, and now, sitting on such a soft sofa, the pain was coming back again; it was like an unwelcome college friend, calling up after fifteen years of non-communication and announcing that he'd just got divorced and was looking to get in touch with his old buddies again. Taking his mobile phone, he dialled Johnny's number.

It was 10am. Mack's body clock refused to allow him the luxury of sleeping off the excesses of the night before and had woken him an hour before. He had showered, packed the few belongings he had bothered to take out of his suitcase and gone to knock on Johnny's door. No reply. When he had gone to reception, they had given him a note which Johnny had left for him, saying that he had already left for Memphis and would see them there. The itinerary allowed for an overnight stay in Memphis before moving on to their next gig in Jonesboro. There were 400 miles between the two cities, so he could understand the thought behind Johnny's early start, but it seemed strange that he hadn't mentioned it the night before.

The mobile phone went through to Johnny's voicemail. Mack left a brief message for Johnny to call him back, terse enough to portray his intended impression: that he was not very impressed.

He nodded to Harpo, coming through the door from the stairs. Mack noticed one or two of the other guests staring. He saw Harpo through their eyes for a moment, and took in the image. There was no doubt that you would have to start with the hair. A huge frizzy mass of small greying curls, shaped into an oval; somewhere between an afro and a Mohican, with the bushy moustache giving the impression that his hair had given birth. The combined result looked as though it could adorn a hedge at the entrance to a stately home, if only Harpo had been able to stand still for more than a few minutes. Indeed, Mack had a feeling that he would be just as good at topiary as he was at hairdressing, should he ever put his mind to it.

How long must Harpo spend each morning working on his hair? It seemed to be perfectly smooth around the outside, like a giant glass dome balanced on his head. The clothing he had chosen for today was a shiny grey suit with tight trousers and a white shirt. He had bought himself a bolo tie while in New Orleans, boot laces round the neck in the traditional southern style. The black leather laces were fastened by a silver mount featuring a gold head of an American Eagle, with a gold rope surround. The overall image this ensemble created was a London mod from the sixties who had climbed into a teleportation booth with an American country singer and the two had got mixed together. Was there another person walking around somewhere who was the opposite of Harpo: 60% country singer and 40% mod? Mack shuddered as he wondered what the other guy would look like, all rhinestone and winkle-pickers.

Pouring himself a free cup of coffee from the pot at reception, Harpo nodded a morning greeting, and sat on the opposite sofa.

"Good night last night?" Mack asked him.

Harpo sipped at his coffee, staring forwards, ignoring Mack's question. Mack hadn't really expected an answer, but it was still fun to ask. It was virtually impossible to be rude to Harpo. His response would invariably be to simply ignore you. Mack often wondered why he was friends with the man, he got so little back from him. Loyalty is a powerful drug. Only occasionally would Harpo break – usually without warning – and then it was best to steer well clear of him; the ire that had so clearly built up inside him over a period of time would be unleashed on some poor unsuspecting shop assistant or railway guard who happened to push him over the edge.

The lift bell chimed, the doors opened, and Jay and Julia stepped out, both dragging cases behind them, engaged in polite discussion. The previous evening, Mack had gone to Julia after his conversation with Jay, and rather clumsily suggested that Julia return to their hotel

236

with them from the Maple Leaf; to his delight, she had accepted. When they had stumbled into the hotel, however, she had booked her own room, kissed him on the cheek with a knowing look, and sashayed off to bed. It was as if she was telling him off, but without closing the door to possibilities completely.

Jay looked much the worse for wear, the contrast with Julia's immaculate appearance bringing his hangdog look into sharp focus. She sat next to Harpo, and it seemed for a moment as if their hair had become independent of their heads and were growling at each other. Jay put his baggage down behind Mack's sofa and poured two coffees. He gave one to Julia, then stood in front of the sofa, holding the cup and rubbing his chin with his eyes closed. Harpo continued to stare forwards, barely acknowledging Julia sat next to him.

"Good night's sleep?" Mack asked, looking at Julia to address the question to her.

Jay, still with his eyes closed, his hand now having reached his forehead but still rubbing firmly, replied, "No. Thank you, but no. Of course not. Wholly insufficient, frankly. Christ, I sound like you now. I think I've been on this tour too long. Oh, my head hurts."

Mack and Julia smiled at each other. The moment caught Mack by surprise. It had been such a natural thing to do, yet the fact that it was such an easily shared moment meant that they must be connecting. They had noticed the same thing – that Mack had asked Julia how she was feeling before his old friend, Jay. Did this show that Julia was becoming more important to Mack than Jay was? So soon? The fact that they smiled at each other meant that they were aware of the two-person clique that was forming, and wanted to acknowledge it to the other. They had each begun to remove their own personal walls, just a little bit, and only for the other, and that one smile represented the laying of the very first bricks of a new wall, this time big enough to surround the two of them.

Mack's heart beat faster for a few moments as the enormity of her even being in that hotel dawned on him. If he had any doubt as to why she had come back with them last night – and he had plenty of doubts, his entire body was riddled with them – then they disappeared in five seconds of eye contact and realisation. In that moment, Julia had said yes. Yes, you may proceed to get to know me better. I have assessed you, I have tested you, and the early signs are promising. So yes, you may assume that I am willing to go on a journey of discovery with you.

He held her gaze for as long as he could but her will was stronger than his, so he eventually turned to Jay and said, "All set then?" He looked at Harpo to silently repeat the question, and realised that Harpo was smiling broadly at him. That bastard didn't miss a thing. Mack smiled coyly back.

"Yeah," said Jay. "As I'll ever be. Harpo, do you mind taking the first shift? It's going to be a long drive today, and I think I'd be better in the second half than I would in the first half."

"Not a problem," said Harpo.

"Where's Johnny?" asked Jay to Mack.

"I don't know," he replied, standing and pulling his shirt down over his denim jeans. "Well, I do, he left a note saying he left earlier to get to Memphis before us and make sure everything's okay."

"Oh. Oh, I see." Jay seemed a little put out at this information, as if he didn't like not knowing Johnny's movements. He noticed Mack looking at him and quickly resumed his cheery disposition. "Ah, he's a good lad, is that one," said Jay. "Almost hard to believe he's yours, sometimes."

Mack glared at him.

"Joke! Sheesh, some people are so touchy in the mornings."

Beneath his hair, Harpo grinned.

Later that afternoon, the aeroplane that Johnny had taken from New Orleans airport that morning finally touched down in Washington.

The previous evening in New Orleans, Kent Nicholls had made a few phone calls and discovered that Al had gone from New Orleans to Washington on the last flight of the day. He had passed this information on to Johnny, who had decided to follow him immediately, and hoped that Kent would be able to track down where he was in Washington by the time Johnny arrived there.

Disembarking from the plane, he had immediately turned his phone back on and read a text containing an address in the Wheaton-Glenmont suburb of Washington. Kent Nicholls seemed to have favours that he could call in from people in almost every city in the world. They had found out that Al had gone to Washington because the people that had given him a room in New Orleans (an ex-roadie who owed Kent a 'favour' for not telling his partner about a particularly salacious party after a Kiss concert in Birmingham) had overheard a telephone call.

It was too late to go and see Al now, and so Johnny had asked the cab driver to take him to a hotel somewhere near the address he had been given. He had booked in, eaten a meal, watched an American football game in the bar for a while, then gone to bed. The next morning he was up and had breakfasted, and asked reception to call a cab to take him to the address.

Johnny had decided that he would not tell the others where he was going. He didn't want to admit his concerns to Kent Nicholls, but the only other person that he had been keeping informed was Jay. His father had known of some of the diversions, although obviously he hadn't known the real reason for them. And yet Al always seemed to know that he was there. So, to be safe, he had decided to tell no one else of this trip, and had simply left a note at the hotel reception for his father saying he would see them in Memphis.

Sitting on the plane, staring at the clouds, Johnny had been troubled. It was the first time he had lied to Mack. Well, the first time in earnest, anyway. It felt odd to deceive his father in order to help him. But Al Smart had blackmailed his father all those years ago, whether on his own or on behalf of someone else.

He told the cab driver to keep going past the address and to stop three properties further on. The road was a cul-de-sac in the shape of a U, with a large turning circle; this house was halfway up the second arm. The driver went past the address he had been given, to the end of the cul-de-sac, and dropped Johnny off in the turning circle.

He paid the fare, taking a business card so that he could call the cab driver again. As he watched the cab drive away from him, Johnny felt very conspicuous. Wheaton-Glenmont was a leafy suburb, full of properties which stood on their own, surrounded by immaculate grass; trees were dotted everywhere, along the sidewalks and as central features of many of the lawns. It was not possible for him to get close to the house without risking being seen, and so he stayed a distance away, at the edge of the turning circle. He was in full view of at least half a dozen houses surrounding the turning circle, but he could see back down the cul-de-sac to the front door of the wooden-fronted house that was supposedly the current home of Al Smart, as of yesterday.

With nowhere to hide from the twitching net curtains, and no way of looking like he was doing something other than waiting, Johnny sat on the sidewalk, rested his arms on his knees and put his head in his hands. He didn't have a plan other than to confront Al, but even that seemed like it might be difficult. He certainly wasn't going to knock on the door again; that tactic had failed twice already. So instead he would wait until Al, or at least someone, came out of the house.

Forty-five minutes later the front door of the house opened. Johnny immediately recognised Al Smart from the photos he had seen. The sun was glinting off his teeth. He was wearing denim jeans and a jacket which was unbuttoned. Jumping to his feet, Johnny ran closer to the house, keeping a large tree between him and Al. He didn't care if he did look furtive now, the neighbours could think what they liked.

Another man came out with Al. He was tall and unfeasibly thin, wearing a white shirt which seemed to be mottled, but Johnny realised it was stained. Al was wearing a baseball cap pulled down as if to hide his face. Johnny was close enough to be able to catch snippets of their conversation, and it seemed they were arguing about something, Al being on the defensive. He was promising something, and Johnny guessed that his tenure as a guest at their property was probably going to be a short-lived one.

The tall man opened a garage door, and Al went inside. All was quiet for a few moments, and then suddenly Al came out of the garage on a bicycle. He wobbled down the driveway like a newborn lamb trying to stand, then turned left, away from Johnny. He would have to go for a few hundred yards back up the road, then round the two corners of the U before heading back down towards the main road. The garage door closed from the inside.

Johnny knew he wouldn't be able to catch up with Al, even though he clearly hadn't ridden a bike for some time and was pedalling only very gingerly. As soon as he would get near, Al would see him and cycle away. Instead, he would have to cut across two gardens to reach the entrance of the cul-de-sac and cut off Al's exit. Johnny looked to his left, at the large house two doors down from the one that Al had just come out of. The driveway went up to a double garage and onwards round the side of the house towards a high picket fence, separating the front from the back. A car was parked round the side, seemingly backed up against the fence.

Johnny ran up the driveway and round the side of the property. The car was an estate; Johnny jumped up onto the front bonnet, barely missing his stride and up onto the roof. Two paces later he jumped off the end of the car and over the fence.

As he flew through the air, Johnny immediately realised the stupidity of jumping over a fence without first checking what was on the other side. The detritus of a small child at play covered the floor of the yard that appeared below him.

Sitting in a sandpit at the side nearest the fence was a girl of about four years old. She had her back to the fence, and was holding a delightful, if rather sandy, tea party. Her happy face was briefly a picture of confusion as a shadow covered the small table and chairs she had so meticulously laid out.

The shadow was immediately followed by two legs, as Johnny tried to avoid landing on the girl's head by aiming his feet either side of her. He succeeded in avoiding contact with the girl; however, Mr Shnuggums, a purple stuffed elephant who had up to that moment been behaving himself impeccably was not so lucky and bore the full brunt of Johnny's foot. The poor unsuspecting elephant was knocked from its chair and sent spinning to end up face down in the sand. The little girl and Lady Daisy, a cheap Barbie imitation, looked on in shock.

Johnny rolled forwards, expecting to hear the girl screaming at any moment. It didn't come, however, and he looked back to see the girl sitting, open-mouthed, staring at him. Deciding there was not a great deal he could to do to put things right, Johnny jumped to his feet and ran across the lawn at the back of the house. Behind him, the little girl picked Mr Shnuggums out of the sand, brushed him off, and returned him to the party; the conversation now turned to how rude some people can be, as she poured a fresh imaginary cup of tea.

Another picket fence lined the back of the garden, but a tree offered Johnny easy climbing; he was over it in seconds, and into the garden of another house. He knew if he could get to the front of this house, he would be almost on the road at the entrance of the cul-de-sac, hopefully in time to catch Al before he got onto the main road. Running across the lawn towards the side of the house, he saw a door in the inevitable picket fence. Reaching it, he drew back the bolt and opened the door. As he ran through, he looked to his right. A hedge ran down the length of the lawn separating this house from the next, and over it Johnny could see Al cycling down the road, now looking a little more confident and nonchalant.

Johnny stopped for a moment to catch his breath. He didn't really do exercise, and just running that short way had got him out of breath. He reckoned that he easily had time to creep down the lawn behind the hedge before Al got near.

Crouching, Johnny ran over to the hedge. He then followed its line down the lawn towards the road. To his left, he could see the main road, and noticed that there were no cars in the driveway of this house. Halfway down, he stood up carefully to check on the progress of Al.

Unfortunately, he did so just as Al looked his way. Seeing Johnny's head poke up from behind the bush, Al stood up on the bike, pulled hard on the handlebars, and pedalled as fast as he could.

Johnny started running down the lawn. He had about thirty metres to cover to reach Al, who was on the far side of the road about forty metres away, building speed to try and get past Johnny.

Johnny ran onto the sidewalk as Al had almost reached him, but on the other side of the road. Johnny realised that the bike was travelling too fast now, and he wasn't going to be able to run quickly enough to stop him.

Desperate, Johnny ran diagonally across the road to cut off the angle, then dived as he neared the far side of the road. Al was already in line with him as he left the ground, and was going at some pace. Reaching full-length, Johnny managed to grab the end of Al's jacket, which was now billowing backwards.

He managed to get a good grip of the jacket, and as he landed heavily on the concrete, he pulled Al backwards. Unused to his balance on the bike, Al kept hold of the handlebars, pulling backwards and upwards, resulting in a wheelie. The bike reared up, throwing Al off, and Johnny let go of his jacket, his own momentum carrying him into a bush.

Johnny heard a sound like a cabbage being chopped in half as

Al landed on his back and his head whipped backwards onto the pavement. Quickly getting to his feet, Johnny ran over to the lifeless body. He checked for a pulse, and realised that Al had been knocked unconscious by the fall. He ran to the main road and flagged down a cab that was driving towards him.

He told the cab driver that he had been walking past and seen this man knocked off his bike by a car that didn't stop. Together they managed to lift Al into the back seat of the cab and once Johnny had reassured the driver that he would cover the fare, they took him to St Mary's Hospital. Johnny sat in the back seat as they drove, his mind whirling and confused, unsure whether to be elated because he had finally found Al, or concerned in case he could be arrested for assaulting the man.

Chapter 34

From the window of Theresa's Roadside Café, Mack looked out on a bright sunny day. He could see nothing but crop fields stretching out for several miles until his gaze was greeted by a range of low-lying hills, covering the horizon like a sleeping cat in front of a fireplace.

The previous night in Memphis had been low-key. Johnny had not arrived as expected, and his mobile phone seemed to be switched off. Jay had told Mack not to worry, as Johnny was quite capable of looking after himself and was no doubt busy sorting out more arrangements for later on in the tour. Mack's mood was pretty much the same before Jay's well-meaning suggestion as it was after. A mood that a kind person may have described as being uptight, but Harpo would have called 'grumpy bastard' had he been asked.

Comfort was taken from the fact that Julia was sat next to him. The original plan had been for her to drop in and out of the tour on certain dates, coinciding with Kent Nicholls. Instead she had made some calls and stayed on the tour, travelling with the three musicians from New Orleans to Memphis, and now on towards Jonesboro, where they were to play the next gig. She and Mack sat in the back of the car and talked. Harpo only commented once, to offer the suggestion that the two of them were like having the bloody radio on, and had they noticed that he didn't ever put the radio on. Mack told Julia that being insulted by Harpo meant she may have been accepted into the brotherhood of the band.

As soon as they arrived at the hotel in Memphis, Harpo had walked out into the city. Jay stayed in his room and watched movies, saying he needed a night off the partying. Mack thought he might have been sulking because Julia had booked a restaurant for her and Mack, but he knew Jay would understand eventually.

The restaurant was expensive, a recommendation from an old

college roommate of Julia's, but Mack asked for somewhere special. They had shared two bottles of Mayacamas Ridge Pinot Noir 2008 and a multitude of memories and life stories over a delicate three-course meal that lasted the entire evening. They felt as though they were diving deeper and deeper down into each other, and were as hungry for each other's thoughts as they were for the tarragon lobster bisque.

Julia had not used her room that evening. The fact she had wasted money on booking the room did not overly concern her.

The next day Jay and Harpo had shared the breakfast table on their own. Harpo read the personal ads section of a local newspaper and made the occasional note with a red pen, while Jay read the album reviews section of *Rolling Stone* magazine.

It was only a seventy-five mile drive to Jonesboro. They had left the hotel around 10am, and after crossing over the Mississippi river onto Route 61, they had turned left onto Route 63 before stopping on the outskirts of Jonesboro at Theresa's Roadside Café.

It was Kent Nicholls who had called Julia and suggested that they stop at Theresa's, where he would meet them. Mack had disagreed on principle, but Julia told him not to be so silly.

Harpo sucked noisily at his home-made chicken soup, seeming to cheer up with every mouthful. Jay, ever the adventurer, was trying – and enjoying – fried green tomatoes and hot wings, a speciality of the house (and every other house, given the menus they'd seen over the last few weeks). In-between them, Kent Nicholls nursed a strong black coffee, sunglasses still in place, his heavy black leather coat protecting him from the air conditioning. The three of them were squeezed onto one side of the eating booth.

Opposite them sat Mack and Julia. The waitress placed a ham and Swiss cheese sandwich on pumpernickel in front of Julia, and ribs and steak in front of Mack, then topped up everybody's coffee. After thanking the waitress and waiting until she had gone back into the kitchen, Mack swapped his and Julia's plates.

As he nibbled on his sandwich, Mack looked at his fellow diners sat around the table in the eating booth, each lost in their own worlds: Julia, next to him, their thighs touching unnecessarily, tucking into a mound of meat that would have made a werewolf blanch; Harpo, opposite in the window seat, cocooned in his own world, uninterested in making any alterations in his character in order to be accepted by Julia; Jay, on the outside, if not the character opposite to Harpo then certainly a considerable distance away, always happy, always quipping, determined to squeeze out every drop of experience into his trip of a lifetime. And then, diagonally opposite him, sat on the middle of the blue plastic seat, was Kent Nicholls. A legend in his own lunchtime. A man, without whom, the world might be a very slightly better place.

How had he managed to end up sitting at the same table as that bastard? For so many years he had avoided all aspects of the outside world, a self-imposed exile to protect his family. But when would the protection no longer be needed? Only when others were strong enough to know the truth, should it ever reveal its disgusting face. And that may be never.

This man – could he use such a word? – this scumbag typified everything about the outside world that he had been avoiding. Vain and nasty, the journalist was essential to promote the music, but to be avoided at all costs in case he poked his nose into the wrong places – which he would undoubtedly try to do. Irrespective of the history between the two of them, he understood that a journalist had a job to do; a job which, with unknowing irony, his own son had set up. Mack took a bite of his sandwich and decided that he would give Kent Nicholls something to write about in order to stop him from uncovering the one thing he should *never* find out about.

Swallowing, he looked at the journalist. Kent Nicholls had his arms folded on the table in front of him with his head down, and was staring intently into his coffee. Mack took a swig of coffee and prepared to play the game.

"So, Kent. How is our article coming along? Got much to say about us yet?"

Kent Nicholls grunted and raised his head. "Our article? My article, ya mean. Don't think you're having anything to do with it. You just happen to be the subject. At least you could be, if you'd actually talk to me."

"I'll give you an interview," said Mack. "But I've been thinking about it. I've got a deal to propose to you."

"I don't do deals. I'm a journalist. I write what I want to write, from my perspective, the way I see things. That's why people read me, because I'm not a goddam sycophant."

Mack took a small bite from his sandwich. He stared out of the window for a few moments before swallowing, then turned back to the man that he hated more than anyone else he had ever known. With Kent Nicholls it was sometimes best to pause for a few moments before speaking. Somehow this man had the most extraordinary knack of getting his hackles up with almost every utterance that came from that pretentious, arrogant mouth. "You've put a bit of effort into this article," he said eventually. "I'm guessing someone is expecting something from you. So why don't you climb down off your high horse for a moment, hear my suggestion, then you can decide."

Behind the shades, Kent Nicholls' eyes narrowed. Only Harpo, who had turned to look at him, could see this clearly. The journalist didn't speak, which Mack took as a sign that he should continue.

"It's an offer to you, as a rock journalist," Mack continued. "Suppose I proposed the following deal. You have two choices as to how we conduct the interview. Firstly, we could conduct a typical interview. You know the sort of thing – you ask questions you know I won't answer, I'm guarded all the way through, you make up half the stuff later. The way you usually work."

Mack folded his arms, placed them on the table and leaned on them, moving his head towards Kent Nicholls, who took a slow sip of his coffee in retaliation. "You get a boring interview and have to put your spin on things to make it interesting. Neither of us look particularly good and you get an article out of it, but not a great one, hardly one good enough for the anthology that you are undoubtedly trying to put together. And I'm guessing that there aren't many articles from the latter part of your fading career that would feature." Mack was staring straight into where he guessed Kent Nicholls' right eye was.

"Or there is another way," said Mack. "You sign a pre-interview contract which states that I will be allowed to censor the article you have written. I will then speak to you frankly and openly, will throw caution to the wind. Because I would know that I would be able to review what I have said and take out any excesses or things I regretted saying to you, I would therefore be able to talk totally freely. You could even do it while I was drunk, so that I would be even more lax and indiscreet. No holds barred, I'd tell you everything, be totally candid, but with the right to take some of it back. You get much more out of me, we both benefit from a great article."

"You can't give the interviewee the right to censor an article, that's a golden rule," Kent Nicholls replied, almost without pause.

Mack shook his head, sadly. "So change the rules. Which would you prefer? Guarded and unrevealing? Or pissed and frank. Believe me, I've got a few opinions to air. Come on, don't you fancy yourself as some sort of visionary journalist."

Kent Nicholls thought for a moment, but only a moment, as if this idea had occurred to him already. "I couldn't trust you not to censor the entire damn article," he said. "And you sure as hell couldn't trust me to keep your secrets out of print forever."

The two men glared at each other for a moment. Jay was looking at Mack, a piece of green tomato dangling from the end of his fork. Kent Nicholls straightened up, continuing to keep his sunglasses, and therefore presumably his gaze, pointed towards Mack. Harpo carried on noisily sucking his soup from his spoon, pausing only to dip in some bread. Underneath the table, Julia had placed her hand on Mack's thigh, squeezed very gently as a sign of encouragement, and then continued with her meal.

"Fine," said Mack, eventually. "Don't say you didn't have the choice. Right, what do you want to know?" The sandwich bore the brunt of his feelings as he ripped a portion apart with his teeth.

"You wanna do this now? In front of everyone?" Kent Nicholls' tone was one of amusement.

"Why not. Given that I'm unlikely to say anything interesting, let's get it over with. You need some material for your article. I don't care about the publicity, because I'm not doing this for money or fame. I've had both, and they're not all they're cracked up to be. But I do want to appear in a good light, don't want to let people down. So get on with it, and let me give you something you can use."

"Fine by me," said the journalist, and Jay thought he might not have been the only one to hear a little menace behind his voice. "Seems to me your son means a great deal to you."

"Of course he does. Was that a question? If so it was a pretty stupid one. Have you started yet?"

"Okay," he began. "Why don't we start with something easy. Like what was it that led you to becoming a hermit for over a decade before your son rescued you."

Rolling his eyes to the ceiling, Mack turned and looked at Julia, as if seeking strength. She returned the look with a passive face, giving no indication of her feelings. He read this as meaning, 'It's okay, you say whatever you want, I'll be here to support you'. He smiled to himself. A lifetime ago, that same look from Jude would have been interpreted by him as saying, 'Try not to say the wrong thing this time'. He wondered which had changed more in the intervening years: him or the world.

"Okay, Kent," he said, "I'll try and sum it up for you. If you promise to shut up and not be annoying for a while."

"I can but try, my man," said Kent Nicholls, taking a leather-bound notepad from inside his heavy coat. To get to the notepad he also took out a packet of cigarettes with only one left inside. He took out that lone cigarette, placed it behind his ear, and started to fiddle with the empty packet.

"Failed already," replied Mack. "Never mind."

Placing the remnants of his sandwich back on the plate, Mack leaned back, his head able to rest against the top of the blue vinyl cushioned seat. The angle made his head tilt back slightly to look up and out of the window, eyes focussed on the clear blue sky.

"We used to have a lot of fun, Al and me," he began, talking at the window. "In those early days, it was a real giggle, being in a band. You ask anyone who has been in a band before, you'll be hard pushed to find anyone that regrets it. It's a great experience, everyone should do it once." He glanced at Kent Nicholls. "Possibly except you. I can't imagine anyone enjoying being in a band with you."

Kent Nicholls nodded slightly.

"I remember the first bad gig we had. I was so pleased. We were doing a mix of our own stuff and covers, just to get the gigs – Al singing, me on guitar, and we had bass, piano and drums too. We'd only done fairly small stuff, mates' parties and the like, but someone booked us for a wedding. We couldn't believe our luck. Turned out the two families hated each other. They spent the entire evening at opposite sides of the room while we played, just glaring at each other. The best man's speech had been awful, apparently, he was too drunk to stand up, and two of the page boys had a fight while the photographer was trying to take their photograph. In the end two of us had to guard the kit in case it got nicked while the other two loaded the van."

"Forgive me for interrupting this reminiscing," said Kent Nicholls, in a voice that sought no forgiveness. "I wasn't asking about your early days, or even the Mamal hits. Sorry, *hit*. I thought you'd like to focus on the new music. So, I think you'll find the question was 'What happened to drive you underground?'"

"I decided to focus on making music for myself, that's all. After all those years of trying to make music that Al liked, or the record company liked, or teenage girls liked, I decided to do it for me."

"Christ, you weren't kidding," said Kent. "That really is fucking boring. Let's try a different tack, see if we can get something useable out of this travesty. So what happened between you and Al?"

Mack turned. Kent Nicholls hadn't written any notes but was instead playing with a piece of gold paper that he'd presumably taken from the inside of the cigarette packet.

"I showed Julia your article, you know," Mack eventually replied. "The one that split the band up."

Jay wiped barbecue sauce off his sticky fingers and onto his napkin. Harpo had finished his soup and was sticking a dirty finger into his mouth to try and remove an awkward piece of chicken that had lodged itself between his back teeth. Julia just watched. They all noticed Kent Nicholls smile at Mack's last comment.

"You have the fucking nerve to ask me what happened between the two of us?" said Mack. He was trying so hard to keep his cool; he knew that he was being baited, and yet it was so hard to keep it in. He felt Julia's hand on his thigh again, this time squeezing a little harder. He reached under the table and held onto it.

"Hey, just doing my job, man. It was just an article, just words," said Kent. "It's not like I took any pleasure from the way Al took it all to heart." The half of his face that protruded from beneath his sunglasses was now forming a most unpleasant leer.

"Yes you did. You knew perfectly well what you were doing. I'm only pleased that I got some payment for it in advance. How is the jaw, by the way?"

Kent Nicholls snapped his head towards Julia. She smiled sweetly back at him. "What?" she said, feigning innocence. "Sure, I told him. It's not like it's a secret. Everyone knows about your dodgy jaw. Except I didn't know the full story until last night. The full reason why Mack gave it to you. That kinda makes things look a little different." The eyes narrowed, the lips came together, and the smile became sarcastic.

"Oh does it," replied Kent. "Now, I'm trying my very best here, girlie, but I do seem to be struggling just a bit to see what the hell this has got to do with you, just because you've gone native and are fucking the talent. You've got a job to do. Why don't you take some goddamn photographs instead of stuffing ya fat face?"

Mack began to stand up but Julia pushed down on his leg, forcing him to sit back down. "Easy, Mack," she said. "It's okay. He won't be the first ignorant bastard to speak to me like that. You two need each other. That's all that matters. So give him his story, then he can go and leave us alone."

Us. She had said us. The word cut through Mack's anger in an instant. He suddenly felt no longer afraid of this man in front of him. It had been so long that he had someone to fight with, so long carrying the solitary burden of protection on his shoulders. For years now he had been taking the punches on his own, his hands bound, unable to fight back. But now he seemed to have found someone who might want to stand next to him.

Remember the plan. Give the bastard something to keep him occupied so that he wouldn't peek into other corners of his life. The man knew nothing about what happened in that hotel room; give him something else to look at so he wouldn't go poking around.

"Okay," he said, in the calmest voice he could muster. "As I believe I may have suggested before, shut up, if that's at all possible, and listen. How would you put it, with your ability to mangle and destroy the English language? Let's get this thing done." Mack was talking quickly now.

"I didn't go underground, didn't go into hiding, nothing like that. I just got divorced, and simply didn't go out much for a long time. Stayed in and made music. But my kind of music − not for anyone else, for me. I stopped caring about how the listener would hear the words and just wrote down what came into my head. It was hugely liberating, and I'm still learning about it."

"So why did you get divorced?"

Mack stared at the man for a moment. Kent Nicholls continued to fiddle with the piece of gold paper. It was starting to really get on Mack's nerves. "Wow," he said. "I'd honestly forgotten what it was like to be interviewed by a rock journalist. It's like trying to talk to a puppy wearing earplugs."

"I have to say," said Jay, daring to verbally step between them for the first time, "that is one of the worst questions I think I've ever heard one person ask another person. Do you really think he's going to answer that?"

"Nah," Kent replied, smiling and staring at his fingers as he folded the gold foil. "He hasn't got the balls."

"Okay," said Mack, "I will give you an answer. I had an affair, and my wife, quite rightly, kicked me out. That's it. End of. Okay?" Mack ate the last mouthful of pumpernickel sandwich, as if to underline the finality of his statement.

"Yeah," drawled Kent Nicholls. "Okay. Sure. And that's an answer that ain't gonna make the finished copy."

"You want stuff for your article or not?"

"You know what?" said Kent Nicholls. "I don't think I do, actually. In fact, not the sort of trite crap you seem to want to feed me. I think I got enough already. Know what's the most important asset a rock journalist needs?" Nobody answered. "These," he continued, and pointed to his eye.

"What," said Mack, "a pair of clichéd sunglasses?"

Julia giggled.

"No," he said, in a voice that no one would have mistaken as being friendly. "It's what we see that we write about, not what we hear. Not what musicians tell us, for sure. And I've seen quite enough of this sad, jaded little tour to be able to construct an article that my editor will be only too happy to run. I'm not sure Johnny would like it, mind you, but hey, what can ya do. I'm sure he won't be blamed for the failure of your comeback."

As Kent Nicholls was talking he glanced down at his hands, only partly concentrating on folding and refolding the gold paper. He had clearly done this many times and his fingers moved as if on autopilot. Mack had also been watching his hands more and more closely, until the point when Kent carefully placed a gold origami unicorn on the table in front of him.

Mack stared at it in silence for a few moments. He had seen an origami unicorn twice before in his life. Once was in the film *Blade Runner*. The other had been a gift for his son from Al a long time ago in his old front room, 'made for him by a friend of Al's', Jude had said. It had stuck in his mind because it was such a significant moment in the film; now it was a memory that came searing back into his mind like a branding iron. Everything around him disappeared from his vision as he stared at the gold foil, shaped and folded into something beautiful, yet representing something so utterly repugnant.

Awful realisation created the most sickening feeling in his stomach. Kent Nicholls had made that unicorn for Al. It felt as if some huge piece of a giant jigsaw had collided into place with a loud clang and a cloud of dust, but the picture it revealed was horrific. And yet totally logical. How had he not put these pieces together before now? Mack struggled to control the urge to lunge at the man opposite him and throw him through the window.

When he looked back at Kent and spoke to him, his voice was like Jay had never heard, like none of them had ever heard. Harpo shuffled carefully to the edge of his seat, his limbs tense, ready to move quickly if needed. If a voice could shake, then Mack's voice was shaking now.

"Tell me, Kent," he said. "Do you like films?"

Kent Nicholls turned his head. "Sure," he answered, caution in his voice now. He too could tell that an abrupt change had come over Mack. "Why do you ask?"

"Any particular favourites?" Julia could feel his hand shaking and she held it firmly, not understanding what was going on, what had caused Mack to react like this. It was as if he was trying to stop something evil from taking him over.

"Not really," Kent said slowly, then picked up his coffee cup and drained it, as if preparing to make a quick exit.

"Yeah. Right." said Mack. "Well, I reckon you're a science fiction fan. And I'll bet you've been a fan of *Blade Runner* for a long, long time now. Would I be right?"

With a sudden movement, Kent brought his empty coffee cup down on top of the origami unicorn, crushing it. And in that moment, by that act of instinctive, belated concealment, Mack knew what had really happened all those years ago when Al had come back into his life; why his friend had become part of such a terrible thing. And who was really behind it.

He grasped Julia's hand so tightly that she let out a gasp of pain. Mack did not notice. Staring at the disgusting sunglasses, his mind felt overloaded as he fought the desire to grab the man in front of him, to take him with his bare hands and inflict serious pain on him. But he knew that to do so would be impossible. Not because of the consequences for himself – he was a long way past any concerns of that nature. But to do the sort of damage to Kent Nicholls that he felt such a massive desire to inflict would mean the secret that he had been protecting for so long would come out. Johnny would learn the truth.

While Mack struggled to control himself, Kent Nicholls took his moment and slipped past Jay out of the booth and walked quickly from the cafe.

Chapter 35

Johnny paused for a moment outside the door to Al's room. He had tried to visit the previous evening, convinced that this conversation was going to unlock the entire mystery. Knowing why Al had been in that hotel room would prove that his father had not been having an affair, but was the victim of blackmail. He needed to find out what his father was being blackmailed over before he could do anything else; needed to be clear on what he would be unearthing. What secret could be so far reaching that his father would go to such lengths to protect it?

The objective had changed. It was no longer a mission to reveal the truth in order to help his father. It was a mission to discover what that truth was. He would then decide what to do with the knowledge.

Upon arriving the previous evening, the doctor had told him that although they had not needed to operate on Al, they were taking a scan in order to rule out internal bleeding within the skull, and that Johnny should come back the next day.

The scan showed that Al would be fine. There was no serious damage so the doctor gave the all-clear for Johnny to go on up. They also presented Johnny with a considerable bill, which he had agreed to pay in order to get Al admitted.

Now that he was finally going to be able to ask Al some questions, trapped in his hospital bed, Johnny was a little nervous.

The events in that hotel room had overshadowed his entire childhood. He had realised this only recently, like only becoming conscious of your own accent when you move to a different area of the country. Living with his father had been a wonderful upbringing in so many ways, but it had also been different from other kids at school. Johnny didn't want to be different, he wanted to be accepted. The desire to break free, to be unique, crept up on his friends during their teenage years. But Johnny had always felt different, so the effect of puberty on him was actually the opposite, creating a desire to be normal, having a dislike of things not being in their proper place. And Johnny had a particular memory which was not in its proper place.

Taking a deep breath, he pushed the door to the side room and walked in. Johnny had not seen Al up close when he was chasing him. The baseball cap had performed its disguising duties well, and Johnny had been in a panic when he and the cab driver were putting Al in the back of the cab. This was the first time he had been able to take in the gaunt face, thin from years of drug use; it was split by bright white teeth, like a newly painted white door on an old terraced house. Al was sat up wearing a white hospital gown, and turned towards the door when he heard it open.

When Al saw Johnny enter the room, his first reaction was to look away and curse under his breath. Then he turned back to Johnny and smiled at him, sheepishly.

Johnny stared at the man. Something lit up in the back of his mind. Something dark, buried deep in the very recesses of his memory, something that had not been released for a very, very long time.

"I know you," said Johnny, simply. He was staring at the man, stunned for a moment.

"No you don't," Al replied, his tone friendly, jovial even.

"I do. We've met before. When I was a kid."

"No. We haven't," replied Al, in a voice that seemed to want to cajole the listener into changing the subject. "You probably just saw a movie I was in. Happens all the time."

"The teeth. I can picture the teeth. They've not changed. The rest of your face has. But not those teeth. I recognise you from somewhere."

"Hey, I am here, ya know," said Al, laughing nervously. "This is me you are talking about, have some respect, would ya." Al's accent was American, but with a hint of Somerset on certain words. He pronounced 'about' as 'a boat'. "You've probably just seen me in a movie."

There was silence between them. Johnny was thrown for a moment, confused. The younger man walked fully into the room now, still studying a face that meant something but he did not know what. He picked up a chair and brought it to the end of the bed, before sitting down.

"I suppose I should say thanks," Al replied. His voice was slow, and with a slight rasp. He did not come across as a man in the full rudeness of health, even before banging his head. "Thanks for bringing me here."

Johnny didn't answer for a moment, as if rebalancing himself, then said, "Thought you might be mad at me for making you hit your head in the first place."

"No," said Al, as if he was forgiving someone for standing on his toe. "No. Not your fault. You've been trying to find me for a while now, ain't ya. And now you have. Got to give you credit fer that." That smile again, those teeth again.

"So you do know then – that I've been looking for you."

Al didn't speak. The smile wavered for a moment. His brain seemed to be trying to force a message to his mouth, but it was not getting through quickly enough.

"How?" said Johnny. "How did you know?"

Al looked to the side, smile gone, avoiding Johnny's stare. His tone abruptly shifted from over friendly to guarded. "Just because you've found me doesn't mean I have to tell you anything."

Johnny leaned over, getting into Al's eyeline. Al looked back to the front.

"Why can't you look me in the eye?" Johnny asked.

Al turned his head slowly and looked at Johnny's left eye. Then he turned away again. "I don't want to do this," he said. "Why do you think I've been hiding from you? I've nothing to say to you. Go away."

"You've been hiding," Johnny said, "because you know something. I need to know what."

"No," said Al, looking at Johnny again. His voice revealed that he was getting agitated. "No, you do not need to know. You do not need to know anything. Go away now, and don't know stuff. Alright? Just fuck off and carry on with not knowing."

"I'll leave you alone if you answer a question. One single question. One."

"No." Al was staring ahead again, past Johnny's shoulder.

"It's a very easy question." Johnny spoke slowly now, constructing the sentence carefully. "Why were you in the hotel room with my father and the woman he was having an affair with?"

"No."

"No what? You weren't in the room?"

"No. I. Was. Not. There. Now fuck off."

"But my sister saw you. Why were you there?"

No response. Johnny sat on the bed and stared at the man in front of him, arms folded, a picture of defiance. He had come into his father's life and, if not ruined it, then certainly changed it. He felt no more sympathy for the man. He no longer wanted to understand him. He just wanted to know what was going on.

"Why did you go and see my father again?"

"You said one question. I answered it. Fuck off."

"But you lied." Johnny was now staring hard, and he saw Al's eye twitch. "You lied." Fighting the rising anger and indignation that was building up inside of him, Johnny kept his body very still, arms on lap, fingers clenched tightly together, and stared at the man who was refusing to meet his glare.

Neither of them spoke. They maintained their positions for at least two minutes. Eventually, it was Al who broke.

"Go away, Johnny. Leave me alone."

"Tell me why you were in that room."

Al looked at him, his voice softening. "I told you, I wasn't. Now go away. You don't want to know anything. It's better for you to not know things. Now go, please."

Standing, Johnny crossed to the window and looked down at the car park below. A lorry was collecting the rubbish, lifting up the large blue bins and tipping the detritus into its waiting mouth. This was not going anywhere, he thought to himself, except to prove that Al was definitely in the room when Mary had entered. So why had Mack said he wasn't? His mother didn't seem to know he was there either. Mary had never thought to mention it to anyone; she just saw what she thought was her father having an affair and told her mother, who never discussed it with her again. But Mack knew that Al was there, and had lied about it. Why? What was he missing?

And then a realisation hit him.

Johnny stayed at the window, but turned slowly to address Al. "He didn't have an affair at all. Did he?"

Al first looked at him, then resumed his position of folded arms, staring straight ahead.

"That's it. Isn't it?" Johnny continued, his voice becoming more animated. He paced the room, no longer looking at Al, but instead looking at his hands as he gesticulated. "He didn't have an affair. If you were there, he can't have done. Yet all this time he's pretended he was. He gave up his marriage. Allowed everyone to think that he was having sex with that woman. Became a recluse. All for something he didn't actually do." He paused for a moment, then said, almost to himself, "Why?"

Al flicked his eyes nervously towards Johnny for a moment, then watched through his peripheral vision as the young man walked around the front of the bed, right into Al's line of vision. Johnny leaned forwards, resting his arms on the end of the bed.

"Another thing," said Johnny, calmly, slowly, deliberately. "How did you know when to leave? In Galway. In New Orleans."

Al was looking out the window now, like a child refusing to eat his broccoli.

Johnny continued staring at him, realisation driving confidence. Eventually, he said, "And how do you know who I am?"

Al returned his gaze but the tips of his ears were burning bright red – the giveaway.

"Never introduced myself to you when I came in just now. But you knew me, didn't you. You knew me."

Nothing. Al just sat, arms folded, staring at the window, impassive.

Johnny realised that he was not going to get any information from Al. He also realised in that moment that Al was not the person he needed to be talking to. It came to him suddenly, in a moment of embarrassing clarity, who had been driving the car when Al had escaped from him in New Orleans. His father. It was Mack who was trying to keep the secret.

Standing, Johnny looked at Al one more time. The familiarity just would not turn itself into a memory, and yet he knew they had met before. He turned to walk out of the room when Al spoke once more. This time his voice was plaintive, pleading, quiet.

"Johnny."

Turning around, his face hard, Johnny saw a man who had been through more ordeals in his life than he could imagine. A broken man.

"Look," Al said, in a quiet voice, a voice that wanted to correct

259

his past but knew it could not. "I'm not telling you anything, but just know this. We didn't want to do it. Kimberly and me, it wasn't our idea. It was his. We didn't know what he was going to do, that he'd go that far. We just had to make the best of it, to find a way to get out of it. If you learn things...trust me, you don't want to learn them...you're better off just forgetting the whole thing. Walk away. But you are stubborn bastard, just like your father. So if you do find out stuff, please know it wasn't our doing. Okay? Don't judge me. Don't judge me." He was crying now, sad, lonely tears, of someone who has lived with a memory for far too long. "Just don't judge me. It wasn't my fault."

Johnny turned and walked out of the room without another word. He pushed the button to call the lift, travelled down in silence with three people in white uniforms, and left the hospital through reception, barely noticing what was going on around him. In the car park, he took out his mobile phone and retrieved his father's number. They would be in Jonesboro now, preparing to move on to the next gig in Pittsburg, south of Kansas City. Nervously, he dialled, cursing when he went straight through to the answerphone. Mack was on the phone.

Had Johnny looked back into the room a few moments after he had left, he would have seen that Al was also holding a mobile phone to his ear. He had managed to get through to Mack first.

At around the same time, five hours ahead in the UK and therefore 3.30pm, two children were noisily coming to the end of their afternoon nap. Their mother put down the telephone that she had been holding. Had she been successful in dialling the number of her father's mobile phone, she too would have found it engaged. Instead, she had been sitting at the dining room table for half an hour trying to decide whether or not to make the call.

However, Mary would not get to hear that 'caller busy' message, because instead of pressing the 'call' button, she pressed the 'cancel' button and went to attend to her daughter, who had been woken by her brother crying.

Chapter 36

Lying down on his hotel bed in Pittsburg, a college town near Kentucky, Johnny made an effort to close his eyes, and looked for sleep. It was there somewhere, hiding; shy, as if afraid to come out. So many things had rebounded across his mind since talking with Al that morning, so much had happened. Or rather, so much had not happened, but even that seemed important right now. Thoughts kept running around his mind, popping out even though they were not wanted, and sleep seemed to be cowering in a corner of his mind waiting for the all-clear.

So his father had been the one trying to stop him from finding Al. The secret which Johnny was trying to uncover in order to exonerate his father was a secret that his father himself did not want uncovered. Why? What could have been so important that it required the sacrifice of his family unit?

His father had been in contact with Al all along. How long had this been going on? Had Mack got back into contact with Al when he knew he was going to America? Did this mean Mack knew that Johnny was looking for Al? Did he know why? What was he so desperate to hide?

They were questions he had to ask his father face-to-face. And yet it felt as though there was the one question he would not be able to ask.

After calling Mack outside the hospital, he had tried again and again. Finally and reluctantly he had left a message. He had then called Jay, hoping he wasn't driving. By that time of the morning, he reasoned that they would have left Jonesboro and be on their way to Pittsburg, a five-hour car journey.

Jay was relieved to hear from him. They'd been worried, wondering why he had turned his phone off. He asked Johnny if he had heard from Mack. Johnny was surprised when Jay asked him this, as he was calling to speak to Mack. Jay had explained that Mack was not with them, having told them to go on ahead. He'd asked Julia to travel with Jay and Harpo, and had said that he'd meet them all in Pittsburg. They had tried to argue but Mack wouldn't budge – he wanted to hire his own car and make his own way there. Jay said Mack was in a strange mood; that he had been sullen all the previous day but wouldn't admit to anything being wrong. He and Kent Nicholls had almost come to blows in the restaurant, the journalist leaving very suddenly after Mack had told him to go.

This confused Johnny's mind even more. Kent had been the one telling Johnny where to find Al. Mack had been the one telling Al when Johnny was coming. What the hell was it between those two? What had happened for Kent and his father to be playing such games?

Jay was speaking to him from the passenger seat while Harpo drove and Johnny could tell that he couldn't speak too freely, presumably because Julia was in the back of the car. He ended the conversation with Jay, then sent him a text message saying: 'Something wrong, don't know what. Must find Dad.'

Johnny had arrived in Pittsburg early evening and had checked into the hotel. He walked in the bar to find Jay, Harpo and Julia but Mack wasn't with them, and he didn't arrive at all that evening. Eventually, they had to take the decision to cancel the gig. Johnny was becoming increasingly fraught.

There was the tour to think of: sixteen further dates to be honoured, as well as the showcase gig in Los Angeles. All four of them were worried beyond logical thinking, each struggling to think what on earth they should do next.

Only Johnny had an inkling of what the real reason for his father's disappearance might be – that he was hiding something from them. Or was he hiding from something?

As he sought out the joyous wave of sleep, that feeling of succumbing to an all-consuming tiredness, his brain continued to hum quietly. If only he could remember where he had seen Al before, could work out what it was that Mack was so desperate to keep concealed. But he was also beginning to realise that he may have made a monumental mistake in trying to uncover the truth of what really happened in that hotel room.

Mack stood at the top of the metal steps, overlooking the beach in South Wales. He had almost fallen to his knees when he first looked over the bay that seemed so fresh and new. He had not seen it since he was a child, the power of memory and remembered love for his father almost overwhelming him.

Leaving the hotel in Jonesboro two days ago, he had driven back to Memphis, and from there travelled halfway back around the world, staying in hotels and grabbing last-minute flights on one-way tickets. And yet more than this, he had travelled half a lifetime. It was now 8pm, with around an hour of light left before the sun disappeared behind the tall cliffs, and he had been travelling for nearly sixteen hours.

As soon as he had received the telephone call from Al, lying in a hospital bed, he had realised that the events of that one week many years ago were now very close to catching up with him, and that important decisions were required. Only one objective remained, had always remained. Johnny must never be allowed to find out what had happened in that hotel room.

It seemed so obvious now that Kent Nicholls had been the person behind everything awful in his life. He had been controlling people then and he was controlling Johnny now. What was so totally and overwhelmingly galling was the success with which the odiously revolting little bastard had contrived events. If Mack had followed his instincts in that cafe the truth would have come out: the reason why Mack had such a desire to get his hands round that bastard journalist's throat and squeeze and squeeze and squeeze. All would have been revealed. And, as Kent Nicholls knew only too well, that was not an option. All of this, from what happened in that hotel room to now, had all been set up for revenge, to hurt Mack in the one place he was vulnerable: his family. He was one sick bastard journalist.

The danger of Johnny uncovering the truth had now become a realistic possibility. Through the blur of his hatred, there was one thing that Mack felt he could be certain of. It was him, and only him, that

Kent Nicholls wished to injure. Anyone else was collateral damage.

This meant that if Mack was not around, then there would be no joy, no pleasure in telling Johnny, as Mack would not be there to see it, to be hurt by it. With Mack out of the way, he truly believed that Kent Nicholls would not tell Johnny anything. There would be no pleasure in it for him.

After so many years of sacrifice, of taking the blame, of being seen as the villain when he was really the hero, what was the point of stopping now? Like adding a cup of water to the ocean, one more sacrifice on top of the last fourteen years should hardly be a problem. Besides, he had so much more to protect than he had to give up. Even if it meant the ultimate sacrifice: to sit on his secret beach and let the incoming sea claim him. The power of his love for his family, all of his family, was so strong that he was willing to take any action necessary to protect them. Any action necessary.

One thing was certain, he couldn't make decisions of such magnitude while surrounded by the very people it would affect. As soon as he had seen that origami unicorn that Kent Nicholls had made, he had realised that he had been the person blackmailing Al and paying Kimberly. Suddenly, the tour, indeed, the world, had felt like it was closing in around him. The stress, the muzzy head that had been fading in and out now came back as if for the kill, crowding his mind, making it impossible to think straight. He had only one instinct, to remove himself from everything that was bearing down upon him. To get himself away from the tour, for starters. As for leaving the world altogether, that was a decision yet to be made. But it would have to be made soon.

He took the first few steps down towards the beach where he was going to have to finally make those decisions, where he would have to stop hiding and confront his memories, memories of that hotel room and of the last time he had felt so out of control of his own life.

Chapter 37

Closing the door quietly behind him, Mack left the house. The events of the last week – Al appearing again out of the blue and the American woman, Kimberly, threatening him – had left him deeply troubled. He was angry, upset, and confused – a mixture of emotions that he was not equipped to handle.

He'd left Johnny at school that morning. Mary was at school too; he'd seen her leave with Stretch. Everything had been under control, so how could it all have gone so wrong?

He had clearly underestimated Kimberly. It wasn't really Al's fault, he knew that, and yet he was the root cause of the whole thing. Those royalties had nothing to do with Al. Those songs were not hewn from his soul. The old Al knew that. So why was he asking for a share now? It didn't make any sense – it seemed to be so much out of character. At least, from the character that Al had once been, that Mack had once known.

He had been firm and stuck to his principles. And yet things were different now, principles had become irrelevant. The stakes had been raised above anything he could have imagined or believed possible, all in that one phone call from Kimberly.

He drove down the street towards the hotel, so confused, so blurred in his thinking he was almost hysterical, and yet so focussed on his panic that he didn't see Mary standing by the side of the road, watching him drive past. She was supposed to be at school, so the possibility of her not being there didn't allow his scrambled brain to notice her.

Driving into the car park of the hotel, Mack followed the instructions he had been given, parking in front of the row of rooms, lined up in a separate block round the side from the main hotel. The door was opened by Kimberly, who was wearing a dressing gown, her cropped hair still wet as though she had just stepped out of the shower. Mack barely noticed her intense sexuality. She looked at him for a moment, then turned and walked back into the room, not saying a word. He followed, letting go of the door as he did so, not noticing that it did not actually click shut.

The room was bright and large, with two twin beds plus a writing desk and chair. Past this was a door to the bathroom. Mack walked past Al, sitting at the desk, and looked into the bathroom. He closed his eyes for a moment and took a deep breath, steeling himself. Then he turned and walked to the window, stopping between the window and the bed upon which Kimberly was now lying.

"This is complicated, Mack." Al looked at the floor as he spoke, softly.

"No it's not. It is very simple." Mack's legs were spread, his hands folded. Mack looked like he was about to explode. "Just tell me why I'm not ripping your fucking head off right now."

"Unfortunately, I do have a few reasons. As you well know."

"Try me. I'm on a very short fuse."

"Because if you do, you won't get the pictures. And you want those pictures, you really do. And I want you to have them, so I can get on with my life."

Mack closed his eyes again and sighed deeply. He opened his eyes again and looked at the woman. "Who thought this up? Can't have been you two, you're not intelligent enough."

"Thank you, darling," replied Kimberly.

She leaned forward, and he could see down her dressing gown to her breasts. He found it a simple task to avert his eyes, knowing that she wanted his eyes there.

"I'm just a foot soldier. Just doin' ma job." She leaned back on her hands, allowing the dressing gown to fall open further. It was as if she had no idea that she was so exposed. Except, of course, she did. She knew exactly how to control the effect her body could have on men, which is why Mack did not look.

"But you're right," she continued, "Al here isn't bright enough to think of it by himself. His acting career hasn't exactly been doing too well of late, you see, so he rather needed the money to pay us back. Your money, to be precise."

"And who is 'us'?" said Mack.

"Mack, she's talking crap," said Al. "I don't know who is behind this, and if she does know, she ain't gonna tell either of us. Look, honestly, I'm sorry it had to come to this. I didn't know they were going to do this. I don't think even Kimberly knew they were going to go this far. I don't have any choice, they just want my money – your money. All I did was pick him up, I didn't know what they were going to do. Don't judge me, mate, please – these are total bastards we're dealing with here. So let's just get it over and done with. Here. I don't want to have these anymore anyway. Sick of even having to have them on me."

He threw a large brown envelope onto the bed. Mack went to pick it up but Kimberly moved herself down the bed, putting her thigh on top of the envelope. "Not until we see the money, sweetheart," she whispered to Mack. She lifted her other foot towards him, the lower part of the dressing gown falling aside, her dark pubic hair being revealed, the dressing gown now virtually lying on the bed underneath her naked body.

"Isn't this something you've been wanting to see for a while?" said Kimberly. "Most men seem to." Her voice seemed unconvincing, as if this was an act, a role she expected herself to play.

Mack raised his head and closed his eyes, steeling himself again, trying to stop himself from throttling this awful woman, teasing him in this way at such a terrible time. He did not feel in any way aroused, instead he just felt his anger rising at the provocation, at the way she could use such base and deplorable tactics at a time when she was party to things that he could hardly believe any human being could have done.

Suddenly, a voice – a small, familiar voice – came from the other side of the room. "Shit," it said.

Mack turned to look and saw Mary stood in the doorway. The word cut through the gloom in the room purely because it was so unexpected. Mary continued to stare at the scene in front of her. "Shit," she said again, then turned and ran out of the room.

Mack took one step towards the door, then realised that he could not follow, could not leave the room. He put his hand to his forehead and closed his eyes.

Kimberly began to laugh. "Now that is priceless – priceless." Mack turned quickly, reached down, and grabbed her by the throat with one hand. She reached up and tried to scratch his face but his spare arm easily knocked her hands away. He squeezed her throat, not enough to block the air completely, but just enough to make her gurgle and choke.

"You. Bitch," he whispered. "What have you done, you, you…"

Al sat still in the chair. "Alright, Mack," he said softly, "that's enough. As much as I have wanted to do that myself on many an occasion, I don't think it's going to be too helpful. Let her go."

Mack let go and stood back sharply, as if shocked by his own action. Blood rushed through his ears and he tried to gain control of his senses. Breathing hard, Mack spoke to Kimberly as slowly and deliberately as he could manage.

"If you ever show any sign of enjoyment from this again, I will fucking kill you. If I even ever see you again, I will kill you."

"Alright sweetie, alright. Jesus, that hurt," said Kimberly, any hint of allure now gone from her voice. She sat upright, shuffling to the back of the bed and leaned back against the headrest. She rubbed her neck with one hand and wrapped the dressing gown around her with the other. "It's only business, man," she rasped.

Reaching into his inside pocket, Mack pulled out an envelope. He threw it at Al. "£200,000. I hope you spend it on heroin and choke on your own vomit."

"I always was a sucker for the rock and roll clichés, Mack," said Al, handing the envelope to Kimberly.

She took out its contents and began counting the money while Al continued talking. "All that time we spent in the band was just a game, wasn't it. I was so busy trying to be you that I lost myself. I…I'm sorry that it came to this, mate."

Mack simply snorted at him and picked up the brown envelope. He opened it, and saw that there were approximately ten photographs inside. He could only glance briefly at the top photograph – the contents were too awful for him to focus on. It was of a naked boy. And standing over him was a man, also naked, but with the head and shoulders out of the picture. He could see who the boy was, but he could not identify the man. He could not bring himself to look at the other photographs. One day, he vowed to himself, I will find that man.

His legs gave way and he sat on the bed, the photographs falling back into the envelope.

Al had been watching his old partner and his own energy now seemed to leave him. Turning to Kimberly, he said, "Now give me my pictures. Then he can take what is his, and we can all get out of here."

Kimberly stood up, opposite Mack, in between the two beds, ensuring that there was at least a bed between them. She opened her robe and let it slip from her shoulders onto the floor, leaving her stood in front of them completely naked. Her breasts were implausible round and pointed upwards in a way that could not be achieved naturally. Then she squatted to the floor and put her fingers between her legs, searching.

Mack was not looking, not interested. Al muttered "Christ," and looked away. Then Kimberly stood up, holding a small plastic tube. She took off the lid, shook out a roll of film negatives onto her hand and turned to Al.

"I know you've been looking through my stuff ever since we got to England, trying to find this," she said. "That was the only place I knew you would never get to." She smiled at him again, the teasing, nasty smile that she must have practised so often. "There was no way I was going to let you in there under any circumstances."

"Just let me have it."

Kimberly threw the roll of film to Al.

"Christ," he said, catching it, and quickly wrapped it in a napkin.

"On here," said Al to Mack's back, "is my career. What's left of it. Photographs of me and a number of Hollywood's leading ladies. If these photographs were to get out in any way, not only would my career be over, but there is every chance that certain individuals who actually run the money that goes around Hollywood would make sure my life would be over too. This is the only reason I came back." He paused. "Had I known the lengths they were willing to go to, I wouldn't have come back at all. I would rather have taken the consequences myself. Honestly, Mack, you've got to believe me, I'm so fucking sorry any of this happened."

"We picked the wrong schmuck to blackmail," snorted Kimberly. "He didn't have any money, but when we did our research, I discovered you did." She lifted her head back, the better to look down her nose at him. "And frankly, you've been a bit of a disappointment too. All this effort for £200k? Can't see why the boss was so keen to nail you. He must have his own reasons."

"How do we know these are all the copies?" said Mack, still not turning round or looking up. "You could have duplicated these photos or you could have taken copies of those," he said, turning and pointing to the negatives that Al now held.

"Because she knows that if she tries this again, I will kill her," said Al, looking at Kimberly. "I almost did this time. You can drive a man to the edge once, but try it again and he sees no reason not to go over it." He turned to Mack. "I'm sorry. I know that means nothing, but it does happen to be true. Why don't you take what's yours and leave."

Mack stood up and turned to them both. "I have two questions. Who is the man in the photograph? I assume he is the person behind all this."

"Just do as Al suggests and take what's yours, honey," said Kimberly. "He don't know the answer, and I ain't tellin'."

"Then just pass him a message. Tell him from me that if I ever find out who he is, I will...I will...fucking..." His voice trailed off.

"I'd leave it, if I were you. This doesn't suit you. Christ, you can't even bring yourself to say it out loud. Your heart's too good, you can't compete with him. He's a total bastard."

Mack put the envelope in his jacket pocket. Then he went over to the bathroom and stopped at the doorway, looking in, his arm leaning against the door frame for support.

"What did you give him?" he said, not turning round.

"Don't worry," said Al, "he's just been asleep, and he won't be waking up for another few hours."

"The whole time?"

"Yeah. So they tell me. The whole time. He should not remember a thing."

Walking into the bathroom, Mack bent down and kneeled next to the body on the floor. It was wrapped in a blanket from the hotel bedroom, but underneath the blanket the body was naked. Mack fought against the overwhelming urge to go back into the bedroom and use his fists on them both, knowing that would only bring worse consequences. He also knew there was no advantage in going to the police, as there was no way of proving where the pictures could have come from. Pictures of his son, naked, in disgusting poses, being abused by a man whose head always remained out of shot. He was only thankful that Johnny had been unconscious throughout the horrific experience – it gave him a chance, a hope that none of this would stay in his memory. And if that flicker of hope came true, he would dedicate the rest of his life to making sure his son never found out what had happened to him.

He put his arms underneath Johnny, scooped him up close to his chest, and stood up. He walked back through the bedroom, not looking at Kimberly or Al, and out of the room. In order to protect Johnny from the truth of what had been done to him, he couldn't let anyone else know either, just in case. The stakes were too high. No matter what the consequences, he would protect his son from any memories that may have embedded themselves through the fog of the drugs they had given him. He would create a new reality over the events of the last few hours – a reality that would apply to everyone involved in Johnny's life. He had to protect his son no matter what the cost to himself, and thereby try to give Johnny a life free from the terrors of recollection.

Chapter 38

Mack stepped off the bottom step and onto the beach. He took the rucksack off his back and opened it. It contained a bottle of Jack Daniels, several packets of cigars handmade in New Orleans, plus a disposable lighter, a jumper, and a fedora hat. He put the fedora on his head and walked down the beach across the large pebbles.

Following his instinct to get away from everything that was boring down into his mind, Mack had flown into Heathrow airport, taken the fast train to Cardiff, then a local train along the South Wales coast to get to Tenby. From there a bicycle had been bought from a second-hand store and he had ridden for a couple of hours. He carried only a small rucksack, his larger bag and guitar having been stored in a locker at Cardiff station. If you don't know if you're coming back or not, then leaving your bags behind makes each and every option truly possible.

This was also the thinking behind throwing the bike into a hedge. If he came back up the metal steps and needed the bike, he would still be able to retrieve it. But if he didn't need to, then it would be unlikely to be found, at least for a while.

In this way, Mack felt confident that he had left no trace of his movements since leaving Heathrow airport. He had not permitted himself any thinking time, diverting his thoughts with various means, including newspapers and puzzle books on the flight and train journeys. He had wanted to save the complete thought process for one session, a session that he wanted to take place in the surroundings that he knew would be the most conducive. This also gave space and time for his subconscious to do much of the reassembling of his life and his priorities.

It was as if he was saving up the internal debate, savouring the decision he was going to have to make. And yet by travelling so far from the people that would be affected by the decision, to somewhere so isolated and yet so full of his own memories, he knew that all eventualities, all possible decisions, were truly open to him.

The small cove was just as he remembered it from his childhood – the high cliffs on either side leading down to the sea and the large, slippery rocks which covered the right-hand side of the beach. They lay in the same way that they had from the moment they had fallen from the cliff, half buried by sand, enormous and ever-present, like the weight of a thousand smuggler's souls – those same rocks which obscured the cave that Mack knew to be there.

The timing of the tide was the one major imponderable. It was entirely possible that the incoming sea would have already crept up the beach far enough to cover the entrance to the cave, and Mack would not have been able to reach the secret beach. He knew that the height between high and low tide along the South Wales coastline is one of the highest in the world – the incoming sea rises more than seven metres at times – and the cave would be impossible to get through from approximately halfway between the high and low tide. Had Mack arrived as the tide was halfway through its journey up the beach, then he would have to wait around twelve hours before being able to secure his seclusion.

More importantly, at high tide the sea would cover the entire length of the small bay, trapping anyone still on the beach, giving them no means of escape from the rising sea. By going through the cave, Mack was giving himself a few hours to make a decision. And if the decision was that he had to continue protecting his loved ones, then he would not return through the cave before the incoming tide cut him off. This would be his deadline.

He was in receipt of grim luck. As he arrived at the bottom of the steps he looked down to see dry sand. The sea had retracted from this spot some time ago, allowing the sun to dry out this part of the beach. The sea was on its way back in.

Walking quickly across the sand and over the piles of large boulders, he reached the cliff face. There was the cave, unchanged from the picture in his memory. He could see through the cave, which sloped downwards at an angle into the rock, away from him. This meant that the cave was not easily detected from the steps or the beach, and Mack recalled the feeling from his childhood of being the only person in the world that had ever been there. Ducking through the opening, he was able to stand upright as the height of the cave quickly increased. The roof was fairly level but the floor dropped away quickly as the incoming sea, over many years, had eroded the rock closest to it first.

The other end of the passage, some ten metres away, ended approximately two metres above the sand. That hadn't changed either, and the memories blew around his mind like a warm summer's breeze. He picked his way down the narrow passage, over the uneven rocky floor, and stopped for a moment at the mouth of the cave, surveying the scene in front of him.

The beach was just as he remembered, if not even more beautiful. The sand stretched in an arc in front of the attacking sea to his left. It was at least four hundred metres to the far side, and the sand disappeared on three sides underneath large rocks and boulders that had fallen from the cliffs; events unseen by human eyes. His childhood memories had been pockmarked by the delights that these edges of the beach held: rock pools, crabs, hidden crevices and high points for lookouts. The fickle pleasure of sandcastles was not for him; instead he would explore the joyous abundance of nature for hours on end.

And then, past the rocky extremities rose the cliffs, vertical, allowing no possibility of pathways or steps. The metal staircase built to allow access to the smaller bay which he had just left had not been replicated on this larger beach, as the cliffs did not yield even for a small section. He saw the cliffs on the far side of the bay reaching out into the sea for several hundred metres, the top of the cliff getting lower as if it were a small child easing itself into the water gently.

He stood still for a moment, balancing himself against the sides of the narrow cave to drink in the view', a wash of emotions coming over him as the sea now washed over the sand. The feeling of latent joy that came from childhood happiness clashed against the arguments that had been battling to make themselves heard.

Taking off his shoes and tying them around his neck, Mack jumped down onto the faultless sand. There were rocks rising out of the ground to his left and right but nature had determined that the area in front of the cave would be smooth.

The sun was still strong enough to allow Mack to strip completely naked. He knew that the sea was nearing low tide, and that high tide would therefore be at around 3am. More importantly, he had until a little before midnight to get back through the cave. If he did not get through the cave and back up to the higher beach of the smaller cove next door, then he would not be leaving the beach at all, and the sea would claim him.

He walked slowly over the sand into the middle of the beach towards the sea. He stood, watching the waves coming up to his feet, then retracting again, like a stray dog nervously approaching a stranger who might have food. The waves seemed to grow in confidence as they surrounded his feet, then grew wary again, stopping some distance short. Further out, the sea was starting to boil, the wind goading, encouraging the sea to behave mischievously. Mack knew that in a few hours' time, the entire bay would be covered by those large, threatening waves, and that even swimming out of the bay would be dangerous, if not impossible.

Turning, he looked up at the cliffs. The sun was now dipping and half the beach was in shade, the late evening rays of the sun visible against the dark cliffs behind. Only now, as he studied the strata of the rocks and the cliffs, did he start to allow the thoughts to permeate through to his conscious mind. He observed the lines in the rock and the way that the cliffs seemed to stop at the sand, as if resting on the beach floor; however, it was the cliffs that went down into deep roots, and the sand was the real fraud.

One week had changed his life, but these rocks would be there forever. They would change, inevitably but imperceptibly, and the cave would very slowly get bigger, eventually forming an arch; everyone would know about this beach then, but that would take eons. The weight of the surroundings began to sit on his shoulders, on his head, and in his mind. The gravitas that he needed grew inside of him as the memories came back, memories that he had kept just out of reach for such a long time.

Protecting the real events of that week had taken his life away from him. He had accepted the consequences, accepted the blame that wasn't his to take. For what he had to protect, it had been worth it. And now the very person who had the most to lose from finding out the truth was close to discovering everything.

He walked to the far side of the beach and studied the rocks more closely. He could tell that the beach was sloping by the dark horizontal line that ran the entire length of the cliffs at the side of the bay, forming a triangle with the sand. That line had been created by the high tide; the rocks above it were dark but those below it were lighter, where the sea had eaten away the plants and lichen that attached themselves to the cliffs, leaving their mark at the height of the tide.

Mack noted grimly that this line, showing where the seas would eventually rise to in just a few hours' time, was above the top of the cave, on the cliff now on the other side of the bay from where he stood. It also ended about two metres up the cliff face at the back of the beach. Anyone on this beach at high tide would be swimming. Or not.

This stood as a stark reminder that he had come here to make a decision. A decision that could result in him leaving the beach in a couple of hours and having to tell Johnny the truth – a truth which could potentially have terrible consequences for his son, who, up to now, had shown no memory of that awful day. He had often wondered whether his son's unusual mannerisms had been an exterior revelation; that there was a memory buried deep down, a vague memory through the drugs that Kent Nicholls had given him. Mack had only one desire in the world, and that was to prevent those memories from coming to the surface.

And so the other decision would be the one that would result in keeping the truth hidden for evermore. He could only see two options at that time: he had a few hours to either find some more possibilities, or to make a choice between black and white.

Walking to the back of the beach, he sat down heavily on the sand and leaned against the base of the cliff. He unwrapped the covering from a packet of cigars, carefully putting the cellophane into his coat pocket. Taking a dark, slim cigar from the packet, he lit it, inhaled, and leaned his head back. Slowly he blew the smoke into the pale blue evening sky.

Epilogue

Glancing at her watch, Mary walked uneasily along the path by the side of the river. She had a further hour before she was due to return to Phil and the children, and had been away for an hour already. It was the longest she had been separated from her children since David was born, and it was making her uneasy. That morning, Phil had told her that he was getting fed up with her brooding about the problem and that she needed to take a couple of hours out to think, and then to make the call to her father.

Two swans landed flapping and spluttering on the river surface. It was as if it was the first time they had ever pitched onto water and were unsure if they would sink or float on this strange new surface. Mary didn't notice any wildlife, whether it was the swans, the dragonfly that circled her warily, or the fox that crept through the long grass at the far end of the field on the other side of the river. It was a fox that had strayed a long way from home and was anxiously picking its way back across the fields towards its den in the distant woods, its work done for the day.

Mobile phone held tightly in her hand, Mary found a grassy spot at the side of the path between two large clumps of reeds, spread out the coat she was carrying, and sat down on the bank of the river. Behind the path was a small wood, and to her left and right she could see for many hundreds of yards. There was no one else in sight – only the flies and the fish would be able to hear her telephone call.

Taking a big sigh as if preparing to dive underwater, she dialled her father's number. Her heart was thumping and yet she felt glad, confident that she was doing the right thing. It was time. Time to end the absurdity of their silence. Time that she finally embarked upon a relationship with her father.

Her father. Even that sounded amazing. Of course he was her

father. There was absolutely nothing to suggest that he was not, and she didn't know how she could have allowed such a notion to have gained such a firm hold in her mind. The realisation that what she had seen that day in the hotel room was not all it appeared to be had begun a chain reaction of new thinking, which in itself allowed an entirely new view of the world to gestate inside her. Endless possibilities which had quickly whittled down into clear, focussed facts. Mack was her father. That fact seemed to be at the centre of it all.

She held the phone to her ear. It rang a few times, and then she heard his voice. It thanked her for calling, told her that he must be busy and couldn't take the call right at the moment, and asked her if she would be so kind as to please leave a message.

Acknowledgements

This book would not have been written without the support of my family, and can only be dedicated to Susie, Ella and George.

It also required the understanding of my colleagues at Ovation Finance Ltd.

The story and my confidence in it benefited hugely from the help of David Lloyd in particular, who, showing great fortitude and understanding, read the first draft and gave invaluable contribution. Further drafts were helped by the input from Jo Hague, Callie Willows, Bev Stoves, Joe Pontin, Julie Wild, Adam Roberts, Damien Davies and Matt Budd, and I'm grateful to them all.

But without my parents, George and Maureen Budd, none of this would be.

Find out more about the author at www.cbudd.co.uk

Lightning Source UK Ltd.
Milton Keynes UK
UKOW04f1937301013

220119UK00004B/136/P